Inside Out

D1202625

Susan X Meagher

Inside Out

THIS TRADE PAPERBACK ORIGINAL IS PUBLISHED BY BRISK PRESS, BRIELLE, NJ 08730.

COVER DESIGN AND LAYOUT BY: CAROLYN NORMAN

FIRST PRINTING: MAY 2014

ISBN-13: 978-0-9899895-3-4

By Susan X Meagher

Novels

Arbor Vitae
All That Matters
Cherry Grove
Girl Meets Girl
The Lies That Bind
The Legacy
Doublecrossed
Smooth Sailing
How To Wrangle a Woman
Almost Heaven
The Crush
The Reunion
Inside Out

Serial Novel

I Found My Heart In San Francisco

Awakenings: Book One
Beginnings: Book Two
Coalescence: Book Three
Disclosures: Book Four
Entwined: Book Five
Fidelity: Book Six
Getaway: Book Seven
Honesty: Book Eight
Intentions: Book Nine
Journeys: Book Ten
Karma: Book Eleven
Lifeline: Book Twelve
Monogamy: Book Thirteen
Nurture: Book Fourteen
Osmosis: Book Fifteen
Paradigm: Book Sixteen

Anthologies

Undercover Tales
Outsiders

Acknowledgements

As always, a group of people helped me drag this book across the finish line. My wife is responsible for too many tasks to list, and my gratitude to her is immeasurable.
I'm also very grateful to Peyton Andrews, Cheri Fuller, Denise Spradley and Nancy Jean Tubbs for their many helpful comments.

Every journalist who is not too stupid or full of himself to notice what is going on knows that what he does is morally indefensible.

~ Janet Malcolm

Chapter One

THERE WERE BILLIONS OF dollars on the table, daring someone to invent a shock collar for toddlers. Obviously, it'd have to be completely hidden, and you could only use it until they could speak well enough to rat you out. But imagine the peace of mind!

Kit Travis watched little Joshua bang his chubby hands against the low glass enclosure that protected a seemingly oblivious group of penguins from kids like him.

There might have been more rambunctious, daring, fearless, and energetic three-year-olds, but if there were, Kit had nothing but sympathy for their parents.

From the corner of her eye, she spotted Satan's cousin, strolling along, enticingly holding aloft animal-shaped balloons, drawing kids to him like bees to honey. Madison, Joshua's calm, pink-clad older sister snapped out of her sluggish, dreamy state to follow him—zombie like, ignoring Kit's increasingly frantic demands to stop.

The Pied Piper-like demon turned a corner, and Madison disappeared from view. Trying to work out the geometry in the fractions of a second available to her, Kit decided that Joshua's attention was locked in. He was determined to break the glass with his frantic pounding, and she was confident he couldn't make any progress in the thirty seconds it would take to corral his sister. There were no other people around who could help—all of them having the brains to do something indoors when the forecast was for a major storm—so she went for the greater peril. Losing a kid had to be worse than a little property damage.

Running full-tilt, she chased Madison down and grabbed her. After tucking her under her arm like a football, she wheeled around and ran back, with Madison crying bloody murder. When she rounded the corner, Kit froze in place.

"Joshua!" In the ten seconds she'd been gone, a parent had parked a stroller right next to the kid, who'd used it to climb up and hoist his leg over the top of the glass. He balanced there for a fraction of a second, then fell—right into the water.

Splash!

The pond was shallow—thank God. Joshua lay on his back, slapping his hands into the water while he kicked his feet. He seemed to think he was at a swimming pool, seemingly completely content to slap at the water.

Kit flew to the pool, trying to think of ways to pluck him out while not screwing up worse. Madison obviously couldn't be trusted, so Kit kept her tucked under one arm while she leaned over as far as she could, managing to grab Joshua's ankle. He wasn't a particularly big kid, but she had to use all her strength to hoist him up one-handed. He fought tooth and nail, not wanting to end his impromptu swim. With him wriggling around like a flounder, she didn't have the strength to actually haul him over the wall with just one hand. But Madison, a proven flight risk, prevented her from using both.

A golf cart screeched to a halt, and a waft of pungent burnt rubber floated over to tickle Kit's nose. Two guys in green uniforms jumped out, one of them speaking into a walkie-talkie. His voice shook when he said, "The pond is clear. Repeat. The pond is clear. Code Red cancelled. Repeat. Code Red cancelled."

The stroller owner, a thirty-something mom, ran up to them, grabbed Joshua and turned him right side up. "What is wrong with you?" She was so angry her pale cheeks bore bright red splotches.

"I was trying to catch this one." Flustered, Kit momentarily forgot the girl's name, so she resorted to bouncing the horizontal bundle in her arm. "When that one jumped in."

"I'm calling Child Protective Services." If the woman's cheeks got any redder, they'd burst. Her eyes, full of what seemed like actual hatred, could have set paper aflame.

As strong as her desire to defend herself was, Kit had the presence of mind to tend to the kids. Madison was still screaming, and Kit set her down, then got to her knees to try to calm her. It had to freak a kid out to see her brother almost drown. "Panda balloon!" she cried, pointing in the direction of the long-gone vendor. "Panda!"

Blinking, Kit stood, trying to absorb her crash course in the paucity of childhood empathy. The guards were both talking at once, the woman who held a wildly flailing Joshua was still lecturing her, and, emerging from behind a kiosk, she spotted Daniel, the father of these creatures, blithely yapping into his cell phone. The second he spied the kerfuffle, he started running toward them. "What in the hell happened?" He grabbed Joshua from the stranger. "He's drenched!"

Kit tried to explain, realizing how damning they were as the words tumbled from her lips. "Madison ran away and Joshua climbed in when I was…gone."

"Gone?" His eyes were nearly out of his head. "You left him?"

"She was holding him upside down like a doll," the tattletale said.

"You're the one who gave him the step-ladder!"

"You left a baby unattended!"

It was Kit's turn to lob another accusation, but she was fresh out. When you did something so stupid, it was hard to keep up in a battle of wits.

Daniel looked as if he was struggling to tamp down some very dark urges. He spoke slowly and in such a quiet tone, it was a little frightening. "Do you think you can take Madison and manage to get the car? I'll take Joshua inside and buy him a dry T-shirt." His gaze shifted to his daughter, then back to Kit. "Try not to lose her again, okay? You can't just let them wander away. You have to watch them."

Given the crowd, and the uniformed guards, Kit didn't think it prudent to slug him. But before the day was out, her new boyfriend would be kicked—to the curb.

—⁂—

Asante sipped at his drink, regarding Kit with interest. His cocoa-colored eyes shone in the candlelight, with the flickering light making his warm brown skin glow.

He was a careful interviewer, never leading, paying rapt attention to every word, every nuance. "You'd never met the kids?"

"Never. Daniel and I have only been out three…no, four times. He had this whole plan for how to introduce us. Like he put a ton of thought into it." She took a sip of her drink, thinking back to those conversations. "The main reason I liked him was because he seemed like such an adult. He's the first guy I've met who put his kids' needs first."

"Yet today he showed up with both kids—no warning?"

"None at all. We were supposed to go to brunch, but we were driving to the zoo with the pair of them before I knew what hit me."

"Got it." He nodded, and Kit half expected him to whip out his ever-present Moleskine notebook to start jotting down his thoughts. "How long had you been alone?"

"Not sure. As soon as we got there, the kids started begging for food, but it was only eleven. He said their schedules would get messed up if he fed them too early. Two seconds later he got a call he had to take." She pondered the timeline. "It was noon when I got back to the car... so he must've been gone for about forty-five minutes." She shook her head. "He acted like I'd thrown the kid into the pool."

"I know you're angry, but you drift off to take calls all the time. I can't count the number of times I've been sure you were never coming back."

"True." She took another sip of her margarita, considering her answer. "But if they'd been my kids, I wouldn't have wandered away until I was sure the person I was with was comfortable watching them. I'd warned him, repeatedly, that I was skittish around kids."

Asante made a little noise, like he sometimes did when he didn't want to openly contradict her. "Most people can babysit for a few minutes. It's not like he tossed a couple of chimpanzees at you."

"Same thing! Well, the little one at least. He climbed onto that stroller like it was a ladder. A kid that little should not be able to practically vault a three-foot-high barrier!"

Snickering, Asante said, "Vault? Is that really the right word?"

"Yes!" She jumped up and used the back of her chair to illustrate. As she swung her leg up, she clipped a server in the butt. "Shit! I'm so sorry!"

She grabbed the guy's arm, but he peeled her hands away, while stabbing her with a withering look. "No problem." When he moved on, he held his tray a little tighter.

"Sit down," Asante hissed. "You've had enough trouble for one day."

Kit slunk down into her chair, then drained her drink, wincing when the tequila hit her empty stomach. "I liked this guy. Really liked him."

"Who does he work for?"

"Osborne-Utah. Policy advisor. Not the top guy, I don't think, but he goes on all the overseas trips."

"Pretty big job. Maybe you should give him a pass on taking a call."

"I would, Asante. You know I don't mind waiting." She dropped her head into her hand. "It sucks. He was the nicest, smartest, most age-appropriate guy I've been out with since…you know."

Asante leaned over and gently massaged her shoulder. "Don't be so dramatic. This is probably the worst day you'll have with the kids. You'll look back on this and laugh."

Leaning her head back, Kit gazed at him through slitted eyes. "There was nothing funny about it. Once he got home, he called and reamed me a new one, going on and on about how his ex would make his life miserable over the whole thing."

"You almost let penguins eat her baby," he interrupted, still ineffectively hiding a laugh.

"Duly noted." Kit lifted a hand to signal their waiter for a refill. "I understand he was upset; anyone would have been. But he was an asshole about it. He lectured me for a good fifteen minutes. I couldn't get a word in to explain how quickly everything happened."

"Troubling." Asante nodded sagely.

"Right. I understand that I screwed up. I understand he was upset. I even understand the need to dress me down over the whole thing. But I can't tolerate being lectured to like an employee."

He shrugged. "Everybody has their own ways of dealing with stress. Maybe he goes into lecture-mode."

"Don't like it," Kit said briskly. "But I'd be more willing to give him a pass if he hadn't made such a big deal about his ex."

"You weren't there," Asante reminded her. "He might have been exaggerating how bad it was."

"Don't think so," she said thoughtfully. "Before, when he talked about her, he made her sound like a perfectly rational woman. Today, she's a raging bitch who'll bring this up in court; the judge might order supervised visitation; they'll probably have to get the child psychologist involved again, etc., etc."

"Did you know the divorce was so contentious?"

"No! He made it sound like they'd grown apart and had both moved on. That was a huge lie." She closed her eyes tightly, fighting a headache. "They don't send you to mandatory family counseling because you're doing a bang-up job with the kids."

"Wow." His eyes grew big. "You need that like you need…I can't think of anything that's bad enough to compare it to."

"Too true. It'd be one thing if his wife were dead. I'd try to get over my aversion to kids and learn to be a good stepmother. But I won't be with someone whose difficult ex is looming over me. That's way, way more drama than I'm willing to put up with."

As was his habit, Asante clapped his hands together, then made a sweeping gesture. "Then move on. You'll find someone else soon."

"Soon?" Kit tried to keep the bitter edge from her voice. She hated the fact that it had begun to creep in, and was determined to avoid letting it spill all over her friends. Her laugh sounded a little brittle, but it was the best she could manage. "It's been four years. Four long years."

"You've dated a lot. Don't make it sound like you've been in a dating desert."

"Oh, I've had dates," she said, her sarcasm nearly dripping from her words. "Significantly older guys who assume every youngish woman will fulfill every thwarted fantasy they sublimated during their first marriage; thrice-divorced guys paying so much alimony they can't afford a new pair of shoes; guys who want a babysitter more than a girlfriend; guys who need a babysitter more than a girlfriend; and that rarest of creature, spotted only once; the never-married, childless, social drinker—who feared commitment like I fear bats. Face it, Asante. The good ones have all been taken."

"Not true in the least. I predict we'll both be married within the year. There are at least two wonderful men in DC. We just need one of them to be gay."

Grumpily, she added, "With my luck, both of them will be."

—⁕—

Kit left her apartment at eight o'clock sharp on Monday morning, took the elevator down to the first floor, and nodded at the always busy morning doorman. Using her key, she unlocked the lobby entrance to the office, pleased to see the place buzzing with activity. The nerdy guy with the awesome Afro and the gabby girl had obviously just gotten in, and were standing by the coat rack, waiting for someone to tell them what to do. She was going to have to learn their names. Just because they were interns didn't mean she could treat them like widgets.

Denise, her lead researcher, had her phone jammed up against her ear, but she could communicate quite effectively while doing something else. She waved, and both interns tentatively approached. While jabbering away, she mimicked instructions to them. What a gold mine she was. Besides being top-notch, she had a strong aversion to anyone goofing off. It was awfully nice to have an enforcer on the staff.

Marcus strolled in, bearing a box of donuts. He was going to be the death of her. It was hard enough to eat healthily without him loading the office up with delicious crap. Who would choose plain oatmeal when you could have a warm, glazed donut? She tried not to look. She'd had her oatmeal. She wasn't hungry. But the damned donuts were practically begging to be eaten. Grousing to herself, she took just a half. Small victories.

When Marcus was settled, Kit took her laptop over to him. "I wrote a piece this morning on the impasse over that bill to curb emissions on light trucks. Can you take it off my computer and get it up on the website?"

"Where are you hiding it?"

"It's on my desktop. I should have just sent it to you, but my Internet was crawling this morning."

"Don't you want Donna to look at it first?"

"Ehh…" She noted her editor's absence. "I wanna get it up. It's not very long. It won't kill me if I have a typo or two."

After leaving her machine with Marcus, she walked over to her office manager's cubicle, amazed to find it empty. The main door flew open and Nia rushed in. "Babysitting bullshit." Kit knew not to ask for details. When Nia was late, there was always a valid reason.

"Don't worry about it." She put her hand on Nia's shoulder, able to feel the knotted muscles. The woman was wound as tight as her box braids. "I'm going to head over to the Hill. I've got meetings with Ashman, Simpson, and Bales. Then I'm going to try to find somebody to have lunch with. Someone has to have the scoop on how they're going to get this budget done on time. I'll leave my phone on vibrate. Cool?"

"We're good." Nia let her gaze glide across the room and land on Donna's empty desk. "If our editor gets here." She tossed a hand up in the air. "If not, that new intern, the tall girl with glasses, seems to know how to cross her T's and dot her I's."

Kit poked her in the shoulder. "If neither one of us can remember these kids' names, we're screwed."

Nia leaned back in her chair and smiled up at Kit. "Then we are screwed. It's all I can do to remember my kids' names. Everyone else's is extra credit."

—∞—

Kit tried to check her watch during her meeting with Representative Bales. The guy had a head full of knowledge, but not enough personality to light a forty-watt bulb. How had he ever won an election? He must have been from an all-Amish district, and no one ever saw him on TV.

They were in his office, in the Cannon, her favorite of the House office buildings. It was the oldest and had a dignified, storied air that always made her think important things were being accomplished inside. The public areas were especially lovely, where a big rotunda let sunlight spill in, illuminating huge marble columns, and polished marble floors. But the individual offices showed the darker side. The heating and air conditioning systems were a joke. Today, a hot, early September morning, had most people shucking whatever clothing they could get away with. Eighty degrees outside, about eighty-five inside. An ugly water stain covered a large piece of the wall behind Congressman Bales' chair, and paint flaked off all the way to the floor. That was a perfect analogy for Washington. Luster and beauty on the outside; rot, decay and ugliness when you probed past the facade. She laughed at her dark thoughts. Maybe she just knew too much. Government was much prettier when you merely had a fleeting acquaintance with it.

She finally managed to extricate herself while there was still time to find a lunch date. Distracted as she scurried down the hall, it took her a minute to notice that nearly every person she passed gave her a look. A weird look. Surprise, sympathy, censure... What in the hell?

Kit looked at her phone, seeing forty voicemails. The maximum. A hundred and twenty-five e-mails. Oh, my God. Aliens must have landed on the White House lawn. Nia picked up on the first ring.

"Have you heard?" When Nia panicked, you could only hope the worst thing was that aliens were now running the government.

"Heard what?"

"You've been outed."

"What?!"

Two staffers walked past, both tittering when she yelled.

"I'm not sure who had the story first, probably Mudge. Now it's everywhere. The genie's out of the bottle, Kit. I'm so sorry."

"Yeah. Right. Later."

She clicked off, put her phone back into her bag, and slunk out of the building. Now what?

—⁂—

It might not have been the smartest thing to do, but whenever Kit was troubled she took herself offline. The phone messages could pile up, people could be banging on her office door. She didn't care. They'd all still be there once she'd sorted things out.

Her favorite place for reflecting was Rock Creek. It wasn't a huge park, but it ran down a long strip of urban Washington and you could get there on the Metro. It was a perfect place for meeting an inappropriate lover, or dropping a suitcase full of money to shepherd legislation through the House. Dark, dark, dark, she reminded herself. Not all legislation was bought and paid for.

Part of the reason she liked the park was because it hadn't, technically, been created. It was a little bit of nature that Congress had the foresight to protect over a hundred years ago, when Washington's sprawl threatened to pave over every bit of greenery. If that's all they'd done that year, it had been plenty.

It took a bit of walking to get past the jogging, biking and inline skating exercise addicts that Washington was peopled with. But she'd been here many times before and knew just where she needed to be—at the most isolated part of the creek. Away from roads, people and noise, with only the rush of the water to calm her jangled thoughts.

Consciously zoning out, Kit sat on a boulder for a long time, letting the hot sun and tinkling water soothe her. Then she allowed herself to take it all in. She was no Pollyanna. Being outed had been inevitable. When you traded in political gossip, you quickly learned there were no perfectly guarded secrets. Still, she'd managed to pull it off for almost ten years. Now she'd have to deal with the repercussions. Fun times!

—⁂—

That night, Kit sat in her apartment, wading through the personal messages that had piled up. There were about two dozen, but only one she could bear to return. She texted Asante, assuming he'd be up. It was only midnight.

"I hope your day was better than mine."

In seconds, the little ellipsis showed he was typing. "I wasn't shot, so…yeah. Call?"

Using the phone as it had originally been intended, she hit his button. "Wanna do a piece on what happens to an anonymous political blogger who gets outed?"

He paused for a few seconds. Asante was too good a reporter not to be tempted. He was also too good a friend to jump in with both feet. "Uhm…we can talk about that later. How are you?"

"Not great. But not horrible. I knew it would happen, but I still almost barfed in the hallway of the Cannon when I heard."

"Barf would improve the Cannon. Want me to come over? Or meet for a drink?"

"No, I don't think so. Tomorrow's gonna be horrible. I should get some sleep."

"It'll be okay, Kit. Your newsletter is like crack, and your blog's very well respected. Knowing you're the face behind the cute graphic won't hurt much at all."

"Maybe. But it's going to be weird. A lot of my sources will feel betrayed."

"Yeah, yeah, that's true. But they'll still talk." He chuckled. "Maybe even more than before now that you're famous."

"Ugh. You know that's the last thing I want."

"Yeah, I do. Still, I'll never understand why you got into political reporting. You're the vestal virgin in the fame whore rodeo."

She laughed. "Good one. I'd better hit the rack. In the morning, I'm gonna have to make some calls that I really, really don't want to make."

"Like?"

"Mmm, my parents, my sister, my brother. I've got some 'splainin' to do, Lucy."

Dead silence. Then Asante quietly said, "You're shitting me. You've never told them?"

"Nope. They're won't be happy."

"Kit! You've lied to your entire family?"

"Not technically. They just don't know anything has changed."

"Since when?"

"Since I was full time at the *Globe*."

"That's been ten years!"

"Time flies."

"They honestly think you're still a print reporter?"

"Well, I do kinda work for the *Globe*. I get two or three bylines a year."

"How…who…why?"

She bristled slightly. "You know why. They'd prefer not to know what I do, and I'd prefer not to tell them."

"You're guessing at that, Kit."

"I'm not about to spend every visit defending the Democratic Party, liberal ideas in general, and my beliefs in particular. So we talk about other things."

"Uhm…I swear I'm not trying to be rude, but you don't have other things."

You could try to bullshit Asante, but you'd be wasting your time. "That's why our visits are short, but sweet."

"They're going to be hurt," he warned.

"I don't think so. My family isn't like yours. We're more like colleagues."

"I'd be angry if a close colleague didn't trust me enough to tell me he had a secret life."

Kit let out a short, wry laugh. "I didn't say close colleagues. Just colleagues."

Chapter Two

KIT STOOD IN FRONT of her full-length mirror, assessing herself as carefully as she did a story she was about to post. She wasn't going to find an eligible guy at a fundraiser for the biggest gay and lesbian political action committee in the country, but gay men paid much more attention to how a woman looked than straight guys did. Sadly.

Except for an occasional elegant wedding, she hadn't been to a formal event in four years. In her former life, she'd been to so many that she thought she'd never want to attend another, but that didn't turn out to be true. Maybe the fact that this one was for gay people made it more compelling, but she was frankly excited about getting dressed up and dancing.

She probably should have taken the time to have her hair trimmed, but it wasn't yet at the crisis stage. If she used product, it didn't cover her eyes. It was a shade darker than it had been during the heat of summer, reminding her of how many weeks it had been since she'd been able to indulge in her favorite activity; lying on her roof-deck to soak up the sun. Without that temptation, she spent most of her weekends inside, catching up on work. The sun might be harmful, but she was certain overwork was just as bad.

The fine lines at the edges of her eyes had grown a little more prominent, but she could still pass for thirty. Thirty-five on a bad day. But that big four-oh was looming much brighter on the horizon than she liked. She hated being hung-up on age, but something about this birthday was weighing heavily on her; yet she didn't have a clue how to snap out of it. By summer, it'd be over. She'd be a woman in her forties. Shaking her head to dislodge the annoying thought, she went into the bathroom to freshen her lipstick. Asante was going to have a date who'd pulled out all the stops to look as good as possible. He would have much preferred a guy, but she couldn't help him there. He was pickier than she was, and that was saying something.

She'd asked Asante fifty questions about what most lesbians wore to a formal event, but he'd been uncharacteristically vague. He, however, was wearing a new tuxedo, and since Kit was his date she was determined to match him in style.

She'd never worn anything quite like what she had on tonight, but she felt good in it. The top was dark blue, velvet, and fitted. It was also strapless and almost backless. The skirt was voluminous, coming just to her knees, with wide, multicolored stripes of satin, and a dark blue, wide belt. She'd bought new shoes, and they were surprisingly comfortable—for heels. Comfort was a must, because Asante was a darned good dancer and had gobs of energy.

The door buzzed, and she went to let Asante up. When he entered, he stood back, looked her up and down carefully and whistled. "For the first time I can remember, I wish I was straight."

"That's the nicest lie you've ever told me." She twirled around, preening. "I've forgotten how good it makes me feel to really dress up."

"You look amazing, Kit. Truly amazing."

"So do you. Simple elegance." She reached up and brushed some flakes of snow from the shoulders of his topcoat, watching a few more vaporize on his shaved head. "We're totally unprepared for this crazy weather. Who could have predicted snow in October? You need a hat, and the only thing I have that won't look stupid is my unlined rain coat."

He frowned. "You don't have a coat?"

Exasperated, she said, "Of course I had one. A nice camel hair one. But someone knocked a glass of red wine all over it at the end of last winter. I haven't had a chance to buy a new one yet."

"Why didn't you call me? My sisters could've fixed you up with no problem at all."

"I'm such a dunce!" Asante's family had lived in the Washington area since before the Civil War and was firmly ensconced at the top of the professional class. Both his sisters were members of a prominent sorority, along with other social organizations and philanthropic groups, and they were constantly in formal attire.

"Don't worry about it. We'll take a cab."

"No, no. It's not far to the subway. I can use this as a lesson to remind myself to buy an adult coat. I'm too old to be able to get away with just a parka."

"You're not too old for anything. Now put on that raggedy raincoat and let's get shakin'."

—◊—

When they entered, Asante was herded to a red carpet for photos, but Kit pried his fingers from her arm and scooted away. She was a foot away when Asante called out, "Photos don't really steal your soul!"

"Says you." She found the most distant wall and plastered herself along it, safely out of harm's way. Yes, she was paranoid, but she'd spent far too long having people notice her. Fame sucked.

When Asante's picture-taking was finished, they entered the ballroom, where a cloud of aftershave briefly overpowered her. That was…different. She was around men all day, but most politicos didn't wear cologne. They'd rather be bland than turn off even one person by wearing the wrong scent.

The room was filled to the brim with men, most of them in formal dress, a few pulling out the stops to don kilts or even white tie. When she looked more closely, she noted a decent number of women, most of them in pantsuits. "Am I the only person in a dress?" she asked, pulling Asante close to whisper in his ear.

"Of course not." His head swiveled as he scanned the crowd. "Right over there. Those ladies are dressed to kill."

Kit had to stand on her tiptoes to see over the generally taller men. "Those are drag queens!" She slapped at Asante's shoulder. "Wow. They're lots hotter than I am. How do they get hips like that?"

"I have no idea. But I think you're prettier. I like a woman who looks a little more…natural."

"You don't like women at all, buddy." She playfully popped him on the shoulder. "Can I buy you a drink?"

"Sure. Scotch and soda."

"You got it. I just have to pry my wallet out of this tiny purse." She held up her bag, barely large enough for a credit card and her keys. "You could make a fortune if you designed formal dresses with pockets."

"Even I know that would never work. You'd ruin the line." He slinked an arm around her shoulders. "You should have worn a tux. Like her."

Kit followed his eyes, spying a tall, substantial woman in a well-fitted tux. "Not a bad idea. But I'd look like I was in a boys' choir. You've gotta be tall to get away with that."

"Wouldn't hurt to be gay, either," he said, chuckling. "I don't think most guys want to fight with their girlfriend over who gets to wear the studs."

She got their drinks and they wandered around the room, with Asante introducing her to a bunch of his friends and acquaintances. After an announcement floated over the crowd stating that it was time to take their seats, they worked their way to their table, fairly near the stage. "Nice spot," Kit teased. "I guess they don't want you to have to walk too far to get your award."

They sat and he leaned over and spoke quietly. "I'm really glad you came with me. It takes another reporter to understand how hard I worked on that story."

His multi-part story on homeless gay youth had run a few months earlier, drawing praise from all—something that Kit knew was tough to do. No matter how unbiased you tried to be, you always made someone mad. "I do. And I'm proud of you. To get a mention at the White House press briefing was a big deal."

He ducked his head, always a little embarrassed to be recognized for his achievements. He'd been summa at Georgetown, and Kit knew his family was disappointed he'd become a reporter instead of a lawyer or a doctor, like most of the Lewis men. But he'd shrugged that off, followed his heart and had become a well-respected reporter. Just one of his many admirable qualities.

"Thanks. I'm glad I did it, and I'm doubly glad I did it in the summer. Freezing my butt off to interview kids at four a.m. doesn't sound like a party."

Kit regarded him for a minute. He might protest, but if he'd had to stay outside all night in ten-degree weather he would have done it. He did what he had to do to get a story.

Someone leaned over in front of Kit and said, "Asante?"

"That's me."

"Bailey Jones." The woman stuck her hand out and Asante stood to be able to shake. They chatted above Kit's head for a moment. "Congratulations on that fantastic series you wrote."

Kit looked up while they spoke. Bailey was…unique looking. As tall as Asante and pin-thin. Her dark blue velvet suit was probably made for a man—a gay man— but it fit her perfectly, making her look even taller than she was.

She definitely had the kind of angular, boyish body that lent itself to menswear, but her pearl white satin shirt added a hint of femininity. The skinny black tie whisked that away immediately, though. Kit assessed her carefully, really studying her. Nah. She could never get away with copying Bailey's look. For formal events, she'd have to stick with skirts—with no pockets.

Both Bailey and Asante sat down, and Asante made introductions. Kit shook her hand, commenting, "We should have come together. Your suit is almost the same color as my bodice."

Bailey wore big, tortoiseshell, nerd-chic glasses, and her eyebrows rose enough to pop over the frames. "I think that's the first time I've ever heard anyone use bodice in a sentence."

Asante chimed in. "Kit's a reporter. She loves using words most of the world has forgotten—if they ever knew them."

As he spoke, a woman approached from behind and tapped him on the shoulder. "Asante? Natalie Ramirez. Congratulations on your series. It was wonderful."

"Thanks. I really appreciate being recognized."

"There was a lot of competition this year, but I think your series stood out head-and-shoulders over the rest."

Bailey twitched her head, then pulled out the chair next to her. "Here's an empty chair, Nat. Sit down for a second."

Natalie walked around them and Kit was pleased to see she was also wearing a dress. With her tanned skin, Natalie's off-white, spangled sheath really made her stand out in the crowd. As she sat down, her dark eyes slid up and down Bailey's body. "You look wonderful." Her voice was a little throaty, almost sultry. Kit sat up, attentive, hoping she was about to see her first lesbian seduction as Natalie eyed Bailey like she was a tasty steak. "You never wore velvet when you were chasing me around campus." Darn! No seduction.

Bailey smiled at Kit and Asante as she shrugged her shoulders. "Natalie was my first love. I got to make all of my mistakes with her."

Natalie patted her cheek loud enough to be audible. "Not all of them, sweetie. You're single again. Be quiet."

What? That was a strange thing to say. Must have been some private joke. You could never sort through the references old friends used. It was like a different language.

Bailey shrugged, not looking bothered in the least. "Sad but true. Before you spill all my secrets, let me introduce you to Kit Travis."

Natalie started to take her hand, but stopped abruptly. "Kit Travis? The Kit Travis?"

Bailey stared at her curiously. "Are you… Should I know who you are?"

Kit's color rose as her stomach sank. She should have prepared better. Asante would have had fun making up a fake name for her. "I'm only well known to news junkies. I write a blog and a newsletter about Washington politics."

"Not a newsletter," Natalie said. "The newsletter. For years, everyone's been reading it, but no one knew who wrote it. That gave it an edge that people loved." Her dark eyes landed on Kit. "We found out who she was a couple of months ago. It was a big, big deal."

"It wasn't that big a deal." Kit hoped they'd move on.

Natalie wasn't to be dissuaded. "Of course it was. It made the national news and all of the major papers." She addressed Bailey. "You probably don't understand how important the newsletter is. A staffer told me that people in the White House scan the headlines in the major dailies, then actually read the *Daily Lineup*."

Kit could feel herself blush. "That's probably an exaggeration, but I hope it's not."

Natalie gave her a long, probing look. "Are you here with Asante, or are you…a member?"

"I've been a member for years. I've even got an Equal Rights Campaign Fund T-shirt I wear if I'm in town during Gay Pride."

"Really?" she purred, looking remarkably pleased. "I've never seen you at anything."

"This is the first event I've been to. Once I 'came out,' as it were, I realized I didn't have to be so careful about everything. It's nice to be able to just live my life without trying to do everything anonymously."

"You've been a member for years? Did Senator Brearly know his girlfriend was an ERCF member?"

Ugh! Damn, she hated going through this again and again. It took some convincing to get her mouth to contort into a benign smile. "He was my boyfriend, not my jailer."

Natalie just looked at her, not adding a word. Maybe she was a reporter too. She clearly knew how to make someone feel uncomfortable enough to keep talking.

The silence got to Kit and she added a little more. "We broke up four years ago, but I get the feeling people think we're still in daily contact." She tried to remove any sting from her smile. "We're not."

"But you were together a long time. How long was it?"

"Eight years."

"Wow. Eight years is forever. I guess that's why I still see articles referring to you as his girlfriend."

Give it a rest! "I was with the guy for a long time. Now I'm not. That chapter of my life is over. Forever."

Bailey shifted so she blocked Natalie's view. "I don't know who Senator Brearly is, so that chapter of your life never existed for me."

Kit let out a sigh, very grateful to Bailey for blatantly changing the subject. "You're obviously not in politics."

"I vote." She had a darling smile. Really sweet with a slightly impish quality. "But that's my only connection to politics. I'm a systems architect." She waited for Kit to comment, and when she didn't speak up right away, Bailey added, "Computer nerd."

"The biggest." Natalie peeked around her shoulder. "She takes computers apart for fun."

"I do not! I play squash for fun."

Kit's mouth dropped open. "I play squash! I haven't met another woman who plays since college."

"Do you live in DC?"

"Yeah. Foggy Bottom. You?"

"Near Dupont Circle. Wanna play?"

Kit reached into her tiny purse and extracted a business card. "I'd love to."

"I think you can beat her," Asante said to Bailey. "Every time she plays she complains about getting her butt kicked."

She elbowed him playfully. "That's because I have to play with guys who are younger, faster, bigger, and…"

"Better," Asante chimed in.

Kit made a show of looking Bailey over. "You're definitely younger, and taller…"

Natalie interrupted. "She's not as young as she looks." She got up and put her hand on Bailey's shoulder. "We're the same age, but everyone thinks I'm older."

Kit looked up and spent a moment surveying Natalie. She did look older than Bailey, or maybe she simply seemed more mature. Whatever it was, she didn't have a thing to complain about. Natalie was a knockout, pure and simple. Bronze-hued skin, deep brown eyes, chestnut hair with enough wave to make it curl attractively around her shoulders, and a sharp, perceptive gaze. She looked like the gorgeous DA from a TV police procedural. But even though she was pretty, Kit couldn't see her and Bailey as a couple. Maybe it was just her lack of familiarity with lesbian couples, but they didn't have that "we belong together" look.

"Well, you both look younger than me, but so does everyone else here." Kit realized how grumpy that sounded, and added, "I've got a birthday coming up and I'm not looking forward to it."

Asante put his arm around her shoulders. "Kit's from such good genetic stock that forty probably isn't a third of her expected lifespan. She won't be middle-aged for another ten years."

Bailey looked at her for a second, then said, "You look much younger than forty. My ex will be forty this year and she'd trade with you in a second."

Natalie tapped her on the top of the head. "That's one of the reasons you're single. You say what you think." She stood up and started to leave, but something about Bailey's hair caught her eye and she stopped. "I can't believe you spent so much time getting that suit tailored just right and then did such a haphazard job on your hair."

Natalie did have a point. Not that anyone should mention it in public, of course, but Bailey's hair didn't match the rest of her. From the front, her sandy-colored hair looked okay—plain but okay—but lots of strands had escaped from the haphazard braid.

Kit watched, amazed, as Natalie unfastened the band and ran her fingers through the braid, letting the hair fall where it may. Taking a brush from her purse, she stood there in the crowded ballroom and brushed the hair carefully, with Bailey not giving any sign that it bothered her. Actually, she leaned back against her friend, like she was getting a good head rub. If a friend came up and started screwing with her hair, Kit would have decked her!

Diligently, Natalie separated the strands into three equal parts. "I wish I had a spray bottle to get the fly-aways," she grumbled. "Something you could have easily done at home." She snapped one of the hanks a little harder than she had to, but Bailey just smiled placidly. "I guess I've gotta use this again," she said, frowning as she finished and replaced the band. "If you would have blown it dry, it'd have more volume and you could wear it down."

"Not interested."

"How can you not be interested? You fussed over that suit like a new baby. Then you stick your hair into a sloppy braid."

Bailey tilted her chin to be able to look into Natalie's eyes. "I can't see the back of my head. When I look in the mirror—I'm super. That's all I care about."

Natalie brandished the brush, like she was going to bonk her on the head with it.

Kit watched them, amazed. Bailey acted like a kid being tended to by a disapproving older sister. Strange.

"I've done all I can." Natalie bent and kissed Bailey's cheek, then rubbed a faint lipstick print away. "Don't play with your phone during dinner." Then she strode away, elegant and self-possessed as she glided across the room.

"I have two older sisters." Bailey grinned as she watched her thread her way back to her table. "But Nat's convinced she's the third."

Kit was still trying to think of what she'd do to someone who embarrassed her like that in front of strangers. Maybe the difference was that Bailey didn't look embarrassed in the least. Either she was a very cool customer, or she was just used to being treated like a dog being groomed.

A stream of people came by to congratulate Asante, and, thankfully, no one else seemed to recognize Kit. Or if they did, they didn't make an issue of it. At one point, Kit shifted her gaze, noting that Bailey had scooted her chair back a little and now had one ankle crossed over a knee, her phone propped against her calf, texting so quickly her fingers were a blur. Apparently, Natalie's warning had no effect.

Soon, Asante directed his attention to the guy who sat next to him. Asante was a great date when he wasn't tempted by an available guy, but when he was— sayonara. Kit hoped the seat next to Bailey stayed empty so she'd have someone to talk to—if she could get her to put that phone down.

—⁓—

Bailey had to use all of her skills to focus only on keeping up with the conversation. It was tough trying to ignore the way Kit's eyes twinkled when she laughed, or the way the pin-lights made her hair gleam like gold. Too bad it was so short. Why would you do that to really good hair? She laughed at herself. Who was she to criticize another woman's hair?

Other than the short hair, Kit was exactly Bailey's type—slim, delicate, and fair, with finely sculpted features. She'd never had a girlfriend who looked like that, and that made it all the more exciting to sit there and lust after her. Those warm brown eyes kept landing on her, making her skin prickle, as if they actually emitted heat.

As she'd told Kit, she'd never heard of the ex-boyfriend, but he was obviously history. The forceful way she'd said that part of her life was over must have meant the straight part of it. And she'd said something else…something about being out now. If she was famous enough for Nat to know her, being at an event like this meant she was comfortable being openly gay. Niiiice.

—⁕—

After dinner, conversation stopped as they started handing the hardware out. Bailey tried to pay attention, but awards dinners were so boring. They'd started handing out the awards a half hour ago, but, from the list in the program, they'd barely started. Her chin was propped on her hand, and she tried, unsuccessfully, to stop a yawn.

Kit leaned over and whispered, "You look bored to death."

Nodding, Bailey told the truth. "I'm not really very connected. I've only been in town a couple of months, and…this isn't really my thing. I've been doing some work for ERCF but most of this stuff's over my head."

"You're really not into politics."

"Not really. I mean, I know I should be…"

"Let's go get a drink."

Damned good idea! "Right behind you," Bailey said, smiling to herself as they threaded their way through the jumble of tables.

After getting their drinks, Kit guided Bailey to a relatively quiet spot a few feet away from the still-crowded bar. "Even if you don't like politics, it can be fun to watch people try to work the room. Do you recognize any of those people?" She pointed at a gaggle of guys looking as if they were fighting to get a tiny bit of recognition from a striking-looking woman in a dark suit.

"Uhm…the woman looks familiar, but I'm not sure where I've seen her."

"That's Sarah Meadows. Pundit. Big deal. Very big deal. The superstar of the liberal media. Now stand here for a minute and watch people kiss her ass."

"She has a nice one, but why are people kissing it?"

"Because she's got a popular nightly show. Watch." She laughed, a throaty, sexy chuckle. "That's Congressman Roberts' chief. He'd blow Sarah for a chance to get his guy on her show. But it's not going to happen. Roberts is a solid liberal, but he's got no personality. The only way he'll ever get headlines is if he gets caught boffing an intern or two." Kit slapped Bailey on the shoulder. "Check it out! Senator Shipman's chief's literally blocking Roberts' guy out. Like a nursing pup trying to starve the runt! Brutal!" She threw her head back and laughed. "God, I love politics."

"Sarah looks amused. Like she's enjoying the attention."

"You don't get into this game if you're not a fame whore. Well," she said, shrugging her shoulders, "You might start out with noble goals, but they get perverted pretty quickly."

"How about you? Fame whore or perverted idealist?" Bailey tried to make sure she was giving Kit a teasing smile.

It took her quite a while to answer. When she did, she seemed a little somber. "I was never very idealistic and I hate being famous." Her face slowly brightened into a warm grin. "I guess I'm an outlier."

Bailey didn't care if she was selling her soul to the highest bidder. She was cute enough to make you ignore any sin imaginable.

—⁂—

Asante led Kit around the dance floor like they were in a contest. He was a little more skilled, a little more willing to really put himself out there, but she wasn't very far behind. Luckily, not many people knew Bailey, and no one seemed to notice she'd locked her focus onto Kit and was now happily imagining cutting in and taking Kit for a slower, closer, more sensual… A bop on the head stopped her daydream cold.

"Put your tongue back in your mouth," Natalie chided. She sat down next to Bailey. "On second thought… Go ahead and drool over her. Having someone like her on our side would be huge."

"I'd like her on my side, on my lap…" Bailey chuckled when Natalie gave her a warning look. "You can tell a lot about a woman when you watch her dance." She couldn't stop looking. Kit was shaking her butt like a woman who felt very, very comfortable with her body, and that was always a turn-on.

"I don't think you understand how important she is. If we could get somebody on the inside, who could nudge the right people at the right time… I'm telling you. It would be a very big deal."

Bailey smirked at her. "I'm giving a lot of my time to ERCF, but I'm not going to pimp for them. I'd love to go out with her, but not just to have her do your bidding."

"You can do both. You're all about multitasking."

"Only in some areas." She reluctantly turned away from staring and faced Natalie. "Why do you know her ex? Were they in the tabloids or something?"

Natalie blinked. "You really don't know him?" Scowling, she said, "You've gotta get your head out of your computer and into politics. This is a political organization, Bailey. You've got to pay attention."

"I'm paying attention now," she said, giving Natalie a big smile.

She sighed heavily. "Not for the right reasons." Bailey had years of experience in ignoring Natalie's mother-hen qualities. If she waited her out, Nat would respond, even if it was reluctantly. "All right," she groaned after a few seconds. "Henry Brearly was a left-leaning Republican congressman from Boston. In case you haven't been paying any attention, leaning even a little left is rare for a Republican. When one of Massachusetts's senators got picked for the cabinet, they had a special election and he won—pretty handily, if I remember correctly. It was off-cycle, so it was easier for a newbie without a huge organization to sneak in. He also didn't have to spend the kind of money he would have had to come up with in a national election."

"How do you remember this stuff?"

"It's important. Anyway, he was just re-elected, and while he's liberal for a Republican, he's starting to drift further and further to the right. Everyone says he's positioning himself to run for president."

"Fascinating. But you know I don't care about that. I'm interested in Kit."

She rolled her eyes. "I don't know a lot. He's a politician, not a celebrity. They weren't hounded by the paparazzi when they were together."

"Then why do you know about her at all?"

Natalie waved a hand in front of herself. "The senator is a good-looking, young guy. There were lots of fluffy personality profiles in the press. And since he was a unicorn, a liberal Republican, even the left-leaning press liked him. Kit was always on his arm at official functions, but they never married, and that made people wonder."

"Why?"

Natalie looked like she wanted to pinch her, but she behaved herself—this time. "Because politicians get married. Period. If you don't, everyone assumes you're gay."

Grinning, Bailey said, "Looks like people assumed the wrong person was gay." She turned again to watch Kit dance. "I just hope she's single—and likes nerds."

—∞—

Late that night, Asante and Kit stood together on the Metro platform, freezing. It wasn't really that frigid, but the first cold front of the year always seemed worse than it was. Asante put his arm around her and she burrowed into his body, trying to soak up any warmth he could spare. "You've gotta get a coat, or a boyfriend. Or are you going to give women a try?"

"Huh?" She looked up at him, able to see the tiny nick he'd made under his chin while shaving.

"You're going on a date with Bailey. I thought maybe you were expanding your options."

She made a dismissive grunt. "We're going to play squash. That's hardly a date."

"Bailey thinks it is."

Kit pulled away and stared at him. "Why do you say that?"

"You said something about coming out and how much easier it was to live openly. As soon as you said that, she asked you to play. Date."

"No, she asked me to play to stop Natalie from grilling me about my ex-boyfriend. No date."

"Date," he said, nodding confidently.

"Lesbians don't have boyfriends."

"Ones who've come out of the closet might."

"Asante." She bumped into him, making him step back to get his balance. "Don't even tease about that."

"I'm teasing, but I'm also being serious. I guarantee she thinks you're gay. If you don't want to have an uncomfortable evening, you'd better find a way to come out—as a straight girl."

"Ridiculous," she muttered. "Straight people can be supportive of gay rights, you know."

"I know that. I'm just saying…" His big, brown eyes danced with impish charm. "Date."

Chapter Three

BAILEY DIDN'T CALL TO arrange a match. She texted. That made it harder to drop in the fact that Kit liked dudes. She sat at her desk, staring at her phone for a moment. "Match on Weds?" didn't leave a lot of room for elaboration.

"Sure. My club?"

"OK. Where?"

Kit sent the particulars, then went over in her head, once again, what she'd said at the dinner. Asante was letting his fanciful imagination get the better of him. If Bailey had as much trouble finding a squash partner as Kit had, that would explain away her interest. And if she did think it was a date, Kit would find a way to make it clear she played for the other team.

—m—

Being beaten by guys was one thing. Being thrashed by a gangly, long-legged woman who looked like Bambi on ice was quite another. How had Bailey so effortlessly trounced Kit's best efforts? And she said she'd only been playing for a few years. Infuriating!

Bailey truly did look like a lanky high school boy who hadn't yet grown into his body. In her gym clothes, she would have more easily passed as the captain of the computer club than an athlete. Nothing but long arms and legs. But her reaction time had been uncanny; not to mention how tactically she played. She was clairvoyant!

Kit waited for her in the lobby, licking her wounds while pondering her new squash partner. Bailey was decidedly unique. When she stepped back and really thought about it, Kit guessed lesbians would be seriously into Bailey. The big glasses and the way she haphazardly gathered up her sandy blonde hair into a clip gave her a look—a sharply androgynous look that lesbians probably found appealing. If Kit could get her out of those glasses, cut a few inches from her hair… Maybe a blunt cut that would take advantage of how straight it was. While she was at it, she'd dress her in something a little more feminine. Not ruffles and lace, but there were plenty of things that would keep her androgynous but still make her look like a woman. Just a few changes and she'd be really attractive. But Bailey clearly wasn't into looking girly. When she exited the locker room in her street clothes, she looked just like your nerdy younger brother. A blue oxford cloth shirt, open at the neck, a yellow knit tie, loosely knotted, a pair of dark jeans and brown suede ankle boots. She definitely had a look.

"How about a drink?" Bailey asked. "Winner buys."

"Ha! I knew you were going to offer that. That's why I tanked it."

"I'll bet you did." Bailey slipped into a navy blue stadium coat, then moved over to a mirror to add a colorfully striped wool scarf. Intently focused, she spent a few moments buttoning and tucking to make sure a whisper of air couldn't get in. Someone needed to tell her it was fifty degrees outside.

Bailey then put her hand on the small of Kit's back and guided her to the door. As they got close, Bailey jumped ahead to open the door. That was weird. Guys didn't even do that very often. When they hit the street she put her hand on Kit's back again, directing her to go south. Then they walked next to one another, and Kit's brain processed their interactions for a minute.

Not knowing any lesbians was leaving her at a huge disadvantage. Bailey was…butch…or androgynous or something. Maybe it was a thing for her to act…gallant? To be a little like guys used to be, when they dashed in front of a woman to open a door. The question was—did she do this for all women? Or just the ones she was interested in. Kit didn't have a damn clue.

They went to a nearby pub, Kit's choice. "I've been here a couple of times," she said as they entered. They were barely through the door when her favorite bartender called out, "Vodka and cranberry, Kit?"

Bailey cracked up, snickering when Kit said, "That complete stranger must be some sort of psychic!"

Bailey held up a pair of fingers. "Make it two." When they sat down, Bailey leaned over and spoke conspiratorially. "There's a place by my apartment where the bartender knows what drink to bring me based on my facial expression when I cross the threshold."

"Thanks for trying to make me not seem like a lush."

"Maybe I'm just confessing to being one too."

Their server brought the drinks, and Kit held up her glass and they clinked them together. "To friendly bartenders with good memories."

"I'll drink to that. And most other things."

There was a moment's silence. That was awfully common when you were with someone you didn't know. But Kit's reporter's instinct never let an opportunity pass her by. Time to interview. "Tell me about this job of yours. Did you say you were a systems engineer?"

Bailey sipped at her drink. "Kinda. I was an engineer, but a few years ago I switched to systems architecture. It fits me much better."

"Is that like a regular architect?"

"Yeah. A little bit. In systems work you tend to be more of a generalist as you go up. You lose your sharp focus and learn to step back and look at the whole picture."

"Mmm." She squinted at her for a moment, trying to determine what she really understood. "That doesn't tell me much. I need more details."

"I can do that." She must have really loved her job. When she started to talk, her eyes glimmered with interest. "Let's say you want to put in a system that keeps track of the documents your office creates. I'd meet with the big guys, the managers, to hear what they were trying to accomplish. Then I'd work with the users and the supervisors to figure out what they currently have and what they need to get the end product they want. A million things can go into that – hardware, software, security, access, you name it."

"But you don't do the actual work. You're like the project manager."

"That's pretty true. I've gotten good at being able to communicate with non-technical people, but I also have to do a lot of really wonky stuff." She chuckled. "Because the really techie people have to be spoken to in their native tongue— machine language."

"That's pretty interesting stuff. Been doing it long?"

"Ten years?" She squinted in thought. "My ex would say twenty, since she thought I worked a hundred percent too hard." Her easy smile disappeared and the kind eyes hardened.

"That sounds bad."

"More like sad." She looked over the top of her glasses. She did that a lot, looking a little vulnerable when she did. Her eyes were so damn pretty, a pale, clear blue. Why cover them up with frames? Kit would have worn contacts if she had eyes that nice.

"Wanna talk about it? I love to listen. It's a calling."

A bit of the smile came back, but she looked a little unsure of herself. "Really?"

"Sure. Of course. I really am interested."

Cocking her head a few degrees, Bailey said, "But you don't even know me. Why would you be interested in my broken heart?"

Kit batted her eyes. "That's how you get to know people. I'm not much for small talk. I want to know people."

Bailey leaned back in her chair, giving Kit what looked like a truly puzzled gaze. "That's not the way most of my friends are, but I'll give it a go."

"Great." She put her chin in her hand and said, "Spill it."

Hands raised in warning, Bailey said, "It's not a very exciting story. You've probably heard things like this a thousand—"

"Spill…it," Kit urged, scowling. "Every story is exciting if it affects someone deeply."

"Oh." Her pretty eyes opened wide. "Then this one's super exciting." She took a sip of her drink, swallowed, then began, "Julie and I met at Share Me not long after the company was founded."

"Ooo. The masters of social media. Aren't they in California? Every time I see the wunderkind founder he's in shorts and a T-shirt. I figured he must be somewhere warm."

"Yep. Silicon Valley. I was just out of college, starting my first job as a systems engineer. Julie was in marketing, but she's a total nerd too. She was a few years older than me and had taken a big risk to switch to a start-up. There were only thirty people there when we met at the new employee orientation."

"Wow! How many now?"

"Thousands. We got in right when they started to gear up. Rode it until we were too tired to work another day."

"Ka-ching!" Kit didn't have a huge interest in business, but even she had paid attention when the stock started out at eight hundred dollars on the first day of the IPO. Someone who'd been there at the beginning would have gotten a load of options. Bailey had to have some serious bank.

Blushing, Bailey looked away. That was so cute! Like she was embarrassed to be a success. She'd never make it in Washington with that kind of attitude!

"Not really," she said, still blushing. "If we'd stayed for a few more years we both would have gotten crazy rich. The options I have are worth a good chunk, and I'm not sorry I left. Money's never been my primary motivator. Share Me had gotten too big for me. I get off on starting things, not tinkering with things that are already in place. So I wanted to find another start-up. Julie wanted to sell some options so she could kick back and focus on having a baby. She thought it would be a good idea to get away from the stress of the job for a while."

"A baby, huh? You two were obviously serious about each other."

"Very much." Bailey nodded soberly. "We'd been together about four years at the time and both wanted a child. But things didn't work out. Julie couldn't get pregnant, no matter what we tried. " She closed her eyes and seemed to think for a minute. "We had six…no, seven IVF cycles. She got pregnant with the last one, but lost it just a week after we got the positive test." Bailey put her hand to her forehead and rubbed it for a few seconds. She looked so sad Kit almost reached over and hugged her, but that was way too forward with someone she barely knew.

"We tried for four long years. By then, Julie was thirty-eight and was starting to get spooked about the higher risk of birth defects. So she wanted to go for an open adoption."

"I know a couple who've done that. It worked out great for them."

"Sure, that's true for many…probably most. But read a little bit on the Internet and you'll find horror stories of birth mothers changing their minds after a week or two. Lots of states allow a whole month to renege. I didn't want to go that way. I wanted to use a surrogate or have a fetus implanted. We just couldn't agree."

"And you broke up because of that?"

"No, not exactly. I have a tendency…" She looked up over those big glasses again. "To work a lot." She sighed heavily. "To work instead of anything else. Julie'd been warning me for years, but it's darned hard to go home when your whole team is slaving away. We'd planned a big trip to China." She blinked. "Did I mention she was Chinese-American?"

"No."

"She was. She can trace her people back to laying the transcontinental railroad, and even prospecting for gold."

"That's…amazing."

"Yeah, her family history is like a history book on California." She took a breath, frowning. "After she left Share Me she had so much free time that she spent hundreds of hours doing genealogical research, tracking down every lead she could find on her family. We were going to spend a month in China, visiting any spot her ancestors were connected to."

"I have a feeling I know where this is going. Big trip planned... workaholic..."

"Yeah. Good guess. I'd cleared the trip, of course. But we were months late on a big project at my new company, Pictogram. My boss promised he'd reimburse us for any money we lost from canceling." She frowned. "Not canceling. Deferring." A determined, sober expression covered her face. "You can't turn your back on your team at a critical point. You just can't."

Kit tried to take any sting from her words. "But you turned your back on Julie."

"That's what she thought." Her voice rose. "But she wasn't even working at the time. Delaying a month would have made no difference at all!"

"But it did to her."

Bailey sank down in her seat, defeated. "Yeah. She was a very quiet person, a logical thinker. We never, ever argued." She sighed, looking so sad it was hard to watch. "Maybe that should have been a danger sign. I got home on the day we were supposed to have gone, and found a note. She said her plans were as important as mine, and she was going alone."

"Ouch!"

"Yeah. Then I got a note from her after she'd been gone about a week. She said she didn't miss me as much as she thought she would. That I was gone so often, it wasn't much different than being thousands of miles away."

"Double ouch!"

"Yeah. Now here comes the bad part." She swallowed, then shifted her gaze to the table. "When she came home, we had it out over her leaving. Instead of apologizing, she said she'd thought it over and had decided she couldn't trust me to put her and a baby first."

"Damn, Bailey! That's cold."

"I sure thought so. But that's how she was. Once she figured out the right answer, she went for it. She didn't trust me anymore." She looked up, pain filling her features. "Last I heard, her baby's due in a month or so."

"Open adoption?"

She nodded. "Just what she wanted, and she didn't have to put up with me second guessing her."

"That must have been awful for you. Is that when you moved?"

"Not right away. I moved out of our house, of course, and tried to find another, but I obviously wasn't into it. I was sleeping on a friend's sofa, working more than I ever had, trying to work instead of feel. But you can't keep that up forever. It finally dawned on me that I'd never be happy living in the area. I knew I'd run into her and her baby." She shivered roughly. "I wouldn't have been able to take that."

"Did you come here for a job?"

"No. I just moved. Natalie talked me into it. My family's in Pennsylvania, so it was a chance to be closer to them. I needed my family to get me through it." A ghost of a smile settled on her lips. "I don't really like the east coast, but seeing my family more has been just what I needed."

"Who do you work for?"

"Oh." She nodded. "I thought I'd said I was independent. I've been taking jobs as they come up. Luckily, Natalie knows lots of people and she's introduced me to people who run departments at think tanks and various branches of the government." She showed that shy smile again. "I'm not great at networking and bullshitting my way into jobs. So far I've had more work than I can manage, but that's all due to Nat and her contacts."

"Are you happy here?"

She shrugged. "It's okay, but Silicon Valley's tough to beat."

"I've never been there, but I'd bet the weather's better."

"Every damn day," she agreed, showing a sweet smile. "You really are a good listener. I haven't told that whole story to hardly anyone."

"I'm glad you told me." She lightly touched the back of Bailey's hand. "Really."

"I don't mind talking about myself, but I guess I've gotta feel…mmm…safe."

"I'll take that as a compliment. So…what are your plans for a baby?"

Bailey held her hands up. "I don't have any. After we broke up, I realized I was doing it mostly for Julie. She was so into it I kinda got dragged along."

"Just like that?" Kit snapped her fingers. "Dream gone?"

Nodding, Bailey said, "That's what made me see it was Julie's dream. I didn't want it enough to be a single mother."

"I'm sorry you got your heart stomped on to learn that." Kit took a quick look at her watch. "I hate to rush, but I've gotta go listen to a bunch of policy wonks at the Pentagon at eight in the morning. Do you mind if we settle up?"

"I've got it." She took her wallet from her back pocket and left a few bills. "Since you're a regular, I'll leave a good tip." Then she stood and drained the last inch of her drink. They walked out together and stood in the coolish, damp night.

"We'll have to play again," Kit said. "Even though you beat me like a drum, you're fun. Much less serious than the guys I generally play with."

"How about next Wednesday?" She pulled out her phone and checked something. "I can do the same time."

Kit had no reason to demur. But Asante's words kept coming back to her. How did you wedge in the fact that you were straight when a woman just wanted to make a date to play squash? "Yeah. Wednesday's great." She took out her own phone and went to her calendar to enter the time. Just as she slipped it back into her bag Bailey appeared, an inch from her face. Soft lips met hers, and if her startle-response had been just a little sharper, she would have yelped like someone had stomped on her foot. Her eyes widened and she stepped back, stunned. But Bailey was already gliding down the street, heading toward Dupont Circle. "See you then," she called, waving.

Kit's hand went up and moved in an approximation of a wave. Stupid, stupid, stupid! Damn Asante and his accurate predictions! She stood there, her lips tingling slightly from the soft brush of Bailey's. Now what?

—⁂—

The next afternoon, Kit was meeting with one of the National Desk editors at the Post, and she swung by Asante's desk, surprising him. He looked up, then leaned back in his chair. "It's weird seeing you in my building." He noted the big ID tag she wore. "Ooo…the seventh floor, huh? Wanna tell me who, what, when and why?"

She moved around to perch on the edge of his desk. "Oh, sure. You know me…old gabby pants."

He stuck his lower lip out like a three-year-old. "Just here to taunt me about getting to talk to people at my own paper who don't even know my name?"

"Nope. I'm offering a late lunch or an early dinner. Knowing you…probably a late lunch. You always forget to eat when you're working on something big."

His head cocked. "How do you know I'm working on something big?"

Kit ran her hand over his shaved head. "Because you've been very closed-mouthed for a week or two. When you've got something big going on you're like the Sphinx."

He got up, put his jacket on and took her by the elbow. "Officially? No comment. But you're right about lunch. Are you eating real food these days?"

"I am. I'm finally at my ideal weight. You may try to put the ten pounds I lost right back on me in any way you wish."

They stood by the elevator bank, waiting. Asante's eyes narrowed and he nodded. "Gotta be a burger. Haven't had one all week."

They rode down in the elevator with a car full of people, but none of them spoke. As they exited, Kit said, "There was a weird vibe in that car. Did somebody die?"

He shook his head slightly, warning her off. When they got outside he said, "Lots of somebodies. Another round of layoffs/buy-outs is supposed to fall this week. And this time they're rumored to be looking to cut some big paychecks."

"What do you mean by big?"

"Editors. Or assistant editors at the very least. Big names."

"Big names?" She saw a list scroll through her head of all of the assistant editors she could think of.

Asante snapped his fingers in front of her eyes. "I know you're already writing the story, but that was off the record."

"What?" she squawked. "You didn't say that. You definitely didn't say that."

He put his arm around her shoulders and gave her a quick hug. "Well, I'm saying it now. I promise I'll call you the minute they make the announcement. You can have the story already written. Just plug in the names."

"Wow. Editors, huh? This shit is getting real."

"It's already real. And if I get fired, I'm coming to work for you."

She bumped him with her shoulder. "You know I'd love to have you. But you'd hate writing about national politics. No one cares about DC as much as you do. The local beat's perfect for you."

"Sadly, you're right." He sighed. "I love my damn job. I just hope I get to keep it."

They went to one of their old standbys, ordered at the counter, then chose a booth. "I like it here at four o'clock," he said, looking around at the mostly empty spot. "This might be my new lunch time." He picked up his soft drink and took a big gulp. "Always better from the fountain. How was your squash game? Did Bailey crush you?"

"Like a bug. She's about nine feet tall, and has arms that are a foot longer than mine. It would've been embarrassing for her if she hadn't beaten me."

"Yeah, that's you," he snickered. "Always concerned with your opponent's feelings."

"Fine. She's substantially better than I am. Satisfied?" She stuck her tongue out.

"You gave in awfully easily. That's not like you."

"I have bigger fish to fry. I'm not going to say you were right about it being a date, because I'm not sure you were, but is it common for lesbians to kiss casual friends on the lips?"

His eyes widened. "Kiss…like how?"

"Mmm, like you kiss me. Quick, dry, almost a glancing blow."

He nodded, his brow furrowed. "All of my friends kiss hello and goodbye. But I don't know a lot of lesbians. Do straight girls not do that?"

"No," she admitted. "At least my friends don't. We kiss on the cheek, never on the lips."

"I guess it could be a gay thing." He rubbed his head, a tic he fell into when he was pondering something. "Did she act like it was a date?"

"Not a bit. Totally casual. We chatted about what brought her to DC, then I had to go. She gave me a quick kiss, then took off."

"So…the question isn't whether she thought it was a date. The real question is why didn't you tell her you were straight?"

"I would have. I definitely would have. But we talked about her the whole time. I had to get up at the crack of dawn, so I had to get going before I could wedge it in."

Their burgers were delivered, and Asante started loading his up with every condiment he could get his hands on. Kit waited to speak, knowing he wouldn't be able to listen when he was so focused. The man loved his burgers. He took his first bite, moaned in pleasure, then put the burger down to wipe his hands. "If I asked a guy out, and I liked being with him, I'd kiss him in a way he'd know I was serious. Maybe you're right. Maybe she didn't think it was a date."

Kit started to eat, letting his assessment settle in her head. He was probably right. She could tell Bailey her status next week. No rush.

—m—

The next time they played, Kit did a lot better. This time, she actually reached double digits in one of their games. Still, going down 11-5, 12-10, 11-3 wasn't a good day at the office. Luckily, it was fun playing against Bailey. She didn't act like they were performing brain surgery or deactivating a bomb, like so many guys did. Clearly serious about her game, she could still laugh and joke while she was kicking ass.

After showering, they met in the lobby of the club. Normally, Kit would have hung out in the locker room to wait, but being with Bailey was starting to feel like being with a guy, and she would never strip in front of a guy she wasn't sleeping with. "Do you have time for a drink?" Kit asked when Bailey emerged, her wet hair twisted into a knot and secured to the back of her head with a clip.

"Not really." She bit at her bottom lip. "I shouldn't have come out at all tonight, but I needed to get my blood moving. I haven't left my apartment in two days. Really tight deadline."

Kit took a second look at her clothing. A white shirt with a broad blue stripe, a deep red paisley tie and dark, wool slacks. Polished loafers covered her bright red socks. This is how she dressed to dash out of the house for a squash game? What was wrong with sweats? She looked more like a model for GQ than a computer nerd.

Looking at her oversized watch, Bailey made a face. "How about this? I should be finished with my project by Saturday. I'll make you dinner to make up for not being able to go for a drink tonight."

"Dinner? Really?" Dinner at a woman's house on a Saturday night was a date. Especially when the woman dressed up to meet you to play squash.

"Sure. I'm a pretty good cook, and I don't get to show off much. Are you free?"

Kit found herself telling the truth. Unfiltered. "Yeah, I am. But are you sure about this? That's a big payback for not being able to get a drink."

"I'm a giver." She leaned in close and placed another gentle kiss on Kit's lips. Was this one a little longer than the other one had been? Or was Kit waiting for it this time? How in the hell were you supposed to know? There should be some sort of chart you could check! "I'll text you my address. Bring wine," she added, floating away with a wave.

Kit stood there for a minute, her mind going in fifty directions at once. There was only one thing she was sure of. She had a date on Saturday night.

Fuuuuck.

—m—

Asante was unrelenting. Kit felt like she'd been caught committing a felony and was now facing the judge. "You're playing with her, Kit, and that's not like you."

"I'm not trying to play with her," she said for the third time. "How was I supposed to shoehorn it in?"

"You just put it out there. Why are you being so coy?"

"I'm not! We finished our match, she couldn't go out, so she offered dinner. I was trying to think of a reason not to go, but nothing came to mind. It seemed dumb to refuse just because I don't want to sleep with her."

"You should have told her as soon as she invited you."

"Oh, dinner?" she said, roleplaying. "I wish I could, but I go over to the Tidal Basin on Saturday nights and blow guys. I can't go more than three days without dick."

"Damn, that's a weird place to go." He gave her a puzzled look, making her feel even dumber. "How about, 'I'll have to check. I've been seeing a guy and we usually get together on Friday or Saturday...'"

"That's a total lie!" She wanted to shake him. "I don't want to make shit up, Asante. I want to be friends with her. And I don't want to try to build a friendship by lying."

"She's a lesbian, who thinks you're coming to her apartment for a date. Trust me," he said, his brown eyes narrowed, "she'd rather have you tell her a little lie than feel like an idiot if she hits on you."

In silence, Kit let his words swirl around in her head. He was right. No doubt about it. Totally right. But she knew she wasn't going to make the call. She told very important people very unpleasant things on a daily basis—but she didn't have the guts to tell Bailey she was straight. Why? Damned if she knew.

Chapter Four

KIT HAD A HUNDRED THINGS to do. Maybe a thousand. Writing and editing a daily political newsletter was like having a truck bearing down on you at great speed. Constant pressure. Hours of phone calls, e-mails and meetings, not to mention managing a staff. But nothing could hold her attention the next day. Instead of writing, she spent the majority of her time doing a rigorous personal inventory of her sexual orientation.

At almost forty, she could state, with one hundred percent certainty, that she'd never had a single sexual feeling for another woman. She'd never kissed a girl, had never wanted to. Lesbian porn, on the few occasions a college boyfriend had tried to use it to heat her up, left her cold. She had good girlfriends and had warm feelings for them, but had never wanted to see them naked. Women were sometimes pleasurable to look at, but looking at them was like viewing art or fashion. There was no sexual vibe. At all.

So what was up with Bailey? Kit had made an innocent mistake at the dinner, but she'd had several opportunities to correct it. She should have called moments after that first, brief kiss. It would have been simple. "Hey, I'm hoping I didn't give off the wrong impression, but I'm into guys." Or she could have done an honest variation on Asante's advice and said something like, "At this point I'm free for dinner, but if a guy asks me out, I'm going to have to cancel." Women did that kind of thing all the time. It would have been simple. Really simple. But she hadn't, and now she was clearly going on a date. With a woman. Why? She didn't know. She truly didn't know.

—⁂—

Kit had never been in a lesbian's apartment. That was weird to admit, but she'd met very few lesbians in her career, and the few she'd come in contact with hadn't seemed interested in being friends. And she wasn't going to try to find a lesbian friend just to tick another minority group off her list.

Inside Out

Bailey's apartment was in one of the new buildings that had popped up along New Hampshire Avenue in the last few years. It looked like a condo building, but the rental market was still strong, and many buildings were staying rental until people came to their senses and refused to pay astronomical prices for no equity. Kit imagined the building was filled with the usual Washington habitués: single government workers, married congressmen who'd left their families back in their home states, or lobbyists. Given how nice the building seemed, probably lobbyists. Yuck.

Nervously, Kit waited while the doorman buzzed, then told her to go on up. It was a chilly day, but she was sweating a little when she knocked on the door. Her imagination had been running wild all day, letting her dwell on all sorts of scenarios. In the one that had settled in her head during the bus ride over, she'd decided that Bailey had a place like one of the computer masterminds in a thriller—lots of slate gray, a high-tech entertainment center, four or five computers doing everything from turning on the lights and sound system to vacuuming the floors.

Bailey threw the door open, and Kit forgot about the apartment and her nerves. Bailey looked like she'd very carefully tried to look both cool and casual. Kit had dressed to impress enough times in her life to know how difficult it was to pull off some casual flair. There must have been a store somewhere that sold clothes that looked good on tall, thin women as well as men not afraid to look gay. Really, really gay.

Bailey's violet and white checked shirt and shiny, violet silk tie were covered by a snug gray collared vest. Stiff-looking blue jeans and shiny black cap-toed boots made her look a little Victorian. Once again her hair was twisted into a haphazard ponytail and secured to the back of her head with a pen. So... Victorian gentleman with a nerdy girl's hairdo. Unique. Really unique. But that was part of the allure. Kit was sure of that now that she was standing in the doorway, taking her in. Bailey was one hundred percent unique, and in a town full of people who seemed like they'd been rolled out on an assembly line, she was a welcome breath of fresh air.

"You look nice," Bailey said, her eyes slowly scanning up and down Kit's body. Immediately, a flush covered her cheeks. She hadn't even considered that Bailey was checking her out, but she definitely was! Tongue-tied, she slid past her and tried to get her bearings. Looking around the stark room, she saw that

38

her fantasy had been just that. The apartment was sleek and high tech, but the furnishings were more like the apartment of a post-grad geek.

"Let me take your coat," Bailey said, sliding it from Kit's seemingly paralyzed body. As the coat left her she stood there, completely out of her element. "Give me just a minute and I'll get you a drink. I've got a timer about to go off." She jogged across the living room, her big boots thumping along the hardwood floor. "Take a look around if you want," Bailey called out as she entered the kitchen.

To get some control, Kit walked about the apartment, perusing it like she was at a museum. "Did you do your own decorating?" She hoped Bailey said "no." The decor was tragic.

"Almost everything is rented," she called back. "Natalie promised she'd have the place all ready for me, but she got busy and just called a service that threw the minimum in here. If I like it enough to stay, I'll buy my own stuff."

There was a table with four chairs in what should have been the dining area, but Bailey had crammed all of the furniture into a corner, and placed the upturned chairs onto the table. Next to a desk, a big whiteboard had been affixed to the wall, now filled with a maze of diagrams colorfully created with a wealth of markers.

A bookcase sat against the wall, filled with plastic toys and puzzles. Kit recognized some of them as space thingies, but the action figures of scantily clad, buxom women hoisting swords of impossible proportions really took her aback. Bailey looked like she could have been in a period drama on the BBC, but this stuff should have been in a junior high school boy's room! Were lesbians in general into stuff like this? Somehow, Kit had a hard time picturing Ellen and Portia's mansion decorated with plastic toys. But Bailey could give Ellen a run for her money when it came to dressing, so maybe…

Next to the bookcase stood a utilitarian desk with three monitors whose screensaver showed a blue telephone booth that careened from one to the next. Kit had no idea what it was, other than another clear sign of geekiness.

Bailey appeared next to her, making Kit start and clutch her chest. "You scared me!"

"I did? It's just the two of us here. Who'd you think it was?"

"Well…you. But I thought you were in the kitchen."

"Not now." She pointed at the monitors. "Are you a Doctor Who fan?"

"Doctor what?"

"Not what…Who." She grinned. "That could be a comedy routine. British sci-fi series?"

"No," Kit said, wishing she were a fan so they'd have something in common. Not only didn't she know any lesbians, she didn't know any geeks. "I thought the phone booths in England were iconically red."

"They are. That's a police box. It's a great series." Bailey's eyes danced with interest. "I like the early doctors the best, but I'm hooked no matter who the current guy is. I've got every one available on DVD."

Kit had zero interest in science fiction, but she thought she could fake some. "Maybe we could watch one or two episodes after dinner."

"We could…" Bailey looked a little unsure of that prospect. "But you wouldn't get much out of it if you didn't watch the whole first series. You've gotta let it build." A sweet smile settled on her face. "I'll lend you the first series. If you like it, I'll dump the whole box on you. Hundreds of episodes and specials. You'll be busy for years if you get into it."

"Super!" There wasn't a show on earth that she'd be that interested in. Actually, she probably hadn't watched several hundred hours of TV in her whole life. Unless you counted political shows. Her TV was locked onto her favorite news channel and rarely budged.

—⁓—

Whoever said lesbians couldn't do more than load up a crock-pot had never met Bailey Jones.

They'd moved the dining table to the living room, stuck the chairs where they belonged, then Bailey'd put the pot she'd cooked in on the table. Clearly, her gay man tendencies didn't extend to home decorating. No place mats, no napkins. But Kit didn't have a single complaint. She lustily dug into a delicious roast chicken, accompanied by caramelized onions and potatoes. "I don't know who taught you to cook, but they should be generously thanked."

"My mom taught me. Actually, she taught all of us. My oldest sister's the best, but don't tell the middle one I said that."

"This is really delicious. I can cook, but I wouldn't say I'm very inspired."

"Julie didn't like my cooking very much; she said it was too heavy. But I guess that makes sense. Eastern Europe and China don't share a lot of culinary roots."

"Your family's from Eastern Europe?"

Bailey nodded. "Poland."

"Is Bailey...a Polish name?"

Chuckling, Bailey shook her head. "Not a bit. I was named after a character on a TV show. My mom liked the name, mostly because it was different. She went into labor when the show was on and took that as a sign." Her mouth curled up in a half-grin. "Sometimes she's easily influenced." She pointed her fork at Kit. "What about you? Kit's a nickname, right?"

"No. That's the whole thing. Hey, speaking of nicknames, the night we met Natalie said something that seemed out of place, but I didn't get a chance to ask about it. Does she use a nickname for you?"

Smiling, Bailey said, "Yeah. We went to college together. Long before I changed my name."

"You changed your name? What was it before?"

"Kwiatkowski."

"Oh." That was a real tongue-twister, but Kit wasn't sure if she should comment on that.

"They used our first initials and five letters of our last names for our e-mail addresses. That made mine B. E. Kwiat. A lot of people started to call me Be Quiet." She shrugged. "It was funny when I was eighteen."

"It's still funny. It's nice to have friends you share a history with."

"Oh, we share a history all right."

"I just realized I don't have any friends of Polish descent."

Bailey took a bite, chewing a potato quickly. "I'm from a little town around Scranton, and nearly everybody was Polish. I didn't know how difficult my name was until I got to college."

"Did people make fun of it?" Kit asked, trying to be sensitive.

Bailey blinked slowly. "No. They just couldn't spell it. It got in the way, so I decided I had to pare it down."

Kit laughed, finding Bailey's nonchalance cute. "I think you did more than pare it down. There's no resemblance."

"I guess there isn't. I decided to go with something anyone in America could spell, and wouldn't take too many keystrokes. Three and a half seconds for Kwiatkowski, barely one and a half for Jones. No contest."

"That seems very..." She tried to think of a word that wasn't insulting. "Pragmatic."

"That's probably the best word to describe me. I'm very proud of my Polish heritage, but I'm not going to waste a couple of minutes every day typing my name. If my girlfriend's name had been easy, I would've switched to hers. But Mimi, my college girlfriend, was a Schroeder. No improvement. I guess I should've waited to meet Julie. Wu is pretty darned universal."

Kit had no idea how to respond to that, since it was clear that Bailey was completely serious. The woman was beyond practical.

"Tell me about blogging for a living," Bailey said. "You're the first blogger I've ever met. Professional, that is. Everybody has one that most of them never update."

Kit laughed at the truth in that. "Some days I wish I didn't have to update mine. But content is king. You've gotta grab your readers with something new every time they come to the site."

"Do you write about everything? Or do you have a specialty? I looked at your blog, of course. You've got a nice design."

"Thanks. It cost enough." She took a sip of wine, thinking it was about time to refresh the layout. "I've got two tracks. One is a newsletter that comes out five days a week. Keeping that up is like bailing water out of a sinking boat. Then I have a blog, where I can be a little more reflective."

"Is it just you? That sounds like a lot of work."

"It is. There's no way to run even a small newsletter on your own—and mine isn't small. I've got a staff that keeps growing, making me spend more time than I'd like managing people."

Bailey looked puzzled. "Don't you do the writing?"

"Not all of it. The newsletter is an 'all hands' kinda thing. For the blog, I write most of the big pieces, and all of the opinion stuff."

"Wow." She shook her head. "I've gotta say, I thought people worked hard in Silicon Valley, but DC's just as bad. You must be busier than a one-armed paper-hanger."

Kit laughed at her colloquialism. "Usually. But my staff does a lot. I've got a couple of researchers, a junior and a senior editor, a tech guy, and an office manager. Then a bunch of interns. They do as much as they're capable of. Sometimes they're more trouble than they're worth, but I like helping kids get a start."

"Where does the money come from? Ads?"

"Uh-huh. The usual for a blog. I hate having all of that stuff littering my pretty site, but the ads pay the bills."

Bailey looked like the concept of monetizing the blog was just reaching her brain. "Don't tell me you have to go beating the bushes, looking for sponsors."

Laughing, Kit shook her head. "I did for a while, but couldn't handle it. I hired a firm that manages the whole thing. Costs me a good chunk, but it's worth it." She dropped her head, like she was exhausted. "It's bad enough trying to keep up with the sewer pipe." While picking her head up again, she let out a soft chuckle. "My term for the constant onslaught of information poured onto us."

Bailey'd been raptly gazing at her, but her furrowed brows showed she'd gotten lost. "I really don't know anything about politics, so I'm not sure I get the concept. Tell me about a typical day."

Chuckling, Kit said, "There isn't one. That's what I like about it. But, in general, we spend the whole day making and fielding calls, following up on leads, reading, thinking about what we read, deciding if any of it merits passing on, and then deciding what to say about it."

"Five days a week," Bailey said, shaking her head. "That's a lot of work."

"It's actually seven. When I got so busy I thought I'd snap, I hired a weekend staff. The weekend edition isn't as comprehensive as the daily, but it lets me start Monday with a clean slate. I found a couple of reporters who freelance and needed a steady gig. That was a couple of years ago, and I'd have to say they've saved me from an early grave."

"I didn't guess it was that grueling." She smiled, her white, straight teeth highlighting her clear, pale skin and piercing blue eyes. Bailey clearly hadn't spent her youth smoking and chugging coffee like most fledgling reporters did. She probably didn't eat junk food like it was crack, either. "But, like I said, I've never been into politics."

"It's crazy busy. And there's always some event I should be going to at night. Parties, book launches, benefits. I refuse many, many more invitations than I accept, but I have to go to more than I want to, just to stay in the game."

"You should have majored in computer science," Bailey said, grinning. "You can go days without talking to another soul."

"I might not mind that. Actually, I'd like it. Now that I'm out, I'm offered a decent number of talking head gigs. I'm not sure why, but I've really been in demand."

Bailey gave her a look that was hard to characterize. For a moment, Kit was sure she was going to say something, maybe even something suggestive. But she just took another drink of her wine and leaned back in the chair, gazing at her exactly the way a guy would.

—⁓—

After finishing dinner, they relaxed in the living room, working on the second bottle of wine Kit had brought.

It was time to spill it. Bailey was sitting much closer than her other women friends did, and Kit could feel her interest. She couldn't put the feeling into words, but there was a vibe Bailey gave off that you'd have to be a fool to miss.

Kit leaned over to pour some more wine to fortify her nerves, and when she sat up Bailey had slid over a little closer and put her arm onto the cushion behind Kit's back. Oh-oh. There was a part, a part bigger than she was comfortable admitting, that wanted to keep her trap shut and see what happened. But that wasn't playing fair. She had to gut it up and tell the truth.

"It's dawned on me," she began, struggling to get command of her voice, "that you might think I'm gay."

She couldn't look. Kit kept her gaze on the coffee table.

"Might?"

Fuck. She snuck a glance and saw an eyebrow raised in a fierce, unblinking gaze.

"Yeah. I just got the feeling…"

Suddenly, Bailey was up and across the room in two seconds flat. Now she stared at Kit from a chair, farther away but more able to glare hotly at her.

"Why did you lie to me?"

"Lie? I didn't lie."

"You certainly did! You said you could live openly now. You said you'd come out of the closet."

"About my identity! My name, not my sexual identity. I'd been doing my blog anonymously for years, but I got outed. That's all I meant."

"You said you marched with ERCF in the Pride parade!"

Kit blinked, trying to recall what she'd said. "I've never done that." Finally, she recalled the context. "I said I have an ERCF T-shirt. I wear it during Pride weekend to show I'm a supporter. A supporter of gay rights, not a member of the club."

Those vivid blue eyes burned a hole in her flesh as they lit and held her in place. "You knew that's not what I believed. You knew I thought you were gay."

44

It was hard to speak when you were mortally embarrassed. But Kit forced her tongue to work. "Asante told me you'd think that."

"Fuck Asante," Bailey spat. "I'm asking about you!" She leaned over, her gaze growing impossibly more heated. "What did you think?"

This was so damned mortifying! "I wasn't sure at first. But after you asked me to come over for dinner, I…I assumed you thought I was gay."

"Why did you accept then? Did you just want a meal?" She stood and walked over to the door, taking Kit's coat from the hook. "I hope you enjoyed it. Bye-bye." Dead blue eyes fixed on her, all heat, all spark completely gone.

"No! I…I swear I wouldn't have done anything differently if you were a guy."

The spark came back in a nanosecond. Her cheeks flushed pink with anger. "A guy would have assumed you were straight!"

"Come sit down. Please."

Still carrying the coat, Bailey flopped down onto her chair. But she didn't speak. She stared, glumly, into the distance.

"The same sort of thing happened when I first met Asante." Kit cringed when she heard how earnest she sounded. Like she was begging for her life. "I thought he was hot, and when he asked me to lunch I assumed we were on a date. It wasn't until the third time we got together that he told me he was gay."

"That has nothing to do with this situation. Nothing."

"Yes, it does. Really."

Bailey finally looked at her again. Her gaze was still flat and cold, but at least they were making eye contact.

"He waited until he was confident I was trustworthy. He wanted to make sure I was…I don't know…open-minded, I guess."

"I've met straight people," Bailey said dryly. "Several of them. Some of my best friends are straight—"

"Knock it off!"

"No, you knock it off! There's no reason to hide being straight. None!"

"Yes, there is." Kit had no idea this was going to come out, but she was in this far, why not go all the way. "Something happened when you kissed me goodnight after our first match. I'm not sure what it was, but…" She grit her teeth, annoyed with herself for being so inarticulate. "I wanted to see what happened next."

Bailey didn't say a word. Her chin tilted, vivid eyes locked on Kit. Finally, after Kit felt like she'd squirm out of her skin, Bailey quietly said, "What did you want to happen?"

"I'm not sure. But there was some kind of electricity in the air. Something new, something different was going to happen, and I'm not the kind of woman who walks away before I know the end of the story."

Bailey maintained her fervid gaze. "Even if the story means you have to use me to get it."

"No! I wasn't using you. We just met, Bailey. It's not like I married you before telling you I was straight. You can't tell me you're deeply invested."

"No, I'm not. But I've been fantasizing about getting invested." Her stare was still heated. "Doesn't that count?"

"Yeah, yeah, it does." Kit dropped her head, the reality of what she'd done hitting her hard. "But you know the truth now." Somehow she found the courage to put it out there. "Is there any way we could…see what happens?"

"What…exactly are you saying?"

"I liked it when you kissed me. I'm not sure what that means, but I definitely liked it."

"Good to know." Bailey stood and shook Kit's coat, like she was knocking dust from it. "I wish I had time to kiss all the straight women in Washington, just to see if any of them dig it—but I can't swing it."

Shame filled Kit to overflowing. On the verge of tears, she got up, snatched the coat from Bailey's hands and headed for the door. For a moment, she thought she heard her follow. But the only sounds that accompanied her to the elevator were her own sobs, muted as she exerted all of her will to stifle them.

—⁓—

It was crazy to be this upset. She hadn't cried when her grandfather died last year! But here she was, plunked down on a bench in front of the Dupont Circle fountain, sniffling like a baby.

It wasn't that she was very invested, either. Yes, she'd spent a lot of time thinking about Bailey and about what it meant to be going to her home, but she didn't know Bailey well enough to be this hurt. Kit lifted her chin to see a couple of guys getting ready to bed down for the night. Living on the streets in November gave them every right to cry. But they quietly surrounded themselves with blankets and big pieces of cardboard and got on with it.

Forcing herself to get down to the emotional truth, she admitted she wasn't hurt. She was humiliated. For her, that was worse. She'd shown Bailey her belly —and Bailey had taken a bite out of it. Dating sucked. And dating outside of your orientation clearly sucked even worse. Being vulnerable was for fools. From now on, she was going to stick with the program—more middle-aged, divorced workaholics who wanted someone to help raise their kids. Super.

—⁓—

Kit got nothing done the next day. Nia, her office manager, walked into her office at the end of the day and looked at her for a few seconds. "Is everything okay? You were zoning out all day." They had a very good working relationship, but they rarely spoke of anything personal.

"Sure. I'm fine. Just a little off. I'll be back to normal tomorrow." Her phone hadn't buzzed, but she acted as if it had. "Gotta take this. G'night."

Alone, she sat at her desk for another hour, going over what had happened with Bailey. She jumped when her phone did buzz, and her heart started to race when she saw the text.

"Sorry I was so rough with you last nite. Truce?"

Texting back madly, Kit wrote, "Absolutely. Drinks?"

There was a delay. A longish delay. But finally, the reply came through, "1537 17th St. NW 9 p.m."

Hands shaking, Kit closed up her computer and headed to her apartment. There, she took a shower and tried to get some dinner down, but she was too nervous to do more than pick at a salad. At nine, she was seated at the bar, working on her second vodka cranny when Bailey arrived.

"Martini. Sahara dry," the bartender called out the moment her lanky frame crossed the threshold.

Bailey raised a finger and pointed at him. Then she went to a small table, and Kit got up from the bar to join her. "I was hoping the bartender was wrong on the drink you needed."

"Nope. Chris should have been a shrink or a minister. He can read people like a book." Her drink was delivered, and she took a tentative sip. "Makes my liver hurt, but it's just what the doctor ordered." She placed her hands on the table and cleared her throat. "I want to apologize."

"No, no. This was all my fault. I screwed up, and I'm really sorry."

Bailey raised a hand. "No, I let an old memory catch me off guard. That wasn't fair to you."

Just knowing there was an unexplored fact lying around pulled Kit out of her mea culpa mode. "An old memory? Wanna tell me about it?"

Her smile was sweet. Open and pure, and full of warmth. "You really do like to listen, don't you?"

"I do. Listening is my hobby and my profession."

"Okay. It's about Natalie."

"Got it."

"I refer to her as my first love, but she wasn't my first lover. She chickened out."

"Chickened out of…?"

"Having sex. We were at Cal Poly together and started to hang out during our freshman year. I was terminally crushed on her, and sure she felt the same. We fooled around a little, just kissing and stuff, skipping classes to have time alone—the usual. Then, when I was so frustrated I thought I'd explode, she said she couldn't go further. She'd decided she wasn't gay."

"Oh, shit," Kit moaned, dropping her head into her open hand. "You must have been crushed."

"Of course I was. My first heartbreak." Her eyes filled with sadness. "But I got over her, and eventually met a woman who wasn't confused about her orientation."

Kit reached over and gripped her arm, squeezing it tightly. "I'm so glad."

"It worked out fine. I think Mimi and I were more compatible than Nat and I at that point in my life. Fast cut to a year later, and Natalie showed up at my dorm room, crying her eyes out. She'd fallen in love again, with a woman, and didn't know what to do. I'm not sure I pulled her out of the closet, but I definitely helped her get comfortable."

"That's so sweet!" Kit reached over and gripped her arm. "That shows your good heart."

She brushed past the compliment. "It was hard for her. She's first generation Mexican-American, and her parents had a lot of adjustments to make just to live in America. The gay thing was way, way over their heads. But she eventually followed her heart, and her parents got used to it. They still don't like it, but they got used to it."

"That would make anyone skittish."

She smiled again. "A little more than that. I'm kinda neurotic about being played." Kit gripped her arm again, holding on tight. Bailey carefully loosened each finger, saying, "I bruise easily. A sincere look is plenty."

Kit adopted the most sincere one she had. "How's this?"

"Not bad," she said, chuckling. "That's enough groveling."

Kit took a breath. "I wasn't playing you. But I should have been honest."

"Yeah, you should have been." Her gaze sharpened. "Even if I hadn't had a bad experience with a straight girl, I wouldn't have liked you playing me. It feels like…" She tilted her chin, deep in thought. "My sexual orientation is a part of me. A big part. Having someone act like she shares that…" She shook her head. "I can't explain it. But it sucks."

"Lesson learned. Next time I meet a lesbian I'll make it clear I'm only familiar with one vagina."

Bailey slowly revealed a half smile. "And I'll try not to be so gun-shy. I really overreacted, and I'm sorry."

Kit patted her hand, then gave it a squeeze. "We're good."

"Let's start fresh," Bailey said as she took out her phone and pulled up her calendar. "Can we make another squash date? It's hell finding a woman who can play worth a damn, and I'd like to keep playing you until I find her."

Tension gone, Kit felt completely free to slug her on the shoulder.

—m—

The next afternoon, Kit texted Asante. "Need a meet-up."

It took him an hour to respond. "Home by ten. Too late?"

"Good. I'll be there."

She spent the rest of the day jumping from one silly task to the next. Nothing could hold her attention. Writing about the president's trip to an economic summit in Europe was like writing about particle physics. Something she knew nothing about and had no wish to learn. At a loss, she knocked off early, trying not to let Nia's open-mouthed stare guilt-trip her.

The only thing she could think to do was exercise. That sometimes let her work through a jumbled brain. But it didn't work well today. Twenty laps of the pool had her gasping for breath, but her mind was just as sloppy as it had been when she'd jumped in.

A home-cooked meal might make her feel a little more settled, but she'd have to go to the store and that was no fun at seven o'clock. But almost anything from the grocery store was healthier than delivery, and she was determined to keep her weight where she wanted it.

The closest grocery store to her apartment had an excellent salad bar, and after loading up a container with mostly vegetables, she got into the checkout line. A couple in the next line was giving her the once-over. Don't let it bother you. The lines were moving very slowly, letting them whisper and try to act like they weren't both gawping.

It was stupid to let it annoy her. She knew it was stupid. She'd chosen a profession where you got a certain amount of notice. Plus, she'd had a long relationship with a man who was in the public eye constantly. Those had been choices she'd made. Trying to make the result of those choices disappear was never, ever going to work. But it had only been a couple of months since she'd been identified as the *Daily Lineup* editor and she still didn't have a good tactic for dealing with being recognized for that. Maybe it would feel better to just grab the bull by the horns. Turning her head, she locked her gaze on the woman. "Hi," she said, trying not to look like she was stark raving mad. "Do we know each other?"

In a flash, the color drained from the woman's cheeks. "No!" She laughed nervously. "We just thought you were…" Squinting a little, she asked, "Are you?"

"The *Daily Lineup*? *Capitol Ideas*?"

"Yes! We love your blog."

"Oh. Well, thanks," Kit said, wishing she could disappear.

"We love it," the guy added, a silly-looking grin on his face. "I work at State, and everyone reads the newsletter. Everyone," he added. "All the way to the top."

"Thanks. I appreciate that."

Now they got to continue standing a few feet away from each other, with nothing more to add. The guy obviously had the smaller tolerance for uncomfortable encounters, because he said, much louder than he needed to, "I forgot to get milk. Come with me," before tugging the woman from the line. They both waved, like they were going on a little trip.

Kit watched them go, then heard a woman behind her quietly say into her phone, "You thought she was cute when we saw her on TV a couple of weeks ago, remember? Yeah, I guess she's okay. But she looked a lot better on TV. Younger. I thought she was only around thirty. No way. She's gotta be pushing forty."

Fighting the urge to make it clear she'd been at the office for twelve hours and hadn't planned on being evaluated, Kit got hold of herself and made a decision. Never speak until spoken to, and never, ever voluntarily introduce yourself to people. No good could come of it.

—⁓—

It was a cool, windy night, but she couldn't wait to talk. At nine forty-five Kit paced in front of Asante's apartment, dismayed that he still wasn't home. She'd be lucky if the cops didn't pick her up, since she looked like an addict desperate for a fix. A whistle finally pierced the still night. Asante. He was almost a block away, but Kit could recognize his long, lean frame and confident swagger. "Why is it only women who stalk me?" he asked when he got close.

"Damned if I know. One of the mysteries of the ages is why you're single."

Smiling, he put an arm around her shoulders and they walked to his front door together. Once inside his apartment, he hung up their coats, led her to his sofa and sat down. "Spill it. You look like you're about to burst."

"I am." She nodded emphatically. "I really am." Her lips pursed and she found herself strangely inarticulate. "I…I have a crush on Bailey."

His eyebrows rose and he instinctively scratched at a spot on the back of his head. "You do?"

"Yeah." She took in and let out a slow breath. "At least I think I do. I…want to see what happens."

Asante put his hand on her knee and gazed into her eyes. "That's a funny way to put it."

"I know. But I don't have a better way. I know she's interested in me, and I want her to stay that way." She looked into his eyes, silently pleading for understanding. "I want to see if anything can happen. To see if I can be interested in her."

"Is that something…" His head tilted to a dramatic angle. "Is that something you can just…do? You can just…what? Give it a whirl?"

"I'm not sure. It might be a whim, but I've spent more time thinking about her than I have about the last ten guys I've been out with—combined. That has to mean something."

"Does it? I think about you a lot, but I don't want to have sex with you. Maybe you just like her. Like a girl crush."

She could feel herself blush. "I want her to kiss me. I really want her to kiss me."

He sat there quietly for a few moments, clearly digesting the news. "Uhm… again, not to throw cold water on this, but I'm going to guess Bailey wants to do more than kiss. Are you up for that?"

Kit held a hand up. "That's something I'll think about when the time's right. For now, I'd love to see how it feels to kiss her."

"Bailey knows this?"

"Yeah. Well, kinda. We had a bad evening when I told her I was straight, but I think we got through that. I told her just what I've told you."

"And she still wants to see you?"

"Not sure. She said we can play squash again. I'm hoping there's more."

Asante scooted over and put his arm around Kit's shoulders. "Don't be hurt if there isn't. If I were in her shoes, I wouldn't be able to hang out with you."

"Thanks," she grumbled.

"Sorry, baby, but I couldn't. If I was into a guy and he'd never been with another guy…no way. I'd be very, very leery of an adult who wanted to experiment."

"You can say it. I'm too old to have my first crush on a girl. Even people at the grocery store comment about how old I look."

He pulled back and gave her a puzzled look, then continued. "Age has nothing to do with it. But it sounds like a very tentative crush. That's the part I wouldn't like. It'd be one thing if you said you'd spent your whole life hiding these desires and just now felt able to express them. But that's not true, is it?"

"No." She slapped her hand across her forehead and slowly lowered it. "Not at all. I'm a thoroughly straight woman who wants to kiss a girl."

"That would ruin the deal for me. But maybe Bailey's more open-minded than I am." He kissed Kit on the temple. "I hope she is."

Chapter Five

THERE WAS NO PERCENTAGE in playing around with a woman who had, at best, an inkling she might be able to be into women. That was a sucker's bet. Bailey was willing to be friends, but she was determined to make it clear they were only going to play squash.

Both of them had busy schedules, and three weeks passed before they found another time to play. That Wednesday, they played an excellent match, with Kit taking a game, and keeping the other two close. As usual, they met in the lobby afterward. Kit looked up when Bailey exited the locker room, a hopeful expression on her face. "Drinks? Dinner?"

"Mmm, not this time." Bailey added no explanation. "But I've got two days free next week if you want to schedule another match."

"Uhm…sure."

A child could have seen she was disappointed, but Bailey closed her mind to that. She would not let Kit get too close, and she would not lead her on. Doing that was just as unkind as Kit's playing her had been. Maybe more.

—⁂—

Asante had spent that Sunday with his sister and brother-in-law, watching the Redskins and having dinner. Since they lived fairly close to Kit, he dropped by for a nightcap. They'd both been busy, and hadn't seen each other on their regular schedule. But one of Asante's many wonderful qualities was that he went out of his way to see his friends.

Kit had taped one of his favorite shows, and they sat on her bed, drinking port and watching a British costume drama. Kit wouldn't have bothered on her own, but sharing it with Asante made it something she looked forward to.

"The Duchess of Leicester is going to be ass-deep in alligators if she keeps putting up with the Duke's bullshit." Asante shook his head mournfully. "That woman has to learn to stand up for herself."

"I feel sorry for her. She knows what she wants, but she doesn't know how to get it."

"Projecting?" He raised an expressive eyebrow.

Chuckling, Kit said, "Probably. The Duchess is a bit of a whiner. She used to drive me crazy, but now I see the fix she's gotten herself in."

"Your crush hasn't eased any, huh?"

"No, if anything, it's gotten worse. I just don't know how to get past the barrier she's put up."

Asante sat up, crossed his legs and sat there for a moment, gazing at Kit. "She put up a wall because she felt she needed one." He reached out and put his hand on Kit's leg, then gently massaged it. "You probably don't understand this, but I bet she's not looking at this like she would another lesbian who was interested in her. It's really difficult to try to develop something with a straight person."

"But everybody is a straight person until they show they're not."

"That's not true. I knew I was gay long before I knew what sex was. If that's true for her, it'll be hard for her to open up."

"What do I do?" she moaned.

"You lick your wounds and move on. If you're interested in finding out if you can be into women, find a different one. Find one who came out when she was older. She might be more understanding of your situation. I don't mean to be cruel, but you screwed this one up."

She patted him absently. "You're not being cruel, you're being honest. I just wish you were wrong."

—◆—

Finally, after two more matches with Bailey refusing to socialize afterward, she agreed to go out to dinner. Having a drink or a bite to eat once a month seemed like a good schedule for making it clear they were just friends.

It was Tuesday of Thanksgiving week, and they'd played early, with both of them famished when they'd finished. "I'm driving home tonight," Bailey said as they walked down the street, looking for restaurants without a throng fighting to get in. "Let's find a place that isn't already serving turkey. I'll get enough of that at home."

"I'm taking the train home tomorrow evening," Kit said. "Are you sure you have time? I don't want to hold you up."

"Yeah, I do. I like to leave after traffic's calmed down. I thought I'd take off around ten."

"Then let's find a place that isn't serving turkey, but has plenty of caffeine."

A little searching found a mostly empty spot, not far from Bailey's apartment. They sat at a bistro-style table while Bailey surveyed the menu with deliberate speed. "What are quenelles?" She looked up over the frames of her glasses.

"Mmm, kind of a dumpling." Kit looked at the description. "They're good if they're light."

Bailey closed her menu. "I think I'll stick with soup and a salad. I don't want to have a heavy quenelle sitting in my stomach all the way home."

After they'd ordered and received their drinks, Kit sipped at her wine, while Bailey had a cup of tea. She brought the cup to her lips and blew across it for a few seconds. "What's been going on in your world? I haven't seen any banner headlines for a few days." She shrugged. "That's the only way I know if something big is going on. The size of the type in the headlines."

Kit nodded. "Don't feel bad. Most people don't read the paper anymore. That's why you can graduate from the best journalism school in the country and be lucky to make minimum wage."

"Someone sounds bitter," Bailey teased. "I know you make more than minimum wage."

"Luckily, I do. And, in the spirit of the week, I'm very thankful that I do. To answer your question, national news is slow around Thanksgiving. My newsletter has a very chauvinistic view, so all sorts of stuff might be going on in other places, but I don't have to cover it. I can't imagine how much work that would be."

"Do you really like politics? Or is that just what you fell into?"

"Like it," Kit said. "Really like it. I've always been a news junkie, and national politics has always been my thing." She chuckled. "As soon as I could read, I'd be at the breakfast table trying to figure out the morning paper."

Bailey smiled. "I can empathize. I was always taking things apart to see how they worked or trying to read my older sisters' science books. It was really, really nice to find something that interested me as a kid and still holds my attention."

"Yeah, that's exactly it." Their salads were delivered and Kit took a taste of hers. "Good. That's a nice goat cheese."

Bailey played with the various ingredients of her salad, tossing away the ones she didn't like and re-arranging the ones she did. "Tell me about this boyfriend. The politician."

Kit blinked in surprise. "Okay. What do you want to know?"

"Mmm." She took a bite and chewed thoughtfully. "What was it like to write about politics, then go home to a politician?"

"Ahh...work/life balance. Good question." She considered it for a moment, then said, "It worked out fine with Henry, because he generally liked to leave work behind when he came home. But that's pretty odd for a politician."

"I'd bet. Most of my work here has been for political groups and trade associations. Those people are obsessed. Actual politicians must be much, much worse."

"They are. I've taken a vow to never date another politician. Not gonna happen. Ideally, I wouldn't date someone who was even marginally in the game. But that's tough in this town." She let out a sigh. "Work's grueling enough. Twenty-four hours of it's insane."

"I get that. Julie was in marketing, but she was consumed with Share Me. Our relationship improved a lot when she left the company." She focused very intently on her salad, thinking of Julie and how things had been for them. "I think you've got the right idea. Dating outside of your profession is probably best."

"But you've gotta admit it's nice to have someone understand what the heck you're talking about when you're trying to explain something technical."

"Yeah, yeah, that's nice, but I think it'd be enough to have someone who was interested in you. If you're really into a person, I bet you wouldn't mind listening to stuff you didn't know that much about."

"Maybe," Kit allowed. She snuck her fork across the table and speared the olives Bailey had discarded. "Last time we talked, you were telling me about the project you were working on. How's it going?"

"Eh." She made a face. "I'm stuck."

"Really? Stuck...how?"

Bailey looked up curiously. "It's pretty technical."

"Good. If you can explain it to me, it might help you sort it out."

She'd never considered talking through a technical problem with a civilian. "Okay. But just remember..." She grinned, feeling shy but a little excited. "You asked for it."

—∞—

Kit used all of her mental strength to stop herself from yawning. It wasn't that Bailey's project wasn't interesting. It was. And letting her bounce ideas around for the past two hours had been remarkably engaging. But Kit had been up since six, and had to get up even earlier to get her work done before taking off for Boston. But she had the impression Bailey had made a breakthrough. Luckily, their table was covered in white butcher paper. The restaurant would not have appreciated having her whip out three different colored pens to start drawing on real linen.

"Did you get this part?" Bailey asked, her gaze landing on Kit as she tried to stifle another yawn. "The part where the user has to log into this other system to gain authorization?"

"Yeah. I got that." Amazingly, she was able to understand exactly what Bailey was talking about. On a very, very topical level, no doubt, but she still understood. "But the user isn't going to like having to use a separate password. They'll wind up writing it down on a sticky and putting it right on their monitor."

Bailey chuckled at that. "I don't know why people find passwords so difficult. You just think of a phrase that means something to you, use the first letter of each word, then add a favorite number and symbol."

Kit batted her eyes at her. "Is that all? So I just have to remember a phrase, a number and a symbol, and make each one different for every kind of system I have to log into? That's all?"

Rolling her eyes, Bailey said, "You can have four or five of them and then keep the number and symbol static. I use the intros to some of my favorite shows." She chuckled. "I bet there are more passwords with some variant of the Star Wars or Star Trek intros than a super computer could tabulate." She took a glance at her watch. "Eleven o'clock! How'd that happen?"

Kit reached over and took one of the pens, then drew an arrow at a complicated part of the diagram. "Working through this part took about a half hour." She tossed the pen back, smiling when Bailey caught it on the fly. "It was fun watching you work. It's so nice to know that someone in this town actually does something real."

Bailey started to put her pens back into her messenger bag. "I've never thought what I do is very concrete. To me, it's all ideas and concepts."

"Politics sure isn't about making anything. That diagram might be the most concrete thing to come out of this town all day."

Bailey looked up and showed a warm, full smile. "It helped a lot to think this stuff through. You're a very good listener. And you ask insightful questions. That's what let me look at the workflow with a different perspective."

"My pleasure. Now let's get out of here and get you on the road."

They paid the bill, got into their coats and went to stand in front of the restaurant. "I had a great time tonight," Bailey said. Her eyes scanned across Kit's face like she was assessing her for pattern recognition. "We'll have to do this more often."

"Any time," Kit said. She stood there, not sure if she should offer a hug.

But Bailey wasn't indecisive. She pulled Kit into a hug, then kissed her cheek. "Have a good Thanksgiving."

"I will. Now get going! I don't want you driving all night."

"Okay. See you." She took off, loping down the street, with Kit watching her until she disappeared around a corner.

There was something mesmerizing about that woman, and Kit was determined to hang in there to see what happened. Something would. There was some kind of energy bubbling just under the surface. With a happy grin on her face, she walked home, thinking of Bailey's diagram and the delight on her face when she'd figured out whatever had been troubling her. That had been a very nice way to spend the evening.

—⁊⁊—

On Thanksgiving Day, Kit lay on her childhood bed, delaying her arrival at the dinner table as long as possible. She'd been home for less than twenty-four hours, but it seemed as though she'd had at least a dozen arguments with everyone from a seven-year-old niece to a ninety-four-year-old grandfather.

Actually, that wasn't true. The extended family didn't really argue. They made statements, declarations, pronouncements—that you either ignored or responded to mildly, depending on your order in the hierarchy. Voices were rarely raised, true feelings always hidden. Maybe that's why she was drawn to politics. It felt like home.

She hated to whine about the holidays. So many people had it much, much worse. But it was never a box full of fun to be in Boston. Other than faking an injury, she was out of excuses. Time to join the group. She got up, fluffed her hair and went into the dining room. Her brother-in-law Craig was the first to see her, and, as usual, he took the first swipe. "Do your people celebrate Thanksgiving?" He chuckled fiendishly. Kit didn't think that Craig really ascribed to half of the crap conservative pundits spewed, but he loved to act like he did— just to pull her chain.

This was her first visit home since she'd been ID'd. Her entire record was all there in black and white for him to read—and torture her with. Given some of the barbs he'd hit her with, he'd gone to the archives to load up.

"I like Thanksgiving just fine." Kit walked over to the bar and mixed herself a stiff one. "I just had a few things I had to take care of before dinner."

"Trying to rally the troops? I assume most of the people who read you are sitting all by themselves today in rent-controlled New York City apartments. I bet you don't have a lot of people in your demographic who have a God to thank."

Kit counted the spaces at the children's table, hoping there was an extra chair for her. But her six nieces and nephews filled the smaller table, leaving her to sit with her siblings and their spouses, her parents, and her grandparents. It was a darn shame they had a dining table that could seat ten. If she had her way, she would have taken a plate and sat in front of the television. But holiday dinners were sacrosanct in the Travis home, and you had to take your assigned seat and play your part.

It wasn't all bad. Her mom was a really good cook, which allowed Kit to try to ignore the cross talk and concentrate on the food. Sometimes that actually worked.

And yet, it was uncomfortable. It always was. It always had been. Being the only liberal in the family made it worse, but in her heart she knew she'd stick out even if she worked for a right-wing think tank.

She resembled her mother quite closely, so she was fairly sure they were genetically related. But often times she felt like a foundling. A child they'd happened upon and had taken in as a charitable act. The childhood stories she'd most identified with were Dickens' tales of orphans struggling to stay on their guardians' good side. She knew that was silly, in a way. No one had ever beaten her, or even spoken to her harshly. She just wasn't one of them.

They'd barely gotten through their salad course when the doorbell rang. Kit's father got up, grumbling to himself, and set off for the door, undoubtedly rehearsing a lecture for the poor soul who had the temerity to show up at two o'clock in the afternoon on Thanksgiving Day. When Kit heard laughter coming from the hallway, she was sure she was hearing things. Surprise turned to ire when she saw her father standing in the doorway with the senior senator from the state of Massachusetts, the Honorable Henry Adams Brearly.

"I won't be but a minute," Henry said, full of his usual good cheer. "I just came by to drop off a little something to make your holidays bright."

"Come in, come in," Kit's mother urged, paling a little. "Join us."

Adding another person to the family gathering at the last minute might have actually killed her mother. Her favorite thing was order, predictability. Kit blinked in surprise at the hold Henry still had over the clan.

Henry held up both hands. "If I could possibly get away, you know I'd stay here all day, Marjorie. But Caroline will have my hide if I'm not home soon."

"Oh, I wish she could have come with you. We haven't seen her since the wedding."

It still rankled to have had her parents go to her ex-boyfriend's wedding.

"I wish I could have brought her, but she's a little under the weather these days. She's as sick as she was with Jake. It's going to be tough to talk her into having a third, but I'm going to try."

Kit's dad slapped him on the shoulder. "You got started late, but you're certainly not letting any grass grow under your feet."

Steaming, Kit provided the alternate translation for that sentence. Since our daughter wasted so much of your time, refusing to marry you or have your children, it's great to see you found a fertile replacement.

"I think three is the ideal number," Henry said. "You and Marjorie had the right idea." His eyes finally landed on Kit, and he gave her a sincere-looking smile. "Why don't you walk me back out to my car? I haven't seen you in ages."

She tried for lightness, but was fairly sure she wasn't succeeding. "I'm lurking around the Capitol almost every day. You don't have to come all the way to Boston to see me."

Her father gave her a sternly disapproving look. "We'll hold dinner for you."

Kit took the path of least resistance. As always. Old habits were the hardest to break. She got up, folded her napkin and followed him out to the front of the house. "Seriously? You had to come during Thanksgiving dinner? You know dinner time is etched in stone."

He winced. "Sorry about that. I thought it was at four or five o'clock." His grin was, as always, charming. "I was trying for the first cocktail, well before the cheese ball made its appearance."

They went out to the driveway, with the shock of cold air actually feeling kind of good. "What's going on? You know you can reach me any day of the week."

"Nothing. Nothing." He looked distracted, or maybe he was dissembling. Sometimes it was hard to tell with him. "If I had a reliable tip that Eddie Don Jackson's family had a weekend retreat near Tupelo that was affectionately named Lynchburg…would you be interested in the details?"

For the better part of a year, people had been saying that the next Republican nominee for president was going to either be Henry or Eddie Don Jackson, the governor of Mississippi. Henry's people were undoubtedly working like bloodhounds to find any dirt on Jackson and eliminate him from the race as early as possible—and vice versa. "I can't see a story there, Hank. I don't get the point."

He got a fiendish gleam in his eye. One she hadn't seen very often. "That's because you don't know there were lynchings on the property as late as 1940."

"Disgusting, but I still don't see the story. It's no crime to have your weekend retreat on a parcel of land with a bad history."

"It is when there's a nice new sign, showing a black figure hanging from a tree, that says Welcome to Lynchburg. I can't prove he put it there, but I've got pictures showing it right next to the driveway."

Politics was such a filthy business. Eddie Don Jackson was a Grade A asshole. Anti-choice, anti-immigrant, anti-gay. She was certain the country would be in significantly worse shape if he were its next president. But this kind of slime turned Kit's stomach. And yet, it was her job to let people know what she'd learned about all of the candidates—no matter how it came to her. "I take it you don't want to be caught sending me the pictures."

He reached into his pocket and extracted a flash drive, which he handed to her. "Smart girl." He cuffed her on the chin, opened his car door and got in. "Always good to see you, Kit Kat."

She had to force herself to say it, but she did, "Congratulations on the new baby. I hope you have twins. Then you won't have to convince your wife to have another one."

He gave her a quick salute, started the car and took off, roaring down the quiet street in his huge, American car.

—∞—

Kit had only been back in her chair for a moment when her paternal grandmother said, "It must make you kick yourself when you see how well Henry's doing."

Oh, please. Not more of this! "I'm happy for him, Nana. He has what he wants, and so do I."

"His wife was on the cover of The Hub just last month. On the cover," she repeated. "That could've been you."

"I don't want to be on the cover. Of anything. That's not who I am."

"Oh, pshaw." She dismissively waved her hand in the air. "Everyone wants people to look up to them. Being a senator is the best job in the country, and a senator's wife is even better. You get all of the respect without doing a bit of the work."

Kit took a sip of her wine, while giving her grandmother a mild shrug. Sometimes silence worked. But not today.

"You'd honestly rather write about important people than be an important person?"

"Uh-huh." A slight head nod respectfully underscored her point.

"You've got no fight in you. I knew Henry would see that. I just hoped you'd have a couple of babies before he realized how weak you were."

Another shrug.

"It's a fine mess you've gotten yourself into. No husband, too old to even attract one who wants a baby, and no real job."

Kit tried to tune out, to think of a snippet of music or study the pattern on the china. If she cowered like a victim, her grandmother usually got tired quickly and moved on to other complaints. There was nothing the old woman hated worse than an adversary who wouldn't fight back.

But she was full of ire today and kept right on going. "And don't try to convince me that writing those gossipy little articles is a real job."

Nana had a point there. Part of the newsletter was insider gossip. Kit mentioned every minor player's birthday, made a big deal about engagements, weddings, births, anniversaries and deaths. Almost like a small town newspaper. But giving the under-under-under secretary of defense a moment in the limelight sometimes made him call you when he had a story he wanted to place. But even her little gossip rag sometimes shone a light on things that wouldn't otherwise get any play at all. Maybe one important thing for every hundred pieces of crap—but it still mattered—to Kit. "That's my job, Nana."

"It's not real. You can't even hold it in your hand! Craig had to put that stupid computery thing up to my face to even see the thing."

That was kind of funny. Perversely. What in the hell made the guy tick? What kind of weirdo got off on winding an old lady up? But it wasn't just Nana. Many members of the family thought her job was illusory. They'd made that crystal clear when they'd found out she wrote the newsletter. The funny thing was that they hadn't thought that when they assumed she was still working for the *Globe*, and only getting a couple of articles a year into the paper. What did they think? That the *Globe* paid ten thousand bucks per column inch?

"I'm happy with my job," she said quietly.

Her maternal grandfather, the staunchest, most rock-ribbed conservative of them all, scowled at her. "You don't have a job, you have a bully pulpit. You're just a water carrier for the administration. Craig printed off some of the things from that so-called blog and sent them to me. Shameful."

Kit was tempted to look Craig right in the eye and ask him why he got so much pleasure from torturing her. Henry always insisted he had a crush on her. She fervently hoped that wasn't true. Even the thought of it sickened her a little.

"I can understand that it might seem that way to you, Grandpa, but I'm still a reporter, not a cheerleader." This was such a waste of time and energy. They were a legacy media family, and having a newsletter or a blog would never be anything to brag about—no matter how many page views she got.

Her sister-in-law piped up. "Nana's got a point, Kit. You don't have much time left if you want to get married."

"True," she said, contorting her face into a smile. "Forty is the new eighty." She mentally kicked herself for snapping off a smart reply. The only way through this was to lie down and take it. They eventually got bored with kicking an inert body.

"It's not that you look old. But men are suspicious of women your age who've never been married. They figure there's something wrong with them. Maybe you should tell guys you're divorced."

"Good idea. I'll start doing that." She took a big bite of turkey, hoping the Travis prohibition against speaking with your mouth full would allow the conversation to veer off into another direction.

—⁓—

Bailey was going to be back home on Sunday afternoon, and getting the text asking to play a match to end the holiday week had been the highlight of Kit's trip. She called a car service and snuck out of the house just after dawn, leaving a note bidding them all a fond farewell.

Bailey must have overeaten while visiting her family, because she was a step slow all night. For the first time, Kit beat her, even though it took all three games and she only accomplished it by two points. But a victory was a victory, and she was ecstatic.

As she always did, Kit went into one of the cubicles to dress, then went to the lobby to wait. While standing near the main door, a pair of guys walked past her, with one of them nudging the other. Kit heard, "*Daily Lineup* chick."

People were so odd. Like she wouldn't hear them talking about her from just feet away. They stood there, obviously checking her out. "Don't think so," the other guy said. "Doesn't look like the picture."

She was about to go settle the argument, but that seemed silly. When a guy couldn't tell the difference between a cartoon and a photo, it was probably a waste of time anyway. So she moved away and sat down, idly thinking that she'd give half of her salary to go back to being anonymous. Maybe three quarters.

Bailey came out a few minutes later, flopped down in a chair next to her and said, "I hope you remember the deal. Winner buys."

Thoughts of the guys evaporated as Kit focused on Bailey. Maybe they were back in the habit of having a drink. Nice! Kit patted her pocket. "I've got two hundred and fifty dollars in cash. My grandmother parses out cold hard cash for every holiday. Where would you like to spend Nana's money?"

Clearly shocked, Bailey said, "I don't want you to spend your present."

"I want to. Not all of it, of course, but let's go someplace decent and have a real meal."

"You can pay for drinks. We'll split dinner."

"I think you might be Nana's real relative. You're just as thrifty as she is."

"Thrifty? Two hundred and fifty dollars is a lot! My grandmother gives me five dollars for my birthday, then I sneak it back into her purse when she isn't looking."

"My dad's mom has survived two husbands, and come into a heap of cash with each. She could paper the walls with hundreds and not make a dent."

"Wow," Bailey said, shaking her head. "My grandmother has to save up to have the early-bird dinner at the diner. I think we come from different circumstances."

"Maybe. But my Nana proves money doesn't buy happiness. She's the crankiest old bird you'll ever meet."

"Cranky?"

Kit shrugged. "That's the nicest word I could think of. She's really an extortionist. She's been trying to control us with her money for years, but my brother obviously pushed her too far."

"How'd he do that?"

"Mmm, he wants a weekend house on the Cape, and thought he could talk her into buying it for him." She chuckled. "He's such a dope. If he'd go visit her every few weeks and let her talk—she'd buy him the whole Cape. But he can't figure that out. At dinner, she made a big announcement that since my siblings and I should be self-sufficient she's going to rewrite her will to leave her money to her great-grandchildren."

"Really? She's going to cut you out completely?"

"Seems like it…but she still gave us all cash, so I'm not sure how serious she is."

"But you're…okay with it if she does? Damn, if my grandmother was handing out sacks of money, I'd like a little."

"Oh, I could use the money. I'm not paycheck to paycheck, but I run lean." She considered the issue for a second. "But I'm not going to try to play her. If the kids want to grovel to claim a share—more power to them." As a thought occurred to her, she smiled as she recounted it. "One of the things Henry taught me was that people could only take away your dignity if you let them. Nana's not gonna get mine."

—m—

The place they chose wasn't very fancy, but it was a step up from the bars they'd been to. "Tell me about your Thanksgiving," Kit said. "Did anyone disinherit you?"

Bailey smiled and shook her head. "No, there's not much in the Kwiatkowski coffers. But I really do enjoy having a holiday with my family again. When Julie and I were together that wasn't possible."

"Because…?"

"Oh. That's just how it was. Every holiday was spent in Milpitas."

"Milpitas?"

"Her parents' home. It's near San Jose."

"Every holiday?"

Bailey's eyes grew wide. "I can't imagine what would have happened if we'd made other plans." She put her hands on her head and tossed them into the air, as though something had exploded.

"Really? That bad?"

"Worse than that, really. I'm underplaying it. I would've been happy to stay with Julie until the bitter end, but her mother…" She acted like she was buttoning her lip. "If you can't say anything nice…"

"I'm glad you had fun with your family. But I'm sorry you had to lose Julie to get them back for the holidays."

"What about you? Tell me more about your weekend. I know everyone isn't disinheriting you."

Kit took a sip of her drink, deciding what she wanted to share. "There are worse families than mine, but I wouldn't mind having somewhere else to be."

"Really?" Bailey looked genuinely sad. "Lots of arguments?"

"Not arguments per se, but I'm the only liberal in the family. I've never been the favorite, but they liked me better when I was with Henry. Having him elevated me slightly."

Suspiciously, Bailey said, "That can't be true. How were things when you were younger? Before Henry."

"About the same." A weak laugh punctuated her sentence. "Emily, my sister, is fifteen months older than I am. She was smarter, taller, prettier, and more gifted in every way. I wasn't just in her shadow, I wasn't on the same street."

"No!" Bailey reached across the table and grasped Kit's forearm. "Maybe you imagined that."

"I don't think so. Emily started violin lessons when she was little—like six or seven. I lusted after that violin, waiting for the day I'd get to start lessons. But when my time came my mother said that since Emily was doing well and would advance into the next group, and I'd be a beginner, she didn't have time to take us to separate lessons. I got to play the recorder." She made a face thinking about the hour or two she'd spent with the dumb thing. "Then my brother came along, sixteen months after me. The first boy on either side of the family. If they'd had a crown, he would've been wearing it."

"I hope that isn't true. Kids can infer a lot of slights that aren't really that bad. Maybe you were just really sensitive."

Stopping to think for a few moments, Kit agreed. "I was pretty sensitive. But I don't think I was making it up. One small example: my parents missed my high school graduation because my brother was playing in an important baseball game. Don't you think they could have split up—so that one of them could have been there for me?" She had to force herself to show even a semblance of a smile. "They didn't dislike me, they certainly didn't abuse me. They just…" It was hard to think of a way to put it that didn't seem like she was begging for sympathy, which she was not. "Things would have been better if there had been more space between us." Smirking, she added, "We're not religious in any way, so I'm not sure why they had us in such quick succession. But I'm pretty sure I was a timing mistake."

Bailey looked like she could cry. She pressed her lips together, looking truly upset. "I'm really sorry your parents didn't let you know they were crazy about you." She touched Kit's arm again. "I'm sure they were. Sure of it."

Kit was pretty darned sure her parents had never been particularly crazy about her. But it felt fantastic to have a friend who cared enough to try to make her believe they had been.

Chapter Six

THINGS WERE STARTING TO ease between them, with a real friendship developing. Kit had been wanting to have Bailey over for dinner, and finally felt they were at the point she could do it without stressing out over it. But on the day they'd chosen, Kit found herself babbling away on the walk from the health club, unable to maintain the chill attitude she wished she could pull off.

"Nice place," Bailey said upon entering. "I like it when an apartment looks like the person really lives there, rather than just passing through."

"Thanks. I've tried to make it homey."

"I like your Christmas tree. I didn't bother to put one up."

"Oh, thanks. I love the smell. I'm usually rushing to get it over to the chipper for the last recycling day in January. I'd keep one all year if I could."

Bailey stood near the door, looking around reflectively. "This is a nice building. It's got some character."

"Yeah, it does. This is one of the few big apartment buildings in this part of Foggy Bottom." They stood at the big window in the living room. "Look down there at those cute little row houses."

"I wouldn't mind having one of those," Bailey said. "But I'm pretty happy to rent."

"I would have rented, but Hank wanted to buy. We tried for a place on a lower floor, but got outbid. But we liked the building so much we waited until another unit came on the market."

Bailey turned and looked around. "It's a nice sized place."

"I wanted to go for a two-bedroom, but Henry's New England thriftiness required the smallest place we could stand. Since I have to pay the whole mortgage now—I'm glad he won that argument."

After slipping off her coat, Bailey moved around, casually checking the place out. "You must've been here for quite a while." She met Kit's eyes. "I remember you've been single four years."

"Yeah, it's been...wow." She paused to think. "Almost ten years."

"It looks like you're well settled." Bailey continued to walk around, investigating. Kit was going to follow her and give her the provenance of every piece of art or kitsch she owned, but Bailey seemed happy to poke about on her own.

"Do you eat pork?" Kit called out after she went back into the kitchen. Chuckling, she added, "I guess I should have asked that before I made dinner."

Bailey's voice floated through the room. "I eat everything. Need help?"

"No, everything's ready. It needs another fifteen minutes, then we're good." Everything was ready because she'd spent a small fortune to buy a pre-cooked pork tenderloin, scalloped potatoes and French green beans from the most expensive gourmet shop she knew. Now she just prayed it still looked edible after warming up in the oven.

Suddenly, Bailey was at her side, swiping a slice of avocado off the salad. "Do you work from here?"

"Not really. For the first couple of years I worked in the apartment, but eventually I needed to hire a researcher. Then an assistant. When I had to hire an editor I couldn't justify all of us banging into one another up here. So when the dental office on the ground floor came up, I rented it. The commute is sweet."

"I love it when I can work from home. Can I…open the wine I brought? Or do you have something else you'd…"

"Oh, yeah. Good idea." She mentally slapped herself. It had been four long years since she'd cooked for anyone, having been very careful about not letting her dates think she was going to take up where their ex-wives had left off. No chance of that with Bailey.

Bailey poured the wine and they drank a glass while the oven did its work. Finally, the timer buzzed and Kit got everything portioned out onto plates.

"This looks great." Bailey eyed the food appreciatively as Kit moved past her into the dining area.

"Then let's get to it."

They sat and Bailey made a few enthusiastic comments, then lowered her head and really dug in. During their post-squash dinners, Kit had grown to like watching her eat. She had very good manners and could pace herself when she needed to. But when she was comfortable, she ate like she'd been on a three-day fast, with sparks nearly flying from her fork. It was strangely adorable.

"Really good," Bailey said, cleaning her plate before Kit had made a dent in her portion.

"There's plenty more." Kit twitched her head toward the kitchen. "Go help yourself."

On her way past, Bailey squeezed Kit's shoulder. "I like that you didn't get up to serve me."

"I want my guests to feel at home. Go for it."

Bailey filled her plate with easily as much as Kit had originally portioned out. Her metabolism must have been set on hyper-speed, given that she looked like she could have just escaped from a refugee camp, yet ate like she was in a pie-eating contest. She sat down and plowed through this plate in a more leisurely fashion, now just determined and focused rather than frantic.

After dinner, Kit took their bottle of wine and they sat on the sofa in the living room. She took a drink, finding her mouth dry as a rock. "Uhm, I've been thinking…"

"Good. Thinking is often helpful."

"About us," Kit added, hearing her voice break like an adolescent boy's.

"Us?" Bailey's head cocked slightly.

"Yeah." Some of the tension that had been building dissipated when she moved around a little. "I can tell you've decided I'm not dating material." She looked up and met her eyes, seeing kindness and maybe even a hint of understanding. "But I'm…interested in you. More all the time."

Bailey nodded her head, looking very serious. "I uhm…had a feeling that might be happening." She crossed her leg by placing a calf upon her knee, then dropped her head, breaking their eye contact.

"It's true. I can't get you out of my head."

"I don't want to make light of how you're feeling." Bailey looked up, her eyes filled with tenderness. "But it sounds like you want to visit a place that I live. I've lived here every day of my life, Kit, and it feels strange to have someone say that she wants to…vacation here."

"Do you still like me?" Kit asked, staring into her eyes.

"Of course I do."

"If I was a lesbian, would you be into me?"

The slightly wary look in Bailey's eyes eased. "Yeah, I really would."

She'd been rehearsing the speech for days, and Kit thought she had it nailed. "Then why can't you approach this like you would anybody else you were starting to date? You never know what kind of crazy you're gonna get when you first start out."

Chuckling, Bailey said, "And you're saying that I know what kind of crazy you are?"

"Yeah. No one comes with warning labels. A stranger can hide all of her issues. But with me, you already know the biggest thing I have to deal with."

"I think it's me who has to deal with that—if you change your mind."

Once again, her expression turned sad. Just seeing how vulnerable she looked made Kit's heart clutch in her chest. "That could definitely happen. But I'm not a kid, like Natalie was. I'm a mature woman, and I'm comfortable with my sex drive, wherever it leads me."

"And it's leading you to me. Just me. Not other women."

"Just you. My interest in you grows every time we see each other." Scooting closer to Bailey, she lowered her voice. "Every time."

Clearly skittish, Bailey moved back a couple of inches. "I'm having a hard time getting my head around this. I haven't had to deal with the 'is she or isn't she' issue since I was eighteen. I haven't missed it, either."

"That part is for me to handle. You just have to deal with the 'am I or am I not cool enough to keep her interested' part." When a ghost of a smile split Bailey's lips, Kit allowed herself to relax a little. If they could tease about this, it would go much, much easier.

"I'm not wracked by self-doubt." Her smile grew. "I think I'm plenty cool. But people don't switch sexual orientations overnight. You had to have had some crushes on girls when you were young."

"None," Kit said, shaking her head.

"There had to have been some times you thought about women in a sexual way."

"Nope. Just you."

Bailey got up and paced around the apartment for a minute, mumbling to herself. "How is that possible? You're turning forty and out of the blue decide to have lesbian sex? Is this a mid-life crisis? Or have guys turned you off so much you're willing to try anything?"

"No, I don't think that's it." She took a breath and gave words to the insight she'd had just a few days before. "I've been limiting myself to men. Never giving women a second thought. Maybe that wasn't smart."

"What?" Bailey's brows popped up. "You've limited yourself because that's how you're oriented." Her determined look eased. "Isn't it?"

"I don't know. I honestly don't know. But it seems that it might be smarter to find someone who you're attracted to—without ruling out half of the world."

"Be my guest," Bailey said, shaking her head. "If women were only five percent of the population I wouldn't change my orientation. You make it sound like a supply and demand problem." She got up and went to the window. "That seems nuts. Just nuts." She shoved her hands in her pockets and rocked back and forth, clearly agitated.

"You're working yourself into a frenzy." Kit patted the sofa cushion. "Come sit down. You're making me nervous."

Rolling her eyes, Bailey did as she was asked, but she sat even farther away than she'd been before.

"I hope this isn't a mid-life crisis, since I'm planning on living much longer than eighty. I've still got three of four grandparents, and a full complement of aunts and uncles."

"I remember Asante saying you had good genes."

"I do. And yes, the supply of men I'm interested in is a little thin. But not enough to do something that I'm not interested in." She took in a long, cleansing breath. "It's more that I opened my eyes to a possibility I'd closed off without giving it any serious consideration."

"You're honestly telling me you've never, ever considered being with a woman."

"My very first inkling was the first time we played squash. You kissed me… just a quick, friendly touch. But it was the first time a woman who could potentially be interested in me kissed me. It was like a light turned on. A whole new realm of possibilities." She let her gaze roam up and down Bailey's body, taking in her checked shirt with the sleeves rolled up to expose lean arms, and the narrow, knit tie. "I really like you. You're fun and smart and kind and thoughtful. If you were a man—I'd be chasing you so hard you couldn't possibly outrun me."

"But I'm not."

Her voice dropped another few notes, taking on a sexy purr. "No, you're not. And that's part of what attracts me. You're not like a man at all, but you're kinda…boyish."

"That's…" She trailed off and looked away. Kit waited for her to speak again. She clearly had something to say that was hard for her to get out. "I guess that's a good word for it."

Kit waited again, but nothing more came. Without doubt, there was more on Bailey's mind, but she wasn't willing to give it up. Maybe they hadn't built up enough trust yet.

"At first, I thought I could give you a makeover. Maybe convince you to wear women's shoes and get you some different glasses. With just a few changes you'd look like a runway model." She shifted, getting a little closer. "But once we got to know each other… When I got to know your energy…" She closed her eyes for a second and let her mind fill with her fantasies. "Now, I'd cut your hair so you'd look even more boyish. I love the way you look. It's…really, really sexy."

"Because I look like a guy." There was a certain suspicion in her tone, and Kit rushed to reassure her.

"No. You don't look like a guy." She let her gaze roam across Bailey's face, her jaw, her elegant neck. "You look like a woman—who's really boyish. I've never been attracted to someone who looks like you; I'm not even sure I've ever noticed another woman who looks like you—but the way you look really, really works for me."

Now Bailey leaned in, and her voice became gentler. "I love the way you look, too. If I could change anything about you I'd try to convince you to grow your hair out. I love long hair." She grinned sheepishly. "I guess you can't change what attracts you."

"No, you can't." A soft rustling sound accompanied Kit's scooting still closer. "Let me show you how attracted I am to you." She put her hand on Bailey's cheek, amazed at the incredible softness of her skin.

Bailey took her hand and held it between both of her own. She had the hands of a pianist. Soft and delicate, with elegant, long fingers. "Only if we go really, really slowly. Like a glacier."

"During climate change?" Kit asked, trying to make her smile.

"Before. I'm not kidding. I will not get too far into this until I'm sure you're willing to put up with all of the bullshit that comes with dating a woman."

It was hard not to laugh at that. "That won't be a problem. I'm a big girl."

"I'm not joking."

"I know that. But look at the facts. I'm self-employed, not overly influenced by my family, and I don't belong to a disapproving church." She had to touch that smooth cheek again. "It's been a very long time since I cared what people thought about my dates."

"I'm not making light of this." Bailey's eyes narrowed. "Same-sex dating is complex. For everyone."

"Fine. It'll be complex. I'll deal with it."

Bailey still hung onto her point doggedly. "Dating a woman is tough. Dating me is even tougher."

"What's so tough about you?"

"The way I…look." She swallowed, and Kit's heart ached again when she saw the fragile look on her face. "It's not easy."

"Okay." She nodded soberly. "I'll gird my loins." Something hit her and she took a breath and spit it out. "I don't want you to get the wrong impression about this. I'm not saying that I'm a lesbian. I'm pretty certain I'm not. I'm just attracted to you."

A small smile settled onto Bailey's mouth. "And any other woman who wears a tie."

"I've seen other women in ties." She made a cutting motion with her hand. "Nothing. I'm into you." Bailey didn't complain when she moved even closer and tentatively slid her arms around her shoulders. They were nose-to-nose, with Kit's heart racing so fast she felt like she might have a stroke. But this was… compelling.

Bailey felt so different than a guy. Her body was smooth and lean, no bulky muscles making her all lumpy. And her scent was sweet, very womanly. Her complexion would have been the envy of a model, not a wrinkle to be found. But it was her eyes that drew Kit in. Like she'd taken in the whole world and had tucked all sorts of secrets inside, just waiting for Kit to discover them.

Then those lovely eyes closed, and Bailey's pink lips parted. Kit moved toward her and sighed when their lips touched tenderly. It felt amazing. A sweet softness she didn't have words for. And Bailey didn't push, didn't even try to escalate things. They simply shared a tender intimacy that struck Kit right in the heart.

Bailey slowly pulled away, then put her hand on Kit's cheek and gazed into her eyes for a long time. A tiny smile revealed itself, then she closed her eyes and placed another soft, sweet kiss on Kit's lips. She breathed in, and Kit almost swooned when she felt Bailey's chest press against her own. If the blood hadn't been pounding in her ears, she would have felt Bailey's heartbeat. God, she'd missed being intimate with another person. It was glorious to share yourself with someone you were starting to care for.

Bailey's fingers were sliding along the side of her head, threading through her hair. They were still just inches apart, and Bailey's eyes were locked on hers, unblinking. Her voice was a soft purr. "What do you think?"

"I feel like I'm high. I could burrow into your arms and stay there for a week, perfectly content."

"Was that really the first time you've kissed a woman? Your very first?"

"Very first."

"You're not going to recall some long-repressed fantasy you've been tamping down since you were a girl?"

"No fantasies." She tried to pull her back in for another kiss, but Bailey resisted.

"Slowly," she soothed. She put her hands on Kit's arms and gently pushed her away. "Let this sink in. Call me in a few days and let me know how you feel about it."

She blinked up at her as Bailey stood. "You're…leaving?"

"Yeah." She smiled, then moved over to the front door. "Pre-climate change, remember?"

Kit stared at her, stunned. "You are nothing like a guy."

"Probably true." Bailey walked back over to the sofa. "I don't think this will be as easy as you seem to think. I've never dated a guy, but I'm sure it's really, really different." She reached out and pulled Kit to her feet for a gentle hug.

"I'm willing to do whatever it takes to see where this leads." Kit looked up into Bailey's clear, bright eyes. She was the perfect height. When they snuggled, Kit would be able to put her head right on her shoulder.

"Then there's a chance there will be an us." She kissed Kit's cheek, then went back to the door. Turning the knob, she added, "I really hope there is."

—⁂—

The next day, Kit was in her office, fielding phone calls, trying to scare up a new source for a story. It was a darned good story, but she refused to print even the most compelling item if she didn't have two sources or some credible physical evidence.

Every time she had a moment where her brain wasn't otherwise occupied, her thoughts turned to Bailey — picturing the way her eyes closed when Kit moved in for a kiss. There was some very serious sex appeal wrapped up in that nerdy package.

Her cell phone buzzed, and she was tempted to ignore it. Nia answered the office phones, but every once in a while a business call came in via her private number. She checked the display, saw that it was an unknown number and took a chance. At worst, she'd have to hang up. "Hello?"

"Kit?"

Just one word. But after spending eight years with someone, one word was enough. "This is getting to be a habit," she said, chuckling. "Don't worry, I won't say your name. I'm assuming you want anonymity, since you're not calling from your office or your cell."

"Yeah, that would be best. I hate to be all cloak and dagger, but the more people know about you, the more they want to take you down."

There was a moment, an almost imperceptible flicker of time that made her miss their former intimacy. Not because she wanted him back; breaking up had been a clearheaded choice that she didn't regret. But when you had a long relationship with someone and switched over to being purely business associates, there was always going to be something missing. Something important.

Henry had known her very well, as well as anyone in her life ever had, and she'd loved him deeply. A few years ago it would've been unthinkable that she'd be dreaming of a sexual relationship with Bailey; Henry had fulfilled both her sexual and emotional needs. It surprised her, but she felt strangely guilty to have just a few hours ago kissed those sweet, womanly lips. Like it was somehow a betrayal of Henry. Emotions were strange things.

"It's been a while," he said. "I haven't seen anything about that issue we spoke about."

"That issue needs some verification. I've got someone looking into it, but until I'm certain of the facts, I can't move forward."

He wasn't good at hiding frustration. "Give me a break! You've got pictures."

"It's probably not a good idea to be too definite about what you know of this matter. I'm on it, and if it's valid I'll go with it. But I need more than your word."

"That's not how it used to…"

He really sucked at this cloak and dagger stuff. If you wanted to fly under the radar, it was probably unwise to reveal that you and the reporter on the phone used to be lovers. She did him a small favor. "I know I used to publish things from just one source, but I'm trying to step up my game, dammit!" She chuckled softly, knowing that wouldn't translate in a transcript.

"Right. That's what I was going to say. You're changing the rules on me."

"I'm changing a lot of things. Time marches on. Stay tuned."

She hung up and sat perfectly still, staring at the wall for a minute. The questions Bailey had posed came back to her. It seemed very hard for Bailey to believe that not only had Kit been very much into having sex with men, but also that she'd never fantasized about being sexual with a woman. But it was the God's honest truth. If Hank had lost that first election and stayed a district attorney in Boston, they'd still be together—happily together. She was certain of that. But politics had changed him, and doing all of the dances one had to do to be connected to a politician had changed her. Changed her in ways that harmed her. Yes, politics had ruined their relationship, but he hadn't sulked for long. He wasn't the type. She'd never doubted that he'd loved her; she'd also never doubted that he'd find someone new. Quickly. She'd been right on the nose with that prediction. Sadly, she'd known it would be tough for her to bounce back. Now, four years later, she was trying out for the other team.

—∞—

For the second time since she'd moved to DC, Natalie dragged Bailey by the ear to shop for clothing. Nat believed that you needed to buy one nice outfit a season, and you had to buy it right when the new things reached the stores.

Bailey's first choice was to find things in second-hand shops. Her second was to only buy items that were on sale. But Natalie was unbending. She insisted that the most attractive things were long gone by the time the sales started.

Washington was much more formal than Silicon Valley had been, meaning fewer jeans and sweaters and more slacks and jackets. If it had been up to Natalie, Bailey's clothes would have been more unisex, but that was one area where Bailey would not give an inch. She'd made the choice to dress the way she'd always wanted when she'd moved to DC and was not about to change.

They went to a nice menswear shop in Georgetown, where Nat had a passing acquaintance with the manager, who made sure Bailey was treated well. It was the perfect spot for her. Almost everything was slim-cut and European-styled, the look that fit Bailey best in every sense. A very thin, very gay guy and she could trade clothes. Luckily, there were enough guys like that in Washington to keep a whole store in business.

She'd decided on a pair of salmon colored twill slacks and a plaid shirt with all the colors of Easter; now she had to let Natalie poke at everything else in the store.

Their salesman had abandoned them long ago, and now Natalie was idly considering shirts that hung on a long rack. "I assume you think Kit's just unaware of her lesbianism?"

This was Natalie's new focus. She clearly thought there was a key to unlocking Kit's interest, and she was determined to find it.

"No, I don't think that. She seems to know herself pretty well."

"Then what's in it for you? You meet some tech-types at your jobs. If you're involved with a straight woman you won't be watching for signals that a real lesbian gives you."

"I can multitask."

Natalie turned and gave her a long, appraising look. "I'm being serious. Why even play around like this?"

Shrugging, Bailey told the simple truth. "I really like her. She's the most interesting person I've met since I moved, and it seems silly to ignore that."

"I know she's your type physically, but don't let that blind you."

"I'd have to be blind to not have that influence me."

A scowl was Nat's only reply. Bailey walked over to her and spoke quietly. "I'm not going to lie to you. At this point, it's mostly physical. What I know of her I like, but the physical attraction is what's compelling. But I think there's more than that, and I don't think that's just my hormones talking."

"You don't have much experience. Why not get out there and date a boatload of women? You're smart, you're pretty, you've got money and no obvious faults. Spend some of that capital while you have it."

"I'll take that under advisement."

"You don't have to humor me," Natalie said, obviously a little wounded.

"Okay, I won't." Bailey looked her right in the eye. "I can find my own women, Nat. I love that you care, but you're not going to change my mind if I choose to go forward with her. But thanks for trying." She gave her a playful cuff and took her items up to the cash register. It was kind of fun to let Natalie boss her around when it came to clothing; she drew the line when it came to women.

—⁂—

Now that she'd had a tempting taste of her, there was nothing Kit wanted to do as much as chase Bailey—preferably around her apartment. But Bailey was as elusive as anyone Kit had ever been attracted to. It had been two days since their kiss, and if Kit had counted how many times she'd wanted to call—well, it was embarrassing to admit how large the number was. In a way, it was good that Bailey wasn't more receptive, since Kit hadn't had a moment to spare. The Christmas party season was in full tilt, and there were some invitations she couldn't even consider declining.

On Friday night, she and Asante stood in a long line that snaked down a narrow street in Georgetown, supplicants waiting to enter the storied home of Asante's publisher.

"We should have hired a limo," Asante said, shivering in the cold.

Whispering, Kit said, "The people in back of us came in a limo, and they're out here with us. The only people who can cut are those with security details. Oh! There's our favorite former vice president and his lovely…what did we decide she was?"

"A Terminator. No way she's got blood running through those veins. Look how big his security detail is. Are we paying for that?"

"Probably. In one way or another."

"I heard they were going to try to confiscate cell phones tonight. Good luck with that."

"They wouldn't have five guests," Kit agreed, chuckling. She took out her phone and started to make notes. "Run up to the front of the line and scope it out for me, will you? I've gotta tag people for the newsletter."

"No way! I'm not your intern. Besides, I don't know half of the low-level operatives you do." He put a hand on her back and gave her a gentle push. "I'll hold your place in line. Have fun."

—⁂—

Hours later, Kit had exhausted every possible bit of gossip she could wring out of the party. A melting ice sculpture caught her eye and she instinctively snapped a photo and sent it to Bailey. Then she started to worry. Was that too casual? Should she have called instead? She hadn't been so skittish about a crush since she was twelve, but she didn't know how to calm down and act like herself. Thankfully, she only had to sweat for a few minutes. Her phone buzzed with, "What in the hell is that?"

"Capitol. Looks like Coliseum in Rome now."

"Where are you?"

"G'town."

"Nightcap?"

"Love to."

"Address? I'll pick you up."

Smiling like a cat who'd just swallowed a canary, Kit texted her location. She'd played it right. Her elation only lasted a moment, then she hightailed it for the bathroom. She always carried a tiny disposable toothbrush—just in case. Tonight, she fervently hoped she'd soon have her minty-fresh lips firmly attached to Bailey's.

—⁓—

Forty-five minutes later, Bailey texted. "I'm here. Should I force my way inside?"

"Ha! Be right out."

Asante had cornered one of the big editors of the paper, so Kit waved discretely, got her wrap and allowed the tuxedoed doorman to escort her down the stairs to the sidewalk. Bailey was waiting a few yards down the street, behind police barricades and a couple of security guys, wands at the ready for latecomers.

"This was the best idea I've had all day," Bailey said, grinning lasciviously. "Do you always dress like this for work?"

Kit had almost forgotten she'd had to go full-tilt in the formality department. "Yep. Every day." She made a quick twirl, then dipped her heavy, black velvet wrap, showing a bare shoulder.

Bailey stood there, gazing at her with a slightly vacant look in her eyes. "Nice," she finally said. "Really nice."

When you had a date look at you that way, you were making progress. So far, the difference between dating men and women was very, very small, and that was a huge relief. It was much easier to navigate a path you'd trod many times.

—⁓—

Kit knew the area pretty well and guided Bailey to a dark, quiet, sophisticated place off M Street. "Glad I dressed," Bailey said as they threaded their way through the crowd. "I thought a suit would be dressy enough for this part of Georgetown, but now I'm wishing I had a tux."

"You look great." Kit let her gaze travel up and down Bailey's body. "Beyond great."

"Thanks," she said, looking a little shy.

They wound up in the far corner of the bustling place, with pale violet lighting painting the brick wall behind them. "This place is really pretentious, but it's always a good place for me to tag people."

"I'll go get drinks. What would you like?"

"Someone will be over. It might take a while, but drinks are so expensive I'm always glad they don't rush." She took out her phone and started to make notes. "My battery's almost dead, but I see the former director of OMB over there and I want to make sure he gets tagged."

Bailey gently removed the phone from her hand. "Why don't you have a case that gives you extra battery power?"

Kit looked up. "Didn't know there was one."

"There is. And you're going to have one by Monday. Early Christmas present." Her grin was so cute it was almost impossible not to pull her down for a kiss.

"Let me finish. Then I can devote all of my attention to you." She took the phone back and completed her text. "All done. Unless someone really important comes in, I'm off the clock."

Once again, Bailey took the phone. "Mind if I look?"

"At…?"

"What you're texting." She went to the message Kit had been adding to for the past four hours. "Hmm… Lots of names of people I haven't heard of and a few even I know." She handed the phone back, grinning. "They must be super famous."

A server came by and Bailey gave Kit a brief look, asking for permission to order for her. "We both like vodka," she told the server. "Surprise us with something."

He stood there for a moment, giving them an assessing look. "I'll be right back."

Kit watched him leave, thinking of how nice it was to be with someone who took charge. Few things irritated her more than a date who never did.

Pointing at the phone, Bailey said, "Now comes the big question. Why were you texting people's names all night long?"

"I'm getting the impression you haven't taken a look at the *Daily Lineup*, have you."

"I should… It's just not something—"

"It's okay," Kit soothed. "No need. If you're not into politics it would be like reading the phone book." She turned her phone around, saying, "One of the things we do is 'tag' famous people wherever we see them. Especially if they're with someone you wouldn't expect to see them with." She typed for a few moments, then turned the phone again and craned her neck so they could both see. "We keep this document in the cloud all day, and add to it constantly. Then my overnight editor decides which tags are important enough to leave in. I check it before it goes out in the morning, but my night staff writes most of the copy."

"Why does it matter that Mike Mullvaney was with Mark Rukovitch?"

"Oh. Mullvaney is a lobbyist for big tobacco and Rukovitch used to be Surgeon General. Rukovitch is probably going to join up with the enemy."

"Just because someone saw them together? Isn't that a leap of logic? Maybe they…" She smiled sweetly. "Play squash together."

"Maybe. But since one of my guys saw them having lunch in a very downscale place near Mullvaney's offices, I bet I'm right." She shrugged. "We'll put it under the strange bedfellows section. People can assume what they will."

"And…" She looked like she was about to say something she knew would cause offense. "This is journalism?"

"I'm afraid it is." Kit put her phone away. Their server delivered their drinks, which Bailey paid for before Kit could get her purse open. "Thanks," she said as they toasted. "Delicious. Really, really good."

"I think I'm going to have to learn how to make these." She inclined her glass toward Kit. "Tell me more about this…" Playfully, she made air quotes before saying, "Journalism."

"It's clearly not what I did at the *Globe*. And my journalism teachers wouldn't be proud of me. But this is the way things have gone in the last ten years. I certainly don't see them going back to the old way, so I had to join in or drop out." She took another sip of her very tasty drink. "I joined in." She looked up when something caught her eye. "Incoming."

"Huh?"

"Secret Service. Someone important's coming in."

"How can you tell?"

Kit gave her a puzzled look. "How can you not? The haircuts, the suits, the earpieces, the blank expressions on their faces. Don't make any sudden moves or you'll be face down in a nanosecond."

"I hate being face down," she said, chuckling. "Who is it? Anyone I know?"

Kit watched as a space opened and a stylishly dressed woman sat at a chair that had miraculously opened for her. A man stood behind her, trying not to appear inconsequential. "Big policy advisor. I heard she was getting protection, now I see it in action." Pulling her phone out, she added to the tagged list. "I won't mention the protection thing, of course. Just that she's here."

Tentatively, Bailey said, "You do…more…substantive things, don't you?"

"Damn, I hope so!" Kit laughed. "Sucking up and gossiping is only about ten to fifteen percent of my daily output. But it's the part everyone reads. Sadly."

"Do you go to a lot of parties and stuff to find out where people are?"

"More than I'd like, but I have a legion of snitches who feed me things. I got burned once, repeating something a guy told me. Now I'll only print gossipy sightings if my sources give me a photo."

"And people do that?" She looked adorably confused.

"Yep. I get four or five times as many items as I could possibly mention. No one ever leaves junior high school. Sad, but true."

"Uhm, I don't want to burst your bubble, but there are a lot of people out there—me included—who didn't participate in that junior high stuff—then or now."

"Then you're very lucky you don't want to be a member of the permanent ruling class here. No one over the emotional age of thirteen need apply."

—⁓—

It was late when they left the bar, almost midnight. Bailey knew Kit got up super early most days, but she still seemed bright and sharp and bubbly as she prattled away on the 32 Bus. They'd never taken a cab, which she found kind of funny. But Kit had never suggested it. Maybe she was really concerned about the environment.

Even in the unflattering glare of the bus' lights, Kit looked fabulous. It must have sucked to not be able to throw on a parka on a cold night, but her strapless cocktail dress made Bailey very glad Kit chose looking good over being warm. Luckily, she seemed not to mind, although Bailey was still cold in a wool suit and lined raincoat. No one ever said fashion was fair.

When they arrived, Bailey was mulling over her next move. Kit didn't seem nervous, and she wasn't acting any differently from the way she'd been before they'd kissed. But she also hadn't brought it up. As attractive as she found her, Bailey wasn't going to press the issue. The ball was in Kit's court, and if she never hit it back—it'd stay there. All of this was jumbling around in her head when Kit gave her a warm smile and said, "Come up for a minute."

Done, Bailey thought, smirking as they walked past the doorman, who smiled and greeted Kit by name.

When they went into the apartment, Kit stayed right by the door. Her voice dropped into a sexy purr as her warm eyes scanned Bailey's face. "I've been thinking about how it felt to kiss you since the minute my lips left yours."

Wow. This woman was as sexy as sexy got. Bailey wasn't usually tongue-tied around women, but she couldn't do more than offer a smile, trying to make it look sexy rather than dull-witted.

Kit moved even closer. So close Bailey could smell the sweet perfume she wore. "I've got to get to bed, but I hoped I could talk you into a goodnight kiss." Her hands moved slightly, letting her sumptuous-looking wrap drape lower on her shoulders. "What do you think?"

"I think you could manage." Kit was doing the asking, but not the doing. Nice. It was so much nicer to be in control. Bailey slid her hands around Kit's waist and pulled her even closer while she let her hands relish the feel of Kit's body. Slowly, Kit's eyes closed as her head tilted back, waiting for Bailey. Then their lips met, gently and softly. Bailey pulled her in a little harder, the need to press into her body remarkably strong. But she fought the urge and gentled her hold. Glacial speed.

Kit's hands were on Bailey's hips, and she could feel her struggle with herself to avoid doing the exact same thing Bailey wanted to. They were getting somewhere. Somewhere Bailey could hardly wait to get to.

—⁂—

Kit waited until she'd brushed her teeth and had gotten into bed to send a text. "No adverse reactions from a VERY small number of kisses. Maybe we should increase the dosage?" She lay down, too anxious to even close her eyes. Putting herself out like this wasn't something she'd had to do very often. Usually, a guy liked you and immediately started to push as much as you'd let him. Bailey's style was taking some getting used to.

A text came back. "Doesn't sound like a bad prescription. Free this weekend?"

No. Kit was never "free." Nearly every minute of off-time had to be carved out of a completely unpredictable news cycle. But she really wanted to see Bailey. "I can be. What's good for you?"

"Sunday?"

Huh. Sunday. There were an awful lot of hours in a Sunday, and Kit usually spent most of them in her office, catching up on all of the things she couldn't get to when Washington was chugging along on its usual Monday through Friday schedule. She found herself typing, "Sunday's great. What time?"

"Let's have brunch, then see what we're in the mood to do."

Kit stared at the phone for a while. Bailey was apparently asking for the whole day. Certain she'd be digging a hole she'd have a hell of a time getting out of on Monday, Kit replied, "Great! Text me when you want to get together." She switched her phone off and closed her eyes, trying to get her mind to switch off as well. With any luck, Bailey slept until one or two, and Kit could get some cleanup done before they met.

—␣—

Bailey didn't sleep in that late. In fact, she texted at nine a.m., just after Kit had started to dig her way past the first few inches of her in-box. "Up? I'm starving. Swing by and get you?"

Kit stared at the message, desperately wishing it had come three hours later. "Excellent," she found her fingers replying. Then she dropped the article she'd been reading and raced upstairs, determined to look perkier than she felt.

—␣—

They'd eaten far too much, and were now determined to walk off some of the calories. Given that Kit had eaten a whole waffle and three pieces of bacon, she figured they'd have to walk to West Virginia to make a dent. Instead, they decided to go to a museum. "I like lots of different kinds of art," Kit said, once they were outside in the chilly, gray day. "What are your favorites?"

"Mmm," Bailey said thoughtfully. "Probably sculpture. I like almost anything in three dimensions."

"Super. Are you up for being outdoors?"

"Absolutely. I'm dressed for it."

"Let's hit the Hirshhorn, and see if that works for you."

"Sounds good. My cultural exposure has been very, very limited since I moved here. I think that should change."

"Washington has a little something for everyone. I'm confident we can find something that resonates with you."

They weren't too far from the museum, so they decided to walk. "Did you go to museums when you were growing up?" Kit asked.

"No, not very often," Bailey said, shaking her head. "There wasn't much close by and we didn't travel. I went to Philadelphia on school trips, and that was about all I was exposed to. How about you?"

"I've spent more than my fair share of time looking at paintings. I had a great art teacher in high school, and she took us to every museum in town. It really made an impression on me."

"Art joke," Bailey said, grinning. "A small one, but…"

"If you know impressionism exists, you're doing better than most of the guys I've dated."

"That's my goal. Just trying to stay above the median."

She wore such a confident grin that Kit was pretty sure Bailey wouldn't be happy with anything less than the peak of the curve.

—⚬—

Bailey stood a few feet away from a huge clock, set on an angle. She wasn't great at expressing in words why something reached her emotionally, but this clock did. Kit, normally chatty, hadn't spoken much at all whenever Bailey had stopped in front of a piece. That was a really, really nice trait. Having someone talking like a magpie while looking at art should be illegal.

Stepping back a little, Bailey crossed her arms over her chest and let her gaze grow unfocused. Sometimes sculpture was even better when you didn't look at it too closely. Minutes must have passed, and when she snapped out of it she looked around, finding Kit sitting on a bench, giving her a half smile. Bailey walked over and sat down next to her. "Did I zone out?"

Widening her eyes, Kit nodded. "Way out. I do that too, but usually with paintings."

"Thanks for giving me a little time. I hate to rush when I see something I like."

Kit chuckled softly. "I think I'm learning that about you. If you don't want parts of me to snap off from the cold, you'd better take me inside."

Bailey got up and extended her hand, which Kit took. "There's not a single part of you that doesn't belong right where it is."

—⚬—

The sun set so early it was dark by the time they got back to Kit's apartment. She lowered the blinds and turned on every light in the living room, saying, "I hate it being dark by five. If I keep the blinds closed I can make believe it's still sunny."

"Interesting," Bailey said, nodding. "Delusional, but interesting." She sat in the middle of the sofa, then stretched her long arms out along the back. "Any other easily disproved items on your belief list?"

"Not too many. I'm generally sane." She went into the kitchen and called out, "I can make cocoa, or tea, or coffee. And I've got wine of all colors. What'll it be?"

"I'd better have tea. I've got some work to do when I get home."

"How about peppermint?"

"Sounds good."

Kit used her electric kettle to have the tea ready in just a few minutes. When she brought it in she hesitated just a moment, trying to decide where to sit. The spot right next to Bailey looked the best, so she handed her a mug and settled close.

Bailey took a sip, nodded and gave a lazy, sated smile. "A nice day looking at art, now a good cup of tea and a really pretty woman right next to me. I can't think of a better way to spend a Sunday."

"I can, but I don't want that glacier to melt too fast."

Laughing, Bailey clinked her mug against Kit's. "All things in good time." She sat there, looking perfectly content. Her body language was wide open, with one ankle crossed over the other knee, arms stretched out. She was tall, at least four inches taller than Kit, but she took up even more space than her height would have indicated. This was the part of her that was boyish. The part that made her look like she filled the room, even though she was thin as a rail. It was a combination of self-confidence, optimism and something else. Something Kit couldn't name. But it was compelling. Very compelling.

After setting her mug down, Kit leaned a little closer and said, "Do you have any interest in kissing me? 'Cause I'd really like to kiss you."

Bailey beamed a grin at her, looking like she'd been sitting there waiting for those exact words. "I was just thinking the same thing. You beat me to it." But she didn't move. Not a muscle. She just waited, waited for Kit to come to her. Which she did without a second thought.

Leaning in, Kit brushed her lips across Bailey's relishing the soft, pliable skin. Kit had kissed plenty of boys and men, but she'd never kissed one who acted quite like Bailey. With her half smile firmly in place, she looked like the king of the jungle, contentedly allowing the lioness to approach. Kit had no idea if this was her usual way of being, or if she was letting Kit go at her own pace, but it was damned sexy.

Sliding her hands across the tops of Bailey's shoulders, she pulled her close and gave her a long, lush kiss. After several seconds Bailey took in a deep breath, then tilted her head to nuzzle against Kit's neck. "I love the way you smell. So sexy."

Having Bailey's warm lips trailing across her neck sent Kit's temperature soaring. This was so much nicer than having a guy lunge for you! She'd always felt she had to be slightly on guard. Trying to make sure a guy didn't take more than she was ready to give. But Bailey didn't give off one shred of that aggression. Yet…it wasn't that she wasn't assertive. Kit was certain of that. She was just…patient.

At that moment, there wasn't anything she was holding back. If Bailey wanted to saunter into the bedroom—she was more than willing to go. Kit grasped her face with both hands and kissed every inch, placing a special kiss on the little grin that never faded. Her pulse was thrumming, and after she pressed her lips against Bailey's once again she pulled back an inch and tickled that pink flesh with her tongue. But Bailey didn't open her mouth. She wrapped an arm around Kit's shoulders and pulled her into a warm embrace.

"I'm gonna have to leave soon," she whispered into her ear. "Don't want the glacier to melt too quickly."

"I can find two hundred congressmen who'll tell you climate change is a fallacy. Not just a fallacy, but also that we're entering an ice age. The glaciers aren't melting at all."

Chuckling, Bailey kissed Kit's forehead. "Tell that to my body. It's about to combust."

"Different scientific theory," Kit insisted. She tried to shift and get Bailey into another clutch but Bailey moved away and stood.

"I really have to get going. But I'd love to come back."

"Tomorrow?" Kit asked hopefully. Was she crazy? Her calendar was full from six thirty a.m. until seven p.m. Then she had a reception way out at the Pentagon.

"No, not tomorrow." Bailey took her hand and pulled her to her feet. "I'll call you."

Kit looked up into those gorgeous eyes and nodded vacantly. "Soon. Make it soon."

Chapter Seven

IT HAD BEEN A VERY slow news day. The town was eerily quiet, with Congress in recess and most people gone to their respective home states for Christmas. The only thing looming on the political calendar was the budget battle. Budgets weren't Kit's favorite thing, and she was sure this one was going to be a bruiser.

She tried hard to be impartial. It was tough at times, especially when her heart was decidedly liberal. But she always avoided being the liberal bag-woman. She would never allow herself to be like some of the pinheads who called themselves journalists, but just repackaged talking points from one camp or another and called it news.

Even though she didn't want to be the mouthpiece for the Democrats, when they were in power she had to curry favor. That was the only way to get any information out of them. It made you feel dirty, but it was part of the game.

In the newsletter, she'd been dropping bits of info she'd been fed from a White House policy wonk. It was dry as dirt, and took her a long time to polish it up enough to make anyone without an economics degree bother to read it. Right before she was going to pack it in and go up to her apartment, her source called.

"Hey, it's Edward Tellen."

"Hey, Edward. What's got you slaving away at this time of night?"

"Huh?" He must have looked at a clock. "You call this late?"

"I guess you're right. It's only late if you've got a real life."

"I gave that up when I came to Washington."

Kind of sad. Also, kind of common. "Right. So…whatcha got?"

"Just wanted to touch base. The piece you posted today was perfect! Well, you left a few of the important details out, but I think you got the message across."

She laughed to herself. She'd left out charts, graphs, regression analyses, Bureau of Labor Statistics footnotes and other assorted facts that would have guaranteed not a soul would read it. Thanks to her knocking it down to human language it was getting some play. She'd rushed to get it in on Monday, but thought it better to showcase it to jamming it in late in the day. "It's been up for two hours, and has been linked to…" She checked the counter. "Four hundred times. Not bad for a Tuesday."

"Big, big thanks. I owe you one. A big one."

When a guy who worked in the actual White House owed you one, it was best to claim your prize quickly. Memories were very, very short in Washington. "How about a tour? I haven't been since forty-three was in office."

"Done. Name your date."

"How long will it take to clear security?"

"A few days. Got time before Christmas?"

"Absolutely. How about next Saturday?"

"The twenty-first?"

"Yeah."

"Done deal."

"It's on my calendar. Me and a friend. I'll send you her name, rank and serial number."

"Passport sized photos, too. And Kit, if your friend has a record, for anything, it's not going to happen."

Kit laughed at the thought of Bailey in a line-up. "I think she's clean. I guess this is one way to find out."

—m—

There were not a lot of perks that came with being a political blogger. Yes, she was invited to tons of cocktail parties and luncheons, many of which she had to pay for, and dinners honoring people for the thinnest of excuses were nightly happenings. She chose to go to very few of those. Of course, there were the ubiquitous book release parties, where you got a cup of cheap wine and a cracker or two. You had to go to those, especially for fellow journalists. But it was rare to get invited to anything even remotely "fun." So it was a huge surprise when a friend handed over a pair of tickets to Mixology Fest, which promised an evening at a new bar with an expert in molecular cocktails. Kit normally kept her drink selection pretty simple, but the chance to do something fun—with Bailey—was too good to pass up.

When she'd proposed the event Bailey had begged off, but then she managed to change her schedule around so she could get away. The bar was only about a half mile from Bailey's, and Kit arranged to pick her up at seven.

Arriving at her building right on time, the doorman said, "Go on up. She's expecting you." Kit stood in front of her door for a moment, always needing a bit of time to organize her thoughts. Bailey tended to make her feel like everything was a little wonky, and she needed all of the clarity she could gather.

As soon as she'd gotten off the elevator she'd heard…music, but it wasn't until she was in front of the door that it was clear it was coming from Bailey's apartment. Kit rang the buzzer, got no response, so she slapped the door with the flat of her hand. That didn't work either, so she kicked it a few times. That did the trick. Bailey threw the door open, looking sunny and bright.

"The music's really, really loud." Kit found herself almost yelling.

Dashing across the room, Bailey turned it down many decibels. "I have to have music on when I work."

Kit approached her, always a little tentative at first. Was it understood they'd kiss when they met? Or was that something they did at the end of the evening. She held off, letting Bailey decide.

"Uhm…I'm not familiar with this…style?"

Bailey blinked a few times. "Oh, the music!" She opened a window on her computer and peered at it. "This is a Daft Punk thing. I'm on a channel that plays everything."

"Everything?" Kit looked at the window, seeing words that had no meaning for her.

"Every kind of dance music." Bailey closed a bunch of windows, and the music stopped. "You don't like dance music?"

"Mmm…maybe I do," she said, trying to be agreeable. "I don't know anything about it, but I could learn."

"What do you listen to?"

Truth? Might as well. "Not much. I always have some news channel on in the background and whatever spare attention I have gets diverted there. I should listen to music though. It might relax me." She didn't add that Bailey's music would make you feel like you were smoking crack.

Bailey walked over to the closet and got her coat out. "I listen to music to calm me down once in a while, but usually I like it to wire me up. I get cranking on something and I can feel the beat just amp it up a little."

They walked to the door together, and Kit pulled her to a stop before Bailey put her hand on the knob. She preferred letting Bailey make the first move, but she wasn't locked into being passive. "How about a hello kiss?"

Flushing, Bailey said, "I'm off my game." She leaned over and placed a quick, chaste kiss on Kit's lips. "I worked like a dog today. I'm ready to chill out."

"I can't think of a better place to do that than a bar with free drinks." She reached into her pocket and produced the tickets. "Free!"

—m—

Three hours later, they made their way back to Bailey's apartment. This time they weren't moving as quickly as they had been on the outbound trip. And the path they walked wasn't nearly as straight. Kit wasn't drunk, but she was close enough to be able to see it in the near distance. Bailey seemed about the same; definitely loose-limbed.

When they entered her lobby, she said hello to the doorman as though they were the best of friends. "Armando! How've you been?"

"Good, Miss Jones." He smiled, but the puzzled expression he wore told Kit that Bailey was acting much more effusive than normal.

"You've got to call me Bailey." They got on the elevator. As the doors began to close she yelled out one last time, "Bailey!"

"Maybe the building tells him not to do that."

A frown settled onto Bailey's face. "Oh. Maybe I'd better go back and tell him not to do it if he's gonna get in trouble."

Kit put her hand atop Bailey's and pulled it away from the control panel. "I'll tell him on my way out."

Nodding soberly, Bailey said, "Okay. That's good."

They started to walk down the hallway, with Kit deciding that Bailey was a little bit further down the path to inebriation than she was. She wasn't frat-party drunk by any means, but she was singing a little song and kept giggling at something only she was aware of. They entered and Bailey hung her coat up, then looked at Kit with a confused expression. "Did you come up for a drink? 'Cause I don't think I should have any more."

Kit had actually just wanted a kiss or two, but now decided she should stay for a minute and make sure Bailey didn't go back downstairs and harass poor Armando. "No, I've had plenty." She put her coat on a chair and sat on the sofa. "I can't believe I'm this lit from three drinks."

Bailey sat down next to her. "They were goooood, weren't they?"

Her crooked smile made her look a little goofy. Cute goofy. "They were. I had fun."

"Me too." She put her arms along the back of the sofa, leaned her head back and let out a long breath. When she sat up tall again she turned to Kit, that cute, goofy smile still there. "I have fun with you. Every time." Her expression clouded and she added, "Not the night you told me you were straight, but every other time." Her head shook slowly. "That made me mad."

"But I'm not too straight." She put a hand on her shoulder and pulled her close. "If I was super straight, I wouldn't do this." Gently, she touched Bailey's lips with her own, holding the kiss for a few seconds.

A soft purr sprang from Bailey's lungs. "Niiiiice."

They were mere inches apart, and Kit looked for the sharp intelligence she usually saw in Bailey's clear eyes. It wasn't leaping out at her, but it was still there, just muted. "This is nice." It was so damned nice to kiss someone you were really into. To feel her lips mold to yours; to know she was enjoying the contact as much as you were. Kit held the kiss for a little longer this time, unable to pull away from the sweetness that infused her when they touched. Even though Bailey had a boyish look, when she kissed she was the essence of a woman, soft and tender. Her body was pliable and cuddly, relaxed, as if she knew everything would happen when it should.

"You look really, really good tonight." There was a frankly sexual edge to Bailey's voice and a surge of excitement zipped up Kit's spine. Bailey gently touched her face with a finger, running it all along her forehead, cheeks and chin. "You're such a pretty woman."

"Thanks." Kit basked in the compliment, having learned that Bailey didn't toss them off just to be polite.

"I love that you wear skirts." Her hand was on Kit's thigh, the skirt covering dark tights. "Short ones." She leaned in and kissed Kit with an energy she hadn't shown before. It was…nice, but it took a second to get used to. While she was processing it, Bailey's hand slid all the way up, her fingers tickling between Kit's legs.

Whoa! She froze. Just for a second or two, but Bailey, despite her alcohol-infused brain, caught it.

Suddenly, the hand was gone, then Bailey was gone. She stood, then leaned over, her eyes showing sadness but also resolution. "I don't think this is going to work."

"No!" Kit jumped to her feet and put her hands on her shoulders.

But Bailey slipped away and walked over to the windows to look out. "You know I like you. But I don't think you're going to be able to have sex, and I won't accept less."

Approaching her from the back, Kit kept a respectful distance. "I'm not sure I am either. But I'm sure as hell not ready to stop."

Bailey turned and looked at her curiously. "Why? You know you can have good sex with guys. Why not just find one?"

"I'll throw that right back at you. There are thousands of card-carrying lesbians in DC. Why bother with me?"

Blinking slowly, she murmured, "You know why."

"I think I do."

She moved closer, edging in until Bailey slipped her arms around her and held her loosely. "I'm really attracted to you," Bailey said, sighing heavily. "Much, much more attracted than I've been to anyone since Julie." After placing a light kiss on her cheek she let go and moved just out of reach. "It's hard to find someone who makes me want to get up at five and work like a madwoman so I'll be able to see her."

"That's exactly why I want to be here. That's why I want to go back to that sofa and kiss you again."

Her expression was filled with pain. "I want to do more than kiss, Kit. I want to be able to touch you. To have you want me to touch you."

"I do!"

"Your body turned to stone when I barely grazed you. I could see if tonight was the first time we'd been out but..." Sighing, she shoved her hands in the pockets of her jeans and moved over to the stereo in her dining room/office. The CD started to play, all bass and drums. But it sounded remote, sterile. Kind of like the vibe Bailey was giving off. Kit had never seen a stereo system that needed to be watched, but Bailey stayed right in front of it, looking at a few tiny blue lights on the front of one of the black devices.

Finally, she moved back into the living room, hands once again in her pockets. Bailey went to the window and leaned against it, facing out. "I don't normally talk about things that happened with ex-lovers, but I'm going to make an exception."

Kit moved to stand close, showing she was paying close attention.

"When Mimi and I were first together, we were all over each other like animals." A soft, sweet smile settled on her face. "But that only lasted for..." She frowned, clearly thinking. "A year… no, less than that, since we went home at the end of spring term. When we came back for our sophomore year…" She slid her hands out of her pockets and punched one into the other. "I had to beg for sex." Her eyes met Kit's and she added, "I hate to beg for anything, and having to do that for something that should have held us close—brought us together…" She shook her head briskly. "It got worse as time passed. She had a million excuses — stress, exams, work, worry about her roommate hearing us. All bullshit. We went to student health for counseling and yapped about it for two years…two fucking years," she spat, her eyes flashing with anger, "before she admitted the truth." Her arms crossed over her chest, like she was hugging herself. "She wasn't attracted to me. I didn't turn her on."

"Was she blind? You're so cute, even straight girls can't resist you."

Bailey's expression softened. "Thanks for that. But Mimi didn't feel that way. She loved me, I'm certain she loved me. But she wasn't sexually attracted to me. After another year of her trying to make me feel shallow for focusing on sex, I had to end it."

"I understand. Expressing how you feel with your body is the point of an intimate relationship."

Bailey took in a deep breath. "It took a while to convince myself I was attractive enough for a woman to be interested in. Having the first person you have sex with tell you she's not into you… It really took a chunk out of my self-esteem. Luckily, I met Julie and she made me feel desirable again."

Kit moved a little closer, hoping Bailey might show she was amenable to a hug. But her posture didn't change. Still standoffish.

"I'm not going to go through something like that again. I need a sexual partner."

Kit couldn't stand to have the distance between them. She moved to stand right next to Bailey. Taking her hand, she brought it to her lips and kissed it. "I love being sexual. That's not an issue."

"Are you sure?" She gazed deeply into her eyes. "You like sex? You want it?"

Slowly Kit nodded. "Once I get the lay of the land, you're going to have your hands full—of me." A small smile flashed across Bailey's features, but she seemed to volitionally douse it.

"I don't want to feel like I'm walking on eggshells. Having to pause and think about everything I do ruins it for me."

Kit pressed Bailey's hand to her chest. "That might happen at first. So we wait for a second while I catch my breath. Every bump in the road isn't a fatal crash."

"I can only do this," Bailey said, her eyes locked on Kit, "if you can talk to me about how you're feeling. You've gotta be brutally honest. If I do something you don't like, you have to tell me why. You have to let me know if it's something you don't ever like, or it's too soon, or I did it wrong or…"

"I can do that." She nodded forcefully. "It's not natural for me, but I'll do it."

"Why isn't it natural?"

Kit laughed softly. "Seriously? Are you saying you like to have an audio track when you're making out?"

"Making out." Bailey smiled. "Sounds like we're teenagers."

"I am a teenager when it comes to kissing girls." Taking Bailey by the shoulders, she pulled her close. "You need to be patient with me. You can't threaten me with the death penalty for the slightest glitch."

A gentle smile settled onto Bailey's mouth. "Death penalty? That's a little harsh, isn't it?"

"No, it's not. I feel like we've got something growing here, and if you pull the plug it's going to die." She pulled Bailey in for a long hug. "I don't want you to snuff this out before we see if it's viable."

Bailey's lips were close to her ear and she whispered right into it. "I don't want to lose you. But I'm afraid of being too vulnerable. I don't wanna be hurt again."

"No one does. But every time we try to love someone, we risk pain. A lot of it."

Bailey moved away and looked at her carefully. "That's what you want? To love me?"

That caught her by surprise. She wasn't ready for this talk, but she had to be honest. "I…I'm not sure… I've never been into casual sex, and I don't think I'm going to start now."

"And that means…what?"

"I mean that I've never wanted someone to just sleep with. I'm a relationship kinda girl. But…" She looked into Bailey's eyes, praying for understanding. "I can't predict how I'm going to feel about being sexual with you. I might not…be able to…"

"Okay, okay." Bailey put her arms around her and held her tightly. A deep feeling of safety pervaded Kit and she nuzzled into her. "I think I understand," Bailey said. "You're generally a sexual person, but you don't know if you're going to like something you've never done."

"Exactly." She looked up, scanning her eyes. "Do you understand?"

"I think I do. You're afraid of promising too much."

"Right. That's exactly right. If I could have what I want, we'd have sex, we'd both love it, then we'd grow closer and closer. I want to love you, Bailey. I really do."

"I want the same thing. You're…I'm…I'm so attracted to you it's almost embarrassing."

"Get in line," Kit said, chuckling. "I'm as crushed on you as I've ever been. I think you're just who I've been looking for—in a slightly different package."

"So…you're not just trying this out to see if you like it?"

"No." Kit put her hand on Bailey's cheek and caressed it for a second. "I don't want to just visit for a while and then go home. If we can make a go of it, I want to live in your land."

That goofy grin was back and if Kit hadn't been treading carefully, she'd have her lips firmly attached to it. "Sounds like a sci-fi novel."

"*Journey To The Isle of Lesbos.*" As Bailey's grin grew, Kit moved closer. Confidently, she took Bailey's hand and started to tug her back to the sofa.

"Not tonight." Bailey stopped and put her arms around Kit's shoulders. "I'm not pulling the plug, but I'm suddenly sober." Placing a kiss on her cheek, she added, "You're gonna have to get me drunk again to feel you up."

Wrapping her arms around Bailey, Kit hugged her tightly. "Hang in there with me. I think there's something here."

"I do, too." Bailey kissed her one last time. "We'll just put feeling each other up on hold for a while."

Kit laughed as she squeezed her tightly. "Who says computer geeks aren't romantic?"

—⁂—

It was cold. Much colder than she could comfortably tolerate. But Bailey needed cold, fresh air to let her get her mind around what had just happened. What in the hell had been going on in her head? A few days ago she'd stopped

Kit from putting her tongue in her mouth and now she was trying to feel her up? Kit must think she had a Dr. Jekyl/Mr. Hyde thing going on.

She stopped at the light and stood there, not even noticing when it changed color. What had gotten into her? After a few seconds, her lips curled into an embarrassed grin. Sex had gotten into her and alcohol had let her do what she'd wanted to do for weeks. One drink maximum until they had this sorted out. She was not going to let her hungry libido screw this up. The melting glacier would drown her if she let her body have what it wanted. From now on, her mind had to be in charge!

—m—

Kit and Asante sat on his sofa, sharing a pint of chocolate fudge ice cream. She'd refused when he'd offered her a bowl, but now she kept diverting the spoon from his mouth and depositing it into her own.

"I think it's the same amount of calories no matter whose spoon it's on," Asante teased.

"Not true. Snatching a bite or two from someone else's food has no calories at all. Neither does eating something you don't really like. I read that somewhere…"

"In the Crazy Town Journal." He pointed the spoon at her. "Tell me more about this overreaction. Did you slap her and accuse her of compromising your virtue?"

"Funny. No, it went just like I said. She made a move I wasn't expecting, and I froze."

"Hmm. I don't wanna probe too deeply, but was it something you'd let a guy do?"

"Probably." She thought for a second, sighed, and added, "Definitely. Especially if we'd been out a couple of times. But this is new for me, and I only froze for a second. Literally."

"She seems pretty laid-back. Is she supersensitive or something?"

"Maybe a little, but only about certain things. She's…cautious."

He loaded up the spoon and slipped it into Kit's mouth. "She can't be too cautious if she's willing to see how it goes with you. I couldn't do it."

"I can name a dozen straight guys you'd give a kidney to get naked with."

"Yeah, but that's just for sex. It'd be different if I was really into a guy. I'd be a lot more cautious."

"She seems to think that she's the one who's priming herself for a fall. But I'm the one who's leaping off a cliff here. I'm really into her, Asante, but I'm terrified I'm not going to be able to follow through."

"If you can't follow through, that just means you're not lesbian enough. But if I was in Bailey's position, and you couldn't do it, it'd feel like you were rejecting me. Like I wasn't attractive enough to get you over the hurdle."

Glumly, Kit leaned her head on Asante's shoulder. "I'm remarkably attracted to her. I truly love the way she looks. The other night I wanted to grab her by the tie and never let her leave."

He slipped another spoon of ice cream into his mouth, looked at Kit out of the corner of his eye and sent another spoonful her way. "I've…been wondering about that."

"About what?"

"About why you're attracted to her."

"What's that supposed to mean? You don't think she's cute?"

He laughed a little. "She's really cute. So cute she'd have to beat guys off in a dark gay bar." He chuckled. "Figuratively, that is." As he laughed a little harder, he added, "Probably literally too, depending on the bar. I…uhm…thought she was just doing the suit thing for the ERCF dinner. Kind of a gender-bendy look for a special occasion. But from the pictures you've shown me…" He cocked his head slightly. "She looks more gay than lesbian, and that puzzles me. I'd think you'd be into someone like her friend. What was her name?"

"Natalie. She was more than a friend, by the way."

"I can see why." His grin was strangely lecherous. "If I was into women…"

"You and Bailey share that attraction. But Natalie doesn't do a thing for me. Bailey does." She paused, then made it clear. "I'm only into Bailey. I don't have any interest in finding a woman in general. I want Bailey or no one."

"Uhm…" Kit could tell he was judging how frank to be. But she knew him well enough to know he'd say exactly what was on his mind. It just might take him a minute. "If she had short hair, she'd be a total twink. Do you think it's her…Uhm…maybe you could find a really gay-looking straight guy."

"Thanks." She patted him on the cheek. "You're massively helpful." She pulled away and started to get up, but he snagged the pocket of her jeans and held her in place.

"Don't be mad. I'm just trying to figure this out."

"Figure it out?" Kit took a breath and tried to compose her thoughts. "How in the world do you figure out attraction?"

"Come on. Tell me you wouldn't freak out if I told you I was into...I don't know..." His eyes took on an impish glow. "What if I had a crush on Bailey? Wouldn't you try to figure out what was going on with me?"

Admitting defeat, Kit slumped against Asante's body. "Yeah, of course I would. And I guarantee you wouldn't be able to tell me."

He reached down and squeezed her leg. "Damned good point. I guess it's odd for me since I'm always attracted to the same type of guy. You've always been all over the place."

"You never vary," she agreed. "Big, hunky, handsome guys who look straight."

"You know me well."

"I'll admit Bailey's pretty far out of my normal boundaries. Okay, really far out."

"That guy you brought to brunch last year could have been a lineman for the Redskins. So, yeah, Bailey's out there." Once again, he hesitated. "Uhm...what's up with the way she dresses? Is she...does she identify..."

"Identify what?" Kit sat up straighter to be able to see his face better. "What are you hinting at?"

"Is she trans?"

"Trans...sexual?"

"No, transnational. Of course I mean transexual."

"Uhm...how do I tell?"

He put his head in his hands, moaning softly. "Kit, Kit, Kit. You haven't had this conversation? What if she identifies as a man? What if she's planning on having reassignment surgery? What if she wants to take testosterone?"

Sitting stock still, she let those thoughts ramble around in her head for a minute. "I don't think it would matter. She'd still be Bailey. It'd take me a while, but I could get up to speed."

"I don't know about that. I think you're gonna have your hands full just dating a woman. Having to watch someone you care about go through all the bullshit trans people have to go through..."

"Wait! She made it clear the first time we kissed that she was a woman. She wouldn't have said that if she was trans, right?"

"Mmm, I guess not. But you'd better have the conversation."

"Maybe we did…" She wracked her brain, trying to think of the exact words Bailey had used. "She said something about it being tough to date her because of how she dresses."

"Right. She looks much more like a guy than your run-of-the-mill lesbian. There's gotta be something behind that. It's either a political thing, or a fashion thing, or an orientation thing. And you'd better understand what it is. You can't support her if you don't know where that comes from—and you'll have to support her. There's no way she doesn't get some blowback for being different."

"Damn, and I thought the hard part would be having sex." She settled back down, then snuggled up against Asante. "I've become obsessed with thoughts of kissing her. Honestly, I think about kissing her all day. But…I'm not as confident about the next part."

He put an arm around her shoulders and hugged her tenderly. "There's only one way to find out how much you're into her, and that's to keep going until you don't want to go further. And if you ask me, you're better off knowing where that limit is sooner rather than later."

Kit nodded. "I did ask you. And I'll take your suggestion seriously. Next time we get together, I'm going to figure out some way to ask her if she's…what? All woman?" She slapped herself on the forehead. "I've gotta get some books and do my research. I'm out of my element in this, buddy. No two ways about it."

—⁂—

They were too busy to see each other until Friday evening at the earliest, and even that wasn't a slam-dunk. That night, Kit was stuck at a book party at The Ritz, and Bailey, who'd hoped to be home early, was still involved in a project meeting at RNC Headquarters. After texting back and forth a few times, they agreed to meet at the Lobby Lounge in the hotel at ten.

Kit was ensconced at a table when Bailey entered. They made eye contact and Kit watched her cross the room. It had been a very cold day, and Bailey was dressed for it; wearing a pale gray turtleneck covered by a cream-colored cable knit sweater and dark gray slacks. Smiling to herself, Kit had to admit that she missed the cotton shirt and tie that Bailey usually wore. "Hi," Kit said, waving.

Bailey leaned over and kissed her cheek. As her scent reached Kit's nose, she felt a chill chase down her spine. Damn, it didn't take much to turn her on these days!

"You look really cute."

"Thanks. So do you." She leaned over and touched a pin Kit had affixed to her sweater. "Cute. Does this light up?"

Kit flipped a tiny switch, making her Christmas light flick on and off. "Must have flipped the switch when I put my coat on."

A server came over and Bailey said, "I need a drink and the most calorie laden thing you've got to eat."

"Kobe beef sliders?" the man asked. "With fries?"

"Sounds good. What should I drink with that?"

"Just about anything. We have some good beers…"

"No, I'm not a fan. How about a vodka and cranberry?"

"Great. I'll be back in a flash."

Bailey leaned back in her chair and let out a sigh, finally concentrating on Kit. "Sorry I got delayed. The guys I'm working with at RNC act like the fate of the world rests on finishing their project by the end of the year."

"Tough day, huh?"

Bailey stuck her arms out and stretched for a moment. "Yeah, it was. Besides the Republicans, I had a meeting over at ERCF that went on a lot longer than it needed to. I'm really too busy to waste time listening to people go over the same thing again and again."

"Are you on the books? Or still just volunteering?"

"All gratis. Just helping them figure a few things out." She let out a short laugh. "Seems like they're trying to figure me out, too. After my last meeting, I decided I need to mix it up a little bit and not wear a tie every time."

"Why not? It's your signature."

She laughed, and Kit watched as her eyes almost closed. She loved the way they got all squinty. "I usually meet with their main systems guy, but every once in a while I have to sit in on meetings where they talk about planning and stuff. I was at a meeting last month and a guy was making a point about how careful they had to be to make sure they included everybody. He looked at the woman next to me and said, 'We do a good job with lesbians,' but then he looked right at me and said, 'We also have to make sure we always include trans-people.'" Her eyebrows hiked up above her glasses. "I think I'm sending out a message I don't intend."

The server came over with her order. This time Kit watched her carefully as she interacted with the guy. She got a little brasher, more spirited when she talked to straight men. Like she consciously tried to make herself seem bigger, bolder, less womanly. Her promise to Asante bit at her. She had to ask.

"Have you always been…?" She tried to think of the right word. "Androgynous?"

"Yeah. Always." Almost visibly the wall came up again. Tall. Impenetrable. They were going to have to get past it. They couldn't move forward if they didn't trust each other enough to tell their secrets.

"Uhm…why don't you tell me about that?"

Bailey's eyebrows went up again and she looked a little spooked. "You wanna talk about my…presentation?"

Kit squinted at her. This was like visiting a foreign country. "Presentation?"

"How I look to the world."

"Oh! Your boyishness."

"Yeah." Bailey smiled again, looking a little more comfortable. "I'm starting to like that term. I haven't had one for myself until now. I think I'll co-opt it."

Once again, Kit peered at her carefully, like she could see Bailey's thoughts if she tried hard enough. "I think you're talking about something a little deeper than the fact that you look nice in men's clothes. Right?"

"Yeah. Yeah." She nodded, and when she swallowed, Kit could see her throat move, like her mouth was dry. "Uhm…I've never felt…like other people."

"Other girls?"

"Yeah." She shrugged. "But more than that. I was very much into boy things when I was little. Girls were alien creatures to me. But there was something different—really different about the boys too." She frowned. "I don't mean their sex organs."

"Keep going," Kit said, feeling just a little skittish.

"I got along better with boys, but I knew I wasn't one and didn't really want to be one. I never, ever felt like I was a boy trapped in a girl's body. But I didn't feel like a girl, either. I wasn't in either camp."

"Did you talk to anyone about it? Your parents? Your sisters?"

"No. I didn't have words for how I felt. I thought I was the only one who was like this."

Kit reached over and took her hand, chafing it gently.

Bailey swallowed again. "Being attracted to girls made everything more confusing. But then, when I started high school, I got my uniform. Nothing was solved. I was still as confused as ever. But for the first time, I had the right clothes on."

Seeing the spark of pleasure in Bailey's eyes gave Kit a big clue. "Was there a tie involved?"

"Yep. We wore long-sleeved blue shirts, navy blazers and blue and maroon striped ties." Her expression darkened. "And skirts. But I could ignore the skirt. When I looked in the mirror in the bathroom, all I saw was my cool jacket, shirt and tie." She held up a finger. "That was the first time in my life I felt like I was in the right clothes. When I looked in that mirror, I saw me."

Kit's heart ached for the pain she could plainly see in Bailey's eyes. She thought of her own childhood, and her delight at getting a fairy princess costume for Halloween, her first pair of heels, her first prom dress. Everything she'd worn had felt like it had defined her—properly. She squeezed Bailey's hand. "That must have been so confusing."

"Yeah." She ducked her head. "It was. But from that day on, it got better. It also let me get closer to my grandpa. He was a tailor…old school kinda guy. Gruff. Not much into kids. When I showed him my tie, a little clip-on number, he said there was no way I was going to represent the Kwiatkowski name in a clip-on." When she laughed, her whole face lit up. Seeing the happiness on her face made Kit's heart beat double time. She was soooo crushed on her! "Did he make you a real tie?"

"He did. He'd been retired for a while and didn't have much to do. From that point on, he took me under his wing and taught me about fabric and cut and drape and everything he knew about menswear."

"How old were you?"

"Fourteen, but I was pretty much fully grown. Easily tall enough to wear men's sizes. We started going to thrift shops together, hunting for quality material. I'd save up and he'd guide me to the best stuff available. Then he'd tailor it for me."

Kit knew this was a delicate topic, but her curiosity got the best of her. "Uhm…he didn't try to tailor girls' clothes for you?"

"Oh, no." She shook her head briskly. "He knew nothing about women's clothes. He said the only thing a dressmaker and a tailor had in common was hems."

"I just thought that an old school guy would be more traditional."

Nodding, Bailey said, "I think he really wanted to pass on his knowledge. It made him feel like he mattered again. He didn't have any grandsons…so maybe I was the only game in town." She tossed a hand in the air, like she was sweeping speculation away. "I don't care why he did it. He did it. Of course, everyone else in the family thought we were nuts—at best—but we ignored them." Tears showed in her eyes. "He died of a heart attack when I was in college. He was working on a blue, double-breasted, pinstripe suit for me when he went." Taking a nice handkerchief from her back pocket, she dabbed at her eyes. "That suit was such a find. It was vintage. Right in my grandfather's wheelhouse. I took it back to California and had a tailor out there finish it. It's for special occasions only." Her voice broke when she added, "I'm going to be buried in it."

Kit's eyes were suddenly leaking, as well. "I envy you. I'd give anything to have a real relationship with my grandparents. Any of them."

"It's not too late," Bailey encouraged. "You've still got three left?"

"Yeah. But none of them seem interested."

"That's gotta be wrong. It's gotta be."

"Don't think so. But you can come to Boston with me sometime and check 'em out for yourself."

"I'm ready." She grinned; such a charming look settling onto her face when she did. "I'll wear my pinstripe."

Kit still had a thousand questions. But they'd get to them. They didn't have to figure everything out at once. "Next chance I get…meaning next time I have to visit, I'm taking you."

"And I'll take you to meet my family. I think you'll like them."

"If they're anything like you, there's no question."

Bailey waited a second, as if waiting for permission to dig in. Kit simply smiled at her as Bailey once again ate like she was being timed. Kit had succumbed to temptation and had eaten all sorts of fattening finger food at the reception, but she kept sneaking French fries.

"I'll order you some," Bailey said, a gentle smile taking the sting from what was probably a warning.

"You know what I'd really like?" She tried to show her sexiest smile.

Bailey popped the last of her sliders into her mouth. After spending a moment dabbing her mouth with a napkin, she wiped her hands clean, put her chin in her hand and gazed into Kit's eyes. "I think I've figured you out. I'd like the same thing. Your place or mine?"

"Doesn't matter. Let's settle up and get going."

After paying, they stood near the main entrance and negotiated. Kit wasn't sure which of them hated cabs more, but they'd never taken one. Since they were halfway between their apartments, one of them would have to double-back to get home. Kit spent a moment assessing Bailey. "You look…beat. Are you sure you're into it?"

"I'm okay. I got up at five, but I can rally. I'll walk you home."

"I'd walk to your place, but these heels will kill me."

Bailey's gaze shifted down to take in her dark tights and knee high, black suede boots. A slow smile bloomed. "Nice."

Her voice bore a decidedly sexy quality, and Kit briefly thought it would be well worth the cab fare to spend a few extra minutes alone. Then she thought of an alternative. "Give me a second. I might be able to arrange something." Bailey gave her a questioning look, but Kit didn't spend the time to explain herself. Instead, she cruised over to the front desk.

"How may I assist you?" the perky clerk asked.

"Is Neil Fergus in the hotel tonight? I'm Kit Travis, and I'd like to speak to him if he is."

"I'll check for you."

Kit leaned close and whispered, "I've got a guy…" She made her eyebrows pop up and down a couple of times.

The clerk turned the receiver around and handed it to Kit.

"Neil Fergus. How may I assist you?"

"Hey, Neil. It's Kit Travis. Can you do me a quick, easy favor?"

A soft laugh came through the line. "That sounds like something I could manage. Name it."

"I've got to have a fast, secret meet-up with someone. Just to exchange some info. Do you have a spare meeting room?"

"I'm sure I do. Let me see…yes, I could let you into the Executive Boardroom. When do you need it?"

"I'm in the lobby."

"Great. I'll meet you by the concierge desk. See you in a few."

Grinning with accomplishment, Kit took Bailey by the arm. "Wait here for five minutes, then come up to the Executive Boardroom. We're going in style, Ms. Jones."

Minutes later, Bailey scratched at the door of the Executive Boardroom. Kit flung the heavy door open, then crooked her finger in a "come hither" signal.

"I'm here to exchange some information." Bailey stood in the doorway, her eyes traveling all over the sumptuously decorated room. "What must it cost to rent this for the day?"

"No idea." Kit grasped the shoulder of her coat and pulled her inside. "Time's a wastin', pardner."

With a smirk, Bailey doffed her coat, hat, scarf and gloves. She was settling her sweater when Kit caught her off-balance and pulled her against her body. With a thunk, Kit fell onto the huge table, with Bailey nestled between her legs. "I don't normally sit this way when I'm wearing a tight skirt." Kit fumbled around, trying to pull the fabric down to cover herself, but Bailey caught her hand.

"Wouldn't you rather be kissing?"

Kit looked into her eyes, all other thoughts abandoning her. Only Bailey's sweet mouth had her attention and she latched onto it without waiting a beat. Divine. As always, once she got a taste of her, she lost track of where they were, how they'd gotten there, even the fact that her skirt was nearly at her hips.

Bailey was uncharacteristically forceful, holding Kit's head in her hands as she slipped her tongue inside and probed. What a sweet, sweet tongue. Imagining all of the places that softness would be very much appreciated, Kit rubbed against her, needing more contact. Then Bailey pressed into her, shifting her hips to drive against Kit's body. Whoa! It was almost…almost too much. But she fought through the moment of unease and consciously opened herself to the sensation.

It was fantastic to have those slim, delicate hands roving over her body; sliding up and down her arms, along her flanks, across the tops of her thighs. Kit put her hands under Bailey's sweater, grasped the waistband of her slacks and held her close. Her scent was so intoxicating, such a primal attractant, that Kit's mouth watered at the thought of going further…going as far as Bailey would go. But a more rational, more careful voice made itself heard. They were in a public place. Not the kind of place to have your first all-in sexual encounter. As she started to slow down, the thought hit her. She'd let herself go because they were in a public place. It was safe because there was a built-in brake that would make them keep their clothes on. Damn. She was almost forty years old and was afraid of going to second base. A tinge of shame settled upon her and she held Bailey tenderly in her arms, then nuzzled into her shoulder. "We're getting a little carried away."

Kit kept her eyes closed, afraid of seeing dismay or frustration in Bailey's expression. But a soft, melodic laugh made her head snap up. Bailey looked half drunk and very pleased. "We're getting a lot carried away." After placing a gentle kiss on Kit's forehead, she said, "You make me lose my wits! All of them!"

"Mine were gone when you were taking your coat off." Her mood lightened until she was smiling like a fool. "It feels so good to explore like this."

Bailey stood up tall. She grasped her waistband and fussed with it until the pleats of her slacks lined up, then got her sweater settled as she liked it. "Are you sure? Maybe we're going a little too fast?"

It felt like her penetrating gaze would detect even a fib. "Just for a second. By the time I felt a little out of control it had already passed."

After leveling her gaze, Bailey spoke slowly. "We can go at the pace that feels good to you. We should go at that pace."

"You're right." Kit put her arms around Bailey and pulled her close. "Thank you for caring about me." She looked up into her understanding gaze. "I feel very cared for."

"Then my message is getting through." She kissed her forehead, a cheek, her chin, then the other cheek. "I care for you. There's no hurry."

"Thanks."

They were so close Kit could feel Bailey's warm breath on her cheek. It was clear they were done for the night, but just as clear that neither of them truly wanted to leave. With a tender touch that made Kit's heart ache, Bailey caressed her cheek, then placed a final soft kiss on her lips. "We're doing really, really well," she whispered. "There's nothing to worry about."

Kit looked into her eyes, so full of confidence. "Okay. You're right."

She started to shift her hips to pull her skirt into place. Gallantly, Bailey grasped the fabric and tugged it down when Kit lifted her butt. "See how much I care? I didn't even sneak a peek."

Giggling, Kit pinched her cheek. "You may look like a boy, but a real one would have looked. A lot."

Chapter Eight

BAILEY WAS NO POLITICAL junkie, but she was as excited as a puppy when Kit arrived to take her on the White House tour. "I can never, ever tell my nephew about this. He'd be so jealous he'd explode."

Kit poked her in the ribs. "You should have told me your nephew was into things like this. I blew the only favor I have coming from this guy."

Bailey looked at her for a second. "Did you even know I have a nephew?"

"No!" Now Kit pushed her with both hands, making her stumble. "You're so pretty I want to kiss you whenever I get you alone. Whose fault is it that we don't have time to talk?"

"Mine." Bailey chuckled. "It's all my fault for being too pretty. Guilty as charged."

Edward met them at the assigned spot, and after a thorough pat down, a couple of wandings, and a quick introduction, he led them to the West Wing. Kit had been to the press briefing room a few times since she'd had her anonymity trashed, and had visited an office or two, but most of the rooms were brand new to her.

Every once in a while she could abandon her cynicism and let herself experience the thrill of exploring a hallowed hall of government. Bailey clearly didn't have to abandon anything. She was practically wriggling with excitement. Even Edward, a wizened old hand, seemed to perk up at her enthusiasm.

They didn't get to peek into the Oval Office, but they saw the hallway that led to it. Kit didn't know if the president was there, but it was pretty thrilling to think he was just a few yards away. Maybe she wasn't as cynical as she thought. Or maybe the scent of Christmas, filling the old buildings with the fresh smell of cut fir and spruce trees perked her up.

After they'd whipped through the West Wing, Edward said, "Have you ever been on the public tour?"

"No," Bailey said. "First time here."

"Let's go take a look. You're paying for the house."

Kit smiled, thinking he'd probably used that joke a few million times. But he was going out of his way, and that was pretty rare for people at his level. They had to go through another bunch of agents to enter, showing their photo IDs and waiting for Edward to sign in. But once inside they were pretty much on their own.

They sailed through all of the iconic rooms; red, blue and green, all lavishly decorated for Christmas, then headed for the state dining room. They were just about to enter when a voice sounded down the hallway: "Clear the hall for the Vice President."

"Shit!" Edward's eyes grew wide. "If he sees me giving tours I'm toast. Go inside. I'll come get you after he leaves."

Kit grabbed Bailey's hand and ran into the huge room. Big mistake. There was no place to hide. Dozens of large, round tables dotted the room, but they were devoid of tablecloths. The vice president's voice carried strongly in the long, marble hallway. "Edward! I called you ten minutes ago. I hope you're coming to look for me. We've got deadlines looming."

"Yes, sir! That's exactly what I was doing."

"Good. Good. Duck in here for a minute. I hate to talk in the hall."

Kit almost choked. She wasn't certain what kind of trouble Edward would get into for letting visitors off-leash, but a public execution didn't seem out of the question. She was not going to get her best source for the budget impasse canned. She grabbed Bailey and yanked her, almost knocking her off her feet. Heading for the only possible hiding place, she dove for a big table that held a gingerbread replica of the White House. They were able to fold themselves into small enough parcels to be fully covered by the table, but, again, there was no drapery. Anyone who looked would see two adult women, eyes bugged out, sitting on the floor, holding their knees to their chests like they were impersonating gargoyles. Kit shifted her eyes, seeing Bailey cast in stone, not moving an inch.

The vice president pulled Edward into the room, and Kit could hear his voice lose its terrified tone as he realized his charges had somehow managed to hide themselves. *Don't look at the Christmas decorations!*

For at least ten minutes the vice president outlined the strategy he was going to use to make progress on the budget. Kit itched to get her phone out and record the whole damned conversation, but they'd been warned not to bring them. She supposed this was the reason why. Any stooge could record the VP talking to a policy advisor!

Regrettably, the strategy was what one would have expected. No big deal. The VP was going to try to work on a few key house leaders, while blasting the press with as many items as they could get placed. "You can get something in that newsletter," the VP said. "The one Hank Brearly's girlfriend writes. Kate…what's her name. She's on our side, right?"

"Well, I wouldn't say that," Edward mumbled, knowing his source was within earshot. "But she's very fair."

"I don't need fair. I need biased!" He laughed for a few seconds. "I can't figure why a liberal reporter would be with a Republican senator. What's she going to do when he runs for president? You can't even fake being unbiased when your boyfriend's going for the top job."

"Uhm, I don't think they're together anymore, sir."

"Can't say I blame her. But check that. I see their names linked all the time." A loud slap echoed in the room. "Get back to the task, Edward. Make some noise."

"I will, sir."

"Good man. I like that you came to find me. I respect a man with initiative."

"Thank you, sir. I appreciate that."

"We're working our tails off here. Let's get something to show for it."

"Will do."

Feet shuffled, then the voices faded away.

Finally, after long minutes of statue impersonation, Bailey turned her head slowly. "Why are we still hiding?" she whispered.

Kit started to laugh. Really laugh. If anyone came down the hall they'd hear her for sure. But she couldn't stop. She wasn't even sure what she was laughing at. It wasn't a bit funny that even the Veep thought she and Hank were still together. But hiding under a gingerbread house in the state dining room would definitely go into her "stories to tell at parties" folder.

—⁂—

Bailey insisted on buying dinner, and chose a Thai place Kit had never been. "I want something ethnic, well, different from my ethnic, since we'll have nothing but Polish food for Christmas. My mom really gets in gear for the holidays."

"We're old school too. Old school Pilgrims. My mom cooks very competently, but she's not much for anything even remotely exotic."

"Then let's order the spiciest things on the menu."

They sat down, and after ordering drinks, asked the server to decide for them. "Allergy?" he asked, peering at them closely.

"No," Kit replied. "We'll eat anything."

"Hungry?"

They both nodded.

"Okay. Be right back."

Before they'd even had a drink he was back, delivering soups. "Tom yam kung," he said. "And Tom kha gai." He pointed at one and then the other. "Share."

Giggling, Kit took a spoonful of Bailey's before even trying her own. "I follow orders." Nodding, she added, "Good. Spicy."

Bailey did the same, then shook her head. "Something in yours I don't like." She tasted her own, and smiled. "Just right. No more for you."

"Other than eating Polish food, what do you do for Christmas?"

"Not much. Hang out. Visit relatives. How about you?"

"Our Christmas is pretty traditional. Actually, it's beyond that. More like it's scripted. We eat the same things, visit the same people in the same order, have an open house on the afternoon of Christmas Eve… And other stuff I don't care enough about to recall."

"Hmm… Your mom must really like things to be orderly."

"I'm not so sure of that." She put her chin on her hand and sat quietly for a moment, thinking. "My mom doesn't really have much of a…" She stopped and made a face. "I was going to say personality, but that sounds really awful."

"Your mom has no personality?" Bailey's eyes grew wide.

"That's not fair of me. I'm sure she had one…" Kit shook her head. "That's not even true. Her parents are both really demanding, controlling people. And, to be honest, my dad's the same way. I think she's always tried to follow orders and stay out of trouble." She ate a little more of her soup, thinking about that for a moment. "When the family's together all she does is cook and fuss over things. I've honestly never seen her sit back and enjoy a thing about it. She's as tight as a piano wire the whole time."

"That's tragic," Bailey said, her voice quiet. "Does she have any hobbies? Friends?"

"Yeah, she's got friends, well, not many individual friends, but she plays bridge with a group of women and she's in a golf league." She shrugged. "I hope she gets whatever emotional warmth she needs from them, because it's an arid desert at the Travis home."

Bailey had a funny expression on her face. One Kit had no idea how to read. "I wish you could come home with me. My family isn't perfect, but it's no desert. You know you're wanted and you know they're sad when you leave."

"I wish my mom had a different life. I truly do. But she doesn't seem unhappy." Kit shrugged, feeling out of her depth. "But then I'm not sure I've ever seen her happy."

—⁂—

They took the Metro back to Dupont Circle, then Kit walked Bailey home. "Why didn't you tell me you were driving home tonight?" Kit demanded. "I hate having you drive this late."

"I'm fine. That green curry will keep me up for hours."

"That was some spicy stuff, wasn't it? I'd like to go back there. I love spicy food."

"Me too. One more thing we have in common." She showed her most charming smile. "I think that makes a grand total of one."

"We have plenty in common." They went up in the elevator, and as soon as they got inside Bailey's apartment, Kit pressed her up against the wall and gave her a hot kiss. "We both like that, don't we?"

"We do," Bailey purred, looking like she'd be happy to stay right there all night.

"Then let's do some more of that before I send you on your way."

Bailey's arms slid around Kit's body, holding her close. "Should we take our coats off?"

"No. Just kisses, then get on the road."

"I can live with that." Bailey sighed, then placed long, soft kisses upon Kit's lips, giving her the Christmas presents she knew she'd like the best.

—⁂—

Christmas was in the middle of the week. That meant a long visit. Interminably long. Kit sat in the den, watching her nieces and nephews play with their new electronic toys. It was day three of her five-day stay—the longest she'd suffered through for eleven years—the last time Christmas was on a Wednesday.

Why did she have so little connection to these kids? They'd all spent a decent amount of time together when the older ones were babies. In fact, she and Henry had spent all of the holidays with the family, even going on vacations to the Cape with the whole clan. But since she'd moved to Washington, over twelve years ago, what little closeness they'd had disappeared like smoke.

Seeing the kids for just ten or twelve days a year had to contribute to the problem. It took kids a while to warm up to you, and being with them for just a few hours didn't allow for much bonding time. But as she watched them interact with their parents and each other, she realized it was more than that.

It had been fun being around them when they were little, but as they'd developed their own personalities they'd all begun to seem like their parents—not a good thing. The older kids had bought the conservative mantra hook, line and sinker. No, that wasn't fair. Conservatism and elitism didn't have to go hand in hand. But it certainly did in the Travis clan. None of the kids had even a wisp of a social conscience, which was to be expected of the young ones, but damned odd for high school kids.

They were obsessed with stuff—electronics and designer clothes and expensive cars. Wyatt, the eldest, heading to the Ivy League in the fall, made it clear he was going to go into whatever line of work would get him a Porsche the fastest. Last year, Kit had spent some quality time with the youngest, Allie, reading the book Kit had brought for her. But this year the little snot had learned to read and she'd rebuffed Kit's offer of reading with a curt, "I can read by myself," before snatching the new book from her hands and sauntering away to check it out.

All of the kids fought—with each other and their parents. It was a good strategy, since every one of them got what they wanted if they whined enough. Kit had no idea why her brother and sister allowed that, since whining never worked when they were kids. Who knew? Maybe they wanted to raise their kids a hundred and eighty degrees from the way they'd been brought up. Whatever the reason, they'd managed to spawn a bunch of brats, pure and simple, and being around the group for a full day was not only draining, it was depressing.

She'd been ruminating about a minor fight they'd had on Christmas Eve. The church they allegedly belonged to was having a Christmas party, where families living at a local homeless shelter would be invited to have dinner and receive presents for their kids. She'd waded through the crowds at a big box store to buy the things the church had requested, then wrapped the gifts and labeled them.

Kit proposed that the whole family go with her to serve. They had so much—money, health, luck. The perfect trifecta of American life. But her family not only had refused to go along, they'd teased and taunted her all day long; about how all of them would quit working if people like her would simply give them things, how damaging it was to teach kids to accept handouts, how liberals didn't actually want poor people to progress because then they wouldn't have anyone to feel superior to. Finally, she'd gone by herself, staying until they practically threw her out—just to avoid having to go home.

She was no saint. Clearly. There were many opportunities to be a hands-on volunteer in DC. But she had so little free time she rarely went out of her way for others. Still, when you had the time and the opportunity drop into your lap… The thought kept nagging at her. No one in her family was generous. Not just with the less advantaged, either. They weren't even generous with each other. Sure, her grandmother handed out money at the holidays, but that was merely to exert control. Looking out for number one was the Travis family motto, and it made her sick. She didn't admire anyone in the group, and that was a bitter pill to swallow on Christmas.

The only fun thing to do was daydream about Bailey. It was impossible to think of those pink lips and not want to be kissing them. With a good deal of luck, one day they'd be spending Christmas together. With the Kwiatkowskis. Definitely the Kwiatkowskis. Bailey was pretty chill, but she'd clock Craig for the way he behaved. And Kit would have to clock him for the way he'd harass Bailey. No, to avoid jail time, holidays would have to be spent eating whatever delights Bailey's mom would whip up. Kit was looking forward to it more than she could say.

—m—

Kit raced back to DC on the twenty-seventh, cutting her visit short by two days. She had no pressing need to be back at work, but as she headed into her office on Saturday morning, surprising the weekend staff, she finally felt like she was home. Sadly, Boston had lost that title years earlier.

New Year's Eve found her working until late in the evening. There was nothing going on, but the quiet office let her mind wander enough to compose a few longish pieces for her blog. None of them were time-sensitive, letting her put them aside to be used when she didn't have time to crank out something new. Content was not just king. It was a despot.

After heading upstairs to her apartment, she ordered in, then watched some silly, mindless junk from Times Square. By ten she was beat. Lying in bed, alone, on New Year's Eve found her surprisingly upbeat. For the first time in four years she was truly excited about her prospects. If her desire for Bailey continued to grow at the rate it had been, there wasn't a thing to worry about.

Finally, on Sunday evening, Bailey returned. Kit answered the phone when she saw her picture appear. "Happy New Year!"

"You sound cheery. Did you have a good holiday?"

"I'm back home and no one has given me a hard time about anything for a solid week. So, yes, I'm cheery. How about dinner?"

"I've been eating nonstop since the minute I got home. Might as well keep a good streak going. Where would you like to go?"

"Come here. I'll cook."

"Really? Are you sure?"

"I am. I made a hearty chicken noodle soup this afternoon. Just the thing to warm you up."

"Done deal. When do you want me?"

"Right now. I'll be waiting."

—⁂—

Bailey sat on the sofa, watching Kit putter around in the dining area, putting a few things away. She was very neat. Nice trait. The snug chinos she had on showed off another nice trait or two. While trying to tamp down her libido, she reflected on how remarkably attracted she was to Kit. There was a chemistry between them that she could never remember feeling with another woman. Everything about her was attractive; her body, her personality, her sense of humor. She had it all. If she was gay… Okay, so she didn't have it all. Not sharing the same sexual orientation was kind of a big deal. But when Kit bent over to put some dishes onto the lower shelf of a cabinet…little details like that seemed inconsequential.

When Kit walked behind her to join her on the sofa, she let her hand trail across Bailey's shoulders. Even through a shirt and sweater, her skin broke out in goose bumps. Whoever said chemistry wasn't important—hadn't experienced it.

Kit sat close and cuddled up against her when Bailey extended her arm. "I like this. We fit together nicely."

"Yeah, we do. The night we met, I watched you dance and decided we were the ideal sizes."

A big smile covered Kit's face. "You were watching me?"

"Uh-huh. Like a vulture." She leaned close and whispered into her ear, "I was going to ask you to dance, but every time I got up, someone came by to chat. Ruined my plans."

"Oh, you had plans, did you?"

"Uh-huh. I wanted to wait for the slowest song, hold you close, maybe nibble on your neck a little."

"That would have freaked me out so badly they'd still be scraping me off the ceiling. I'm clearly a look-before-you-leap kinda person."

"You're a lot more experimental than I am. If you were a guy, we would not be sitting this way."

"Then I'm extra glad I'm not a guy." She nuzzled up against Bailey, letting out a gentle purr when she did. "I really like sitting this way. There's only one thing that would make it better…" She looked up, a playfully sexual expression on her face.

"I'm good at taking hints." Dipping her head, Bailey pressed her lips against Kit's, just letting her get used to the contact. Another, louder purr showed Kit got used to it quickly. Nice.

They'd known each other for a while now, but this was the first time Bailey felt entirely comfortable, entirely relaxed, while kissing her. Taking it slow had been a good idea—for both of them. But she was ready to speed things up a little. Kit's breasts pressing against her made her want to jam her foot onto the accelerator and let 'er rip.

Shifting her weight, she moved around until they were face to face. The throbbing between her legs eased as she gazed into those warm, expressive eyes. There wasn't a flicker of indecision in them. Not a glimmer of hesitation or fear. So nice. Bailey moved her hand up to steady Kit's chin. Then she pressed into her, tenderly kissing her again and again. With the tip of her tongue, she urged Kit's lips open, then slid inside. The sweetness, the warmth of her mouth made her start to throb again, but she purposefully held back. Glacial speed. Kit clearly didn't have the same warning posted in her head because she grasped Bailey's shoulders and tried to pull her in as she sucked on her tongue. Really nice. That was the kiss of a woman who liked sex. A lot.

Slowly, Bailey pulled away and lightened her kisses as Kit let out a tiny mew of disappointment. "We have to go slow."

A devilish smile bloomed on her stunningly sexy mouth. "We don't have to. You made the law. You can veto it any time you want." She locked her arms around Bailey's shoulders and placed a scorcher on her lips.

It was so tempting! Having Kit pressed up against her, clearly ready for more, made her shiver with anticipation. With need. But she would not jump in until she was sure Kit was one hundred percent with her. That was non-negotiable. Still, her mouth was dry, her voice shaky when she said, "I haven't changed my mind. We're going to do this right or not at all."

Kit let out a heavy sigh. "If those are my only choices—I think we should do it right."

—m—

Because of the holidays, it had been hard to find time alone with Natalie. Bailey liked her partner, Jess, and they all went out to brunch at least once a month. But she and Nat had a different level of connection, and being alone with her was more than just fun—it was sustaining in some way Bailey couldn't put words to.

One of the best things about Nat was that she was very good at being there when you really needed her—for any reason. Bailey texted her one afternoon, saying, "I need a Nat chat. Can you fit me in?"

A text came back in seconds. "Alone?"

"If possible."

"You at home?"

"Yeah."

"Go buy me a skinny decaf cap. Be there before it gets cold."

Bailey put on a pair of shoes and took off. Natalie was a woman of her word.

Fifteen minutes later, her door opened and Natalie breezed in. "Coffee?" she asked, sticking her hand out.

Bailey got up, put the cup in her hand and kissed her cheek. "You didn't have to drop everything. I just wanted to talk a little."

Nat dropped her coat and sat on the sofa, then took a long drink, smiling with pleasure. "Nice. I was at work at seven, and will probably be there until eight. For lunch, I got to eat a soggy sandwich during a horrendously boring meeting. I think I deserve a coffee break."

Working for a big, corporate law firm gave Nat the power and respect she craved, but Bailey knew her heart wasn't fully in it. But Nat had just made partner and claimed she needed to stick around for a few years to keep making big-time contacts. Then one day she'd be able to move to a boutique firm and hopefully work more human-scale hours. "What are you working on?"

"Blah, blah, blah, and more blah. I know you're not interested. Spill it, Be Kwiat. I know there's a burr under your saddle."

It was so cute when she used phrases she'd heard growing up on a cattle ranch outside San Antonio. It was incongruous to hear, especially when she was wearing a thousand-dollar dress, but that made it even cuter. "I just wanted some…encouragement, I guess."

Natalie's dark eyes narrowed. "About a certain politico?"

"Yeah. Of course." She could feel her cheeks color. "She's all I think about."

"What's the latest? Still making out like you're in junior high?"

"Uh-huh. And I'm good with that. I want to give her a bunch of exit ramps."

Nat put her hand on Bailey's shoulder and looked into her eyes for a moment. "I wish you'd find someone else, Bails. Well-adjusted people don't change their sexual orientation when they're forty years old. There's gotta be something screwy going on in her head."

Bailey shrugged her hand off and stood. On the way to the window, she tried to control her temper. "That's not a very sympathetic viewpoint for a woman on the board of a major gay rights organization. I thought the point of the gay movement was to make it safe for anyone to be who they are."

"That is the point. Of course it is. Is Kit saying she's a lesbian? That she's been in denial?"

"No," Bailey mumbled.

"That's what I'm worried about. It sounds to me like she's experimenting, and I don't want her to experiment on you." She got up and walked over to Bailey, put her arms around her and gave her a long hug. "I don't want you to get hurt."

"I know. I know." Moving away again, she went back to the sofa. "She says she's too attracted to me to walk away." She looked up at Natalie, knowing her vulnerability showed on her face. "That's just how I feel about her."

Natalie sat back down and took another long sip of her drink. "I'm going to zap this in the microwave. Be right back."

Bailey sat there, once more considering her feelings. When Natalie returned, she said, "I've had two girlfriends, and neither of them were my type. I'm not complaining. Both of them were good for me in different ways. But I've never touched a woman who appeals to me like she does. I hate to sound so shallow…"

Scooting over, Nat put her arm around Bailey's waist and hugged her gently. "The first time I kissed Jess, I felt like my lips had found what they'd always been looking for. I get attraction."

"It's that. For sure it's that." Bailey swallowed, then made herself keep talking, even though it was hard for her. "It's more than that, of course. I think she's funny, and usually sweet. But she's kinda prickly sometimes, and I like that. And she's got a lot of nerve. I love to be around women who aren't saps. But right now…" She closed her eyes. "Right now, it's primal. I hold her in my arms and I feel so much…drive. I just want to consume her, Nat. I pull away after kissing her and see that gorgeous blonde hair… Those sexy brown eyes… And her mouth. God," she breathed, barely speaking the word. "I practically have to slug myself to stop from chewing her clothes off when I feel her breasts press into me. I just know her body's gonna be perfect." She sighed. "I've only dated flat-chested, dark-haired, skinny geeks." Laughing, she added, "I've been dating me—with dark hair. I loved both Mimi and Julie, but I lust after Kit…and that's brand new."

Once again, Natalie leaned over and hugged her. "Then go for it. One thing I've learned is that you never know who's going to appeal to you. Or when it'll happen. But I do know you're not guaranteed a repeat. Take the chance. Try to protect yourself, but go for it even if you can't. It's worth the risk."

—⁓—

They played squash again the following Wednesday. As usual, Kit was waiting in the lobby when Bailey sauntered out of the locker room. "I think you're kind of pokey," Kit observed. "I always finish before you. And I dry my hair." She patted the damp arrangement clipped to the back of Bailey's head. "Unlike you."

"I try to keep my head out of the spray, but I obviously don't do a great job." She shrugged. "I might be pokey."

"I might be hungry. Could I interest you in trekking over to Ben's?"

"Ben's?"

Kit widened her eyes. "You don't know Ben's?"

"I don't think so. Is it around here?"

"Not really. We'll have to take the Red Line and switch to the Yellow or Green. But it's worth a trip. Come on." She grasped Bailey's sleeve and tugged her along. "You've lived here too long not to be on a first name basis with the guys at Ben's."

—⁂—

A half hour later, they were digging into their food. Bailey had only a very conservative order of plain French fries. Kit was staring down a chili dog along with chili cheese fries. "I lost ten pounds last year through constant vigilance. I'm about to put it all back on." She grinned and dug in. Some things were worth the penalty.

Bailey sat quietly, carefully removing a fry from her stack and dipping just the edge into ketchup. That wasn't like her.

"You're quiet tonight. Everything okay?"

"Uh-huh." She ate another fry, acting like she needed to devote all of her attention to it.

"Bite?" Kit held up her dog.

A small smile appeared on Bailey's face. She held Kit's hand steady and took a bite. "Good," she said, nodding. "We'll have to come back when I'm really hungry."

"Did you eat before we played? You usually don't have time to."

"No." She took another fry, held it over the ketchup for a moment, then put it into her mouth dry. "Just not hungry."

The place was packed, as always, and fairly noisy. Kit took a look around to see if anyone was listening. Nope. Everyone was busy talking with their friends. "Something's on your mind." She put her hands to her ears and pulled on them. "I'm all ears if you want to talk."

Bailey smiled, but it was a pretty wan effort. "I've been thinking. About…us. About your sexuality."

Warning bells started to ring. "My sexuality?"

"Yeah." Slowly, Bailey pulled another fry out and munched on it thoughtfully. "You don't really fit into a category."

"Category? Like what?"

"Like lesbian in denial or bi-curious."

Frowning, Kit said, "Technically, I guess I'm bi-curious, but I don't like the sound of that."

"No, that's not you." Bailey shook her head. "I think of a bi-curious person as a woman who wants to see what it's like to have sex with another woman. Definitely a visitor. Not very invested."

"Gotcha." She took another bite of her dog. It was too good to ignore, even when Bailey was trying to get something off her chest. Given how she was speaking, more reflective than concerned, Kit's pulse slowed down to its normal level. With her mouth half full, she said, "I'm not that." She chewed quickly and swallowed. "I'm not sure what I am. I've decided not to care."

For some reason, Bailey's expression changed in a second. Now she looked pleased, or maybe even excited. "Really? You're good with not caring?"

"Yeah." Kit covered her hand, then grimaced, grabbed a napkin and wiped off the orange stain she'd left on her pale skin. "Sorry. Yes, I'm perfectly happy to just do what feels right to me. There's no correct answer in the sexual orientation quiz."

"That's good to know." Her smile grew a little brighter. "If you really feel that way, we're going in the right direction."

"I think we are. I'm so distracted I'm not doing my job as well as I should, but I assume I'll calm down as we get more settled."

"Yeah. That feels right." Kit held her dog up, but Bailey shook her head. "Are you settled with me? With how I look?"

"Huh?"

She fidgeted a little, as she did when she was uncomfortable. "You know…we talked about this a couple weeks ago. I thought you might have some more questions…or something."

"Not really. All that matters to me is that you're comfortable."

"Sometimes it's dicey, but I'm mostly good."

"When you look boyish."

"Yeah." She smiled. "When I look boyish. In college, I was pretty androgynous, but never went all the way. I wanted to, though." She lifted her shoulders and dropped them quickly. "Chickened out. I would have tried when I started at Pictogram, since that was kind of a new start, but Julie was definitely not into it."

"Why?" A burst of anger flared toward a woman she'd never even seen a picture of. "What business was it of hers?"

"Eh…it would have affected her. People make assumptions when you wear guy's clothes. At the very least, you stick out in a lot of situations. Julie hated that. It was fine telling people we were lovers, but that was as far outside the mainstream as she could go." Bailey met Kit's eyes. "I don't blame her for that."

Let it go. Let it go. "Okay. So you took the plunge when you moved here, right?"

"Right. That's one of the biggest reasons I moved here, and the reason I got started volunteering with ERCF. I thought it would be easier to jump in surrounded by people from everywhere on the gender spectrum."

"Has it been? Easier?"

"Yeah, I think so. I get plenty of weird looks, and a few nasty comments when I walk around. But so far, nothing I can't handle." She reached out and took Kit's hand. "If we're together…in a relationship…people will wonder what my deal is. Given you've always been with guys, people will make some assumptions."

Kit blinked in surprise. "Like what?"

"I'm not sure." She shrugged. "Like maybe you're into me because I'm almost a guy. I don't know. I can't guess what people will think, but they'll think something." Her eyes bore into Kit. "You've got to be prepared for that."

At a loss for words, Kit merely nodded.

Bailey waited her out for a full minute, then gently asked, "Second thoughts?"

"No. No way." She started to gather up their trash, then disposed of it. After coming back to the table, Kit picked up her coat and started to put it on. Bailey did the same. Minutes later they were outside and started to walk to the subway in silence. At the first alley, Kit pulled Bailey in and backed her up against a wall. With her gloved hand, she reached up and soothed the furrow on her brow. "I love the way you look. I get nasty comments all the damn time, mostly because of things I write. A few more won't even register." She stood on her tiptoes and pressed a firm kiss onto Bailey's lips. "Come on now. Let's walk off two or three calories on the way to the Metro."

They started to walk, with Kit wrapping her hand around Bailey's arm. With her stocking cap on, even a lingering glance would have led passers-by to believe they were an opposite sex couple. Was that part of the reason she was attracted to her? Was it just easier to be with a woman who could pass? Thinking about that made her head hurt. "Do you like keeping your hair long?"

"Mmm. Not especially." Her head shook quickly.

Kit stopped her and gazed directly into her eyes. "If we wind up together—and I've gotta say I'm more attracted to you every time we see each other—and you want to get a buzz cut—you won't hear a complaint from me."

Those pretty blue eyes blinked slowly. "Would you like me better if I had short hair?"

"No. Not at all." Thankfully, that was the honest truth. "I'm fine with the dichotomy. But if I had a vote, you'd at least dry it!"

"I'll take that under consideration." Bailey nodded, a happy smile settling onto her lovely face. That had been the right answer. Score!

—⁓—

Later that night, Kit lay in bed, mulling over the evening. Having a chili dog and chili cheese fries an hour before bed hadn't been the smartest thing she'd ever done. But her complaining digestive system kept her up long enough to really think things through.

What she'd told Bailey was the rock-solid truth. She was more into her with every encounter. Her honesty, her vulnerability, her gentleness. Those traits appealed to her in a way that knocked her off her feet. Bailey's inability to completely claim a feminine identity wasn't a cross to bear. It just wasn't. If they got together, they'd deal with it. This was the twenty-first century and they lived in a cosmopolitan city. That alone would make things much, much easier.

She tried to relax, but a nagging thought kept coming back. How much of her attraction was due to Bailey's amorphous identity? She had no way of knowing. Kit laughed to herself. How much of Bailey's attraction to her was because she was clearly feminine? Probably a good bit. In the end, none of it mattered. Attraction was complex. And even if it wasn't, what good would it do to analyze it? It had been years since Kit had been really attracted to someone. That was the key. End of story.

Chapter Nine

KIT LOOKED UP WHEN a shadow covered her desk on Friday afternoon. "Asante!"

He dropped into a chair, leaned it back and hooked a heel on the corner of the desk. "You look like you need a nice dinner."

"I do?" She pushed her own chair back and started to put a foot up to mimic him. Then she remembered she'd worn a skirt—hoping Bailey'd be free for an impromptu dinner—which she had not been.

"Yeah. Knock off early and act like a human."

She checked her watch. Six thirty. That wasn't all that early. "Okay. What've you got in mind?"

"Indigo. I'll buy drinks."

"Hmm…that won't feed me. I need more than a cherry or an orange slice."

"We'll eat there. They renovated last year. The restaurant's not bad at all."

"A gay dance club? That's what you really want?"

His eyes danced with pleasure. "That's what I really want."

"Hmm…do they play electronic dance music there?"

"Yeah. Usually. Why?"

"That's what Bailey listens to when she works. I've tried listening to it, but I can't stand it for more than two minutes. Maybe I can make myself like it if I listen to it while hanging out with you."

"Don't think that's how it works, but I'll take any justification you wanna make to go with me. I love checking out guys with you."

She stood and started to pack up her computer. "I'm out of practice looking for the big, muscular hunks you like. I might prefer the twinks."

"That's a risk I'm willing to take."

—⁂—

Over the years, they'd been to every gay club in DC. When Kit was thoroughly straight, it was a nice way to be able to hang out with Asante and his friends and not have to deal with straight guys trying to horn in. She wasn't sure how it would feel now that she was…whatever she was. But Asante didn't ask for much. And when he did, she made it her business to comply.

Since she'd dressed carefully that morning, all she had to do was drop off her computer and freshen her lipstick. Normally, she would have spritzed a little perfume on, but that was a waste of time for Indigo. No one would be looking at or sniffing her.

They reached the club well before it started to buzz, and managed to snag a table at the overpriced but very convenient cafe. After ordering, Asante regaled Kit with a story about a lead he was chasing down. "I was trying to blend in, and not let the guy know I was following him. But he walked like he was being chased by a pit bull! As soon as I kicked it up to match him, a cruiser did a U-turn and two seconds later I was kissing the bricks."

"They knocked you to the ground?"

"No, no," he put his hand over hers and patted it. "Don't get in a tizzy. They just put me up against a building."

"Damn it, Asante! That makes me so mad!"

He shrugged, clearly having grown used to being treated like a criminal just because he walked down the street. "My mother told me to never jog unless I was on a track." He could obviously see she was steamed. "I'm sorry I told you about it. I thought it was funny."

"It was…until you were stopped by the cops."

"I can either be angry or shrug it off, Kit. Generally, I shrug it off. Once I showed them my ID, they made up the usual lie about trying to catch a guy who matched my description. They actually apologized. That's a little cause for celebration."

"Forgive me for not breaking out the champagne. If white men got stopped by the cops as much as you have, the police department would be reorganized so fast it'd make your head spin."

"That's not going to happen." He took his fork and gently poked her in the arm. "Come on. Don't be all grumpy."

She forced herself to put on a reasonably realistic looking smile. "I'm not grumpy. See?"

"Very life-like. I know how to pull a real smile out of you. Tell me what's going on with Bailey."

He was right. Thinking about Bailey cheered her right up. "Things are perking right along. We're definitely going steady."

"Ooo…going steady. Pretty wild. Have you been to third base yet?" He got a pensive look on his face, then said, "What is third base with women?"

"I don't know. I'll let you know when I've rounded second."

"Second? You haven't grabbed a little boob yet?"

"I don't think there's enough to grab."

"Really? I don't remember what she looked like in that department."

Kit gave him a wry look. "Why would you? I'm not sure what's under those cute shirts, but I know she doesn't wear a bra. I've had my hands all over her back and there are no straps."

He looked adorably confused. "Really? Is that…? I thought most women had to wear them."

"Apparently not. But whatever their size, I haven't touched them."

"And that's okay with you?"

"Yeah, yeah, it is. We're right on the edge. I think I've proven that I'm not gonna bolt, and she's fairly confident I'm not freaked out by the way she dresses."

Sternly, he said, "Have you had the talk?"

"Yes, Asante, we have." She pasted that fake smile back on. "I followed orders."

"So? What's behind the look?"

"Mmm…it doesn't sound like she's put a whole hell of a lot of thought into it. I'm pretty sure she never took a queer theory or gender politics class in college. She's more of a 'this feels right' kinda person."

"So it's not a style choice?"

"No, it's more than that. But she's not transgender. She said she's happy with her body. She just feels more like herself when she's dressed like a twink."

His eyes almost bugged out. "She said that?"

Kit slapped at him, laughing at the look on his face. "Of course not. But she really does. Last time I saw her, she had on a striped shirt, a bow tie, a tweed vest and a pocket watch." When his eyebrows shot up she added, "She'd never looked cuter."

"What would you have done if that guy you dated last year…what was his name…Gene?"

"Yeah, Gene."

"What would you have done if he'd shown up in the same clothes?"

She laughed, unable to even picture it. "I'd suggest ordering in. No way I'd go out in public with a guy dressed like he was a Scottish caddy in 1900!"

"But it's okay if a woman dresses that way."

Kit linked her fingers together and set her chin on them, beaming at him like she was a pin-up girl. "So it would appear."

"I won't understand this if I live to a hundred."

"You're going to live much longer than that. By the time you're…eighty, this is all gonna make sense."

—⁓—

The next Friday night, Bailey took Kit to a club in the U Street Corridor. On the way, Kit peppered her with questions, but Bailey liked having a little mystery about her plans, and just kept saying, "We'll be there soon."

It was early, about eight thirty, and when they reached the front door, Bailey gave her name to the bouncer, who slapped wristbands on them and stood aside to let them in. The place was loud, with reggae playing through the massive speakers, but she could hear Kit if she leaned over and placed her ear close to Kit's mouth.

"You're a reggae fan?" Kit asked.

"I like it well enough. This is an experiment." She led Kit to the bar and shouted for a pair of espresso vodka shots, dramatically taking two singles from her wallet and slapping them on the bar.

Kit's eyes widened at the price, then they clicked their glasses together and downed them. "A buck a shot if you're on the promoter's list," Bailey said, leaning close. "Only until nine though."

Kit signaled the bartender for a repeat, then took her own singles from her purse. "Who's gonna argue with a two dollar buzz?"

After slamming down another round, Bailey put a five on the bar for a tip, then led Kit to the second floor. This space was a little smaller, with fewer people and loud hip-hop playing. "Like this better?" Bailey asked.

"Better for…?"

"The music," Bailey said. "Do you like hip-hop?"

"Sure. I like just about everything."

Hmm… That usually meant the person liked nothing. This might be a bigger problem than she'd guessed. Not bothering to linger, Bailey led the way again, this time to the third floor. A mellow, bluesy soul tune vibrated the walls and Kit pulled Bailey down to say into her ear, "This is more my style. Want another drink?"

Considering her extremities were still tingling from slamming back two shots in two minutes, Bailey shook her head. "Let's hang out for a while. Full price drinks are only eight bucks if we need another later."

"No problem." There were low chairs ringing the room, and Kit maneuvered two of them so they were facing each other at an angle. That let them sit and almost face each other, but let them speak by leaning over and getting close.

"Nice setup," Bailey nodded, smiling contentedly.

"Lots of practice." The song segued into another sexy, slow R&B classic, with a woman's rough voice crooning loudly. "Good music," Kit said, grinning.

"Cool. I knew I'd find something you'd like if I made an effort."

Batting her eyelashes, Kit said, "You could have just asked."

"I did!" She leaned over and discretely nibbled on Kit's ear, careful to do nothing that might make Kit anxious in a crowd. "I think you've got some of that 'I have to go along with whatever my date likes' thing going on."

"Mmm." Kit closed her eyes halfway, appearing to consider that. "I have some of that in a few areas of my life."

"Well, you don't need to do it with me. When I ask for your opinion, I really want it. Unvarnished."

"I'll give it a try," Kit allowed. "But I don't have a lot of practice."

—m—

On the way home, Bailey let her memories of the night roll around in her head. Things were clicking. If Kit had been a lesbian, Bailey would have already asked her to move in together. But she wasn't. It was sometimes hard to remember that, when Kit kissed her like she'd been with women for years. But it was always lurking in the shadows – a threat that could destroy what they were slowly building.

Kit was wearing a sexy, bright blue dress and surprisingly high heels. Bailey insisted they take a cab, the first one they'd shared. She'd never had any trouble with crime in DC, but she believed in being able to run away from harm, something Kit couldn't have done in those shoes.

While slipping an arm around Kit's shoulders, she let her eyes wander down her body. She'd pay for ten cabs a day if Kit would always dress like she had tonight. Her luscious legs peeked out from the snug dress, and even though

Bailey understood that heels were one more weapon the patriarchy used to render women dependent, they made Kit's legs look good enough to eat. It was damned hard to be a lesbian feminist sometimes.

They arrived at Kit's apartment and went up in the elevator. It would have made sense for Bailey to keep the cab and go right home. But there was no way she was going to miss their goodbye kisses.

Since her ill-advised grope, they hadn't done more than kiss and grind against one another, and she doubted Kit would be the one to advance things further. But even though they only kissed, the end of their dates was Bailey's favorite part. She'd now almost started to salivate on the way down the hall, knowing those sweet lips would be waiting for her when they went inside.

Bailey handed Kit her coat and detoured to the kitchen to get water. Kit drank more water than three people combined, and always liked a glass when she got home. Walking back into the living room, Bailey stopped and stared, her hand almost letting go of the glass. Kit hadn't done anything extraordinary. She was just sitting on the low sofa, legs crossed at the knee. But she was giving Bailey a look that almost screamed seduction. She couldn't put words to what made the look so incendiary, but by the time she reached her, the ice in the glass was tinkling as her shaking hand made it fly around. "Hi," Bailey said, handing over the glass.

"Hi." Kit accepted it and brought it to her lips. Bailey watched her, entranced, as her throat moved slightly with each swallow. "Good." She put the glass down and lay her hands upon her knee.

Again, that was a very routine move. But tonight it was as if Kit had yanked off her dress and told Bailey to come and get it. Anxiously, she sat down and pulled Kit tightly against her body. They usually started off slowly and let things build a little, each time ratcheting up the heat. But tonight the first kiss was hot and the second orders of degree hotter.

Kit opened her mouth and sucked Bailey's tongue in, pulling on it until Bailey got control and began to teasingly probe Kit's warm mouth.

A soft sigh left her lips as Kit tightened her embrace. Their bodies pressed into one another firmly, and Bailey's head swam from the feel of Kit's breasts. Her own chest hadn't changed much from the time she was twelve, but puberty had made some delightful additions to Kit's body. Her breasts weren't overly large, but they were soft and cushy when Bailey pressed against them, making her wonder, as she often did, how they'd feel in her mouth.

Her hand moved without conscious thought, grasping and holding that supple flesh. Then Kit's eyes met hers, the slightest question in her eyes.

"Can I touch you?" Bailey asked, her tongue thick in her mouth.

Silently, Kit covered her fingers, making them compress, then she leaned forward and kissed Bailey hard.

Bailey let herself go, palming Kit's breast and squeezing it until she let out a tiny mew.

"That's good," she whispered. "So good."

Unbidden, both hands were immediately filled, with Bailey maneuvering Kit into the corner of the sofa, so she could press into her while revealing all of the desire that beat in her chest.

This was everything she'd wanted. Kit was fully with her; entirely engaged. There wasn't a doubt in Bailey's mind that they could skip right into the bedroom and ravish each other. But it had only been a few weeks since Kit had frozen and Bailey was determined not to screw this up.

She consciously tried to clear her mind, to focus only on Kit's body. Her lips, her tongue, the way her breath caught when Bailey squeezed her firmly. There were so many sensations her head was spinning. But she waited for a sign. A clear signal that Kit was ready to go further. To make love. Knowing that she wouldn't refuse was one thing. But Bailey needed more. She needed to know that Kit was ready. And everything she knew about her said she'd speak her mind when she'd made it up.

Tentatively, she let her hand glide up Kit's thigh. Such unbelievable softness. She closed her eyes briefly, allowing herself to feel the warmth that radiated just above her hand. Moving the slightest bit, she continued—determined to go until Kit stopped her. But Kit seemed a long way from stopping her. Eyes closed, breath coming a little quicker, an occasional whimper. Her body shifted, and her legs opened the slightest bit, as if daring Bailey to press forward.

Testing, Bailey lightened her touch, then slowly pulled away. "I'm so close to losing my mind."

"I won't tell a soul." Kit pulled her close and kissed her again, daintily sucking Bailey's lip into her mouth and raking her teeth over it.

Bailey shook like a leaf in a strong wind. Every part of her wanted to go for it, to slip that pretty dress from her body and consume her. But this was vitally important to get right. Once again she started to pull away, and this time Kit let her go. Or did she? Kit's hands were on her shoulders, a question in her eyes. But she didn't speak. Didn't utter a word.

"I'm at the end of my rope," Bailey got out.

"I am too." She wrapped her arms around her shaking body and held on tightly for a full minute. "I hate to let you go."

Then ask me to stay!

The tension was unbearable, but Kit didn't say another word. Bailey got to her feet, straightened her hair as well as she could, tucked her shirt into her slacks, adjusted her tie and held onto the arm of the sofa for support. With a deep breath, she walked over to the closet and got her coat. Kit stayed right where she was, her head now lying on the arm of the sofa, like she was unable to drag herself all the way to the door. "Call me," she said, adding a weak-looking wave.

"I will." Their eyes met and Bailey tried to convey a little of what she felt. "I had a great time tonight."

"The club was great, but the last fifteen minutes has put R&B to shame."

"G'night." Out in the hallway, Bailey leaned on the door, afraid she might need assistance to get downstairs. They were close—really close. She just wasn't sure she could get much closer without burning up like a Roman candle.

—⁓—

As the door closed, Kit sank down onto the sofa and hiked her skirt up. The dress was a nice one, and would be a wrinkled mess, but she couldn't wait. Not taking the time to remove her panties, she pushed them aside and slipped her fingers into her wetness, letting out a hiss of pleasure when she touched her overheated sex. She could still taste Bailey on her lips, could still smell her beguiling scent, could still feel how swollen her lips were from those super-heated kisses. She still didn't feel like a lesbian, but she was desperate to have sex with one—just one. The cutest, sexiest lesbian she'd ever seen.

—⁓—

It was a cool, but not cold night. They only lived a little over a mile from each other, so Bailey decided to walk to cool off and calm down. She'd just passed the big statue of George Washington astride his horse and was curving around to head up New Hampshire when her phone played the theme from Doctor Who.

Fishing it from her pocket, she smiled when she saw who was calling. "Miss me?"

"I really do. I know it hasn't been long, but my head's clear now."

"It was foggy before?"

"Yeah. Well, it wasn't my head so much as my..." Kit laughed, and Bailey could just see how cute she looked. "Look. I'm gonna embarrass myself and tell you the truth." Bailey could hear her take in a breath. "I was ready to tear your clothes off tonight."

"I wouldn't have complained. But you knew that, didn't you."

"Yeah, I knew. But I needed to think, to get my bearings for a minute."

"How are your bearings now?"

"Pretty good. My hand's about to cramp though."

Chuckling, Bailey found a low wall and perched on it. This was getting interesting. "Hand cramp, huh? Been writing letters?"

"You weren't even on the elevator when I had my first orgasm. I think I'm ready to have one with you in the room. Wanna come back?"

"And you say I'm the romantic."

"That's perfectly correct. You're the romantic and I'm the sex addict." She laughed for a second. "I'm not kidding about your coming back. What do you say?"

"Mmm, I think you need a twenty-four hour cooling off period. It was just fifteen minutes ago that you let me stumble out the door."

"I know," she said quietly. "I'm being overly careful, but I want to get this right."

"I do too. What are you doing tomorrow night?"

"I was supposed to go to a book launch for the Senate minority whip. Am I ditching?"

"You are. I'll be at your apartment by eight. I don't need to be fed. I just need to be loved."

"I'll do my very best. Don't be late."

—⁂—

When the buzzer rang, Kit almost jumped out of her skin. She would have kicked herself if she could've reached her own butt. There was no reason to be so anxious. This was no different than sleeping with a guy for the first time. She grimaced, thinking about the last time she'd stopped seeing a guy largely because of sex. No matter what happened tonight, at least she wouldn't have a repeat of that disaster. It probably wasn't even possible for a lesbian to come in two seconds and then blame her. She stopped in her tracks. It wouldn't matter if a woman came in two seconds. They'd be on separate tracks, not dependent upon one another. She gripped the back of the sofa for a moment to stop her head from spinning. Sex was going to be very, very different without a penis involved.

Opening the door, she stood there for a moment taking Bailey in. She looked like she could have stepped off the cover of GQ. Under her huge parka, a pale blue shirt, red striped tie, and a darker blue half-zip sweater covered skinny jeans. The jeans were tucked into suede ankle-height boots that Bailey hadn't tied. Casual and classy. As she often did, Bailey grasped the edge of her glasses and held them up off her nose as she swiveled her head up and down, taking Kit in like she was a painting.

"You should wear that every day." Lowering her specs, she nodded, looking even more certain. "Every single day." Leaning in, she kissed Kit very gently. "I know you didn't go to Catholic school, but you look a little like a girl I was mad about in high school." She reached down and tugged on the hem of Kit's short plaid skirt. "I would've gotten a free ride to MIT if I hadn't been so obsessed with her."

Kit draped her arms around Bailey's neck and gave her a longer, more welcoming kiss. "I only have a few skirts, but you really seem to like them, so I thought I'd stick with what works."

"You don't have to do anything special for me. I've never seen you when you didn't look fantastic."

Kit took her hand and brought her all the way inside. "Maybe that's because I spend hours getting ready to see you. You might wake up tomorrow morning and see what a mess I am without tons of prep."

"I like the thought of that." Bailey pulled her close, then kissed her. When she pulled away she touched Kit's nose with a finger. "Not the mess part. The waking up with you. That sounds sweet."

Leading Bailey over to the sofa, Kit paused. "Do you want a drink?"

"I don't think so."

Kit thought they'd have a couple of drinks to calm their nerves. Now she had to skip that step, or admit she needed one. Damn. Being honest wasn't a heck of a lot of fun. "Uhm…" She waited until Bailey was seated, then perched on the arm of the sofa. "I'm a little shaky. I don't want you to think I drink every day. I really don't. It's just that—"

Bailey was suddenly standing next to her, comforting arms encircling her shoulders. "If you want a drink, go right ahead. But if you don't, I bet I can help you relax."

"It's the way you're gonna help me relax that makes me tense." Kit chuckled at the oddness of the situation. Maybe making a formal date to have sex hadn't been the best idea. She should have jumped in last night when they were both clearly in the mood.

"No, no, no." Holding her hand, Bailey led her over to the front of the sofa. "Come over here and lie down." She sat and patted her lap. "Put your head right here."

Tentatively, Kit complied, lying on the sofa with her head on Bailey's lap. "Bailey Jones, Lesbian Psychiatrist."

"I don't wanna analyze you. I just want you to talk to me." Bailey started to thread her fingers through Kit's hair, gently scratching along her scalp as she did. "Tell me everything that's making you tense."

Shifting her eyes upwards, Kit gave her a puzzled look. "Can you really not figure this out? I'm super into you and worried I won't be able to do it."

A warm, understanding smile curled the corners of Bailey's mouth. She had the sweetest damned smile in the world. Her eyes almost closed and hints of dimples appeared on her cheeks. "That's complete nonsense."

"No, it's not!" Kit could feel her blood pressure spiking again. "You're the only woman I've ever kissed, Bailey. Doing more is…" She rolled her eyes. "A big deal."

"Nope. You're wrong about that." Her gentle hand continued to stroke. It was almost impossible to be wired up when someone was lovingly caressing you. "If you didn't like it when we kissed, I'd agree that you'd have a tough time going forward. But you're not that good an actress." Those soft fingers brushed across Kit's lips. "You're into me, and you'll be able to make love." Leaning over, she tried to glower. "You'll not just be able to—you'll really like to. It won't be any different than making love to a man."

"How can you be so sure? I'm a big bag of doubt."

"If you're a sexual person, and you care about someone, and you're physically attracted to them, you can make it work. You just have to turn down your conscious mind a little bit and turn up your body's signals. Let all of those hormones do the heavy lifting." Tickling across Kit's body, she teased, "Come on out hormones. Kit needs you. She wants to punch her bisexuality ticket."

"Not sure that's true."

"What? Being bisexual?"

"Yeah." She rolled onto her side, curling up like she was about to take a nap. "I don't feel bisexual, since that implies you're equally into men and women. I'm more like a vegetarian who eats a hot dog at a ballgame."

"Now that's a unique perspective on sexuality. I've never heard a lesbian encounter as being like eating a hot dog."

Kit laughed at her simile. "I guess it should go the other way. I'm a hot dog eater who wants to try one specific kind of tofu."

"You don't need any of those labels." Bailey's voice was calm and reassuring. "No one ever knows what goes on in people's heads. I'm sure there are millions of straight people who fantasize about gay sex. That doesn't make them gay."

Kit looked up at her. "If a guy blows a guy—that's gay. Even gayer if they…" She made a circle with her thumb and forefinger and inserted her other index finger into it, pulling it in and out a few times.

Laughing, Bailey said, "I think sexuality is complex. Really complex. And I'm absolutely certain sexual orientation isn't binary. I'm a firm believer in letting people self-identify. It's really none of my business if a straight man wants to do a guy once in a while. If he says he's straight—I buy it."

"You wouldn't say that if he was your husband."

"No, I'd say he was cheating on me. I'd break up with him if he had sex behind my back with any human life-form."

"I have no tolerance for cheaters either." She looked up and met Bailey's eyes again. "I'm not going to go out with anyone else. I hope you're…"

Stroking her cheek, Bailey said, "No one else. My ideal situation is us falling in love and staying together until the end. Stability is my favorite word."

"Mine is…" She looked up and batted her eyes. "Bailey."

"I like that. You're winning the romantic award. I'm going to have to work to wrestle it back from you."

Kit pushed herself up, then moved to sit right next to Bailey. "I'm not so nervous anymore. You're good at calming me down."

"I don't want you to be too calm." Bailey tucked an arm around her and pulled her close. "Why don't you tell me what you've fantasized about?"

Kit started to giggle, finding herself unable to stop for a few seconds. "I'm such a goof sometimes. My fantasies have all been one way—you making love to me. Then—I'm done. I never hold out long enough to think about what I want to do to you."

"You'll think of something. You're a very resourceful woman."

Kit snuggled up against Bailey's body. "You're being so considerate about all of this. Asante said he would've sent me packing long ago."

Laughing, Bailey said, "I wish I could say that lesbians were more open-minded than guys are about the conversion of straight people, but that's just not true. I'm sure my lesbian friends will tell me I'm crazy when I tell them about you."

"You haven't told your friends?"

"No." She looked a little abashed. "I'd have to admit how into you I am, and if you find you're not into me…" She shrugged. "Only Nat knows about you."

"And she doesn't think you're crazy?"

A big grin settled onto Bailey's face. "Natalie believes she can talk anyone into anything. She doesn't count."

Kit took her hand and held it, spending a few moments inspecting it carefully. There were a lot of nice parts to Bailey, but her hands were way up on the list. "Why are you willing to take a risk with me?"

"Now that we're into it, it doesn't seem like that much of a risk. It won't take long to figure out if this is right for you; if it's not, we'll go back to being friends."

"Really? It's that simple?"

She nodded decisively. "I think it is. You told me there were lots worse things you could be hiding, and you were dead right about that. If the worst thing about you is that you've never been with a woman, this will be a walk in the park."

"I hope we have a really nice walk in the park. I so want this to work."

Her grin was so cute it should have been illegal. "I can see why. I am pretty awesome."

She was clearly teasing, but there was a part of Bailey that was very, very confident. That was the part that Kit found so alluring. That adorably cocky grin was just begging for a kiss. As usual, their first serious kiss always made Kit feel like Bailey had slipped the key into her lock. Whatever barriers and walls she'd had to put up to get through the day fell to rubble when Bailey kissed her.

Immediately, Bailey took over, pushing Kit back against the sofa as she started to kiss her in earnest. Soon they were moving against each other, pressing their bodies closely together, their kisses growing more fervid.

Then Bailey's hands skimmed over her breasts, making Kit shiver.

"I think we should move to the bedroom," Bailey whispered, her lips close to Kit's ear. "I don't want to roll around here on the sofa. Let's make this memorable."

Kit swallowed. "I... I think it's going to be memorable. One way or the other."

Bailey stood up, took both of Kit's hands in hers and pulled her to her feet. "In just a few minutes, you're going to laugh at how nervous you were."

"If only one of us is going to laugh, I sure hope it's me."

They started to walk toward the bedroom, with Bailey saying, "Mark my words. You're going to wonder why you made such a big deal out of this."

When they entered Kit's bedroom, Bailey walked around and removed every photo that graced the dresser and the bedside tables. Smiling, she said, "I hate to have an audience. I haven't met your family or friends, and having them look at me naked doesn't sound like fun at all."

"You might not know much about photography, but they can't see you."

Bailey reached out and pinched her cheek. "That's what I'm looking for. Your sense of humor is back."

"I might as well laugh. It's a lot better option than locking myself in the bathroom, crying."

Ignoring that comment, Bailey looked around. "No candles? You seem like a candle kind of woman."

"I don't think I have any. I used to use them all of the time, but I got out of the habit."

"Luckily for you, I'm a thoughtful guest. Hold on." She was gone just a few moments, and when she returned with her messenger bag she took out three big pillar candles. "I don't take these everywhere I go. But I like the way they make a room look." She placed them at various spots around the room and lit them. When they were as she liked them, she turned off the overhead lights, then took out her phone and a small metal box. She shoved her glasses up onto her head, then scrolled through her phone until she found what she was looking for. A sensual R&B tune oozed through the little speaker she placed next to the bed.

"Oh, Bailey." Kit's heart skipped a beat. "You're so thoughtful."

Bailey smiled, but otherwise ignored the compliment. "Isn't it nice to have good lighting and music?" Skimming her fingers over Kit's cheeks, she murmured, "You look fantastic in candlelight." Then placing soft kisses on both of her eyelids, she added, "Your eyes are the most beautiful color. Brown and gold and a little green. Like a pretty cat's."

Kit slipped her arms around her waist and hugged her tightly. "You make me feel really beautiful. That's such a nice gift."

"I'm the one who gets to enjoy your gorgeous face. You should probably put a mirror on the ceiling so you can catch a look at how pretty you are. Only seems fair."

Kit placed her hands behind Bailey's neck and leaned back in the embrace. "This is a change I think I'm going to like. You're not in a rush. If you were a guy, you might be looking for your clothes to go home by now."

Bailey stopped like she'd been frozen. It took her a second to even blink. "You can't be serious."

"I kind of am. Some guys are slow and thoughtful and considerate, but others act like they're in a race. Those are the jokers I've been seeing for the last few years."

"Sometimes I'm in a hurry, but that's only to get the first round out of the way." She grinned wolfishly. "Once is usually not enough."

"You haven't yet said anything to make me think this is a bad idea."

"It's not. It's a very good idea." With that, Bailey held her close and started to kiss her again, really getting into it this time. In just seconds, she'd turned up the heat to a point where Kit felt the temperature had risen by ten degrees. Bailey must've been just as overheated, because she reached down, grabbed the hem of her sweater, and yanked it over her head.

The warmth of her body through her cotton shirt made the hairs on the back of Kit's neck stand up. She hooked her thumbs into Bailey's belt-loops and pressed into her. "You're so sexy," she murmured.

Bailey didn't reply, but her eyes took on even more of a sparkle in the candlelight. Soon her hands were working the buttons on Kit's blouse. Her pulse quickened, but she purposefully tamped it down. This was Bailey. A woman she trusted deeply. She'd let men she'd barely known strip her without a second thought. This was safe. *She* was safe.

Cool air hit her skin as her blouse fell open. Involuntarily, she shivered, but was immediately warmed by Bailey's body holding her close. "I'm going to keep going," Bailey said, sounding so sure and forthright. "But you can put up a stop sign any time you want."

Kit's head moved up and down without really telling it to. She was on autopilot, but Bailey seemed to be in control enough for both of them. The blouse slipped from her shoulders, then her skirt fell to the floor. Bailey's shirt and tie joined the pile in what seemed like seconds, then Kit's bra was tossed away, leaving her shaking with nerves.

But Bailey was right there, holding her close, whispering into her ear. "You're so beautiful. Just like I knew you'd be."

Kit lifted her hands and slid them up and down Bailey's back, tickling her through the silky tank top she wore. Their chests rubbed together, and Kit closed her eyes when their nipples hardened and flicked against one another while Bailey rocked her gently back and forth.

Now the kisses that rained down on her took her breath away. She could feel her need, feel how Bailey's desire was growing like a living thing. They were close to the bed, and with a quick movement Bailey yanked the spread away, then pulled the sheet down. Kit found herself sitting, watching raptly, as Bailey kicked off her boots, then shimmied out of her jeans. She stood there in just her underwear, looking proud and confident.

"I thought you'd wear boxers," Kit said, staring at the lean muscles in Bailey's legs.

"I've tried them. They don't fit right."

"Right. Right." Kit couldn't take her eyes off the fuchsia boy-shorts Bailey wore. Knowing her bare body was right behind that thin fabric made her pulse thrum.

Bailey sat next to her, then wrapped an arm around Kit and lay down. It was remarkably cozy being cuddled by Bailey's warm body. For a few minutes they merely got used to each other, then Bailey got down to business again, latching her hungry mouth to Kit's for long, sensual kisses that seemed to go on forever.

Kit reached up and carefully removed Bailey's glasses. "Your eyes are so beautiful," she whispered. "I love to take your glasses off and just look at them. It's like a present—every time."

"I'll wear contacts if you want me to." She chuckled. "Right now I'd agree to just about anything."

Lacing her arms around Bailey's shoulders, Kit kissed her again, exploring her mouth until the pounding of her heart made her a little weak.

"If you want anything," Bailey said softly, "anything at all…just tell me. I only want to make you happy."

"I'm happy." Kit heard how tense her voice sounded.

Bailey smiled at her, her eyes warm and sparkly in the candlelight. "Then I'll try to make you happier." Her mouth covered Kit's, claiming her forcefully. Hands slid down her body, quickly removing her panties and cupping her ass.

She thrust against Bailey's leg, which had slid between her own. A man had never done that, but it was kind of perfect. A nice, sturdy, soft thing to grind against. Being with someone who owned a vagina was bearing unexpected rewards. Kit's overthinking brain settled down as she let the physical sensations envelop her. The smooth, sleek feel of Bailey's body, the softness of her gentle hands, the warmth of her mouth and the slickness of her tongue. Every element of her was different—very different—but very welcome. It was like going to a vaguely exotic place you'd never been before, and finding it fit your tastes in ways that surprised and delighted you.

"How do you like to be touched?" Bailey asked, nuzzling against her ear. "What turns you on?"

Kit couldn't begin to speak. Everything Bailey had done so far was perfect. "Uhm…" She started to laugh. "I have no idea. Do whatever you want. I'm good."

"You're sexy," Bailey murmured. "Incredibly sexy." She ran a hand over Kit's breast, then held it tenderly. "Your body is absolute perfection." She started to scoot down, then her warm mouth covered one of Kit's breasts and she purred when Bailey started to suckle.

It was so nice to be touched by someone who knew how sensitive your breasts could be. Bailey kept her touch delicate, slowly increasing the insistent tugging until Kit shivered with sensation. "Right there," she murmured. "Just right."

It wasn't possible to lie still. Kit moved and shifted under Bailey's weight, wanting more of her, more sensation, more pressure. Then Bailey moved to her other breast and gave it the same appreciative treatment.

Kit's hands glided down to Bailey's ass and suddenly she needed to feel her bare skin. She slipped her hand into her boy shorts and felt the firm muscle that made her slacks fit so nicely. Just like every other part, her ass was lean, but there was enough flesh to grab a handful and squeeze, making Bailey suck all the harder on her breast. "Goood," Kit purred. She'd thought she'd reached her limit, but her limit seemed to expand along with her desire.

Bailey reached down and tugged her shorts off, then whipped her tank off in one quick move. Kit's mouth grew dry as she was faced with a pretty, blank canvas to play with. In seconds she had her by the hips and was pulling her against her body forcefully, unable to get enough of her.

As her driving need escalated, Bailey responded by lying on her side and gently slipping her hand between Kit's legs. "Do you like this?" she whispered when her fingers circled the slippery folds of skin.

"Yes, yes, yes," she managed. "Touch me." Her eyes were closed and she started to shake again. But this time nerves had nothing to do with it. She was so turned on she couldn't lie still; couldn't keep her body from thrusting against Bailey's clever fingers. Kit's arms locked around her body, holding her in place. Without thinking, her teeth raked across Bailey's shoulder, wanting so badly to bite her. Her rational mind knew that was a crazy instinct, but a primitive part of her brain had taken over.

After teasing her until she thought she'd go mad, Bailey's fingers began to move faster, and Kit's hips kept pace with them. She was thrusting against them furiously, her head thrown back, biting her own lip to keep from taking a chunk out of Bailey. "Almost," she finally managed to grunt. Then it hit her—a wave of sensation that started in her belly and spread in every direction at once. Her nipples hardened, her gut clenched, and her pussy throbbed almost painfully. Kit held Bailey so tightly her muscles cramped, then her grip eased until Bailey lay across her chest, softly kissing whatever skin she could reach.

"Kiss me," Kit murmured. Nothing was more important at that moment than having Bailey's lips touch hers. They kissed, tenderly, for long minutes. Kit had never been so needy; so compelled to merge with a lover. She wanted to consume her—body and soul.

After a long time, some of the need spilled away and Kit started to breathe more easily. Then Bailey placed tickling kisses down her belly and Kit braced herself. Before she could even form a thought Bailey was burrowing between her legs, her tongue probing her pussy just like it had her mouth. She opened herself fully—welcoming every touch with gusto. Kit still didn't feel like a lesbian, but she sure wasn't perfectly straight. She didn't think many completely straight women prayed that the woman going down on her would never, ever stop.

Lying together, their bodies heavy from exhaustion, Kit took the clip from Bailey's hair. Gently, she threaded her fingers through the strands. Bailey's head was on her chest, her hair now splayed across Kit's breast. "I've missed this," she murmured.

"Playing with a lover's hair?" Bailey tilted her head up, meeting Kit's eyes. "Have you had other lovers with long hair?"

Kit pinched her butt, making her squirm. "I've missed this kind of intimacy. I love having sex, but this part—the closeness I feel after—that's the best."

Clear blue eyes looked at her carefully. "You haven't had that…in a while?"

"A long while. Not since Henry and I broke up."

"But you have had it."

"Yeah, definitely. I've had three long term boyfriends and they were all good partners."

"Just three?" Before she spoke again Kit could tell she was going to tease her about something. "I thought you people jumped into bed with anyone you could grab."

"No, that's you people. They tell me the gays are completely indiscriminate. Pat Robertson hasn't been lying to me, has he?"

Chuckling, Bailey said, "I like to focus on getting it right with one person. I'm not a grazer."

"Really?" Kit managed to prop herself up a few inches. The exact words Bailey had used hit her and she said, "How little have you grazed?"

"Mimi. Then Julie." She strained to reach Kit's lips. "Then there's you."

Kit's eyes opened wide. "I'm number three?"

"Yep. I hope the third time's the charm."

Kit tried to do her own history in her head. She'd only been with two guys before Henry, but she'd had to zip through quite a few in the last few years. If you didn't have sex by the third date, you weren't going to get a fourth. When she hit double digits she stopped counting and hoped Bailey didn't ask. She didn't seem like the type to judge, but you never knew.

"Everything okay?" Bailey asked, looking up with concern. "You're looking a little…something."

She shook her head and dismissed the upsetting thought. "Yeah, I'm fine. Just letting things settle."

The teasing tone was back again. "When are you going to admit that I was right?"

"You were right," Kit said immediately. "About what?"

"Heh. About your ability to relax and enjoy yourself."

Smiling, Kit squeezed her tenderly. "You were definitely right. Now I just have to figure out how to make you feel half as good as you did me."

"Don't set your goals so low!" That adorably sweet grin was back. Bailey must have escaped ever being in trouble when she was a kid. No one could stay mad at her when she flashed that smile.

"My goals are high. I'm just not confident in my ability to reach them." She lay back down, with Bailey scooting up to be on her level.

In seconds she was being cuddled tenderly, with Bailey saying, "Don't worry about that. We're doing great. I've talked people through some remarkably difficult installations. Making me come is as easy as rebooting your computer. Child's play."

"I just have to hold your start button down?"

"That's about right. Especially when the woman I'm with is as sexy as you are. Not to mention beautiful."

"Go on and mention it," Kit teased.

Propping herself up on her forearm, Bailey gently trailed her hand across Kit's features. "Everything about you is beautiful." Her voice was soft and low, a slight whisper. "Your bone structure, these pretty pale eyebrows, your long lashes, straight nose." She bent and kissed each part in turn, making Kit feel like she was positively cherished. "And you already know how much I love your eyes and your sweet mouth." She touched the corners of her lips, then moved closer and kissed her again. "Sometimes I look at you and you take my breath away. I still can't believe we're lying here together." Another soft kiss. "I'm very, very lucky to be here with you."

Kit's head spun from the effusive, clearly sincere compliments. Bailey wasn't a bullshitter, and that made her words have so much more impact than they otherwise would have. "I think I'm the lucky one." She shifted and began to kiss Bailey, feeling her body start to heat up. It was amazing how quickly you could get back into the mood with just a few hot kisses.

Now that she was relaxed and focused, Kit let herself really look at Bailey. She had the body of a gangly girl on the edge of puberty. A mere suggestion of breasts, narrow hips and long coltish legs that didn't bear an ounce of fat. Only her ass had any real womanly curve, and that was mostly muscle. But she was a beautiful, sexy woman in Kit's eyes.

It amazed her. Stunned her, actually. But it was Bailey's femininity that attracted her. Her smooth skin, unmarred by any discernible hair, no bulky muscle, no musky aroma. She smelled as sweet and fresh as a spring day.

Kit bent her head to touch a pink, protuberant nipple with her tongue and Bailey let out a purr. "Lick them," she whispered, eyes closed.

Taking her literally, Kit spent a long time delicately licking and kissing those obviously sensitive nipples. Bailey squirmed beneath her, moaning sexily as her hips twitched. Kit got into it, pulling a nipple in and giving it a lusty suck. "Gentle," Bailey urged, putting a hand on her head. "They're super-sensitive."

Kit lifted her head and met Bailey's eyes. "I like that," she said, grinning. "I like making you moan."

"Nobody's stopping you." She dropped her head back onto the pillow, offering herself up for Kit's exploration.

It wasn't just her breasts that were sensitive. Everywhere Kit kissed brought out a shiver or caused Bailey to make some kind of happy sound. Kit had played with men before, of course. But the guys she'd been with in the last few years were awfully focused. They seemed to have one erogenous zone—right between their legs. It was exciting to be with someone whose entire body seemed wired for pleasure.

Seeing one of Bailey's beautiful hands lying there, Kit grasped it and covered it with kisses. When she sucked a finger into her mouth and laved it, Bailey groaned like she'd gut-punched her. "You could make me come just doing that. That's so sexy."

Blinking, Kit realized she'd never sucked on a guy's fingers. And she had no idea why she'd wanted to do that to Bailey. But she definitely did, and she definitely loved to make her squirm around the bed like she was unable to remain still for another moment. "I'm digging this…big-time."

"Tell me I'm right." Bailey gave her a strikingly earnest look. Before Kit could say a word, she burst into laughter. "God, I love to be right."

"You're right. You're as right as anyone's ever been." She nestled up against her body. "And for your prize, I'm gonna…" It took her a second to get her hand into position, then she realized she was using her left. Chuckling at her awkwardness, she climbed over Bailey's body and slipped her dominant hand between her legs. "I'm gonna…one of these days…finally! Her fingers touched

Bailey's slippery skin and she got chills when she reacted by shivering and pressing up against her. "Feel good?"

"Yeah. Yeah," she growled. "Good." Her eyes were closed tightly and she kept biting her lower lip, as if it was too intense to bear.

It was a fantastic rush to feel so intimately responsible for another woman's pleasure. Kit felt like she had tremendous power right in the tips of her fingers. Like she could bestow satisfaction with the simplest of gestures.

It was amazing. She knew just how it felt to have determined fingers slipping around your pussy; to feel your lips swell with sensation; to feel that throbbing pulse through your whole body. As different from making love to a man as she could possibly imagine. Bailey was wrong. Dead wrong. This wasn't just like every other time. This was different. Massively different. And very, very exciting.

"Kiss me," Bailey begged, her eyes still closed tightly.

Kit moved to her and covered her mouth with her own, then pulled Bailey's tongue into her mouth and suckled it tenderly. When they broke away, Bailey pressed her lips to Kit's ear and nibbled gently. Her soft voice said, "Mind a little guidance? You're close, really close, but I've got a spot—"

Kit turned her head and kissed her soundly. "Show me." Her biggest fear had been not knowing how to make her come. It was so different approaching a vulva from another direction. Having Bailey show what she needed took the burden off her shoulders.

Bailey's hand covered hers, guiding it to a slightly different angle. Then Kit's fingers were urged lower, to slide inside as Bailey let out a burst of air. "Stay right there," she urged, then her own hand moved up to skim delicately over her pussy, barely touching herself.

Once again, Kit tried to focus, to really take in this brand new sensation. Being inside a woman was kind of amazing. She'd never even considered what it would feel like, but she was fascinated. For some reason, she'd always been vaguely incurious about her own terrain. But now that she was inside Bailey she couldn't be more engrossed. She started to move her fingers, to explore the warm slickness of her, but Bailey gripped her hand and held it tightly. "Stay still. Just fill me up." A small frown formed between her brows, then she started to breathe heavily. Finally, she sucked in a lungful of air and exhaled as she moaned out a shuddering, shaking climax.

Kit watched, transfixed, as a bright pink flush spread across her pale chest. Her nipples were as rigid as pebbles, and a sheen of perspiration covered her hairline. She was beautiful. Simply beautiful.

Bailey's hand was suddenly on her neck, pulling her down for a long, lazy kiss. "I'm still right," she said, sounding drunk.

Kit giggled. "No, you're wrong. That was nothing like making love to a guy. It was different in almost every way."

An eye popped open. "What's the almost?"

After one more kiss, Kit said, "Giving pleasure is universal. But the details are amazingly different."

"Shows what I know." She chuckled softly. "I've never even kissed a guy."

That brought Kit up short. "But you said you didn't sleep with a woman until college."

"Yup."

"What did you do in middle school? In high school?"

"Did you miss the part where I told you I was a geek? I did what most geeks do. Played World of Warcraft with my nerdy friends, dreaming about the woman who would one day show up and make love to me."

Kit kissed her, charmed to think of a young Bailey, sitting in her room, waiting for the door-to-door lesbian to show up. "That's too cute."

"She finally showed up." She grinned toothily. "You just have to go to a nerd college and be willing to answer that door when she comes knocking."

Playfully, Kit knocked on Bailey's temple.

"I would have stroked out if you'd shown up at my door. You would have been far, far out of my league. Mimi was much more my style. A socially awkward engineering major who'd also never been kissed."

"So…tonight was better than a girl who'd never been kissed could do?"

Bailey purred with pleasure, grasping Kit by the waist and forcefully pulling her to rest atop her body. "You've been lying your ass off about not having had sex with women, but you can keep your little secrets."

"Aww…thanks for bullshitting me." She gave her a quick kiss, but when she looked into her eyes, Bailey wore a sober look.

"I'm awfully glad I got to share this with you. The fact that you trusted me enough to be vulnerable with means a lot to me."

"You keep catching me by surprise. I think we're kidding around and then you say something that really touches me." This time her kiss was longer and bore much more emotion. "You've been so patient with me."

"I like foreplay. I didn't know I'd like weeks and weeks of it, but it turns out I do." Pulling Kit down for another kiss, she added, "Being with you was well worth the wait."

Seeing the emotion flare in those pretty eyes made Kit want her all over again. She'd had more than one orgasm with a partner, but it had been years since she'd been able to let a guy rest for a few minutes then go again. Men just weren't made for that. But Bailey…Bailey looked like she was more than willing to take another tumble. Kit started to work her way down, determined to rid herself of any lingering trepidations. But right before she reached her goal, Bailey nearly leapt from bed. "I'll be right back." She scampered into the bathroom so quickly she was a blur.

Kit heard the water run for just a minute or two, then heard Bailey banging around in the bathroom. No more than three minutes after she left she was back, her feet cold and…wet?

"What in the hell?" Running a hand down her leg, Kit wiped away some of the droplets.

"Uhm…" Bailey bit her lip, looking massively embarrassed. "If you're going where I think you're going…"

Kit patted her between the legs. "This was my general destination. Is there a traveler's advisory?"

"Oh!" Now she blushed like a kid. "No, no." Her lips pursed together, then she spit it out. "I thought about this earlier, and decided that you might like it better if I was squeaky clean."

Kit cocked her head. "You weren't…?"

"Oh!" Again she blushed. "I took a shower one minute before I left my apartment. But I'm really turned on and arousal has a flavor…" She scrunched up her eyes. "It's not unpleasant, but I remember the first time I went down on Mimi. It took me a few times to get used to the whole thing." Blowing out a breath, she finished, "I want everything to be perfect for you."

Kit wrapped her in a rib-squeezing hug. "Is it too soon to propose? 'Cause you're the most appealing woman on this earth."

"Nooo," she said, smiling slyly. "Really?"

"Yes. Really." She kissed her once again, relishing the taste of her mouth—clearly having just had toothpaste applied. Did she have a toothbrush implanted somewhere? "I've had guys go down on me and then kiss me, so I have a general idea of the set-up."

Bailey smacked herself in the forehead. "Doh! Of course you do!"

"But I'm very, very grateful for how sensitive you're being. You should rent yourself out to straight women who want to take a lesbian tumble. No one would ever ask for a refund."

"Mmm," she appeared to think about the proposal. "I don't think I'd be good at it if I wasn't into the woman."

"I'm damned glad you're into me." Kit kept her eyes locked on Bailey's as she once again moved down her body. The wacky dash to the bathroom had relieved Kit of the lingering anxiety she bore, and now she knew this would be just one more experience. With a partner like Bailey, no barrier seemed too high.

Settling down between her spread legs, Kit looked up, meeting Bailey's eyes. "I'm going to boldly go where no man has gone before."

That cracked Bailey up, vaporizing the last bits of nervousness Kit still felt.

"If you like Star Trek, I'll propose right now."

"Sorry. That line's fallen into common knowledge." She pressed her lips to the baby-soft skin at the top of Bailey's thigh. "Can I go ahead anyway?"

A sweet smirk had settled onto Bailey's mouth. "Yeah, I think I can get past your limitations."

Kit used her fingers to tentatively explore. She'd never been face to face with a vulva, and she decided that Bailey had a very nice one. Pink as a rose, sparkling clean, with just a little clear fluid near the opening. It didn't look intimidating in the least. She recalled the first time she'd done this with a boy, and felt the last hidden shred of anxiety leave her body. No matter what, Bailey couldn't gag her with it. She started to chuckle, looking up to catch a puzzled look on Bailey's face. "Just thinking about first times. Don't mind me."

"We can do this next time," she said, gently stroking Kit's head.

"No, really. I'm into it." Using her forearms, she propelled herself forward so she and Bailey were almost nose-to-nose. "I'm into you. Kiss me before you send me on my way."

They kissed, with Bailey pulling her onto her body. Kit rubbed against her, loving the soft springiness of her.

"Only do what you want. There's no rush."

"I know that." Lost in her eyes, she stayed with her, kissing her until her heart started racing again. "You turn me on so much, it's amazing." Taking her leave, she slid back down again, having another look. Bailey was going to have to shower again if they kept this up. But Kit wasn't afraid of her body. She was into her. Every bit of her. It surprised and amazed her, but she was definitely into her. Dipping her head, she placed a soft kiss onto those pink folds.

Bailey purred like a cat and twitched her hips. Another kiss, then still another. With each, Bailey showed they were on the same wavelength. So Kit got bolder; using the tip of her tongue to investigate. Why had she been so tentative about this? So worried? Bailey was a delight. Fresh, clean and delicate.

She explored every inch. Fascinated, enthralled. Bailey's skin was so remarkably delicate, Kit felt as if she was kissing something terribly fragile; something she had to be very careful with. Then it dawned on her that Bailey wasn't making a sound.

Looking up, she caught sight of her. Hands curled into fists rested atop her collarbones. Eyes slammed shut, lips pursed; she looked like she was about to jump from a plane. But that wasn't, in any way, the expression of someone who wasn't enjoying herself. Watching her carefully, Kit gently touched her with her tongue again, seeing Bailey's eyes close even tighter. "Are we good?" Kit finally asked.

Those pretty blue eyes stayed closed. "We're great," she said, her voice high and strained. Kit took her at her word and kept trying different things, none of which brought a verbal response. But Bailey's body was shaking roughly, like an explosion was about to rumble through. Going for broke, Kit sucked all of the quivering pink flesh into her mouth and bathed it with her tongue. Seconds later, Bailey clamped her hands onto her shoulders and let out a burst of air, then started to pant. "Wait...wait," she moaned as her flesh pulsed in Kit's mouth. "Yeah. Yeah. Gentle. Very gentle."

Kit lightened up, barely breathing across her flesh, watching, fascinated, as Bailey's body quivered for a full minute.

"I never thought I could hold out that long." She spoke so quickly her words ran together. "I almost lost it thirty seconds in."

Scooting up to wrap her in her arms, Kit said, "I looked up and thought you were about to jump. I didn't know if I was doing what you liked, or if you were trying not to slap me."

"I couldn't talk. I had to distract myself, or I would've come before you even got started."

Laughing, Kit said, "Unlike with a guy, I think I'd be cool with that. With you, I could always go back for more."

Bailey made a sour face. "If I went down on a guy, he couldn't be fast enough."

"Oh, right. I was thinking of…" She made a fist and thrust a finger into it repeatedly. "Finishing fast isn't good if you've only got one chance at it."

Drawing her hand down her body, Bailey said, "You can try to beat my current orgasm record. But trust me—it's a lot more than two."

—⁂—

Kit didn't know the number she was trying to top, but she was exhausted. They'd loved each other in every position she thought possible. Now she was lying flat on her back, unable to move.

"Where's your stamina?" Bailey hovered over her, grinning impishly.

"Gone. Long gone." She reached up and stroked along Bailey's side. "Hey… what's…?" Pulling a little energy from an untapped reserve, Kit sat up and slid her finger down Bailey's pale skin. "What in the heck does this say?"

"That's my tattoo." She turned her head, as if she needed to check it out to make sure it was still there. "Julie wasn't a fan. She didn't want it to be very visible, so I went small and obscure."

Kit turned her head, looking at the letters and symbols that slid down Bailey's hip. It was placed so you would only see it when she was naked—or wearing a string bikini—something Kit thought was highly unlikely. The type was short and dark, but the letters were well-spaced; very professional. Still, she couldn't make it out. It was something computery, that was clear.

<img src="tattoo.jpg"></img>

"I don't get it. It's not English, is it? I know English really well."

"No," she said, laughing softly. "I knew my tastes would change over time, but that I'd always be into computers. So I used HTML to show that a tattoo goes there. You can imagine any tattoo you like."

"Kinda cool." Kit tickled along her ribs. "Super, super geeky."

"Yeah, I know. Geek pride." She fell back to the bed, slipped an arm around Kit and pulled her down next to her. "Are you as tired as I am?"

"Probably. My eyes are crossing. I'm trying to get up the energy to go brush my teeth."

"Don't say I'm not thoughtful." Bailey jumped out of bed with an annoying amount of energy. She came back in a couple of minutes, bearing Kit's toothbrush with a stripe of paste down it, a glass with a little water in it, and another filled with ice and water. "I assume you need water—as always."

"You are thoughtful beyond measure." As Kit started to brush, Bailey walked about the room dousing the candles, then she lowered the volume on the speaker, pressed another screen or two and placed the phone on the bedside table. By the time Kit was finished, Bailey was beside her, fluffing up a pillow.

"Do you need a T-shirt or anything?" Kit put her glasses and brush on the table and fell to the bed with a thump.

"I think I'm good. You've raised my temperature a dozen degrees. You?"

"I can go either way." She looked at the speaker, still playing softly. "You wanna leave that on?"

"I gave it a fifteen minute shut-off. I thought that would be plenty."

Kit's eyes were already closed as she snaked an arm around Bailey's waist and curled up against her. "Fourteen extra. Is this good?"

"Super good." Bailey turned her head and placed a kiss on her cheek. "Sleep well."

"Oh, I will." She snuggled even closer. "I had a fantastic evening. I loved my first journey to lesbianville."

"Glad to have you. You're welcome to come back any time."

Kit kissed all across her bare shoulders, making her giggle. "I'm going to take you up on that invitation. You're a great tour guide."

—m—

Bailey struggled to wake, sporadic clicking sounds nudging her into consciousness. Finally prying an eye open, she realized where she was and who she was with. Half blindly, she stuck her hand out and rested it on Kit's leg. "Is it before dawn, or is the apocalypse at hand?"

Kit let out a soft chuckle. "Before dawn. Go back to sleep." She put her hand on Bailey's shoulder, but it stayed for only a moment. It was clearly needed to furiously type on her cell phone.

Wavering on a thin line between wakefulness and sleep, a few things came into focus. "Did something bad happen? In politics...?"

"Just a normal Sunday morning."

The businesslike way she spoke made Bailey sit up and try to organize her thoughts. "Maybe I'd better get out of your way…"

Now Kit turned and gave her a warm smile. "Sorry if I'm being brusque. I'm in work mode. I had my phone turned off all night, missing the e-mail from my weekend editor, saying she had an emergency and couldn't get in to work. I've got to fill in for her." Leaning over, she placed a kiss on Bailey's forehead, then smoothed her hair away from her face. "I'll go in the living room. You go back to sleep. You look beat."

Bailey didn't want to admit how tired she really was. She was a born competitor, and didn't even like to lose in the "who can work harder" competition. She shook her head. "No, no, I've got a lot of things to do today."

Kit was still just a couple of inches away. "I kind of thought we could hang out. I'm going to be swamped all week, and I wanted to…" She trailed off, but Bailey could see a spark of poorly hidden sexual innuendo.

That was…odd. She was certain Kit would have some amount of… something to get through on the morning after her…whatever. Why were there no terms for your first time having a different kind of sex? Kit was still looking at her, now with a tiny frown lodged between her eyebrows. Time to act like this was normal. "I brought my laptop with me, so I guess I could get some work done here." She forced herself to her feet, wishing a coffee cup was already in her hand. "I could use a T-shirt or something…"

"Super." Kit nearly leapt from bed, then went to her dresser, stopping to switch on her desktop computer. There was a definite gleam in her eye when the big machine emitted a loud, melodic tone. Ahh. She'd wanted to get up and turn it on a while ago, but was being polite. That was a nice trait for a lover to have.

After searching around for a minute, Kit came back to the bed with a long-sleeved T-shirt and a pair of sweatpants. "These won't fit you, but they'll keep most of you warm. I focus better when it's cold, but if it drives you crazy I can crank up the heat a little bit."

Now that the warmth of their bedclothes had left her body, Bailey realized just how cold it was. Kit must've had the air conditioner on! Slipping the T-shirt over her head, and stepping into the sweatpants helped a lot, but they were so short she'd need knee socks to keep her shins warm. "How tall are you?"

Chuckling, Kit said, "I always thought I was tall until I met you. You beat me by a good four inches. All in the legs."

"Do you drink coffee? Please say yes, because I can't leave the house like this."

"I drink enough coffee to power an undeveloped country. And now that you're awake, I'll get right to it."

—∞—

Bailey set herself up on the sofa. It was a pretty good place to work from; comfortable, long enough to stretch out on, and with wide arms that let you rest your laptop as you moved from the left side to the right side to vary your position. She had definitely worked in less comfortable places. But after just a few minutes, she realized she'd need some antifreeze if she was going to spend time in this meat locker. How could Kit stand it?

She didn't have many clothes to add, but she put on the wool ski cap she always carried, then added a thick scarf. That wasn't enough, so she put her sweater on over the T-shirt. That helped, and she no longer felt like the fluid in her joints was frozen. Going back to her computer, she worked until she realized she was shivering. On went the parka. If that didn't help, she was going to go take the down comforter from the bed and wrap herself in it.

Her mood had been broken, and she found herself idly thinking. Kit seemed perfectly normal. Like she had every other time they'd been out. But this wasn't like every other time. They'd had sex! But she was no different than she'd have been if they'd just gone out for pizza. Either Kit was as cool as she claimed to be, or she was under some serious delusions. Bailey found herself gnawing on her thumb, a nervous habit. She'd just have to hang in there and see how the day went. Even if Kit was suppressing her feelings right now, they'd come up eventually. They always did.

She settled down and got back to work. At some point, Kit came by and dangled a piece of cold pizza in front of her. Bailey took a bite, nodded her acceptance and must have eaten it, because an empty plate now sat next to her.

Standing up to stretch, she walked around the apartment just to get her blood moving. It was a nice space, clean and uncluttered, but also warm and homey. The walls were a soothing green, well cared for plants sat near every sunny window, and small mementos from various spots were neatly placed on tables and shelves. When you looked at her home, you'd guess that Kit Travis lived an orderly life. One thing that Bailey noted was that the photos that dotted the walls were all pretty, but every one was of a monument, an historic building or a landscape. Kit wasn't in any of them—nor were any boyfriends or obvious family members. Just Asante and a few women. Then Bailey realized she didn't know Kit's sisters names. Strange. They'd had sex, but neither of them would know who to call if la petite mort turned into la grande mort.

She could hear Kit speaking, so she avoided the bedroom, giving her privacy. A limp-looking pizza delivery box was on the counter, and there was one remaining piece calling her name. After grabbing it, she went back to the sofa, finding that a little problem she'd been unconsciously ruminating over now fell into place. Sometimes you just needed to switch positions to have things sort themselves out.

—∞—

Every e-mail had been answered, every sighting catalogued, every "tag" appended to the proper spot. It was just after noon, and Kit pushed herself away from her desk, then spent a moment stretching her hands, which tended to cramp after a furious typing session.

Well.

Now that she had a moment to think, she let her mind travel back to the previous night. A smile curled her lips while she thought about their amazing evening. Bailey had been right, in a way. Making love was making love. But she'd been remarkably wrong, too. There had to be lesbians who'd be fierce and forceful and focused in bed—like most of the men she'd dated in the past few years. But making love to Bailey had a quality so entirely opposed to that model that it hardly felt like the same act. It was the difference between an action/adventure movie and a romantic French film. Both movies—both meant to entertain—but that's where the similarities ended.

She'd always preferred thoughtful, European films to the car chase, blow-up-the-whole-town kinds of movies that now seemed to fill the theaters, so digging the tender, slow, seductive lovemaking they'd shared made perfect sense.

Lifting a hand to nudge her hair from her eyes, she caught a slight scent on her fingers. *Bailey.* Her smile grew, and she had to go find her…to tell her how great she felt. How relieved. How making love had cleared the decks, as it were. Now they could concentrate on building a relationship.

Sneaking into the living room, she saw her—wrapped up for a walk through the snowy woods, every neuron focused on her computer screen.

Kit watched her for a few minutes, charmed by her rapt concentration. Then she recalled seeing that same expression on her face the night before when

Bailey was burrowing between her legs as though she were on a treasure hunt. Kit would never complain about that laser-like focus. Not when it was such a gift when it was focused on her. Waving, she turned and went back to her office, already seeing her in-box filling again.

—∞—

Bailey squinted at her keyboard, finally realizing it had gotten dark. She got up and turned on a couple of lamps, then walked down the hall. Hearing nothing but the tap, tap, tap of fingers flying across the keyboard, she poked her head into the bedroom. Kit had taken a break at some point to put on some warm clothes. She looked awfully cute in a turtleneck with a scratchy-looking heavy brown sweater over it. "I'm not sure we're going to be good for each other," Bailey said, laughing a little when Kit looked up in surprise. "It's not ideal when both people are obsessive workaholics."

Kit held up a finger, showing she needed a moment to finish something. She typed speedily, checked her phone, typed a few more lines, than pushed herself forcefully away from her desktop. "It can work. Hank and I were both obsessive." She stood up and shook her hands out. "I think it would be worse if one person worked hard and the other one didn't."

"Maybe you're right. I got very used to Julie dragging me away from my computer. I let her be the regulator. That probably wasn't good for us."

"I'm not much of a regulator. No matter how much I do, there's an awful lot more I've left undone. When the person I'm with starts to work, I jump in too." She walked over to Bailey and tucked some of her flyaway hair behind an ear. "Nice hat. How about a long, warm shower?"

Bailey bent over to sniff at her fresh smelling hair. "How did I miss you taking one?"

"You would've missed my knocking down the wall. You have amazing powers of concentration." Kit started to lead her toward the bathroom. When they got there, she peeled off her heavy sweater.

"You're going to take one with me? But you've already had one."

"I have, but I'm freezing and another one will warm me up." She slipped her arms around Bailey's waist and hugged her tenderly. "And I wouldn't mind getting my hands on you again."

"If you're expecting a complaint, you're not going to be happy."

"I think I'm going to be very happy." They got into the shower together, and Kit spent a moment adjusting the temperature and the angle of the spray. Then she plastered herself up against Bailey's body and stood there in the warm water, kissing across her collarbones and shoulders.

"I've been worried you'd have some unpleasant delayed reaction to…last night. The last time I was in this position I had to spend the whole next day trying to convince Mimi that we never had to do it again."

"You're not going to get a repeat of that. I was actually hoping we'd get to do it right about now." She let her hands drift down to cup and squeeze Bailey's ass. "Got a problem with that?"

"Not even a little."

Kit gave her a questioning look. "I thought you said you had lots of sex at the beginning."

"We did. It was the reality of actually doing it that freaked her out at first. She got over her trepidations pretty quickly."

"I'm over mine already. See?" She bent and started to lick and mouth Bailey's breasts.

Bailey started to run her hands down Kit's back, pulling her in tightly. "I like your way a lot better."

Kit looked up, meeting Bailey's eyes. "I'm really, really happy we made love. And even happier that it was smooth sailing."

"Me too."

"Now we can just be normal adults, trying to get to know each other."

Bailey looked down on her as Kit closed her eyes and started kissing all over her body. It hadn't dawned on her that Kit looked at making love like an obstacle that would allow them to move on once they'd knocked it over. But that made sense, given the methodical way she approached things. Kit was no Mimi, that's for sure. Being with a mature, experienced adult was fantastic!

—⁓—

After their shower, Bailey put her own clothes back on. Kit had gone into the living room to find carryout menus, and as Bailey sat on the bed to put her shoes on, she noticed a framed diploma. She had no idea where Kit had gone to school. Strange. Standing, she focused on the name. Kathleen Eleanor Travis.

Heading out to the living room, Bailey caught Kit's eye. "A while ago I asked you if your name was short for anything. You said it wasn't. But your diploma…"

"Oh." She shrugged, chuckling a little. "I changed my name years and years ago. I forget."

Bailey sat down and looked at her speculatively. "Really? Why'd you change it?"

Kit shrugged again. "Just didn't like it. I'd always been called Kit, so it seemed silly to have another name I had to use for official things."

"So it's just Kit?"

"Yep. No middle. Short and sweet."

"Huh. I bet your parents weren't happy with that."

"No idea. Didn't tell 'em."

Bailey sat straight up, searching Kit's eyes. "What? You changed your name and didn't tell your family?"

"Why would I tell them?"

"Why wouldn't you?"

"I was named after my grandmothers, who are both very much alive. If they knew they'd be…hurt, I guess. Why ask for trouble when it's something that doesn't affect them in any way?"

Kit spread the menus out on the coffee table while Bailey looked at the back of her head. Kit acted as if it was perfectly normal to hide something significant from her family. But that wasn't normal. It just wasn't.

—m—

After devouring take-out Chinese food, Bailey moved around the apartment, gathering her things. "You said you have a busy week planned?"

"Super busy. The president and congress are locked in a death match over the budget—as usual. This will be the twelfth time I've covered the annual dustup over the damn thing, and it's getting a little old."

Bailey stared for a moment, confused. "It's January."

"It certainly is. It's months overdue, but they've jumped through all sorts of hoops to keep the government going on a swiftly fraying shoestring." She chuckled. "You really don't follow politics. It's all anyone's talking about."

"Not in my little corner of the world. I haven't heard a peep—and that's just how I like it. So…is there a deadline?"

"Saturday night or the world as we know it will end."

"Huh." Bailey smiled, feeling playful. "Let me know if that happens. I'm not sure how I want to spend my final hours, but I'll try to think of some options."

She slung her messenger bag over her shoulder and walked to the front door. Kit was right behind her, and she pulled her in for a long hug.

"I probably won't get to see you except for our squash match."

Bailey frowned and shook her head. "I'm not sure I can make it. I'm working on a big, secret project for an agency. If I had forty-eight hours in a day it wouldn't be enough."

"Okay. Text me on Wednesday if you can make it."

"That's it?" Bailey was thrown off stride by Kit's casual attitude. "You're cool if we don't see each other all week?"

Her pretty brown/greenish-gold eyes blinked a few times. "Uhm…sure. If you're busy, you're busy." Kit put her hands on Bailey's arms and gave her a long look. "Do you want me to be…different?"

"No, no, you're being really normal. I'm just used to having the first time I'm intimate with someone be a bigger deal." *Oh, damn, do you have to say exactly what's on your mind?*

Kit held her face in her hands and looked into her eyes for a long minute. "I had a great time. A really great time. But I've had a few more first times than you have. Maybe I'm not…" She looked down, clearly embarrassed.

"No, your reaction is perfectly normal. Mature. I'm kind of a rookie."

"I like that about you. I really do. There's nothing jaded about you, Bailey." She stood on her tiptoes and placed a gentle kiss on her lips. "As soon as you have the time, I really want to spend the night with you again." Her eyes clouded with concern. "Maybe I've gotten too used to focusing on work—"

Bailey stopped her explanation with a long kiss. "Don't change a thing. You've got yourself a date."

Chapter Ten

BAILEY WAS TOO BUSY too even consider knocking off early on Monday, but she had to talk to someone. She almost called her sister Kelly, but she couldn't reliably be counted on to keep a secret, and it was way too early to have the whole family find out, so she texted Natalie.

"Got a minute?"

It took several hours for Nat to reply. "Got more than that now. Dinner?"

Bailey stared at the message for a minute. Nat's girlfriend was also not the most discrete person in the world. If they made plans for dinner, it would have to be the three of them. Best to talk to Nat alone. She could easily keep a secret. Actually, she seemed to prefer them. "Can't do it. Phone?"

In seconds, her phone started to play its little tune. "Hi. Thanks for getting back to me."

"Sorry I couldn't do it until now. I was in a presentation that seemed like it went on forever. What's up?"

"Well…" She was suddenly tongue-tied. It felt a little juvenile to call your friend to tell her you'd had sex. But Nat would kill her if she held out. "My dry spell is over. I've had carnal relations with your favorite blogger."

"What?! Good for you! How'd it go?"

"Great. Better than great. No tears, no recriminations. I didn't even have to call student health to get her an emergency appointment with a therapist."

"You never forget a bad experience," Natalie joked. "One woman threatens to jump off a ledge and you think they all will." She paused for dramatic effect. "Of course, you've only had two previous experiences, so your sample size is limited."

"Tease all you want, but which one of us had fantastic sex until the wee hours of the morning?"

"That would be you. Jess and I don't go at it like we're starving anymore. So yes, I'm a little jealous."

"You should be. I can't imagine what this will be like once she knows her way around a woman. Whew!"

"Good for you." Natalie's voice changed, now sounding sincere and caring. "I'm really glad to see you getting some action. You're too cool to be alone when you don't want to be."

"I'm not cool and you know it. But I think Kit really likes me, and God knows I like her."

"Tread carefully, Be Kwiat. You know the drill, so I won't repeat it. But I worry about you."

"I've heard enough horror stories to know it's not the smartest thing in the world to be a woman's first. But sometimes you have to go with what comes."

"I assume you're fantastic in bed, so I'll ask about her. Did she figure out how to flip your switch?"

"My switch is very easy to flip, but yes, I think she could have figured it out even if it wasn't. It was really nice," she added, knowing she sounded like a love-struck teen. "She's dreamy."

—m—

The whole budget process was silly in a normal year, and lots sillier this time around. Weeks of saber-rattling, with each side claiming financial ruin was right around the corner; predictions of every form of calamity; and tons and tons of name-calling. But even though it was closer to political theater than actual negotiations, Kit had to get sources to comment on every bit of news, had to write her own analysis, and had to clip and post relevant comment from other venues. Sometimes she would have preferred to be chasing the "who's pregnant" or "who's dating whom" story for a true gossip site. But Kit had thrown her lot in with politics and that's where she'd stay.

By Wednesday she'd spent hours roaming the halls of Congress, had holed up in dark corners of out-of-the-way restaurants with sources, and had replied to so many e-mails and texts her fingers ached. Her staff had been working just as hard, but they didn't get to leave the office very often. Her job was definitely more glamorous, but meeting a relatively low-level congressional staffer in a greasy spoon diner wasn't all it was cracked up to be either.

It would have been nice to be able to drive when she had to traipse all over DC, but there was no place to park, not to mention the traffic and all of the limited-access streets. So she tried to stick to public transport or the bike share program, not always the easiest thing in the world—especially in the winter. Wednesday evening, she was just about to descend into the bowels of the Metro when her phone buzzed. Taking a quick look, she saw a text from Bailey—from an hour earlier.

"I got free. C U at gym."

"Shit!" she said aloud, but not one person turned to look at her. Washingtonians could be a very chill group.

Texting back, she wrote, "I'm SO sorry! Forgot it was Wed!" She stood there in the cold, waiting for a reply. When none came, she went to catch a train and checked again when she arrived at her station. Still nothing. Kit walked home, after stopping at a deli to pick up a pre-made sandwich. By the time she entered her office Bailey had replied.

"I ran on the treadmill. Same workout. Less attractive than you."

Smiling, she wrote back, "You're too nice to me." Her assistant stood in the doorway, looking like she was about to fall asleep.

"Senator Gregg's chief is on the phone. Pick up."

Kit's eyebrows hiked up. When Nia was curt, they were in trouble. "Got it." She picked up the receiver. "Matt. Talk to me."

"The senator is concerned that the president keeps implying that a small segment of our most productive citizens are being targeted for tax increases."

"Uh-huh." She devoted one half of her attention to his complaint. The other half went to Bailey's incoming question.

"Do you have time to talk?"

"Not now. Gonna be another late night."

"What have you heard?" The voice on the phone shook her awake.

"Nothing. I've heard nothing." That was the truth. She had no idea what he was asking.

"Call me when you can," Bailey wrote.

"Will do. If u need to talk, I'll call tonite. But it'll be late."

"No need. Just miss you."

Kit looked at the phone. A guy would never sleep with you the first time, then admit he missed you just a couple of days later. It was a little odd, but also endearing. "Me 2. Later."

"I can't give you anything if you don't share," the voice said. "We need to know what's still on the table."

Fuck. "Everything's on the table." She hoped they were talking about the same table. Madly, she scrambled through the piles of notes her staff had left throughout the day. This was a real fuck-fest. Which, in the scheme of things, meant absolutely nothing.

—∞—

Kit fell into bed at three a.m. On Sunday morning. In New York City. Where had the week gone? She set her alarm for seven, then called the front desk to ask for a wake-up for five after seven. Her hotel was on Sixth Avenue, in Midtown, and lights kept streaming across her room. They must have had something big going on at Rockefeller Center. Washington was bad, but it wasn't nearly as noisy or frantic as New York. How did people live here? Getting up, she closed the blackout drapes, then took the time to send Bailey a message. She wouldn't normally have done that at this time of the morning, but she knew Bailey turned her phone off when she went to sleep and wouldn't be interrupted.

"Gonna be on TV at nine. CNN. I'll be the one who hasn't slept and looks like hell." Then she plugged the phone in and tried to calm her mind enough to get at least a couple hours of rest. Good thing she was paid for her opinion, rather than her looks—'cause she was going to look like crap.

—∞—

Kit cruised out of the CNN studios at ten thirty, checked her phone and found, amid thirty-five other messages, one from Bailey. "You looked good, sounded better. I like knowing a celebrity!"

"You need to redefine celebrity if I'm one."

"You are! When are you coming home?"

"Now. Going to Penn Station for the noon train. Gonna go to bed and stay there for a week."

"Things that should be fun, but aren't. I bet you're beat."

"Beat hard. I'll call you when I've come back to life."

"Deal."

—∞—

Kit joined the scrum of people trying to maneuver to get to the front of the cab line at Union Station. Cabs weren't her thing, but every once in a while there wasn't a fare that would have been too high. Someone was standing uncomfortably close and she was just about to chew the guy out when she blinked, realizing it was Bailey.

"Share a cab?"

What the hell? She'd been pretty clear. Bed. Sleep. Call when I'm ready. "Uhm…okay. Were you…?" She looked around, like it would become clear why Bailey was there.

"I came down to meet you."

"Oh. That's…really nice." Be polite!

"I know you're tired." Bailey leaned over to speak quietly. "But I was finished for the day and wanted to catch up." A quick look of uncertainty covered her face. "Is this okay?"

Kit gripped her arm and squeezed it. "Of course. It's really nice of you."

She held up a soft-sided cooler. "I figured you haven't had many home-cooked meals this week, so I made you one. Cool?"

Kit let out a breath. Someone she cared for had gone well out of her way to be thoughtful. "Very cool."

—m—

Kit changed clothes, and by the time she went back to the living room Bailey had portioned out dinner and added glasses of wine. She handed Kit a big glass of ice water. "All set," she said, grinning so sweetly it caught Kit by surprise. She stood on her tiptoes and gave Bailey a long kiss.

"Thanks for all of this." She waved her hand over the spread.

They ate while Kit revealed how the budget had come down to the last minute—as expected. But it was done for the year. Thank God.

As soon as they finished, Bailey jumped up and started to clear the table. "Ready for bed?"

It was six thirty. Chuckling, Kit said, "Never been readier." She really hadn't been thinking of sex, or even intimacy. When she was tired she liked to be alone, to do precisely what she wanted, when she wanted. But if she was going to be in a relationship, she had to make adjustments. Being alone for four years had let her get set in her habits. Not good.

They went into the bedroom and Bailey quickly undressed her, then pulled back the covers. "In you go."

Looking up at her, Kit got in and waited. But instead of joining her, Bailey sat on the edge of the bed and bent to kiss her. "Call me when you've gotten some rest."

"What? You're not going to…" She raised an eyebrow.

Bailey laughed softly. "I can't imagine you want to have sex when you're exhausted. And I simply wanted to see you…not have you."

Suddenly, the thought of her leaving was very, very unappealing. "Aren't you tired?" She had to laugh at that. Three year olds stayed up later.

"Do you want me to stay? I will…"

Feeling a little vulnerable, Kit nodded. "I'd really like to sleep with you. It's been forever."

Grinning, Bailey stood and started to strip. Kit looked up at her, puzzled. "Long underwear? It's only about forty degrees."

"I know," she said, leaving the cream-colored silk top and pants on. "Twenty degrees lower than my threshold."

"You didn't have them on the other night."

Chuckling, Bailey said, "I wanted you to sleep with me, not laugh at me. I wouldn't have worn them tonight, but I didn't think I'd be called on to take off my pants."

"Get in here," Kit said, patting the bed. "You're adorable—in any kind of underwear."

Bailey got into bed and spooned up behind Kit. "You're lying, but I'll act like I believe you." She kissed the back of her neck, then her lips when Kit turned her head. "Go to sleep."

With a heavy sigh, Kit scooted back until Bailey was wedged up against her. For the first time in a week, she relaxed. Fully relaxed. Having someone care for you was damned nice, and damned rare.

—m—

When Kit woke in the middle of the night, Bailey was gone. But a note was lying on the pillow. Taking it with her to the bathroom, she blinked against the bright light to read it:

"Surprisingly, I couldn't get to sleep. Apparently I like to go to bed after seven. Call me when you want to get together."

Well, that was cool. It was a very good sign that Bailey didn't lie there, unable to sleep. Being with someone who watched out for herself was as attractive as someone who watched out for you. Bailey was shaping up to be a unique, and very cool girlfriend. Girlfriend. Kit had to laugh at that. She was a little old for a girlfriend. But "woman she was seeing" sounded lame. There had to be a good term. She'd have to ponder that—after sleeping for another day or two.

—⁊⁊—

By Tuesday, Kit felt almost like her old self again. She texted Bailey, announcing her return to civilization. A few minutes later, she got a reply.

"Wanna go on a little trip?"

She stared at the message for a moment. When she was just starting out at the *Globe* she'd spent six months following one of the presidential front-runners around the country, traveling in planes, buses, trains and cars. She'd been to nearly every state fair and rubber chicken gala in every hamlet large enough to shake out a handful of Democratic votes. After the election, the thought of going on a trip of any length had become anathema. Traveling to Boston to see her family was all she was willing to do. But her fingers automatically typed, "Sure. When and where?"

"PA. Friday afternoon."

Ooo. A nice bed and breakfast out in the country…or the mountains. She'd forgotten what Pennsylvania had. All of the states tended to look a little bit alike when you were hitting up two or three states in one day. But unstructured time with Bailey was the lure, and she bit. "I'm in."

"Cool! I think you'll like my family."

Oh, fuck! Kit had completely forgotten that Bailey was from Pennsylvania. It was way, way, way too early to meet the parents! But she couldn't back out now. Damn, dating a woman was so different from a guy it was a whole different endeavor. Guys were happy if you met their parents at the wedding. "I bet I will. Can I see you before then?"

"You can. Tonight?"

"Great. Come be dinner. I mean for dinner."

"Both, please. C U."

—⁊⁊—

They sat at the small table in the dining nook, polishing off the bottle of wine Bailey had brought.

"I've got to tell you again how nice it was of you to come pick me up from the train the other night." She'd thought about the gesture a dozen times, and now believed it was touchingly thoughtful, not overly clingy.

"Oh. Yeah. All part of my reclamation project."

Kit cocked her head. "A little more detail, please. That meant nothing."

Bailey stood, walked over to Kit and took her by the hand. They went together to the sofa and sat next to each other. Bailey put her arm around Kit's shoulders, a move she found she liked an awful lot.

"Here's how it is with me." Bailey's voice sounded both thoughtful and reflective. "I get lost in whatever I'm doing. When I'm involved in something—it can be anything, really—I forget the rest of the world."

"I can be like that too."

Bailey pulled her a little closer and kissed the top of her head. "I can be like that about organizing my sock drawer. It's…difficult. It took having Julie dump me to come up with a plan for how to change—as much as I can change, that is."

"So you go to Union Station on Sunday nights to ride home with people?"

"Yeah," she said, chuckling. She fished her phone from her pocket, and went to a screen. "I tried making reminders to do things at a set time. But that didn't work. So I created a program that reminds me twice a day to connect with someone. The reminder can appear any time between nine in the morning and nine at night. That way I don't expect it—and ignore it." She looked very pleased with herself, but Kit wasn't following very well.

"How did that make you come to the train?"

"Oh." She called up a screen, showing the previous Sunday. "I ignored the reminder that came in at ten in the morning. When I got another at four I thought of all of the people I might connect with. Your name was tops on the list, so I stopped what I was doing and started trying to figure out how to connect with you in the most efficient way possible."

"Amazing." Kit gave her what she knew was a puzzled look. "You have to be so precise."

"Oh, I'm precise. I'm waaaay past precise. I knew you'd be tired, and figured you'd probably refuse if I asked you to hang out. I thought the best thing would be to just show up and ride home with you. That'd give me what I needed and not force you to socialize more than the minimum." She smiled, looking very pleased. "I was glad you wanted to have dinner together. I kinda thought I'd just give you the cooler and take off."

"Bailey! I'd never tell you to get lost after you did something so nice."

Scowling, she shook her head. "You should. Don't let me push you around if you don't wanna be pushed. We'll do much, much better if you tell me what you want—even if it's not what I want."

"Mmm…that's not going to be easy for me. I like to make the people I care about happy."

"Then tell me to shove off if you're not in the mood to hang out. That's what'll make me happy."

Kit snuggled up closer, really liking the feel of Bailey's body. "We're going to have to work to get in sync. Do you honestly put this much thought into everything?"

"Uh-huh." She blinked those pretty blue eyes ingenuously. "I lost someone I loved because I ignored her needs. After we broke up, I talked to a lot of people and figured out that most everyone is kind of like Julie. I'm the outlier, so I needed to find a way to at least mimic the kinds of interactions most people want. It's not natural for me, but I'm trying my best."

"Damn, Bailey you don't seem withdrawn or reclusive to me. Is it really that difficult for you to be connected?"

"No, it's not that I don't want connection. I just get so focused that I forget about it."

"Hey, it was just last week that I forgot it was Wednesday. I've got the same problem."

"Not as bad. You were swamped with work. I can get involved in something totally inconsequential and spend ten hours with it. Then the day's over and I feel lonely…isolated." Her voice took on an earnest quality that made Kit sit up and pay attention. "I'm determined to make myself into a good partner. Give me any feedback you can think of. I'll incorporate it. I promise," she said, emphatically.

Kit took the phone from her and looked at the screen. "What's this list?"

"Those are my prime contacts. Family and friends I care the most about." She flicked her finger across the screen and another one appeared. "When I have a significant interaction with one of them, I check them off. Then the person I need to contact next comes up." She moved the phone so she could see the screen better. "My oldest sister's next up. Luckily, I can tick off every member of my family this weekend." Her face broke into a happy grin. "I'll be way ahead of the game after only a four-hour drive. Sweet!"

Kit watched her face as she spent a moment looking at the screen. You had to hand it to her. Being good with relationships was one thing. Working hard to figure out how to be good was a much more admirable quality.

—⁓—

After squash the next night, they were strolling down the street, looking for a place to eat. As they passed a card shop Bailey said, "Can I run in here for a minute? It's my grandmother's birthday next week and she really likes a physical card."

"A physical card? Like you'd rather send her an electronic one?"

"Don't see why not," Bailey said, looking puzzled. "Same sentiment. I love my grandmother but I really hate having to pick out cards. They never say what I want them to say."

Kit guided her into the store. "Buy a blank card and put whatever your little heart desires on it. Actually buy a dozen. Then you'll have a stash."

"Not a bad idea," Bailey said, her smile brightening. "I love figuring out ways to reduce the time I spend doing things I don't like."

Kit started whipping down the line of cards, quickly choosing a handful that no one would object to. She was concentrating, and it took a second for her to notice a fight brewing.

"I want a refund," a strident voice demanded.

"I understand that," a softer voice replied. "But you don't have a receipt or even a tag from the item."

"I don't need one! Your sign says you accept returns for two weeks."

The clerk cleared her throat. "That's true. But you have no proof you bought this in the last two weeks. They sell these bears all over town."

"Listen," the woman said crisply. "You're going to give me my money back, or you're going to wish you had."

Kit looked at Bailey, whose eyebrows had shot up over her glasses.

"I don't have authority to do that without a receipt. My manager is gone for the day…"

"Then get on the damned phone and have her come back here. Now!"

Bailey started to drift over to the cash register, with Kit watching her—unsure of what she was going to do—if anything. The clerk was no spring chicken, the customer probably in her early thirties. Very well dressed. Obviously on her way home after a long day of stealing candy from babies.

170

"I can't do that," the clerk said. "But I'll check with her tomorrow and see what we can do."

The woman leaned over and spoke like she would to a common criminal. "A mildly bright dog could do this job. Check that. An average dog has the brainpower to run that stupid scanner over a barcode. You obviously don't qualify for a decent job, or you wouldn't be here. So…if you don't want to lose this piece of shit job you'll…"

Suddenly, Bailey was right next to her. "You don't talk to people like that," she growled, looking taller, sturdier and much more imposing than normal. "You owe this woman an apology."

"Who the hell are you?" The woman looked like she wanted to bite Bailey and rip off a piece of her flesh.

"Just a person who can't stand bullies. You have no right to harass this woman for doing her job." She turned to the clerk and her expression smoothed into her usual, placid one. "How much is the bear?"

Hands shaking, the clerk looked at the tag on a fresh toy. "$14.95."

Bailey pulled out her wallet, removed two tens and put them on the counter. "There's your money. You can leave now."

"I don't want your damn money," she snarled. "This idiot's going to give me a refund, or she's going to be out on her sorry old ass."

Gazing at her, looking strangely calm, Bailey said, "You're an awful person. The people in your life might not have the nerve to tell you that, but you really are. You might want to change before you've got no one."

Kit had been too stunned to move, but she got her feet to follow instructions and came to stand next to Bailey. She wasn't sure what she was going to do, but she thought she'd better be close.

The woman reached down, snatched up Bailey's money and tore it into pieces. Then she threw them at her as she stormed out.

The store was silent for a moment, then Bailey started to laugh. "Best twenty bucks I've spent in years," she said, a hearty chuckle bubbling up like a spring. "God, I hate jerks."

They left the store after purchasing ten cards. The clerk had been very circumspect after the bully left. She seemed to regard them with a certain level of suspicion—understandable after seeing how much pleasure Bailey seemed to get from chewing out a perfect stranger. When they hit the sidewalk, Kit grasped Bailey's arm and leaned in close. "That was kinda crazy—but I'm really glad you did it. There's nothing I hate worse than watching self-entitled jerks lord it over people who have a limited ability to defend themselves."

Bailey was still chuckling over the encounter. "I've never done anything like that in my life. I would have wet my pants if she'd taken a swing at me." She laughed harder. "That would've been a sight. Me, shivering like a scared rabbit with that little jerk latched onto my leg."

"Nah. Jerks like that are all bark. I'm proud of you," Kit said, pulling Bailey down to kiss her cheek. "There would be fewer bullies if more people slapped them down."

"Right. But it's the slapping part I'm afraid of." She laughed again. "I'm a little bark with absolutely no bite."

—⁂—

When they could both make it, Kit and Asante liked to have taco night once a week. The day had been switched around a few times, but now they tried to make it Thursdays, which allowed them to watch their current favorite tacky reality show, "Baby Daddy Drama." Junk TV was only fun when consumed with others.

Kit stopped for some Mexican beer on the way to Asante's apartment, and she sniffed appreciatively when she entered. "I smell frijoles."

"Right you are." He kissed her and took the six-pack. "Ready for a beer?"

"I was ready at two."

She shrugged out of her coat and followed him into the kitchen. Asante opened a pair of beers and handed her one. "Salud," he said, clinking their bottles together.

Kit took a long drink. "Ahh." She let out a sigh. "That's good. Slept with Bailey."

Asante nearly dropped his beer. "What? Shut up!"

"I did," she insisted, then took another drink. "My girl virginity is gone."

"Last night? After you played squash?"

Chuckling, she nodded, "Yes, but that was the third time. The first was last Saturday."

He slapped her on the shoulder. "Like five days ago?"

"Nope. The Saturday before that."

"Twelve days ago? And you're just telling me now?"

"The week got away from me. I can't even put into words how busy I was the night we did it. It was right during the budget clusterfuck, but I took the whole night off. My libido won out over my job."

Dashing over to the stove, he tended various saucepans for a moment. "You'd better start talking. I want to know everything. I have to make sure you did it right."

"Like you'd be able to judge. I now have significantly more experience than you do with women."

"It's gonna stay that way." He walked back over and put his arm around her. "Seriously. How do you feel about it?"

Kit looked up into his warm brown eyes. "Good. I feel good. She's very cool, and now that we know we like having sex together…it's onto relationshipville."

"That's it? That's all I get?"

Laughing at his outrage, Kit said, "What more do you want? I've slept with guys—the sex you're into—and you barely asked for names."

"This is different!" Now he put a hand on each of her shoulders and looked at her carefully. "Isn't it?"

Kit took another drink and walked over to peek into the pans on the range. "Ooo, this looks good." Turning, she regarded him for a moment. "It doesn't feel very different. She's smart, interesting, thoughtful, cute, and I'm really attracted to her. And best of all—no ex-wives or lovers she's in constant contact with. And she wanted kids, but changed her mind. So far, she's the person of my dreams."

"Kit." He gave her that puzzled, concerned look again. "She's a woman. Doesn't that say a little something about you?"

"Mmm…I have good taste?" Laughing at his frown, she said, "It's not a big deal. Consenting adults…both in our right minds…why does there need to be a bright line test? Be on one side and you're straight. Sample from the other side and you're gay. That's a false dichotomy."

He looked charmingly puzzled as he scratched at his head. "It's a true dichotomy for me. If we live to be two hundred, I will never confess to having slept with a woman."

"I don't know. If you could find one like Bailey…tall, boyish…"

"Dickless." He gave her a hug, then went over to the range. "I hate to be shallow, but a vagina is not interchangeable with a cock. I'm very fond of one, have no interest in the other."

"That's what I said a few short weeks ago. Apparently, I'm more flexible than I thought."

Asante had to focus to finish the meal. Kit had learned the whole thing could be ruined if she talked during critical points. Once their plates were filled, they went into the living room to watch the junk he'd recorded for consumption.

Kit took a bite and moaned with pleasure. "You must have a little Latino in your background. You do this too well."

"I hope I don't, since an error in my sister's genealogical work would make her lose her mind. Maybe I'm just gifted." He took a bite and nodded. "Pretty damn good." They always sat close to one another, and he was able to lean to one side and rest his chin on her shoulder. "Sure you don't wanna spill some juicy details?"

Kit took advantage of his exposed flank. He was remarkably ticklish. Asante hurled himself upright, slapping at her hand. "A simple no would suffice."

"I love it when you sound like the Dowager Queen." Kit leaned over and spoke quietly. "I'll tell you something really important." She sat up again. "I've forgotten about my significant birthday."

"You have? Really?"

"Yep. Going out with someone younger has made me feel younger." She smirked. "I guess that's why guys go for teenagers."

"How old is she?"

Scrunching up her nose, Kit had to admit the truth. "I'm not sure. Thirty-two, thirty-three? Something like that."

"You don't know for sure? What kind of reporter are you?"

"One that gets distracted every time she's near me. I've spent every minute we have together trying to get to know the real her, skipping the little details that don't matter much. I'm *sure* she's old enough to consent to have sex, my current preoccupation." She grinned, leaning over until her face was right in front of his. He started to laugh, then pushed her back into an upright position.

"I'm really glad you're feeling optimistic. You were going to a dark place there for a while."

"How could I not? Most of the guys I'd been dating had adult children. Gene, the guy I saw last year, had a grandson in high school. I started to get into that mind-frame. Like the end was a lot closer than the beginning." As she thought of Bailey, she could feel her whole affect lift. "Bailey's not just younger, her interests are closer to a college student's than a retiree's. She makes me feel like a kid again. And that's much, much more compelling than her gender."

"But it's gotta be different. Come on. I can't even imagine what I'd do with a woman."

She laughed at him, charmed by his earnest expression. "I think you could figure it out." He was still staring at her avidly, so she added, "Yes, of course it's different. The energy, or maybe the force isn't the same at all. With a guy, there's usually a point where you're really rocking—"

"My favorite point," he interrupted, grinning unrepentant.

"I assume women can do that too, but we haven't. It's more tender than wild. And it lasts much, much longer." Her smile grew. "My favorite part."

"I think you'll miss the rocking part. God knows I would."

"Mmm." She thought about that for a minute. "I don't think so. Don't get me wrong, we didn't just hold hands and cuddle. There were definite peaks of energy. The peaks were a little lower than I'm used to, but there were a lot more of them." He was still giving her a vaguely puzzled look.

"Okay. Let's say you're banging."

"Wish I were…"

She talked right over him. "And the guy's really giving it to you good."

"Got it. But I have to flip it around. I'm giving it to a guy really good."

Kit smirked at his inability to even imagine being passive. "When you start to build up to the big finish, you're both putting out a lot of energy. It gets almost frantic, right?"

"If you're doing it right, yes."

"Exactly. Now I assume you're so good at it that you and your partner climax at the same second, with angels playing their harps, but that doesn't happen for most mortals."

"So I've heard," he teased.

"So…the guy's whipped you into this heated state—"

"I've whipped the guy into a heated state…"

She slapped at him playfully. "I've only been in the passive position. Humor me. So he's really got you going, but he finishes first. The guys I've been with need to rest before they try to repay the favor. But I've lost a lot of steam while he's resting. I mean, I'm used to it, but it's not ideal."

175

"So I rest for a few seconds, fight through the overwhelming desire to fall asleep, then rally to finish him off. If I did it right, he's close, and I focus on making him feel good."

"Right! But when it's two women, you're both putting all of your energy into making the other person feel good—all of the time. Single focus. It just shifts back and forth."

"So…it's better than with a guy?" He looked more than a little suspicious.

"It's different. Very different."

"Different…better?" He was dogged when he was really interested.

"That's a tough one." She thought for a minute. "It was definitely better than anything I've done since Henry. Many times better. But I loved Henry, and that changes things. When you love someone, sex is so much more than physical."

"But from a purely physical standpoint? How does it compare?"

She gave him a sly smile. "When the person you're with has the same buttons —they really know how to press them."

Chapter Eleven

IT HAD ONLY BEEN six weeks since she'd seen her family, but now that she was back east Bailey found she felt better, more connected, if she visited frequently. She normally stayed at her parents' house, but she thought Kit would be more comfortable if they stayed at a hotel. Somehow she couldn't picture Kit digging bunking in single beds in Bailey's former bedroom.

Kit thought she'd be able to skip out of town with no problem, but she was on her phone until they hit a dead-zone in the hills outside Wilkes-Barre. "Nia? Are you there?" She dropped the phone onto her lap and let out a sigh. "I'm so sorry for that. The president named Robert Foxton to head up the EPA."

Bailey turned to give her a puzzled look. "If I should know who that is…"

"Sorry." Kit patted her leg. "I forget you're not obsessed with this junk. He used to work for a law firm that had a lot of big chemical companies as clients. People are losing their shit over it."

"We'll have Internet access. I made sure of it. You can Skype if your phone isn't working."

Kit picked up her phone and looked at it for a minute. "Screw it. The world won't end if I don't post fifty things about the guy."

"We're almost there. You can check in and make sure." She took Kit's hand and brought it to her lips for a kiss. "I'd hate to have the world end before I get to have my mother's sernik."

"I'll try to figure out what that is, but I need a little clue. Anything."

Bailey snuck a quick look. She loved to see the intelligence sparkling in Kit's eyes. Clever women were the best. "Cheesecake. My mom doesn't cook Polish food all of the time, of course, but there are a few things I love and she always whips up at least one of them for me."

They reached their exit, and Bailey followed the signs to the hotel. She was surprised when a kid ran out to valet park the car. "Fancy for Wilkes-Barre."

Once inside, a business-like young guy smiled at her. "Good afternoon, sir."

Bailey didn't comment or correct the guy. Her speaking voice wasn't as high as your average woman's, but it still labeled her as a woman if the listener was paying the slightest bit of attention. "I've got a reservation." She took her wallet from her back pocket, removed her credit card and slid it across the counter.

The kid clearly picked up on his error, as he hesitated a long time, like he was trying to decide if he should apologize or not. He chose not to, but his cheeks turned pink and he snuck a quick glance a couple of times, probably trying to make sure he'd been wrong. "Okay," he said after typing for a few seconds. "I have a superior room for you Ms. Jones. It's on the concierge floor. Two double beds. It's very, very nice."

"I'm sure it'll be great. But I asked for a king bed."

He looked from his screen to her face, frowned, then typed a little more. "I don't have that marked here…"

"I definitely requested a king. It doesn't have to be on the concierge floor, if that's the problem."

"No, it's no problem." He stole a glance at Kit, who had quietly slid across the big lobby and was now lurking near a display of local advertising. "I just assumed you'd want two beds."

Some combination of his words and his obvious confusion hit her and she started to laugh. "Don't get a lot of lesbians around here, do you?"

"No, we really don't," he said, now bright pink. "I'm sorry…we just don't."

"It's not a big deal," she insisted, taking pity when she saw how embarrassed he was. "I'm not an average looking woman. Lots of people get confused."

"I'm really sorry. I was…I just wasn't paying attention." He handed her the key. "I apologize again. I just didn't…" His shoulders rose and fell. "I'm sorry."

She gave him the most reassuring smile she had in her arsenal. "It's fine. Really. I'm used to it."

Another young guy came over with their bags. "Right this way, sir. I'll show you to your room."

Out of the corner of her eye, she saw the desk clerk giving him the "kill" sign. But the bellman didn't get it. He leaned over the counter while the desk clerk whispered to him. When he stood up again, he cleared his throat. "Follow me, ma'am."

Bailey started to follow him after spying Kit near the elevator. They went up together, with the kid prattling on about all of the amenities. He opened the door, paused in the doorway for a moment, then met Bailey's eyes. "This is a king room. Is that what you wanted?"

"Perfect. Thanks for checking."

"No problem. We want to make sure you're happy." When he put the bags down he gave Kit a quick look, then did a double-take and let his eyes linger on her for a few moments. In a flash Kit disappeared, the click of the bathroom door the only sign she'd even been there.

Bailey tipped the bellman, then called out, "All clear." The door opened and Kit brushed by her, picked up her bag and put it on the bed. "Great. I get recognized by the second person I see in Pennsylvania."

"Recognized...?"

"The guy who brought our bags up ID'd me."

"Did he say something...?"

Kit stared at her for a second. "No. You would have heard him if he had. I saw it in his eyes."

"Maybe he just thought you were pretty." Bailey was feeling a little out of her element. Kit seemed...angry.

"Right." She unzipped her bag, yanking on the tab so hard she could have pulled it off. "Was it necessary to have a whole thing about the room?"

"Necessary?" Bailey stood there for a second, trying to replay the conversation. "With the kid?" She pointed at the door.

"The guy at the front desk." Kit pulled her clothes from her bag and hung them up in the closet. "I can't understand why you'd want to tell a complete stranger that we sleep together."

Walking over to her, Bailey put a hand on her shoulder and waited for Kit to look at her. "You mean something personal about you."

"Yes!" She turned and went back to her bag, taking her toiletries and moving them to the bathroom. "I've had sex with a woman three times. That's a little premature for me to claim an identity and broadcast it to Eastern Pennsylvania."

Bailey went to the bed and sat down, needing a minute to let that settle. Things fell into place quite quickly. "You don't want to be here, do you?" Kit didn't reply. "You aren't ready to meet my family."

"Damn it, I feel like we're about to hit the finish line, and I'm barely out of the starting blocks."

She looked so upset; Bailey's stomach was in knots in seconds. How did this get so screwed up? "Okay. Okay. Let's get this all out." Kit stared at her, clearly unhappy. "I wanted to come visit. I thought it would be fun to have you along for the drive. I also thought it'd be good for you to get away for a couple of days and chill. That's it. That's my agenda." She stood and took Kit's cold hand. "If you want to just hang out here and use your laptop to talk to people in your office it's totally fine with me."

The look Kit gave her was filled with suspicion.

"I think you'll like my family, but if you don't want to meet them—no big deal." A thought occurred to her and she went with it. "Check that. We don't even have to stay. I can make an excuse, and we can take off." She paused for a moment. "Now it's your turn. Tell me anything. *Anything*."

Kit rolled her eyes. "That's not easy for me to do."

"I'm sorry if it's hard. But I'm not great at guessing what's bothering you. Just tell me and it'll be over."

"But I'll hurt your feelings." Her frosty demeanor crumbled. Now it looked like she'd cry.

"No, you won't." She put her arms around Kit, who was now a little more malleable. "Unless you tell me you're sick of me and don't want to see me anymore. That'll hurt."

"No, that's not it at all." She took in a big breath. "I'm worried about meeting your family. It seems really, really soon for that."

Bailey sat down and pulled Kit onto her lap. They were just about nose-to-nose when they sat that way. "Why didn't you say that when I asked you?"

"We were texting…" She bit her lip, clearly anxious. "It wasn't until I agreed that you said we were coming here. I thought we were going to the Poconos for a romantic weekend or something."

"We can do that tomorrow," Bailey said, smiling. "We can go find one of those heart-shaped beds and in-room spa tubs."

"You're not mad?"

"Of course not. But I want you to listen to me carefully. You need to try to be frank. Err on the side of hurting my feelings."

"That's really going to be hard. I hate to hurt anyone's feelings. Especially yours."

"It's all a matter of timing. If you'd said you thought it was premature to come, I would have had a few seconds of disappointment. But you hid that from me and now my stomach hurts. I'd much rather have heard the truth a few days ago."

Kit burrowed her head into Bailey's neck and shoulder. "I'm sorry I screwed up. But even if we'd been together for ten years I wouldn't want you to tell a desk clerk that we sleep together. That's way too much information for a stranger."

Bailey looked into her eyes. She was clearly troubled. Probably still angry. "Wanna unwind that thread? Sounds like you might be having a delayed reaction to having sex with me."

Sitting up straight, Kit shook her head forcefully. "No way. I'm comfortable having sex with you. Really comfortable. But I'm also private. Really private. I'm not prudish, but I don't like to talk about intimate things with people I'm not intimate with. I don't think I'll change."

"I don't think I did anything overt, Kit. I just asked for the kind of bed I wanted."

Kit gave her a look that questioned her sanity.

"Okay. That was dumb. When I insist on one big bed, I'm making it clear that we sleep together." She took in a breath, her gut still twisted with anxiety. "I'm sorry. Really, I am. I'm…not used to this…"

"I'm not either, Bailey. I need some room here."

"Okay. Uhm…how do I get a big bed? I really prefer one."

Kit gazed into her eyes for a few moments, then said, "Get whatever bed you want. But get it for yourself. I'll wait in the car. You can call me and tell me the room number."

Bailey let that settle for a moment. "Really? Just getting a room together is too much?"

Kit looked like she wanted to head back into the bathroom. But she slowly nodded her head. "Yeah. At this point, it's too much."

"Would it have been okay if I'd taken the two smaller beds?"

"If that's easier…" She frowned, clearly still miffed. "How can I make this clearer? I don't want strangers to know we sleep together. I think that's a pretty simple request."

Bailey took in a long breath. "Okay. I'll try to reveal the minimum." She kissed Kit's cheek and added, "But I won't hide. Not ever. I've never been in the closet. That's just not going to happen."

"There's a difference between being in the closet and telling people we sleep together. Fair?"

"Fair enough." This topic wasn't closed. It would come up again. But Bailey knew better than to try to work out every issue preemptively. She also knew

181

better than to tell Kit she'd specifically told the kid she was a lesbian. "I'm going to head over to my parents'. What do I tell them? Are we staying or going?"

Kit jumped to her feet. "Let's go get some cheesecake." She stopped and put her hand on Bailey's chest, then spent a moment looking into her eyes. "I want to meet your family. But I'm not ready for the 'this is my girlfriend' talk. Is that okay?"

"Perfectly. They'll ask, but I tend to parse out information slowly. I think we're good."

—⁓—

When they got into the car Bailey said, "My parents live about twenty minutes from here. I'll take you by the mine my mom's father worked in—until black lung killed him. Maybe I should run a guided tour of good places to suffer an early death. We've got more than our share around here."

"I'd pay to listen to you talk for an hour or two. Even about something gruesome." She'd been mulling over the interaction with the desk clerk and was finally ready to talk about it. "Back at the hotel…"

"Yeah?"

Bailey's brow shot up, like she was waiting for Kit to bust her chops again. "I was…surprised that the guy at the desk didn't know you were a woman."

After taking a hand off the wheel, Bailey tugged at the knot in her tie. "Dress like a guy…people think you are one."

"But…" She wasn't sure how to frame her point in a sensitive manner. "You've got a very feminine face. And your voice isn't like a guy's at all. I mean, I could understand it if someone came up behind you…"

"Could you?" Bailey gave her a curious look. "How?"

"Mmm…expectations. You're as tall as a guy, you have lovely, broad shoulders, and you stand…" She shrugged. "Like a guy. Women, especially straight women, often stand with their weight on one foot, or they shift from foot to foot. You always have your feet about shoulder-width apart with your weight evenly distributed. You look like you mean business," she added, smiling wider when Bailey gave her a charming grin.

"I do."

"And, even though your hair is long, you put it back like guys with long hair do."

"Making it look like crap."

"No, no, that's not true. But you look like you want it out of your way. Very utilitarian."

"That's exactly how I feel about it. I want it long, but I don't want to bother with it."

"Right. So from the back I get it. From the front—I don't."

Bailey took her eyes from the road for just a second. She was as careful about her driving as she was about the way she dressed. "It's the same. My height, my affect, being flat-chested… They all add up. Then people go with that impression. Hearing my voice or seeing that my face is pretty feminine often isn't enough to alter their perceptions."

"So this happens often?"

"Yep. More now than in California."

"And you're okay with it?"

"Perfectly," Bailey said, her confident smile all the testament Kit needed.

—m—

Bailey's sister Kelly and her two kids were at the house, along with Bailey's mom. Kit had very good radar for knowing how well someone knew her work. Zack, the younger child, knew it well. Very well. Kit hadn't expected many people outside the Beltway, especially a kid, to have any idea who she was. Maybe she was more famous than she thought. She was definitely more famous than she wanted to be. Felicia, Bailey's mom, didn't seem to have any idea who Kit was. Much nicer.

They were all in the kitchen, jammed around a round table, with Bailey eating cheesecake like she was being paid by the ounce. April, a bored eighth grader, wandered away, but Zack started to pepper Kit with questions. "Have you been to the White House?" he asked, his eyes bright.

She smiled at him. He was in sixth grade, old enough to understand the system, but young enough to not recognize what a mess it was. "Yeah, I have." Her glance slid to Bailey who had a "Don't tell the kid we went on a tour!" look on her face. "I got invited to the big press Christmas party they have. It was funny; hard-boiled reporters all lining up like kids to get a photo with the president and first lady."

"You went this year?" Bailey asked, looking up from her cheesecake.

"Yeah. Didn't I mention it?"

"Nope."

Kit shrugged. "Must've been that week you were practically living in Virginia." She looked at Zack again. "I've been to the White House quite a few times. Actually, I've been to a state dinner. But this was my first time going to the party for the press."

"But you've been a reporter for years…" Bailey nodded, then said, "You were anonymous before, so they wouldn't have known to invite you."

"Right. And believe me, I would have gladly skipped going to the White House in exchange for my anonymity."

"I'd do anything to get to see the White House." Zack's eyes glazed over. "Or the Capitol."

Kit thought she could fairly easily get him in for a good tour, but she thought she'd better hold off on offering. His parents might not want to drag him all the way to Washington. "It's nice. Every once in a while the First Lady shows up and surprises the heck out of the people on the tour."

While Kit was speaking, Zack pulled out his phone and aimed it at her. "I'm gonna post this to my timeline. Nobody will believe you're my aunt's girlfriend!" The flash fired, and Kit was sure she looked like she was about to be the victim of a mugging.

Bailey quickly snatched the phone away, went to the picture and deleted it. "Not for publication. And Kit's not my girlfriend." She spared a sweet smile that went right to Kit's heart. "She's not even a lesbian."

Kelly gave the kid a light slap on the shoulder. "Ask people before you take their picture."

"Sorry." His gaze slid to the floor, fair cheeks coloring. He looked a little like Bailey with his pale skin and innocent expression. But he hadn't gotten the "dress like you're going to a polo match" gene that Bailey clearly had. A big T-shirt and baggy jeans would never grace his aunt's body.

Shit. He was just a kid. How many people could he know? Kit got up and went over to Zack. Squatting down by him, she said to Bailey, "Take one of us together. Don't you believe in freedom of the press?"

The smile Bailey gave her was truly precious. "Firmly."

—⁓—

Near dinnertime Lisa arrived, after having stopped to pick up Grandma. Then Kelly's husband, Mick arrived and it dawned on Bailey that Zack must have gotten his interest in politics from his dad. Zack and Mick cornered Kit to grill her about the state of the government while Bailey used the built-in distractions to make sure she had a few minutes alone with her mom. Her natural inclination was to observe, to let the rest of the family share the spotlight. If Bailey didn't get her alone at some point she could go the whole weekend with barely a peep.

Her mom was a clean freak, and after doing all of the prep for dinner, she had to take the kitchen towels out to the garage to wash them. Just as she'd done when she was barely old enough to get up there, Bailey jumped onto the dryer, and kicked her legs out in front of herself, quietly thumping her heels against the steel.

"So...? Kit's making quite an impression. But if Zack doesn't give her a moment alone she won't want to come back." Felicia chuckled to herself. "Have you known each other long?"

"A while. October, I think. She's nice, huh?"

"Yes. Very." Felicia loaded the washer and put a smidgen of detergent in. "You don't need as much soap as they tell you. You remember that, right?"

"I do, Mom."

"How did you girls meet?"

"At a dinner. For the group I've been volunteering for."

Felicia paused, then looked at Bailey sharply. "That's a gay group."

Bailey nodded. "It is. Kit was just there with a friend who was getting an award."

"Oh." Her hopeful expression fell. "The way you treat each other I was sure something else was going on." She moved to stand in front of Bailey, then put her hands on her shoulders. "I see the look on your face when she talks. It's not a good idea to spend your time hoping to get something from a woman who can't give it to you, kochana."

Bailey leaned forward and kissed her mother on the cheek. "You sound more like great-gramma every day."

Felicia smiled. "She called all of us kochana. I guess it comes back every once in a while. I don't think about it. It just comes out."

"I like it. It reminds me of her." She slid off the dryer and put her arm around her mother. "Kit's not a lesbian. She's very clear about that." Leaning over, Bailey said quietly, "But you don't have to be a lesbian to date one."

Felicia turned and stared at her, open-mouthed. "You don't?"

"Apparently not." She giggled at the stunned expression her mother wore. "I hope you like her, because I'm going to try my best to keep her around."

—m—

There was a flurry of activity in the small kitchen when dinner was close to ready. Just to stay out of the way, Kit moved to the short hallway that led to the bedrooms. Bailey was next to her in seconds. "I like that you're very attentive," Kit said. She almost kissed her, but realized that wasn't the best way to convince the clan she wasn't gay. "Show me your lair."

"It's not a lair. It's a shrine." Bailey chuckled as she led the way. The house was a tiny little space: an eat-in kitchen, a living room containing only a sofa and an easy chair, and a den that had obviously been added on. Kit wasn't sure where they would all sit to eat. She'd only seen six chairs jammed around the table.

They walked down the hallway, with Bailey pausing in front of a tiny bedroom. "This was Lisa's. She had her own room—always. Maybe that's why she never married. She hates to share." She chuckled at her joke, then moved on to the next room. It couldn't have been more than ten by twelve, and was filled to the gills with two beds, two night tables and a desk wedged into the one spare corner. "I was on the right. Kelly on the left. When she went to college I assumed I could move her bed to the garage so I could have a little space. My mother acted like I'd tried to cross her name out of the family bible." She laughed, shaking her head. "All these years later, the place is still ready for either of us to move back in."

"That's so cute," Kit murmured, brushing her lips across Bailey's cheek. "She misses you."

"More like she's worried we'll go bust and have to come home. You'd think she grew up during a famine or the depression."

Kit pushed the door closed and wrapped her arms around Bailey's neck. They looked into each other's eyes for a few moments, then Kit pulled her close and kissed her. "I like you even better after meeting your family. They're so normal."

"They kind of are. Just regular working-class Joes."

Kit moved over to a shelf above Bailey's bed. "What's that?" She pointed at a wooden box with a cord coiled on top of it.

"My first homemade computer." She looked adorably proud of herself. "I'd advise every computer nerd to build one while he or she was still in grade school. When you know the nuts and bolts things make more sense."

Kit stared at her, stunned. "How did you ever...?"

"It wasn't all that hard. When I had it mostly finished, my dad and I worked together to build that nice little enclosure. He doesn't know a thing about computers, but he wanted to help."

Unable to resist, Kit hugged her again, holding on tight. "I'm so glad you got this family." She looked up into her bright, clear eyes. "Really, really glad." Kit let her go, but right before they exited a photo caught her eye. It was of a very young Bailey in her high school uniform, tie knotted perfectly, looking like she knew just how cute she was.

Bailey saw her looking. "I still remember the day I spent in front of the mirror, trying to teach myself how to tie it just right. I couldn't have been happier."

Kit didn't say a thing. She couldn't have. The knot in her throat kept her from speaking.

—⁓—

Back in the car after dinner, Kit said, "I had a very fine time, Bailey Elizabeth. Am I the first person to comment that your mom looks a lot like Martha Stewart? It was kinda weird at one point. I kept waiting for her to say, 'It's a good thing,' but no dice."

"Hmm. I guess she does—a little. Martha's Polish too, you know."

"Stewart is a Polish name?"

"No, I forget her maiden name, but it's Polish. Maybe we all look alike. The sernik was good, wasn't it?"

"Really good. What kind of cheese was in it?"

She showed a shy smile. "Twaróg. It's tough to find, but there are a couple of small dairies that make it. Before I visit a couple of pounds miraculously gets overnighted to my parents. Weird, huh?"

"Very weird." Kit leaned across the car and kissed her cheek. "How Polish are you, anyway? Were your parents born here?"

"Yeah, of course. So were my grandparents. But my mom's grandparents were from Poland, along with some of my dad's great-grandparents. I've got Polish blood on both sides, but it's very thick on my mom's. My dad has a little variety thrown in. Really exotic stuff." She chuckled softly. "Lithuanian and Slovakian."

"So it's been three generations and you still eat Polish food? That's kinda cool."

"Oh! My great-grandmother's only been dead for a couple of years, and she lived in Poland until she was almost an adult. She's the one who taught her grand-daughters to cook." Looking a little wistful, she added, "She was my favorite."

"I think you're the favorite."

"No, no, that's not true. My parents love us all equally." She turned and gave Kit such a shy smile that she had to stop herself from pinching her cheek. "But I'll admit I gave them a heck of a lot less trouble than my sisters did."

Kit gave her a playful slap on the shoulder. "I can't see you giving them any trouble at all…playing games while you waited for lesbians to show up."

"I was a pretty good kid. Kelly gave them a little trouble, but not as much as Lisa. She was a hell-raiser in high school. Always in trouble, arrested a couple of times. Lots of drama."

"One more reason not to have kids."

"Yeah. Really. So when Kelly got caught smoking grass they only freaked out a little. Three years later nobody blinked when I told them I was in love with Mimi. Timing is everything."

"I can see why you like to visit. There doesn't seem to be much drama now. Everyone gets along."

Bailey nodded. "Yeah. We have our stuff, like everyone does. Lisa still likes to bust our chops and Kelly sometimes acts like the forgotten middle child, but we all care for one another. Oh. Sorry about that little thing with Zack. I knew he was into politics, but I didn't guess he'd know you. His focus is usually on making sure I have every gay right possible." She shot Kit a suspicious look. "Are you a lot more famous than I think you are?"

Laughing, Kit said, "I'm famous for DC. My star power went up when I lost my anonymity. I got a lot of press then. A lot."

"But you have to be a real newshound to read your work, right?"

"Definitely. My newsletter's big in Washington, but the blog has more regular people who read it. When I got that burst of publicity, it started to get a lot more hits. Then, when I got some gigs on TV, I shot up to a different level."

"How about in Boston? Do people know you there?"

"A bit. Seems like people know me more for being with Henry. When I'm there, I only get a few people who give me a second glance when I'm out walking around."

"I gave you a second glance, and I had no idea who you were." A sexy smile played on her lovely lips.

Who knew that visiting your girlfriend's parents would make you horny?

—⁂—

When they got back to their room, Kit started to get undressed. "I know I sound like I can't get off the topic, but it was really nice to be with your family. Most of the gay people I know would kill to have parents as accepting as yours are."

Bailey kicked off her shoes and lay on the bed, hands laced behind her head. "I love my parents. More than that, I know how lucky I am to have them." She lifted her head, staring at Kit for a second. "But they're not PFLAG icons or anything. The first time my mother saw a picture of me in a suit she flipped the fuck out."

"Aww…" Kit thumped down on the bed next to Bailey. "Why'd you have to tell me that? Couldn't I have my fantasy of parents who only cared that their child was happy?"

"You can have it," Bailey soothed. "But I'd bet most people fall short of the ideal. Granted, if my parents told me they'd joined a swingers group, I'd faint. Still, my mom struggles with it a little and my dad doesn't say a word. Not. A. Word."

"My poor little babushka."

Bailey's brows hiked up. "Babushka?"

"Isn't that a Polish word?"

Her head shook. "Russian. And why would you call me a headscarf?"

"It just sounded like a term of endearment. Work with me here." She leaned over and kissed her. "Did your boyish clothes catch your family unawares? Or was clothing always an issue?"

"Always." Her eyes closed briefly. "Every Sunday was a fight. The only good thing about wearing uniforms to school was that there were no options. I hated the skirt, but there was no wiggle room. Not true on Sunday. My mom and my grandmothers all thought it was sacrilegious to wear slacks to church." A small smile curled the corners of her mouth. "Only my great grandmother was on my side. 'Let her go,' she'd say. 'She's a good girl. Stop picking! You'll make her bad.'"

"Kinda funny."

"Yeah, she kept us all laughing. I really miss her."

189

"I'm glad she was on your side. Kids need that."

"Who'd you have?" Bailey's eyes were bright with interest.

"Mmm…I learned that you have to stand up for yourself."

Bailey ran a hand up and down her arm, making the skin pebble. "Nobody?" Her voice was so full of sympathy Kit almost cried for her young self.

"Not really. But, like I say, it's hard to complain when you have a lovely house, nice cars, prep schools. All of the benefits of WASPdom."

"None of that matters as much as being loved." Bailey took her in her arms and cuddled up against her back. Kit had taken off her sweater, leaving lots of exposed skin for Bailey to kiss.

"You can love me all you want," she purred. "Hotel rooms make me horny."

"Hold on right there, buddy. I've got something in my suitcase you're gonna like." She slithered out of bed, then quickly got undressed. Going to her suitcase, she pulled out a couple of big candles and set them on the bedside table. "Atmosphere." She popped her eyebrows up and down.

"Candles. Nice." Kit got up and finished undressing, then jumped back into the chilly bed.

"You sound disappointed. Don't you like candles?"

"Sure. Of course I do." She almost chickened out, but Bailey claimed she craved honesty. "Uhm, when you went to your suitcase, I thought you might have something sexy in there."

"Candles are sexy."

Good lord, was she being intentionally obtuse? "Sexier than candles." Bailey was giving her a narrow-eyed gaze. "Given that you like to be boyish, I thought you'd like to…" She looked pointedly at her crotch.

"Oh!" Brow furrowed, she nodded slowly. "I guess I can see where you'd think that. I don't need sex toys, but if you do…"

"No, I've never used them. I just thought—I assumed…"

Bailey sat up and leaned on her forearm. "Kit, you've gotta tell me what you want. If you've got some fantasy or some need, just let me know. If you're used to something bigger than fingers…"

"What?" She held a hand up. "No, no, not at all. Actually, I'm on the narrow side. I'm much, much happier with your talented fingers than…those other things." She giggled. "I actually stopped seeing a guy because his…" She thought better of being blunt and finished with, "Small is beautiful."

"Hmm." Bailey's expression hadn't changed. She still looked suspicious.

"I swear, I don't miss penises." Bailey continued to give her a narrow-eyed stare. Kit hadn't brought up an incident because it was slightly embarrassing, but it was time to whip it out now. "Little secret. The first time you were coming over for sex, I checked to make sure I had condoms. Then it dawned on me that I didn't have to think about birth control. I can't tell you what a relief that was!"

Now Bailey sat up, cross-legged. Her elbows rested on the sides of her knees, then her chin dropped onto her linked hands. She acted like she hadn't heard the diversion Kit had just tried. "Tell me more. You've got some…wish or fantasy or desire you're not being forthright about. Do you normally use a vibrator? A Dildo?"

"I've never even seen one!" Now Kit sat up and faced Bailey. "I had a misconception. I assumed lesbians used sex toys. I've been waiting to see when you were going to spring one on me."

Bailey didn't return her smile. "Did you want me to spring one on you?"

"Mmm, not necessarily. I was just expecting it."

"I can't tell if you're being honest. I really can't."

"Listen." Kit put a hand on her shoulder. "The sex we've had has been great, fantastic, beyond my hopes. We don't need to change a thing. I just thought things would change and I was trying to get myself into the right mind-frame. Every time we've been together I've thought… 'Maybe tonight she'll whip it out.'"

"Is there a part of you that wants me to whip it out? I feel some dissembling."

"No. Not if it's not your thing." Bailey looked so wholly unconvinced, Kit struggled to think of an analogy. "Let's say you smoked. I'm not a fan, but I've seen some people who look super cool when they smoke. If you were one of them, I'd think it was cool, even though I wouldn't have chosen to make you a smoker. But even though smoking can look cool, it'd be stupid to start smoking —hoping to impress me. Get it?"

"Maybe," she said slowly.

"If you normally used dildos or strap-ons or whatever, I know it'd be cool. Just because you are. But I don't want you to run out and buy one for me. No need. Truly."

"My fingers are enough?"

"Definitely." She took Bailey's hand and brought it to her mouth. "Go get ready for bed. Brush your teeth and wash your hands really well. The first night we were together you told me you could come from me sucking on your fingers. Let's see if you were bullshitting me."

Sexy smile back in place, Bailey leapt from the bed. "I'm on it!"

It took Bailey a few minutes, and when she returned she presented her hands for inspection. "You could eat off these things," she teased.

"I love you hands." Kit took one and started to kiss it, letting her caresses linger here and there. "Your fingers are so long and shapely. Like a pianist's."

"Mmm." They'd only had sex three times, but each time Bailey lost the ability to form words the moment she started to get excited. And she got excited as quickly as a teenaged boy.

Kit had been tempted to talk about how different sex with a woman was. But she didn't think Bailey would understand how vast the differences were. If you'd never even kissed a guy, you'd have nothing to compare. But Kit did. And each time the difference amazed her.

Even though men and women were both trying to share their bodies, they went about it in such different ways. Not having a penis on center stage was, obviously, a huge difference. But even bigger was the pace. When women made love they could go quickly or slowly, or switch back and forth. It was almost like moving the goalposts. You thought you were running for a touchdown, then your partner could flip you over and make you completely lose track of where you'd been. Sex changed from being goal-driven into a much more leisurely, sensual experience. One Kit had just begun to explore.

She sucked Bailey's finger into her mouth and bathed it with her tongue. Bailey let out all sorts of funny little sounds, most of them not even close to words. Her eyes were closed tightly, the rest of her body limp. Only an occasional squirm showed she was even conscious.

Kit took Bailey's spare hand and put it on her breast, urging her to squeeze. She took direction very, very well. Her hand compressed repeatedly, squeezing until Kit sucked in a breath. "Too much," she gasped. Bailey's eyes popped open. "PMS," Kit explained. "They get really sensitive."

"Got it." She rolled onto her side and tenderly took one of Kit's nipples into her mouth. "How's this?" she murmured after barely encircling it with the tip of her tongue.

"Nice. You can be a little rougher. Just don't go all-out."

Bailey's gaze shifted up to meet Kit's. "I love it when you talk to me when we're having sex. I want you to always feel like you can ask for anything you want."

"I do." She took her at her word. "I've been thinking about exploring you a little bit. But you've given me a signal you're not into it."

"I have?"

"Just one spot." Kit patted right between her legs. "You hold my hand still. Are you too sensitive for me to explore?"

"No, I don't think so." Her brow was furrowed, making her look quite confused. "I tell you not to move?"

"Yeah. Each time. I start to move around and you put a hand down and hold me still."

"Oh." She nodded. "Right. You get into habits, I guess. When I was learning how to have an orgasm, I'd put something inside. But I never moved things around. Too focused, I guess. So when I feel like I'm close to coming, I like that familiar feeling."

Kit moved her hand, burrowing it between Bailey's legs. "So…I can explore a little?"

"Sure. Of course. I'm a long way from coming now. Perfect time." She lay on her back, opened her legs, then grinned. "It's all yours."

Kit cuddled up beside her, then slowly slid a finger inside. Murmuring right into Bailey's ear, she said, "I love how quickly you get all slippery. I can see why guys love being in here."

"I can't imagine having a guy inside me." She visibly shivered. "Thank God I'm gay."

"Yeah, that'd be a cross to bear for a straight girl." She moved her hand, gently exploring. "You've got all sorts of textures. Like this…" Her finger grazed along a spot that almost felt ridged. "Then these incredibly smooth parts. Like here." Burrowing her face into Bailey's neck, she breathed in, loving the way her scent changed as she got turned on.

Bailey's voice almost cracked, but she could still converse. "You didn't explore yourself?"

"Not really. The first orgasm I had was with my boyfriend. He explored me."

"Really? How old were you?"

"Summer of my sophomore year. What's that? Fifteen? Sixteen?"

"I had four or five years of solo sex until I met Mimi. I guess I was pretty locked-in with my habits."

"And I hardly developed any. Until Henry and I broke up, I always had a boyfriend."

"I'm willing to form new habits." She shifted her hips, then pressed down on Kit's finger. "That feels awfully good."

"No one's explored you? Really?"

"Not a lot. Both Mimi and Julie followed my lead. I told them to stay still and they did." She turned her head and kissed Kit. "Unlike you, who has to indulge her natural curiosity." Another longer kiss followed the last. "I love how inquisitive you are."

"Cool." She spooned up against her again and let her finger move about lazily. "I like finding new ground." Another finger joined the first. "How about that?"

"Good. Feels really good."

Kit had to see rather than just feel. She moved around until her face was inches from Bailey's sex. Then she put both index fingers inside and worked them in and out slowly, varying the speed and the depth. "I love this," she said, amazed at how sexy her voice sounded.

"Remember when I said I'm a long way from coming?" Bailey asked, her voice a little strained. "I might have been wrong…"

Kit moved forward and placed a delicate kiss on her pink skin. "Then I'll back off." She slipped her fingers from her and moved up so they were face to face. "I might not get another chance. I'm going to memorize you."

Bailey pulled her close and kissed her hungrily. "Oh, you'll get another chance. I'm digging this. Really digging it." Another hot kiss followed. "You're showing me things I didn't know about myself."

"Get in line, buddy," Kit said, giggling.

Bailey pressed her to the bed, then gently opened her legs. "Come to think of it, I don't think I've explored you very well. Let's take a peek." She slid inside, then began to duplicate the various ways Kit had just touched her. "Pretty nice neighborhood you've got here."

"I wonder if it feels different at different points in your cycle?"

"One way to find out. I'll come back every day and check." She chuckled as she started to kiss all along Kit's neck and shoulders. "No charge."

"I love playing. No goals. Sex with you is so much more fun than it's been for a long time." Kit kissed her tenderly, allowing herself to focus on the sweet softness of Bailey's mouth.

"I'm having the time of my life." Bailey looked slightly befuddled. Like she was having a hard time keeping up with the conversation.

Kit slid her hand back down and entered her again. "I don't mind having a goal. Let's see who gives in first."

"Bet I do," Bailey said, grinning. "I'm about to pop."

It felt so amazing to have Bailey's nimble fingers slipping around inside her body while her own hand diligently explored. Even though they were playing around, talking and teasing, Kit felt a depth of intimacy that surprised her. Being inside Bailey, exploring her depths, was like being in a sacred space. A space reserved only for people whom Bailey trusted deeply. It was a privilege, and Kit almost misted up. But Bailey's hips started to twitch in frustration, and Kit focused on her. Gently, she tugged Bailey's hand from her own body and placed it right where it was needed. Immediately, Bailey's beautiful fingers skimmed across her glistening skin while Kit continued to glide in and out, slowly. Immediately, contractions nearly pushed Kit out. Bailey bit her bottom lip as her hips twitched sexily. It was clear she was trying to hold off, to make it last, but soon she moaned out a long climax, with her slick flesh gripping Kit, pulsing for long seconds. Finally, she lay still, her chest flushed and glowing with perspiration.

"Fantastic." She met Kit's eyes and murmured, "You know just how to touch me. How do you know me so well?"

Kit pulled Bailey's limp body into a tender embrace. Suddenly, she felt like she could cry, but was able to stop the feeling pretty quickly. They were having fun. It'd be a shame to ruin things by crying. "It feels like I've been doing this all of my life."

Bailey kissed her gently, then stayed right there, gazing into Kit's eyes from mere inches away. "But you don't feel even a little gay?"

That caught her off guard. But she had to tell the truth. This was important. "Not if being gay means you're into women in general. I definitely haven't found myself checking women out when I walk down the street."

"No fantasies?"

She'd thought they were going to have a big, serious discussion. But now that they were talking, she could see that Bailey was just teasing. Much nicer. "Nope.

All I think about is you." She touched the tip of Bailey's nose. "You're keeping me very busy."

"You haven't thought of any memories from childhood? Like having a massive crush on your teacher?"

Kit thought for a minute. "I had a very big crush on my history teacher in high school." She smiled as the memory played out in her head. "Mr. Dillon. Every girl in my class lusted after him."

"You're not working with me here," Bailey teased. "I can't fit you into a category." She poked at various ticklish spots until Kit grabbed her hands and held them still.

"If you behave," she said as she shimmied down Bailey's body, "I'll use my un-categorized tongue to show you a very good time."

"Mmm," Bailey purred as Kit's tongue slid all over her sex. "You can call yourself a Klingon if you want to. Just keep doing that."

—m—

On the way back from Pennsylvania, Bailey pulled out her phone when it chirped. "Oh, my reminder," she said after taking a look. "I keep forgetting to tell you about Nat's birthday party."

"Party?" Kit asked, her stomach doing a flip.

"Yeah. It's Saturday night at her house. Lots of fun. Are you free?"

"Uhm… Tell me more about the party."

Bailey gave her a quick look, then explained, "It's just a birthday party. She has one every year. I think it's a way for her to network, to be honest. She's always expanding the guest list."

"So…it's not just close friends?"

"No, not by a long shot. A couple of hundred people show up through the night. Starts at six and usually lasts until the wee hours. But it's fun. Mostly gay people, but a lot of people from her firm too."

"Uhm…how would we go? Like…how would you introduce me?"

"Nat knows we're dating," Bailey said, sparing a quick glance.

"Yeah, but the other people don't. Would you tell people I was your… girlfriend?"

Scowling, Bailey was silent for a few minutes, eventually pulling off into a rest stop. She shut off the engine and sat there for a moment, with her hands still on the wheel. "I wasn't planning on telling strangers that we have sex, Kit. But I would like to introduce you as…" She sighed and leaned her head back on the headrest. "I don't know. I'd probably just say your name. But it wouldn't be fun for me if I'm worrying about you the whole time."

"Couldn't I act like I know Natalie from something or other and leave it at that?"

Bailey stared at her. "You mean try to not let on that you know me?"

"Not specifically," she said, fighting the urge to jump out of the car and walk home. She hated fights like this more than anything she could think of. "I just don't want people to guess how I know you."

"Then I think you should skip it," Bailey said, turning the car back on. "Maybe you'll want to go next year." She gave Kit a very weak smile, leaving her feeling like a complete jerk. But that was better than having everyone at the party realize Kit Travis was sleeping with a woman. They were way, way too early in the game for that.

—m—

They'd not only had their first extended cold snap of the winter, the tail end of a Nor'easter had caught them. When Bailey texted that Friday afternoon, Kit was ready to ditch the office and finally enjoy some real winter weather. Washington got very little snow, but when a pure white blanket covered the expanse of land surrounding the national monuments, Kit needed to be out in it.

"Wanna get together tonight?"

"YES!"

"Nice reply. Ideas?"

"Let's go play in the snow."

"You're on. I'll come to you. 7?"

"Deal. Wear warm clothes. I'm a snow freak."

That night, she and Bailey were almost alone, standing near the Washington Monument, a vast, pristine loveliness spread out before them.

Bailey stood behind her and wrapped her arms around Kit's waist. They stayed just like that, neither of them speaking for a long time. "I love this," Bailey whispered into her ear. "Being out in a storm, just the two of us. It's magical."

Kit held onto her arms, hugging them close. "It is. I'm so glad we're here… together. Washington is majestic in the snow. I love being able to share it with you." Turning, she draped her arms around Bailey's neck and pulled her down for a kiss. "You look so pretty with your cheeks all rosy. And I must add that you're one of the few women on earth who looks good in a stocking cap." She traced a finger along Bailey's jawline. "Having your hair hidden highlights your gorgeous bone structure."

Shrugging, Bailey said, "I didn't do much to get it, but I'll say thank you anyway." While bending to kiss Kit, she slid her mittened hand along her cheek. "I prefer a less angular face. One like yours."

"Do you like snow as much as I do? It's okay to lie, by the way." She girlishly batted her eyes.

"I don't generally like cold…that's not a secret. But I like snow. Especially when it's clean and fluffy."

Kit cuddled up in front of her, relishing the feel of Bailey's arms wrapped around her. "Tell me about when you were little. Did you go sledding?"

"Yeah, a little bit. By the time I was born my parents had lost interest in doing all of the things you tend to do with your firstborn. So my sisters were charged with taking me sledding and things like that."

"My sister would have pushed me off a cliff if she'd been in charge."

Bailey squeezed her tightly. "You're exaggerating, right?"

"No, not really. I don't remember any of these incidents, but my grandmother loves to talk about how my sister tried to drown me."

"Drown you!"

"Uh-huh. Apparently, it was a serious attempt. We were at the Cape, and my brother was a newborn. My mom stayed on the beach with him, and my dad took my sister and me into the water. I guess he looked away for a minute, then couldn't find me. My sister had pushed me under and was holding onto my shoulders so I couldn't get back up."

"Kit! That's…psychotic!"

Laughing, Kit shook her head. "They say it's pretty common for kids to want to get rid of younger siblings. She wasn't old enough to have any real malice. I guess she just didn't want to share my parents."

"You must have been terrified!"

"I don't remember it, but little things like that might have caused my sleep problems. They say I woke when a pin dropped."

"No wonder!"

"I'm not sure if my mom just had everything under control, or if she didn't trust her, but I don't ever recall having my sister in charge. Besides, Emily always had her own thing going on. I felt like I was an only child most of the time. Or that we were foster kids who didn't have any connection to one another."

"Be careful what you wish for," Bailey said, while giving Kit a squeeze. "Lisa's seven years older than I am, so when I was four, and wanted a safe, slow ride, she was eleven—ready to cut loose with her friends. I usually wound up sitting at the base of the hill, crying." She chuckled. "I felt so much younger. Like she was an adult and I was still a baby."

Kit turned in her embrace. "Ooo, I bet you were an adorable baby. Next time we go to Pennsylvania I want to see some pictures."

"I can arrange that. There are a lot of pictures of Lisa, fewer of Kelly, and about six of me." She laughed softly. "But they're representative. You'll get a vague idea of what I looked like when I was sitting at the bottom of a hill, crying."

Kit stood on her tiptoes to kiss away a few snowflakes from Bailey's lashes. "Wanna see if you've gotten braver?"

"Uhm…how?"

"They don't call it Capitol Hill for nothing. We're gonna be the first ones down it."

"Really? Is that…legal?"

"As our tour guide told us at the White House, we paid for it. Let's hit it."

Bailey didn't seem entirely enthusiastic, but she went along with no argument. A perfect trait in a girlfriend. They walked along the snow-covered mall, no traffic and very few pedestrians out. It was cold and windy, with the snow blowing right into their faces, but Kit could not have been happier. Being outside, almost alone, the glistening white monuments of the government glowing through the snow. It felt like the whole world was theirs for the taking.

She took a quick glance at every trash receptacle they passed, finally stopping at a big pile of junk from some form of festival or protest. There were so many in Washington she had no idea how anyone kept them straight. The trash was actually pretty well organized and she went for the recyclables. "Score!" she called out as Bailey stood there, staring at her like she was mad. Kit held up cut cardboard boxes that had been shortened. Each had a three-inch lip, and she grabbed as many as she could carry. "Now for some waterproofing." Digging in the pile, she found a roll of plastic trash bags that someone had just tossed aside. "This must be my lucky day."

"This must be the day I find out the woman I'm seeing is…what? A pack rat?"

"It's for sledding," Kit insisted. "Trust me. I know what I'm doing."

When they finally arrived, looking like people who'd been rooting around a trash pile, Kit started to prepare the first sled. She was just wrapping a box up in plastic when a guard huffed his way over. "The building's closed, ma'am. Re-opens on Monday morning."

Kit flashed her best, most sane-looking smile and whipped out her press pass. "I'm writing a story about the first major snowfall of the year. We'll just be here a short while."

He looked at her pass carefully, then scowled. "You'll stay off the steps, right? You could get hurt and I'd get written up…"

She grasped his forearm and squeezed it in a friendly fashion. "We won't touch any part of the building. We just want the hill."

Turning his head, he looked at the very modest hill and smiled. "I wouldn't mind taking a turn."

"Come on!" Kit said, grinning. "I'll make you a sled."

"Nah. I'd get caught. You two have fun. Just don't hurt yourselves and sue."

"We're not the types. I promise we won't cause you any trouble."

"That's what I like to hear." He nodded and started to climb the stairs, leaving them alone.

"You're awfully charming when you want to be," Bailey said, smirking.

"I'm charming all the damn time. Now we're going to see if you're still the type to sit and cry, or if you can gut it up and go down headfirst."

"Headfirst?" Her eyes grew wide behind her specs. "I've got a lot in this head that I don't wanna lose."

"Headfirst is the best way, but I'll let you go down like a little girl." She slapped Bailey's butt, then grabbed the plastic-covered box. "Watch and learn." Whooping with glee, Kit hurled herself at the hill, almost knocking the wind from herself as she hit the ground. It was obviously easier to do this when you were ten. But even though many years had passed since she'd flung herself down a hill, the joy was still right there. Snow billowed into her face, and a hunk of it slipped into the collar of her coat. But she loved every second. She leapt to her feet, calling out, "Come on, ya chicken!"

"Yeow!" Bailey shrieked as she started down the hill, bouncing over every bump and depression. There was no reason for her to yell. Her feet kept digging into the fluffy snow, slowing her down so much she was going as slow as a three-year-old.

"Pick your feet up!" Kit called.

But Bailey kept it safe and slow, arriving several seconds later, snow covering her glasses. "I'm blind!"

"You don't need to see when you're sledding. Let's go!" She grabbed Bailey's hand and together they trudged back up the hill. "This time, try it headfirst. It's lots more fun."

"I'll take your word for it. I need every brain cell to do my job. I can't risk losing a few million of them for fun."

"Chicken…chicken…chicken. Bailey's a big chicken."

"I'm making progress," she insisted, after taking a seat on her sled again. "At least I'm not crying."

They kept at it until every box was so mangled they couldn't keep one together enough to even attempt another ride. "That was awesome," Kit said, standing near the steps of the Capitol, looking up at the bone white building rising in front of them.

"Even though I'm still a baby?"

"Yep. You're not brave, but you're willing. That's almost as good."

They kissed again, starting out playfully but quickly gliding into a tender, heartfelt embrace. "This is good," Kit said, smiling up at Bailey's lovely face.

"Very good. Super good." She kissed Kit once more. "Every time we're together, I feel a burst of confidence. Like I could do anything I want to do—as long as you're with me."

"That's the sweetest thing you've ever said to me." She pulled Bailey down for another long, emotion-filled kiss. "Let's go get a little dinner, then go home and get naked. I wanna rock you."

"You couldn't be sexier if you tried." Bailey actually looked a little vacant. Like her brain had taken off to fantasize. "But don't let that stop you."

—m—

They chose a place not far from Kit's apartment. It wasn't quite a sports bar, but it was definitely casual and usually lively on a Friday night. They waited at the bar for a table to open up, each having an Irish coffee to take the chill out.

"Kit?"

Kit turned and saw Melody Kramer, a reporter she'd worked with while she was at the *Globe*. "Hey! What's going on?"

"Girls' night out." She put her arms around the friends who flanked her. "We're sick of waiting for guys to recognize our awesomeness. Every Friday night we go out and have fun. We don't need no stinking dates!"

"No, you definitely don't. Guys are overrated."

"Isn't that the truth?" Melody had clearly had one too many. She approached from the side, able to get a glimpse of Bailey's angular features, even stronger-looking when her hair was hidden under her stocking cap. "Who's this handsome guy?" She put her hand on Bailey's shoulder, almost choking when Bailey turned to face her fully. "Shit! I'm so sorry. I thought you were a..." Turning back to Kit, she laughed nervously. "We've had a couple of drinks. Maybe too many. I can't tell women from men." She actually swayed a little. "Hey, are you still going out with that guy from the SEC? That older guy...what was his name?"

"Gene Slade. No, no, I'm not." Kit knew her cheeks were getting red, but she didn't know how to divert Melody's attention. Bailey had turned back towards the bar, and Kit was unable to see her face. Was she hurt, angry? Did it bother her to hear about former boyfriends? And where was Melody heading with the questions? She felt like the poor sap in a dunk tank at a carnival. Projectiles were being thrown from all directions, and she was sure one of them would swamp her, but there was no way to protect herself.

"I heard Hank's having another baby." Melody made a face. "Jerk. He had a good thing in you. Why does every guy want a twenty-year-old?"

She should have let it go. But it wasn't fair to let someone bash her ex. "Henry's a good guy. Really. He didn't dump me for a younger woman. It was mutual."

"Aww..." Melody put her hand on her shoulder, giving her the kind of smile you'd give a slow-witted person to boost her confidence. "That's sweet that you still defend him."

"It's not that. Really. He's a decent guy."

"It's been years, Kit. You've gotta let go."

"I have!"

"Look. There's a guy at the paper who's just come back from sabbatical. Sweet guy. I'm gonna hook you up."

"No need. Really." Kit stood and started to put her coat on. They had to get out of there. *Immediately.*

"Trust me on this. You'll like this guy. He's been on assignment in Afghanistan and Iraq on and off for years, and he's… Well, he could really use someone like you to help get his feet under him again."

"I appreciate that, Melody. Really. But I'm not interested."

Melody frowned. "You've got a guy?"

"No. Not a… No, I don't." She shook her head, desperate to flee.

Melody had become a good reporter not just because of her doggedness, but by refusing to let a person get away without answering her questions. "You're not dating anyone?"

"No. Not…I don't have a boyfriend."

"Then why not give Eric a try?"

"I'm just not interested."

"Don't give up, Kit," she said, putting her hands on Kit's shoulders. "You're still young."

Bailey stood, then grasped her coat and started to put it on.

"Don't go! We're gonna have dinner," Melody said. "Join us."

"No, actually we were just about to leave," Kit said, feeling like the bar was filling with carbon monoxide. Colorless, odorless, but deadly. Salvation lay outside. "Why don't you guys take our stools? They're hard to get."

"Are you sure? You've barely touched your drinks."

"We're good." She took out a few bills and tossed them on the bar. "I'll see you," Kit said, clapping Melody on the back.

When she turned, Bailey was already outside. Shit!

Kit didn't take the time to wrap up. She opened the door and the cold hit her like a slap. But when she saw Bailey, tears staining her cheeks, she felt like she'd been kicked right in the gut.

"You're ashamed to have people know we're together," Bailey sniffed, searching through her pockets, probably for a tissue.

Damn! She'd been so focused on getting Melody off her back she'd paid no attention to Bailey's needs. "Not true! I just didn't want to talk about my private life with Melody."

"You went out of your way to avoid having to say we were dating. Out of your way!" Sniffling, she started to walk, headed for her apartment.

Chasing her down, Kit grabbed onto her coat and pulled her to a halt. "Not fair! I wouldn't have said Henry was my date, and we were together for eight years!"

Bailey shook her head mournfully. "You acted like I was just a person sitting next to you. You didn't even introduce me." Her tears fell even harder and she struggled to use her mittens to clear them.

"No! It was obvious you and I were there together, but it would've taken another five minutes to introduce everyone. I didn't want to meet her friends, so I didn't bother."

"You can't convince me you wouldn't have said I was your date if I was a guy."

"I wouldn't have had to! In the first place, if I'd been with a guy Melody would have assumed I was dating him. She never would have said she'd fix me up. But that's not true with a woman. I'd have had to make a statement—a statement I'm not ready to make."

"This is why lesbians don't date straight women," Bailey whimpered. "It's not about sex. That part's easy. It's all the rest of it."

She stalked off, with Kit scampering after her. The sidewalks were icy where the snow had been walked on, but she worked to maintain her balance and keep up with Bailey's significantly longer stride. "Come on! Slow down and talk to me."

"I don't feel like talking. I just want to get back to my apartment and blow my damn nose."

Bailey'd been keeping another gear in reserve. She kicked it in, moving so quickly that Kit couldn't begin to keep up with her. But she didn't give up. She just followed her footprints after losing sight of her in the driving snow.

It took another fifteen minutes to reach Bailey's apartment. She'd been there enough times that the doorman recognized her and he nodded as she blew past him. Bailey's door was ajar, and Kit peeked in, assuming Bailey would pounce on her to deliver a good tongue-lashing. But Bailey wasn't in the living room. Kit's heart beat faster as she walked down the hall and heard quiet sobs. Poised on the threshold of the bedroom, her guts clenched when she saw Bailey sitting on her bed, shoulders shaking as tears rolled down her frosty cheeks. "That was humiliating," she sniffled. "Like I don't matter to you at all."

Dropping to her knees in front of her, Kit grasped her hands and kissed them repeatedly. "You do matter to me. So much. I swear I didn't do anything different than I did when I was dating a guy. I never, ever said, 'This is my boyfriend.' That's not something that feels right to me."

"Forever?" Bailey's tear-streaked face gazed up at her, the hurt so vivid it made Kit sick to her stomach. "If we move in together? Buy an apartment? Get a dog? Get married?" Her whole body shook as she coughed out, "Is there any level of commitment that you'd acknowledge? Not to strangers—I know how you feel about that—but friends?"

"Melody isn't a real friend. She's a reporter. That's not the same thing at all."

"Yes, it is." Bailey's voice grew in strength. "It's the same to me. You're trying to shove me into the closet."

"No, I'm not! Look at it from my perspective. I met a colleague at a bar. She starts to grill me about a guy I used to date, then tried to hook me up. I was really uncomfortable, so I wanted to leave. Fast. That's all it was."

"Not to me," Bailey said, once again raising her voice. "You didn't acknowledge me!"

"I'm supposed to tell her—a woman paid to gossip—that I'm dating a woman? It'd be all over Washington in ten minutes. I'm not ready for that, Bailey. I'm just not."

"So I'll be the nameless woman you're hanging out with because you've given up on finding a husband."

Kit grasped her shoulders and held her steady. "If we get to the next step…" She closed her eyes against the tears that spilled out. "And I hope to God we do… I'll introduce you as my partner, or my…whatever title we agree on. It's just too soon. I'm so sorry I hurt you, but it'll get better. I promise."

Sniffling, Bailey sat up tall. "Do you swear you're not embarrassed to be with me?"

"Embarrassed?" She sat back on her heels. Stunned. "Jesus! Embarrassed?" Kit took Bailey in her arms, hugging her until she grunted with discomfort. Loosening her hold, she moved back a little. "How could you say that? How could you even think that?"

Bailey's cheeks were flushed and she couldn't keep eye contact. "Dunno."

Kit gently shook her. "Tell me. You're holding something back."

It took her a few minutes, but Bailey finally lifted her head. "First she thought I was a guy. Then you denied you were dating anyone. A led to B."

"What?" Her head was swimming. "You honestly think I'm embarrassed of you?" She grasped Bailey in a tight hug, her stomach clenching. "I'm proud to be with you. But you have to understand this isn't about you. I'm phobic about talking about my private life."

Staring at her, unblinking, Bailey said, "You swear that's true?"

"One hundred percent. I didn't realize you'd be hurt if I didn't tell her what you mean to me. When we're on firmer ground I'll work to get over this so I can introduce you as my partner."

Looking down, Bailey murmured a few quiet words. "I felt like I didn't exist."

"That's *so* not true. You matter so much to me."

Bailey pulled away, then got up and walked over to the window. She stared out of it for a few minutes, silently. Her voice was quiet when she spoke. "It doesn't happen very often, but every once in a while…it gets to me. I wish I didn't stick out so much." A heavy sigh left her lips. "It would be easier to just be average. Normal."

Kit got to her feet and walked over to enfold her in a hug. "You're perfectly normal. But there's nothing about you that's average." She put her hands on the sides of Bailey's head and kissed her tenderly. "You're extraordinarily bright, extraordinarily pretty, extraordinarily kind. And I'm extraordinarily lucky to be with you."

"Are you close to telling people we're together?" Her bright blue eyes seemed like they could penetrate skin.

"I honestly haven't spent much time thinking about it." She snuggled up against her, burrowing her face into Bailey's shoulder. "Tonight caught me by surprise. Can you be patient with me?"

"I have been. I think I've been very patient. But this caught me by surprise too. I've not…I don't have any experience with how it feels to be in the closet." She kissed Kit's head. "I don't know how to handle it."

Kit looked into Bailey's eyes. "I'll…try to be more prepared."

Bailey nodded, released her hold and started for the living room. "I'm gonna order something for dinner." On the way out she mumbled, "This sure did turn into a shitty night."

—⁂—

Bailey woke on Saturday morning to find Kit lying on her side, gazing at her. "Do you like going to spas?"

While trying to clear her eyes, she sat up. "Has there been a conversation going on that I've missed?"

"No conversation. I was just thinking. It's been so cold and dreary out I thought it might feel good to have some pampering."

"I've got nothing against being pampered." Bailey sat all the way up and tried to corral her hair, which seemed to be headed in several different directions. "But I've never been to a spa."

"Really? Living in California? I thought it was required to have weekly massages out there."

"If it is, I'm way overdue."

Kit sat up, looking a little too perky. She was probably trying to make up for last night's fiasco by being super-cheerful. "Let's give it a whirl. My treat."

"I don't know. Do you have to get naked?"

"Uhm, yeah. Are you uncomfortable doing that?"

"Little bit." She chewed on her lower lip for a second, then told the truth. "I'm careful about things like that. I get mistaken for a guy so often…"

"But that only lasts a few seconds. As soon as they take a real look, everyone sees you're a woman."

"Yeah, yeah." Bailey got up and slipped into a fleece top and sweatpants. "I guess it'd be okay. I just don't like to set myself up for misunderstandings. Makes me uncomfortable…then you have to stand there while the person apologizes…" She sighed. "It can get a little tiring."

"Let me call around and see what's out there. You would like to be really warm, wouldn't you?"

That made her smile. "There's nothing I'd like better."

It took a long time, but Kit finally had what she promised was the perfect solution. After breakfast, they went to a place located in one of the bigger hotels. Kit went up to the desk and spoke to the receptionist for a while, then signaled Bailey.

A woman in a white uniform arrived, said something Bailey didn't understand, then led them down a corridor. They put their coats in a locked closet, then followed her to a frosted door. "This is your room," she said, her accent making Bailey strain to catch her words. "I will knock when time is up."

"Great. Thanks," Kit said. A big grin settled on her face as she opened the door. "Score!"

Bailey entered and smiled, partly at the big spa tub and partly at the pleasure radiating from Kit. "Nice setup," she said. "How long do we have?"

"An hour. But I can ask for more."

"No, that should warm us up." She started to loosen her tie, but Kit moved to stand in front of her.

"My job."

Bailey's smile grew as Kit studiously started to undress her. She seemed to get a lot of pleasure out of doing that, and Bailey certainly wasn't going to deter her. It felt great to watch a woman look happier and happier as your clothes fell off.

Once Bailey was naked, she realized the room was really warm. Being warm in February was something she'd like to get used to. Kit swiftly removed her own clothes, then took Bailey's hand and led her to the tub. "There's a steam room behind that door," she said. "And a regular shower over there. We can move from one to the other."

"Did that woman say all of that? If so, you've got a much better ear than I do."

"No," she said, chuckling. "I looked at the diagram on the website. It's cool, isn't it?"

Bailey stuck a toe into the tub, then let her foot fully land on a step. "No, it's warm. Really, really warm." She could feel her smile broaden. "I love being warm. It might be my favorite thing in the world." She lowered her whole body into the tub, purring when the water covered her shoulders. "I'm going to move here. Just pack my things up and ship 'em over, will you?"

Kit slipped into the water, and let out a pleasured growl. "Oh my God, this feels good."

"Do they have a bulk rate? Like a hundred hours for the price of fifty? If so, sign me up." Bailey stretched out, almost lying down. "My joints are finally loose. First time since September."

Kit moved over and wrapped an arm around her waist. "My Tin Man. All stiff and creaky."

"That's about right." She leaned in and placed a long, lush kiss on Kit's lips. "I'm a happy Tin Man now. Very happy."

"Come sit in front of me and let me loosen you up."

Bailey raised an eyebrow. "You can do that?"

"I think so. Let's find out."

After maneuvering so they could both sit on the bench that circled the tub, Bailey leaned back. Kit started at her shoulders, gently moving them. "Nice," Bailey murmured.

"I don't really know what I'm doing, so let me know if this works."

"You know exactly what you're doing. You're touching me in a nice way. That's always good."

Kit started to press a little more aggressively, working her way down the tight muscles along Bailey's spine. "I love touching you," she said quietly. "I love doing anything that makes you happy." She slid her arms more fully around Bailey. "I'm so sorry for hurting you last night. I'd do anything to have the evening back."

Bailey patted her hands. "It's all right. I just get...sensitive."

"You had every right to be sensitive. I know it hurts worse when someone you care for does something so thoughtless."

Turning her head, Bailey looked into Kit's eyes. "I know you didn't hurt me on purpose. We can let it go now. Really."

"Not until I'm sure you know how much I care for you. How much I hate to hurt your feelings."

Bailey turned all the way around and put her hands on Kit's shoulders. "I believe you. But you have to understand that being in the closet is hard—very hard for me. I was stuck in clothes that didn't represent me for over thirty years. Once I started dressing like the real me..." She blinked and looked away. "I thought I was done hiding."

"But I'm not asking you to hide. I'm just not ready to tell virtual strangers that I've made a big change."

Nodding, Bailey said, "I know that's how you look at it. But that's not how it feels to me. To me...it feels like you're ashamed of what we mean to each other." She cleared her throat. "It's hard, Kit."

Kit grasped her hands and kissed them. "This is the truth, Bailey. I'm not, in any way, ashamed of being with you. I just don't want to tell people yet. It's a timing thing. Only a timing thing."

"Okay." Bailey sank down into the water, letting it rise to her ears. "This is a timing thing too, and I don't wanna waste a minute."

—m—

All too soon, a quiet knock signaled their time was up. Kit had already showered in a cool spray, unable to stand being in hot water nearly as much as Bailey clearly could. Kit slipped on one of the robes the spa provided and said, "Be back in a few seconds." Then she went out to the reception area and negotiated for a few minutes, asking every question she could think of, and making it clear that she needed a sensitive and nonjudgmental therapist. When she felt confident, she went back and announced, "The hits just keep on coming, Ms. Jones. Time for a massage."

Bailey looked up at her, a mix of delight and suspicion in her eyes. "But…you massaged me."

"Not well. You're tight as a drum across your shoulders. I've got everything lined up. Just put on that robe and follow me."

"Are you sure? I hate to think of how much this is costing you."

"Then don't think about it. Come on now, time's a wasting."

They went out by the reception area, and in a moment an older woman in a white uniform arrived and said, "Are you ready?"

"We are," Kit agreed. They followed the woman, quickly entering a treatment room.

"We'll be back in a minute," the woman said. "You can be naked or leave your underwear on if you'd prefer." Then she exited.

Bailey stared at the door for a second. "Why are we in here together?"

"Because we're getting a couples massage. I know I've got a long way to go, but I'm trying to come out in small steps."

Eyes wide, Bailey said, "I'm not sure I'm ready to come out—naked."

"Come on," Kit urged. "I know you're naked under that robe." She pulled the tie and slid the robe from her shoulders. "Now lie down and get ready to relax." Kit lay down next to her and covered both of them with a flannel sheet. In just a second, the door opened and two women entered. Quickly, they started to work, speaking the minimum amount required. Kit turned her head, saw the tense look in Bailey's eyes and took her hand. Then she brought it to her mouth and kissed it, drawing no reaction from either of their masseuses. Almost immediately, Bailey loosened up, and in just a few minutes her eyes closed as the masseuse worked up and down her back.

Kit sighed as her muscles were probed and stretched. It hadn't been hard at all to arrange for the massage. Maybe that was because she'd felt she was protecting Bailey. Making sure no one insulted her had been the only thing on her mind. She wasn't sure if Bailey knew what a big step this was, but she was proud of herself. She'd make progress to make sure Bailey was happy. One step at a time.

Chapter Twelve

THE NEXT WEEK, KIT waited, impatiently, for an invitation. By Thursday, she was getting anxious. Finally, on Friday morning, Bailey texted. "Dinner?"

"Thought you'd never ask! Time?"

"8."

"Out or in?"

"Out. Pick you up."

Finally.

At seven, Kit started to get dressed. Given that Bailey nearly stood at attention when Kit wore skirts, she chose the snuggest one she had. It was cold out, so tights and boots were a good choice. The boots with heels. Bailey liked those. Going through her closet, Kit skimmed past anything that looked businesslike, settling on a V-neck, curve-hugging sweater Bailey hadn't seen yet. With the right jewelry it would be perfect for the occasion.

This was a big deal. She was taking a risk—a big one in her mind. Going to a restaurant with a woman—especially a woman who looked like Bailey—on Valentine's Day was almost like being out.

It wasn't an everyday occurrence, but more and more people recognized her now. Someone would probably take her picture and post it somewhere. But she didn't care. The burst of vulnerability Bailey had shown the previous week still hurt like a wound. There was no way Kit was going to hurt her again. She was going to dress like she would have for a guy, and if people made assumptions—so be it.

She was ready by seven thirty. But Bailey was pokey tonight, not appearing until almost eight. Kit opened the door to find her looking like she was going to work—on a pipeline. Her parka was the usual one; almost to her shins, slate gray with a fur-trimmed hood. Not very dressy, but Kit understood that Bailey was always cold. But a flannel shirt with a red Henley underneath? And stiff-looking jeans tucked into boots that a character in a Dickens novel would have worn? This is what she wore to a restaurant on Valentine's Day?

"Uhm…hi. Aren't we gonna be late? Is the restaurant close?"

Bailey bent over and kissed her cheek. "I thought we'd go get hot dogs at that place." She frowned. "But you look like you think we're going somewhere nice. Really nice. Did I screw up?"

Kit's mood deflated. She walked over to the table, picked up the gift she'd bought, turned and extended it. "Happy Valentine's Day. I'll go change."

Bailey looked like someone had slugged her. "Oh, shit! I had no idea!" She grasped Kit as she passed by. "Damn, damn, damn." Her voice took on a sweet, soothing quality. "You look so nice." She tried for a hug, but Kit needed a second to regroup.

"Open your present. I'll be back."

"No, no, stay. We can go by my apartment and I'll change. We'll go to the nicest place in Washington. Really."

Kit looked into her guileless eyes. "Fine. You call around and get us a reservation." She walked away, knowing they'd be going for hot dogs. Even the worst restaurants in Washington were full on Valentine's Day. The best ones would laugh at you for having the temerity to ask for a reservation.

Ten minutes later, Kit walked back into the room, now clad in more comfortable, less seductive clothing. Bailey gave her a baleful look. "You were fucking with me, right?"

"Right. You need to call in January to get into any place decent on Valentine's Day." She went to the closet and got her parka. "I honestly thought a woman would get it. Like I wouldn't have to drop hints."

Bailey moved in front of her and took her in her arms. "I'm so sorry. I swear to God I didn't know it was today."

Kit gave her a long look. "That's not an acceptable excuse. I can live with your not caring about it, I can live with your wanting to blow it off. I can't live with your lying about it."

"I'm not lying!"

"Bailey, you can't avoid knowing it's Valentine's Day. Knock it off."

"I'm one hundred percent serious." She grasped Kit's arms and held her steady. "I had no idea."

"It's everywhere!"

"Where? Where is it?"

"There've been ads on TV for weeks. I don't watch much, and I've been beaten over the head with them."

"I only watch things I've recorded. I haven't watched a commercial in ten years."

Kit blinked up at her. Odd. "Constant ads in the paper."

"Don't read it. Don't read anything that isn't techie." She frowned. "Actually, I hardly read anything that's printed. Almost everything I read is online."

"There are pop-up ads on every site I've been on."

"Then you're not on the sites I am. The only ads I see are for nerd stuff. And Valentine's Day isn't a nerd holiday."

Rolling her eyes, Kit kept going. "Then at the drugstore. The grocery store."

"Don't go to either. I buy everything online."

"Your groceries?"

"Yep. Almost all of my clothes, all of the things in my apartment. Every gift I give. I'm ninety-nine percent online."

Trying hard to think of an exception, Kit said, "Then at work. Someone had to have flowers on her desk."

"I left my apartment on Wednesday to play squash with you. Other than that, I haven't been out since I saw you on Sunday." She squeezed her shoulders. "I'm really involved with a project. My reminder alarm went off this morning and I was so tempted to ignore it. But I created this one to keep going until I type in a code, then I made the alarm so annoying I couldn't possibly ignore it." She pulled her phone from her back pocket. After bringing up the app, she turned the phone around. Despite her pique, Kit smiled when she saw the reminder. It simply said, KIT in the largest type possible.

"I created this just for you." She pressed a button and an alarm that could have alerted a town to a nuclear disaster squawked out painfully. "I have to type in 'don't be an idiot' to make it stop." After shoving the phone back into her pocket, she put her arms around Kit. "Being connected to you is really, really important to me. I was cranking on something that I've been stuck on, and I was afraid of losing my train of thought. But I saw your name, stopped in the middle of what I was doing, and arranged to have dinner." Her cheeks colored with embarrassment. "I thought I was doing really well. I wouldn't have stopped for anyone else." Her gaze was beyond earnest. "No one."

How could you be angry with someone who was trying so hard? Kit nuzzled into her neck. Bailey hadn't taken the time to dress well, but she smelled great. Freshly showered, clean and sweet. "You're doing very well. I'm being very stupid. Childish."

"No, you aren't." Gently, Bailey stroked her cheek. "Tell me why this means something to you."

Suddenly shy, Kit just shrugged.

"Come on. Please tell me." She held her close and kissed all across the top of her head.

"Sounds stupid."

"That's okay. I won't laugh. Promise."

Kit sighed, then looked up. "It's just a girl thing, I guess. It's almost a competition. Will your guy step up to the plate, or do you have to orchestrate the whole thing? I know it's dumb, but it's validation somehow. It's evidence the guy's as into you as you are him."

Bailey stooped down to pick up the gift Kit had given her. A playful, vaguely cocky smile lit up her face. "Let's see how much you're into me." The longish, rectangular box was a dead giveaway. Bailey opened it and gazed at the bright red tie that bore dark blue writing in neat, horizontal lines. Her eyes narrowed and Kit could see her trying to figure it out.

Moving around behind her, Kit stood on her tiptoes and tied it around her neck. Then she guided her to the mirror. When Bailey looked at her image, a big smile settled onto her face. "Hello, handsome." She smiled at Kit, who was looking into the mirror. "This is really thoughtful."

"I had to scour the stores to find something that wasn't cheesy. I like that you can only read what this says when you're looking into a mirror. I want you to look at yourself and say right out loud that you know how handsome you are when you're rocking a tie."

Bailey turned to snake an arm around Kit's shoulders. Pulling her close, she lavished gentle kisses on her lips. "Thank you," she said, sniffling. "That means so much to me."

"Open your card."

Bailey pushed her glasses up, wiped her eyes with her sleeve, then opened the card and read it. Her eyes met Kit's and she pulled her in for another series of kisses. "I will keep this for the rest of my life."

"Aww, you don't have to do that. I was just thinking of how much you meant to me. It seemed like a good idea to write it down."

"I know it's too late to pull tonight out of the trash, but I bet we could get a reservation someplace nice tomorrow or Sunday. How about it? I'll wear my best suit...you can wear exactly what you had on earlier...I'll bring you armfuls of roses..."

"Armfuls?"

She grinned slyly. "They'll be on sale."

"You don't need to buy me flowers. But I'd love to go out for a nice dinner. I want to be your date. In public," she stressed, in case Bailey had missed the import of the gesture.

"Let's see what we can find." She took her phone out again and spoke to it. "Washington, February fifteen, all neighborhoods, four dollar signs, four stars, two people..."

Kit watched her work. God help her if the power grid was ever destroyed. The poor woman wouldn't know where to turn.

—m—

After hot dogs, they went back to Kit's apartment. They were both feeling frisky and Kit quickly maneuvered Bailey into the bedroom. Bailey let out a scream when Kit snuck her hands under her shirt and started to unbutton her jeans.

"Your hands are like ice!"

"Not for long. There are all sorts of warm places I'm going to have them in about two minutes." She worked at the buttons, having a remarkably difficult time opening them. "What's with this fabric? It's like iron."

"My new jeans. Twenty-two ounce raw denim. I think they can stand up by themselves."

Kit got the last button to cooperate, and Bailey pushed them to the floor. Then she shook them out and played with them for a moment, finally getting them to almost stand on their own. They needed to lean against the wall, but it was still pretty impressive.

"I've never had raw denim," Kit said. "Now I don't think I want it. I like my jeans to cuddle me."

Bailey's eyes were bright with excitement. "I love jeans. I've had raw before, but never ones this stiff. They're gonna crease a lot."

"That's good?"

She turned and looked at Kit like she wasn't sure if she was kidding. "Yeah. That's the point. The fade and the crease."

"They'll be nice if you use a lot of fabric softener, right?"

"Fabric softener?" She laughed. "Heresy! I'm not going to wash these. Probably ever."

"What? You don't wash your jeans?"

"You don't need to. I'll put them in the freezer to kill bacteria. That freshens them up."

"You honestly don't wash your jeans."

"Nope. If I get something on them I'll spot them, but other than that— freezer only."

"I can't wait to see how this little science experiment goes."

"Trust me. In six months they'll be perfect. The coolest jeans in Washington. You'll be able to see where I keep my keys, where my wallet sits, my phone. It'll be sweet!"

Kit gave her a long kiss. "And you'll still be crazy." Playfully, Kit pushed her, giggling when Bailey tumbled onto the bed.

"Gettin' wild, buddy. The neighbors are going to call the cops if we start throwing each other around."

Kit jumped onto the bed and pinned Bailey with her body. "Don't think so. I'm a model tenant." She rolled off and lay on her side, assessing Bailey for a moment. "Speaking of models…your look was really different tonight. First time you've ever looked butch."

"Really?" A small frown settled on her forehead. "You don't think a suit and tie's butch?"

"Not really. You look…" She paused to think of the proper term, but had a little trouble coming up with one. "You remind me of pictures I've seen of Marlene Dietrich in a tux or a suit. Very elegant."

"Huh." Bailey rolled onto her side, mirroring Kit's pose. "That's interesting." She seemed to think for a minute, then said, "Would you like me to look butchier?"

"Nope. It just surprised me to see you lookin' kinda tough. It was a cool look, but I wouldn't want you to ditch your usual. It suits you." She chuckled. "Normally, you remind me of a female Cary Grant. Debonair. Totally classy."

A big smile slowly settled onto Bailey's face. "I think I would have fit in much better in his era. Lots of women wore menswear in the thirties and forties."

"I'm really glad you're in my era. And if you ever want to look tough, go right ahead and try." She started to kiss all over Bailey's face, lingering on a particular spot for a moment or two. "But your face is so sweet, so delicate, you'll never truly look tough." After placing a long, soft kiss on her lips, she added, "And that's just the way I like it."

—∞—

Bailey didn't get home the next morning until well after ten. She'd been itching to get going at seven, but Kit had woken and made her forget her resolve. Now she had to make some sparks fly. Her project was at a critical point, and she was feeling super creative. But first, she had to make a call.

Natalie picked up, sounding half asleep.

"Did I wake you?"

"Yeah, you did."

"Good. That's your punishment for not telling me it was Valentine's Day!"

"Oh, shit." Nat started to laugh. "Did you really blow it off?"

"Blown to bits. Why didn't you tell me?"

"Not my job!"

"You harass me about a million things. Why not the one thing I'd never notice?"

"Did you remember when you were with Julie?"

"She wasn't into it. Actually, she didn't like it. She warned me the first year not to expect anything. Like I would have."

"Sorry, Bails. Are you in trouble?"

"Yeah. But we're going out tonight. I plan to buy her all the flowers still left in the stores and hope that helps."

"Not good enough. You need a real gift. A gift that shows some thought went into it."

"But I'm swamped! It's going to be hard enough to stop working to go out tonight. I don't have time to go shopping."

"Do what you always do when you don't want to do something."

"Genius! Thanks. You're forgiven."

—∞—

Kit leaned against the wall of her building's elevator. "Someone should tell Farm To Table that they don't have to actually burst their customers' stomachs to prove how good the food is."

"We ate a lot," Bailey agreed. "We should have walked home."

"If I didn't have these boots on, we would have."

Bailey grinned at her. "If you didn't have those boots on, I wouldn't be in such a hurry to get home."

The elevator opened, and they went down the hall hand in hand. While Kit tried to get the key in the lock, Bailey pounced on her, kissing every bit of skin that wasn't covered by coat or scarf.

"Give me a half second," Kit begged, giggling like a demon.

She managed to get the door open, then Bailey quickly moved her up against the wall and kissed her furiously.

"Slow down, you beast."

"Can't."

"I thought wine was supposed to be a sedative. You act like you had a double espresso…that's right. You did. Big goof!"

"I love coffee with chocolate cake. Or tort or whatever they called that delicious thing."

"They called it the thing that made me want to unzip my skirt."

Bailey grabbed her again and nuzzled her face into Kit's neck. "I wanted to unzip your skirt the minute I saw you." She reached inside Kit's coat and started to do just that.

"Mind if I take my coat off?"

"Later." Bailey worked doggedly, then slid the skirt down. Her chilled hands landed on the backs of Kit's thighs.

"Yeow!"

"I'll warm you up." Bailey rubbed her body against Kit's like a cat.

"I'm plenty warm. Wearing a coat and scarf inside is an easy way to stay toasty."

Bailey blew out a breath. "You're such a traditionalist." She backed up and helped Kit remove her coat. Then she hung everything up. "Okay. Coats and scarves gone. Let's do it."

"A little slower, please. I love enthusiasm, but I've got to digest some of that dinner." She led the way to the sofa, sat against one end and extended her foot in Bailey's direction. "Take my boots off?"

Putting on an aggrieved look, Bailey sat and got to work. Once the boots had been tossed over her shoulder, she took Kit's chilled feet and put them in her lap. "I like warming you up. Any part of you."

"I like it too." She scooted down a little, loving to sprawl against Bailey. Sometimes she felt like a cat that was only happy when it was plastered all over its owner.

"You know, I was thinking about how upset you were yesterday."

"I'm over it. Totally."

Bailey held up a hand. "I know. But it hit me that you could have either told me it was an important day, or you could have arranged for something." She narrowed her eyes and gave Kit a long look. "Why didn't you?"

"Truth?"

"Yeah. Truth."

She swallowed, slightly skittish about admitting this. "Uhm…I thought of this last night when I was grousing about it. I uhm…think of you as the guy."

"Mmm. I thought that might be it."

Reaching down, she grasped Bailey's hand and held it tightly. "I love that you're a woman. I really do. But I'm used to being the woman in a relationship. In my head, there's only room for one."

"And you're happy to keep it going that way?"

"Yeah, I am. And so far you've been acting just like I expect." She laughed. "Forgetting Valentine's Day is very guy-like."

"Yeah, I guess it is." She closed her eyes and rubbed a spot on the back of her head. "I don't try to emulate guys, but I'll admit that my natural instincts are closer to men's than women's. But every once in a while I'll surprise myself and feel really girly." She met Kit's eyes again. "You'll have to be on your toes."

"No problem. I'm obsessed with you anyway. Might as well be on the lookout for unique behavior."

"Wanna hear about something I did today?"

"Sure. I won't understand it, but I'm happy to try."

"Not work. Personal."

"Personal? You did something personal? With all you've got to do?"

"Yeah. Kinda." She reached into the inside pocket of her jacket and took out a card. "I was determined to make up for screwing up Valentine's Day."

"Oh, Bailey, we've beaten that to death—"

"No, I screwed up. I had a perfect opportunity to show you how I feel about you, and I let it slip. So…" She took in a breath. "I did what I always do. I tried to find someone to take care of it for me." She grinned slyly. "Pretty guy-like."

"How do you—"

Bailey held up a hand. "You can find people to do anything in the world. I used a service called, You Could Pay Me." She chuckled. "I guess they were going with the 'You couldn't pay me to do that' theme."

"You hired someone to buy me a Valentine's Day present? A day late?"

"Yes and no." Bailey nodded. "After I made some poor woman traipse all over DC looking for the perfect gift, I realized that nothing she could pick would mean a thing—to either of us. So I paid her for her time and did it myself." She extended the card. "I hope you don't think I made an error in calling her off. She was sure you'd like a nice pair of diamond studs."

Kit took the card and shook it. "No studs in here."

"I'd be happy to buy you earrings, but only if I picked them out myself. Hiring someone to do something personal would have been insulting."

Kit smiled at her. "If you ever want to buy me earrings, take me with you. I'm incredibly picky."

"Good to know."

Quickly opening the card, Kit saw that it wasn't a card at all. Bailey had taken two different colors of letter paper and cut one sheet down so it served as a liner. On it she'd typed,

Dear Kit,

I could have rushed to buy you a gift, but didn't have time to find something that would mean anything to you. I never want to take shortcuts with you. You're worth the time and the effort and the energy to do it right. I promise to take this day seriously in the future. If it's important to you, it's important to me.

Always your—Bailey.

"Oh, baby."

Bailey blinked slowly. "You've never called me baby before."

Wrapping her arms around Bailey's shoulders, she pulled her close and kissed her. "Is it okay? I'm not sure where that came from. I've never been much for pet names. It just—"

Bailey pressed her into the sofa and lavished kisses all over her face. "It's perfect. I like that you haven't used pet names for other people, but want to for me." Her grin was so remarkably cute. "I'm competitive even with nicknames."

She ran her fingers across Kit's cheek, gazing into her eyes for a long time. "How did you feel tonight? Being in a fancy restaurant on a Saturday night with me?"

"It was good," she said thoughtfully. "I don't care if people make assumptions. I just don't like to make statements."

"For now," Bailey said, narrowing her gaze. "You said you'd be more open when we got to the next level."

Kit pulled her close and placed a gentle kiss on her forehead. "It's not quite like a video game. The levels aren't super clear." When she moved away Bailey was still frowning. "But we'll work things out. You'll tell me what you need, and I'll do my best to get there. It's a process, baby."

"Baby." Bailey smiled and the concerned look floated away. "It sounds a little funny, but I like it." She kissed Kit, then stayed just millimeters away for a few moments. "I'm not very patient, but I'll work on it."

—⁂—

They spent the rest of the weekend together, whiling away so many hours in bed that they woke before dawn on Monday. "What time is it?" Bailey asked when she felt Kit stirring.

The blue glow of a phone lit Kit's face. "Five. I'm awake. How about you?"

"Yeah, I guess I am too. When did we go to sleep?"

"Not sure." Kit stretched and yawned loudly, then flopped onto her back and snuck an arm around Bailey. "I think it might have been like eight." She started to chuckle. "I remember thinking 'One more orgasm's gonna knock me out.' And I was right."

Bailey rolled onto her side and kissed Kit's sleep-warmed cheek. "I'm famished. You barely fed me yesterday. Do you have any food?"

"Mmm. Some dry cereal, and I've got oatmeal, but I don't have any berries for it."

"Do you have sugar?"

"Yep."

"That'll do."

She swung her legs around and ran for her clothes, but as she started to put her underwear on, Kit said, "I have an extra Valentine's Day present for you."

Bailey stood there, holding her suit pants up to her chest to avoid shivering. "Am I waiting for it?"

"Hold your horses, missy. I'll get it." She went to her closet and pulled out a shopping bag. "Extra long sweats and the fluffiest, warmest fleece known to man."

Bailey lunged for them, and started to slip into the pants. "Hey, these really are long enough. But why didn't you give them to me yesterday?"

"I knew I could keep you in bed if you didn't have any casual clothes." Still naked, Kit walked over to her and burrowed against Bailey's warming body. "I've always got a plan."

"I'll just bet you do. But you don't need to trick me to keep me in bed—as long as you're there." She gently kissed the crown of Kit's head. "Thanks for the clothes. I'll leave them here so I'm not always wrapping myself up in your throw blankets."

"Do you need help in the kitchen? Or can I start checking my mail?"

Bailey guided her back to the bed, then covered her with the comforter. "I will deliver coffee and oatmeal. You may start your world spinning."

With a heart-melting smile, Kit looked into Bailey's eyes. "My world spins much better when you're in it."

—⁂—

At six thirty, Bailey stood at the front door, clad in her suit. Even though she was just going home to change, her striped shirt was buttoned at the neck, her new "hello, handsome" tie knotted perfectly. Her hair was kind of a mess, but that was something Kit was going to have to get used to. She was not going to start fussing with it like Natalie always did. You had to allow your girlfriend to make her own choices about something as personal as her hair. And if twisting it into a knot and fastening a clip to it worked for Bailey—that was good enough for Kit.

Kit slid her fingers down the lapels. "You look delicious in this suit. So tall and elegant."

"Thanks. The pin you gave me looks good, doesn't it?"

Kit flicked the little decoration with her finger. "Yep. But you're so cute you honestly don't need any ornamentation."

Bailey's grin was only slightly shy. She knew she looked good. Why deflect a compliment? "When can I see you again?"

"Tonight?" Where had that come from? They only saw each other on Wednesday nights and the weekend. But something had changed in the last few days. Kit needed more. As much as she could get.

"Come to my apartment when you're finished for the day. I'll make dinner." Bailey bent and kissed Kit with such a delicate touch it was like a whisper. "Bring a change of clothes…'cause you're staying over."

"I'd like to see who could convince me to leave."

———

Kit was starving when she knocked on Bailey's door that night. Music was blasting away, some kind of frantic electronic stuff. Her neighbors must have despised her. After kicking the door a few times, Kit finally texted. "Can I come in please?"

Seconds later, the decibels dropped and a stunned-looking Bailey opened the door. "Is it…" Her head swiveled and she looked at the dark windows. "Dinnertime? Did I say I'd cook?"

Kit placed a kiss on her cheek, turned her toward her office/dining room, then marched her to her chair. When Bailey sat, she kissed her head. "Chinese, Thai, Italian, Indian, Burgers. You pick."

"Thai. Anything that looks good to you." She turned her head to look up. "I don't think I had lunch."

"Good thing you ate enough oatmeal for three. Now get back to whatever you were doing. I can entertain myself."

The look on her face brimmed with appreciation. "You're a lifesaver. I'm really on a roll."

"Is your wallet in your pocket?"

Bailey's brow furrowed for a moment, then she shook her head. "On the table by the door. Why?"

"'Cause you're paying for dinner. I've been daydreaming about something hearty and Polish. The least you can do is pay for my Som Tom." On her way out of the room she cranked up the stereo, hearing a muted "Thanks," as she went to order.

Dinner was a little unorthodox. Kit hadn't fed anyone since her youngest niece was a baby. But Bailey was so locked-in, so hyper-focused, that Kit was sure she'd let everything get cold if left on her own. So she sat next to Bailey and stuck a forkful of food up to her lips whenever she stopped chewing the previous bite. It took all of her concentration to be able to feed both of them while balancing the containers on a tray, but she did a darned good job. Bailey must have thought so too. That was definitely a smile on her face as she zoned in again and lost contact with the world.

When Bailey's plate was empty, Kit found a set of headphones lying atop the stereo. After plugging them in, she lowered the volume significantly, then settled them upon Bailey's head. She had no intention of having her go deaf on her watch. Bailey looked up for a just a moment, a guilty look on her face. But Kit pulled the headphones away, said, "I understand completely," kissed her lips and started for the bedroom. She stopped for a moment, standing in the doorway as she looked at Bailey, head bent as she worked feverishly. It hadn't been the most romantic night, but taking care of someone you cared for was pretty darned nice. And just as important as the fun stuff.

—⚊—

It was late, and Kit had fallen asleep several times. She got up and changed into the T-shirt and flannel pajama bottoms she'd brought with her. After brushing her teeth, she went out to say goodnight.

Bailey still wore her headphones, her body contorting in her chair—possibly to the music. Or maybe it was because of the epic fight taking place on her desk. In each hand she held one of her buxom-beauty action figures. They were going at it tooth and nail, possibly to save the world or whatever action figures were tasked with. They were static figures, so they couldn't do much more than bang into one another with their weapons. One held a massive battle-ax, the other something Kit didn't recognize. She was transfixed—while a pang of guilt hit her for snooping. But she couldn't turn away, even though Bailey would definitely be embarrassed to be caught playing with her toys.

Kit almost teared up, watching and listening to the small sounds that came from her mouth. "Pow!" she'd murmur when a particular blow hit the spot. "Oof!" the other character would cry. Back and forth they went until the taller one finally landed what should have been the fatal blow. The weapon came down across the other character's neck, surely decapitating her—if her head hadn't been sturdy plastic. She fell to the desk as the conqueror stood over her for a moment, foot planted triumphantly on her chest. Kit was about to sneak off to bed, but there was a second act. The victor leaned over, touched the cheek of the victim, then lay atop her and started kissing her. Their little plastic bodies clicked against one another as they really went at it. Dissolving in laughter, Kit dashed for the bedroom before Bailey caught her. With any luck, she'd need to rid herself of some of that battle lust, and Kit was just the woman to help.

Chapter Thirteen

BAILEY WAS A WOMAN of her word. She said she'd be at home more often once her big project was finished, and she was. She was always working, of course, but her butt was in front of her computer, not way out in Virginia. That let Kit cruise by when she'd finished for the day and either make a simple meal or order something to be delivered. It was kind of nice to leave her building and be in Bailey's space. Maybe working in her apartment building made things a little too close.

A few weeks passed, with them sleeping together every night. Sometimes that was the only time they occupied the same space, but it was comforting to have that physical bond—even if they were sleeping. One evening, they were curled up together on the sofa, watching a little TV before bed when Bailey said, "Do you know my birthday's Friday?"

Kit turned to her and gazed at the side of her face for a moment. "And just how would I know that?"

She shrugged, looking charmingly juvenile. "Dunno. But I figured you'd be mad if you found out later. You don't have to do anything special, though. Just an FYI kinda thing."

"Oh, sure," Kit said, putting her arms around Bailey and wrestling until she was lying on top of her. "I'll just make a note."

"Well, you can do a little more than that. But you don't have to buy me anything."

"How about dinner? I could take you out, even though you didn't leave me much time to snag a good restaurant, or I could cook for you."

With a sweet smile covering her face, she made her choice. "Cook for me."

─❦─

Kit begged whatever force controlled the lives of mortal men to make Friday a slow news day. Even though she wasn't self-involved enough to believe she had the power to influence the heavens, she was darned pleased when her wish was granted. Nia agreed to hold down the fort while Kit left at the ungodly hour of five to run to the grocery store, then get started with her prep.

Of course she'd bought Bailey a present, despite her insistence she needed nothing. But taking time out of her day, carefully considering the menu, then working diligently to prepare something she knew Bailey would like—that was the real gift. And Bailey was just the kind of woman to realize that.

At eight on the dot, the bell rang. She'd given Bailey a key, of course, but she didn't use it often. They were still a little careful about pushing too far or assuming too much. Kit ran to the door and flung it open. "Happy birthday!" There, in her blue, double-breasted, pinstripe, perfectly tailored suit, stood the woman who held her heart. It was folly to act like they were just dating. Your heart didn't beat a tattoo when you first saw a woman you were casually dating.

Bailey bent and placed a delicate kiss on Kit's lips. "Happy birthday to me. Being with you is the best gift I could imagine."

"Get in here and let me look at you." She pulled Bailey in by the arm and slowly surveyed her. "That is one nice looking coat, Ms. Jones."

Bailey slipped off the dark grey topcoat and slid the sleeve across Kit's face. "Nice material, huh?"

"Really nice."

"My birthday present to myself."

"I'm pleased you didn't skimp on the material. Your grandfather would be proud."

She did a quick pirouette. "He'd be prouder of the suit, since he did most of the work."

Kit nodded solemnly. "I'd have to say that's the best-fitted suit I've ever seen. That style is perfect for your body."

"Yeah." She looked down at herself. "It can't be from the thirties, I don't think, but it looks like it is."

"And I love the tie," Kit said, fingering it.

"My sister. Lisa." On a gold background, hundreds of tiny circles, in every primary color, bore the legend "Happy birthday." Bailey flipped the tail of the tie in the air. "I was really pleased she got me this. She's made it pretty clear she doesn't understand how I dress, and this shows she's trying."

"It's really nice. And it looks great with your suit."

Bailey popped the cuff on her shirt, and pointed to a cufflink. "Integrated circuits," she said, waggling an eyebrow. "Kelly and Mick."

"What's next? Tie tack from gramma?"

"No," she said, chuckling. "But she sent me a card. With a holy card of John Paul II inside."

"A what?"

She made a face, scrunching up her eyes. "I guess you're supposed to call them prayer cards. There's a picture of a saint or someone close to being a saint on one side, and prayers you're supposed to say on the other. He was Polish, you know, so he's been a saint in her eyes forever."

"Nice," Kit teased. "Can you collect a whole set?"

"Probably. I'll check on eBay."

"What about mom and dad?"

With a big grin, Bailey said, "A tin of kolaczki. All of my favorites—cream cheese, raspberry and blackberry."

"If you've got a whole tin, you'd better share, birthday girl. I have no idea what kolaczki are, but if they've got jam in them, I'll like them."

"No doubt. You will eat your fill tomorrow."

"Come in," Kit said, tugging her along. "I made you a special drink."

They went into the kitchen together, and Kit pulled out the ingredients. "I know you like champagne, but I wanted to make it special."

"Ooo. Fancy."

"You betcha." She took a sugar cube, dropped it into a champagne glass, then added several drops of bitters to it. Next, she filled it with the wine, then added a twist of lemon and presented it to Bailey. "Champagne cocktail."

"You've got to drink with me."

"Oops. Almost forgot." Quickly, she made one for herself and they toasted. "Happy birthday to the woman who's so appealing she made me change my entire orientation."

Bailey leaned over and kissed her gently. "Thank you. For everything." She took a sip. "Ooo. I'm loving this. It adds just a little something to make it taste brand new."

"Like you've done for me," Kit said, staring up into her beautiful eyes. "You've made me look at attraction and desire with new eyes. Quite a feat!"

"All in a day's work for Bailey Jones, sexual orientation tweaker. But what do we call your orientation? I know you don't like bisexual."

Kit couldn't help but giggle. "I'd better get used to it, because I passed straight when I started counting the minutes until I could go down on you."

They sat in the living room after dinner, with Bailey continuing to praise Kit's skills. "You know how much I love seafood, and I thought I'd ordered lobster every way possible. But I've never had lobster with champagne sauce, and now it's going to be the only thing I want. You've ruined me!"

Kit basked in the glow of Bailey's praise. The meal had turned out pretty darned spectacularly, if she did say so herself. Cooking for Bailey made the effort well worth it. "We can make it again as soon as you want it."

"I want to keep that taste in my mouth forever." She craned her neck, like she could see into the kitchen, which she definitely could not. "But I sniffed that chocolate cake the minute I walked in. You've put me into a real quandary."

"I'm not as confident of my baking skills. Let's finish the champagne and then try the cake."

"Deal." Bailey leaned back and wrapped an arm around Kit's shoulders. "I really appreciate how much trouble you've gone to for me. That's the best present I could ask for."

"Oh! I almost forgot your present!" She got up and dashed for her bedroom, returning a minute later with a good-sized square box. "Not very romantic, but I'm pretty confident you'll like it."

Bailey grinned as she hefted the box in her hands. "Not too heavy…"

"I don't think you'll guess, but I'm in no hurry."

"Eh…" She started to tear the paper off. "Why guess when the answer's right in your hands." She opened the box and stuck her hand in, then pulled out several pieces of paper. "A train ticket to New York?"

"Uh-huh. Look at the next one."

Her brow furrowed as she read an electronic ticket. "Fantasy Fest? Uhm, should I know what this is?"

"It's a new thing. The guy at the comic book store assured me it'll be as good as Comic-Con."

"Awesome!" Excitedly, she dug in the box again. "Are you sending me alone, or are you going with me?"

"I'm going with you, silly. How can we have a romantic weekend if we're in different cities?"

"A weekend? A whole weekend with you? No sneaking down to the office on Sunday morning when you think I'm asleep?"

"Cheat!" Kit grabbed a throw pillow and whacked her with it. "When I sneak out of bed, I expect you to lie there and wait for me. How am I supposed to get anything done if I know you're awake?"

"I'm not awake for long," Bailey admitted. "The first time you did it I was tempted to get up and make you coffee, then I decided it didn't make sense for both of us to be miserable at five a.m. on a Sunday morning." She showed an unrepentant smile. "Just being practical."

Kit took the ticket from her hand and brushed it across her face. "Are you excited?"

"Oh, damn! I keep getting sidetracked." She sat up straight, put her hands on Kit's shoulders and looked into her eyes. "I'm really, really excited. I went to Comic-Con in San Diego every year. I considered going when they had the New York version in October, but it didn't seem like much fun to go alone." Her head tilted as she squinted a little bit. "But I don't think you're into sci-fi or fantasy or comics. Unless you're hiding your interest really well."

Kit gripped the knot in her tie and tugged on it. "I'm into you. I don't know a thing about those genres, but I'll have fun watching you have fun."

Still peering at her curiously, Bailey said, "How'd you even know about it?"

Kit hadn't considered she'd ask that. She didn't want to reveal the idea had occurred to her after watching Bailey play with her toys, so she skipped to the important part. "I wanted to get you something for your birthday, so I went to a comic book store and grilled the poor kid who works there. He said anyone who really likes sci-fi and fantasy would love Fantasy Fest. You do, so I decided we had to go."

Bailey squirmed around on the couch for a few seconds, then swallowed. "Uhm…do you know about Cosplay?"

"Is that a band?"

"Uh-uh." Her gaze darted around nervously for a second. "It's something that people do a lot of at cons. And since this is called Fantasy Fest I assume there will be a lot of it."

"Is it…something sexual?" Kit asked, her anxiety starting to rise.

"No…well, yeah, it is for some people." She sat there, looking very contemplative. Then her gaze settled on Kit again. "Oh! But not for me. I just like to dress up in a costume. Cosplay. Get it?"

"Uhm…I guess. Like Halloween?"

"Exactly. You dress up like your favorite character. They have competitions and stuff. And sometimes people who like a particular fandom all get together—dressed in their costumes." Her smile brightened, but it still looked a little tentative. "Is this too weird for you?"

"No!" It truly was, but Kit would never, ever admit to that. Everyone had things they liked that other people thought were a little weird. At least Bailey didn't want to be sexual when she was…what? Wearing a mask? How would that work?

"Your mouth says 'no,' but your eyes say 'yes.'"

"No, no, and more no. I can't wait to see your costume. Do you dress up like one of those Amazon goddesses you have?"

"No! I'd look like an idiot. I dress up as Doctor Who. The third doctor, to be precise. Most people now seem to choose the eleventh, but they say you always love the doctor you grew up with, and I got into it when they were showing Jon Pertwee's episodes. He's my guy."

"There's more than one doctor?"

Bailey raised an eyebrow. "I can talk about this all night…but it's okay if you accept that there are many and we move on."

Kit slapped her thighs. "Super! I'll anxiously await seeing you all decked out." She paused for a second. "Do you need me to…dress up too? Does Doctor Who have a sidekick or a girlfriend?"

"Sidekick? Yeah, he has companions. One of the third doctor's best ones was Sarah Jane Smith, who was a journalist. But she didn't have a very distinctive look. She was a great companion, though. Probably my favorite."

"Then I'll just go as a woman who's crazy about Doctor Who…the third Doctor Who, that is."

Leaning over, Bailey kissed Kit repeatedly. "Thanks so much. I can't tell you how good it makes me feel to know you pay attention to the things I like, then try to learn something about them."

"You're all I think about," Kit admitted. They were just a couple of inches apart, and she had no interest in making that distance any greater. She craved being close—just like this. Sharing the same space. Perfect.

Bailey suddenly looked…serious or troubled. Something about her expression just wasn't right.

"Uhm…" She reached into the inside pocket of her jacket. "There's an old Polish custom. On your birthday you give a small gift to the person who's been most important to you that year. Kind of as a way to thank them for making the year special."

"That's really sweet. I've never heard of that."

"Well, you don't spend much time in Polska." She handed Kit a small envelope. "Go on. Open it."

Kit slid a nail under the flap and pulled a simple card out. Inside, Bailey had written, "This has been the best year of my life because of you. I'll always remember this as the year I fell in love."

Looking up at her, Kit saw a mix of excitement and fear flickering in those beautiful blue eyes. "I feel exactly the same." She fell into her arms, kissing Bailey's cheeks, her forehead. Then she placed a delicate kiss on her lips. "I love you, Bailey. I love you."

She ran her hands over Bailey's body, reveling in the contours of it under her suit. Her blue pinstripe. As soon as Kit had opened the door to gaze at her, dressed to the nines, she had a feeling something big was going to happen. Still, she was stunned.

How had this happened? How had she fallen so hard for a woman? She had no idea how it had happened, but it had definitely happened. She was crazy about Bailey. Not in spite of her sex, but not because of it either. It made no sense at all, but she loved her womanliness. Her softness. Her smell. Her taste. And her boyishness. Her forthrightness, her practicality, the way she looked in a suit jacket or a pair of jeans. Her wholeness. The sum of the parts that made her Bailey. She loved every one of them.

"I love you," Bailey whispered. "I'm so in love with you it's caught me by surprise. But it's real. It's very real."

"I've been sure I was in love with you, too, but it felt too soon. Do you know what I mean?"

"Yeah, yeah, I do. And if we were kids it probably would be. But we're adults. Adults who know what we want. And I want you. Just you."

"I want you, too. Only you."

They started to kiss, soon lost in the taste, the smell and feel of the other's mouth. The sensation of soft tongues gliding against each other. Of the quickening of breaths, the beating of hearts. "Tell me what this means to you," Bailey murmured. "What does loving me mean?"

"We're in this together. We're committed." Kit gave her a lazy smile. "No more walking away when we have fights. We stay and work it out." She kissed her again, savoring the tenderness of her lips. "We make each other our number one priority."

"I've already done that. You're my number one."

"And you're mine."

"When will we tell people?"

Kit felt her pulse rate increase. "Can I have a little more time? Just a little?"

Bailey gave her a long look. Then she merely nodded. "You're trying, right? You want to be open?"

"Sure. Of course. I'll tell Asante, but I need time to slide into this."

"Can I tell my family?"

"You can tell anyone you want, baby. I just need to figure out how and when... I have to get the details lined up."

"Okay. I know it's a process."

"I'll try to make it an expedited process. Promise."

Bailey struggled to sit up enough to put her hand back into that pocket. Then she pulled out a tiny red velvet bag and handed it to Kit. "Here's your birthday present."

Giggling, Kit said, "This is a funny custom, but I'm not going to complain." She started to open it, then said, "Unless someone else is number one next year."

"I think it will be you for a long, long time." She jiggled her hand, urging Kit to move quicker.

After pulling the gold strings apart, a narrow, hammered gold ring fell into her hand. "It's beautiful," she whispered.

"I hope you like it. I know you're picky, but I wanted you to have a little something to look at and think of me."

"I love it." Kit leaned forward and placed kiss after kiss on Bailey's pink lips. "Thank you."

"Does it fit?"

It was a small ring, and she tried it on her left hand first. Then the right, where it slid onto her little finger perfectly. "Couldn't be better. I'll wear it always."

"Really? Always?"

Nodding soberly, Kit said, "Always. Promise. And every time I look at it, I'll think of you."

—⁓—

After their cake and some coffee, they spent a long time cleaning the kitchen. Bailey had her jacket off, sleeves rolled up, a chef's apron keeping her tie dry. "This has been a pretty spectacular birthday," she decided.

"Wait until mine. You're guaranteed another present, since no one could possibly make my year better than you have."

Chuckling, Bailey said, "I totally made that Polish thing up."

"What?" Kit snapped a dishtowel at her butt, making her jump. "You made it up?"

"Yeah." She started to laugh. "I wanted to give you the ring and tell you I loved you, but I didn't know how to lead in. I had to come up with an entry point." She shrugged. "I thought it was pretty good."

"I hope you enjoyed your little trick, because I'm gonna expect a present on your birthday every year. A nice one!"

—⁂—

Bailey leaned against the headboard, the comforter pulled up as high as she could get it. She was tempted to go work for a while, but she couldn't compel herself to leave. Not when the woman who held her heart was lying beside her, with a warm, twitching hand draped across her leg.

Kit was so pretty, a classic kind of beauty that would always appeal. The kind of woman who would only get better looking with age. Bailey's heart skipped a beat when she thought of sharing her life with Kit, watching her grow old very, very gracefully. It wasn't something she did very often—usually being deeply rooted in the present or the near future. But Kit made her think about the rest of her life.

She wasn't sure if Kit really understood this about her, but she wasn't the kind of person who needed a lot of variety. She liked to find something that was good and stick with it. It still amazed her that she'd broken up with Mimi, even though their sex life had been non-existent. It had taken a long time, but her libido had finally trumped her need for stability. And if just a few things had been different, she'd be in California with Julie at that moment, changing diapers.

It would be just the same with Kit. They were into each other—very much into each other. Now they just needed to dedicate themselves to creating the best relationship they could possibly have. She was determined to be a good partner.

She'd learned the hard way that you couldn't just assume your lover was happy. You had to work at it.

Bailey slid down until her face was next to Kit's. The urge to kiss her was still thrumming in her heart, but she didn't want to wake her. In some ways, they were still getting to know each other—she still wasn't sure how deeply Kit slept. But she'd learn. She'd learn everything there was to learn about the loving, generous, kind woman she'd pledged her heart to. This was her new project, and she would attack it with every bit of her energies.

—m—

The next morning, Kit answered her cell phone when she saw Asante's picture. "Hey. Hold on a sec." She left the living room and went down the hall to her bedroom, closing the door behind her. "Bailey's in some kinda trance and I didn't want to disturb her."

"No big deal. You go play house."

"No, I can talk. I'm clearly not needed here. In fact, I'm not sure she knows she's here."

"No comprehension on that one," he said, laughing softly. "Wanna reframe?"

"Sure. We got up and I went to check my sites. By the time I got back, she was lying on the sofa, looking up at the ceiling like Michelangelo painting the Sistine Chapel. She's been doing exactly that for a couple of hours now."

"If I did that, I'd be sound asleep within fifteen seconds."

"Me too! But not her. She'll pick her head up every once in a while, make a few notes or draw a diagram, then lie back down."

"Sounds like you're not available for brunch. Unless you want to take her on a stretcher."

"I'm available. I need to get out of here and get some fresh air."

"Great. It's a nice day. Let's go over to the ice skating rink in Georgetown. We can eat and then skate."

"You're on. Swing by and pick either both of us or just me up. Oh. And bring your skates." She paused for dramatic effect. "Oh, that's right. You don't have skates. Because you're not an awesome skater!"

He laughed. "I'm good enough to stay upright. I'll just tag along and let you shine."

"Business as usual. See you soon."

Bailey not only didn't want to go, she was barely able to hide what Kit knew was a relieved look. She was clearly used to working alone, and as Kit got her things together, Bailey took out her earphones and plugged them into her phone. A very satisfied smile settled on her lips and she turned to wave goodbye, even though Kit didn't even have her coat on.

After Asante arrived, they walked over to Washington Harbour to forage for brunch. The only place they could get into was a ridiculously overpriced Americana-styled restaurant that tried way too hard. But there was an open table, and they were both hungry, so they grabbed it.

A server brought fresh OJ and coffee as they divested themselves of their coats, scarves and gloves. Asante, always alert to any change, grasped Kit's hand and looked at it carefully. "What's this? Wasn't it Bailey's birthday?"

"It was. It definitely was." She twitched her finger, trying to make the muted lighting hit the gold just right. "My goofy girlfriend convinced me that there's an old Polish custom of giving someone special a present on your birthday."

Clearly puzzled, he said, "The person with the birthday gives a present to someone else?"

"Yeah. That was the story. Of course, she made it up, just to have a reason to give this to me."

"Why didn't she just…oh, I don't know…give it to you? It's nice, by the way. Very much your style."

She held her hand out and studied it, thinking of the look on Bailey's face when she'd given it to her. "It is." It took her a second to snap out of her musings and get back to his question. "She was a little nervous, I think. And that's because…" She paused and popped her eyebrows up and down a couple of times. "She told me she loved me."

"No! Get out!"

He was so cute. A big, buff guy, very manly looking, who sometimes sounded like a high school girl.

"Indeed, my friend. I'm no longer going steady. I'm…" She stopped, trying to think of what to call their relationship. "I guess we're…what? Girlfriends?"

"I don't know." He took her hand again and looked at the ring. "Clearly not an engagement ring." Looking up, he said, "She didn't ask you to marry her, did she?"

Her eyes opened wide. "I would have mentioned that!"

"Hmm…then I guess you're girlfriends, partners, lovers…I'm not sure."

"Me either. I'd better ask."

Laughing, he said, "There's not a checklist. You are what you think you are."

"Right," she said absently. And that was the problem. She had no idea what they were, and suddenly didn't like the thought of having to figure it out.

Chapter Fourteen

THE DAY THEY WERE going to New York found Kit stuck at a reception at the Saudi embassy for one of her former professors. She looked up and spotted a woman she barely knew, and admired greatly. "Hi, Margaret. Kit Travis."

"Oh, hi, Kit." Under her breath, she muttered, "If there isn't a decent buffet, I'm out of here. How about you?"

"I'm catching the late train to New York, but I've got to speak to Don before I go. He was one of the people who convinced me to give journalism a try."

"You ought to slap him." She chuckled softly and patted Kit on the shoulder. "Don't let my cynicism rub off on you."

"I've been here for twelve years now. I've got my own warehouse full of it. So how are things?"

"Honestly?" She frowned. "I find myself being excessively frank these days. You've been warned."

"I can take it."

"I'm pissed off."

Kit had spoken with Margaret Stevens briefly many times through the years, since they both covered roughly the same group of people. But Margaret had always seemed above the fray. Like she was built of better stuff than your average reporter. Being on the same beat for thirty years and sharing a Pulitzer made you royalty of a sort in the press corps.

"Pissed off by…?"

"The whole damned system." She looked over her shoulder, then lowered her voice. "They're pressuring me to take the buy-out."

"You?!" Kit squeaked. "You're…you're Margaret Stevens!"

A warm smile curled her lips, making her look much more like her headshot. "That and two bucks will get me a cup of coffee. They aren't going to force me to go. But they've suggested…strongly…that it's time." She locked her dark eyes on Kit. "I'm fifty-six. I'd like to work at least…at least…another twenty years. This is what I do. Who I am." She narrowed her eyes, murmuring, "The head of the Joint Chiefs is over there. Gotta go."

Kit watched her scurry across the room, the quality of the buffet forgotten. Journalism was dead when a major daily tried to squeeze out a woman with Margaret's talent and experience. Was the bottom line worth sacrificing every bit of quality? Glumly, Kit checked out the buffet. Second rate. Sighing, she eyed the line of supplicants waiting to greet her old mentor. It would take an hour to get to the front, but she'd be patient and stay. Thanking the people who took the time to lend a hand or an encouraging word when you were first starting out was the least you could do. She just hoped the line moved quickly. She had a three-day party with the third Doctor Who to get to.

—ɯ—

The next morning, Bailey patiently spent their breakfast time going over the schedule, trying to make sure Kit got to attend sessions that might have some appeal for her. "Did you ever like comic books?"

"'Fraid not. Don't think I've ever read one."

"Horror movies?"

"Definitely not. They scare me half to death."

Chuckling, Bailey continued to look at the sheet. "They're supposed to, you know."

"Uh-huh. Well, I find politics scary enough. What else ya got?"

"Fantasy? Like Harry Potter?"

"Not really. Saw the first one, fell asleep."

"Hmm…I suppose it's a silly question to ask if you like anime?"

"Not a silly question," Kit assured her. "I just have no idea what that is."

Bailey slapped herself in the face. "There are so many panels going on that I could literally be happy at six or seven of them—for each session!"

Kit took the schedule from her hands. "And that's exactly what you should do. Pick the ones you like the best, and I'll tag along." She discreetly reached under the table and took Bailey's hand. "This weekend is for you, baby. If you're happy, I'm happy."

With a relieved sigh, Bailey nodded. "There's a sneak peak of a new movie I'm desperate to see, and a panel on a new game for my console I'm itching to try. Let's flip a coin."

Kit had a feeling it didn't really matter if the coin came up heads or tails. Bailey would be happy either way.

—⁘—

By noon, Kit had her fill of watching trailers for sci-fi movies. But she was fascinated by the crowd. Bailey was studiously planning her afternoon when Kit said, "Mind if I grab a bench and watch for a while? I love seeing how creative people are with their costumes." She looked her up and down. "Why aren't you wearing yours?"

"I'm not going to wear it until tomorrow night. There's a big party at a gay club in Chelsea. Pretty much everyone will be in costume." She frowned, looking a little panicked. "Is it okay to go to that? No one will recognize you—I'm pretty sure."

"Yes, honey, I'd love to go. I doubt anyone will be looking for a political blogger in a room filled with people in every kind of costume the world has ever known. We're good—but thanks for asking."

—⁘—

On Saturday night, Bailey started fussing with her costume moments after they finished their dinner. It was ridiculously early to be getting ready for a party, but she was very fastidious about how she looked even on an average day. Obviously, impersonating the third doctor required additional prep. Surprisingly, what was going to take the most effort was getting a rather fluffy-looking blonde wig into shape. Bailey held it in her hand, scowling. "I don't know anything about hair. I want it to be curly…but not too curly. Seventies-style curly."

"I think I can help you out. Pull up a picture of the guy on your computer. I've got a curling iron that can work wonders."

"Really?" She grinned so widely her molars showed. "Damn, I love having a girly girlfriend. You can do all sorts of things I'd never be able to manage."

"Keep the compliments coming," Kit urged, kissing her neck. "You can never go overboard in that department."

They got the wig looking like a reasonable facsimile, then Bailey started to get dressed. Her suit was something to behold, a wide-lapelled, bell-bottomed maroon velvet number that clearly placed her right in the middle of the 1970s. A big floppy bow tie added to her dandy look, and the ruffled white shirt actually made her look more feminine than her usual clothes. But she looked as cute as a bug as she preened in front of the mirror. "You did a great job on the wig," she said once again. "That made all the difference."

"Your suit looks like something from the 'Saturday Night Fever' cast party."

She whipped out a shiny plastic toy from her pocket. "John Travolta didn't have this super-cool sonic screwdriver." She looked so proud of herself Kit couldn't allow the laugh that desperately wanted to escape. Instead, she said what she really felt.

"I couldn't love you more if I tried."

—⁓—

Kit had been in the bathroom nearly an hour, and Bailey was itching to leave. "It's ten o'clock," she said, pressing her face close to the door. "We've gotta get going."

"Honey, parties don't get good until midnight."

"Geeks go to bed early. Really."

"I'm almost ready. Give me two minutes."

"Okay, but I'm gonna be mad if it's over when we get there." She went back over to the chair and continued watching the latest episode of her new favorite show. There was nothing better than finding out about a show she'd missed and being able to buy the whole series and binge-watch it. And a series about a really good-looking woman who can teleport to whatever year she's needed to kick ass —while looking super-sexy—was just up her alley. But she was still antsy, and she got up to rub a little petroleum jelly into her patent leather shoes. She was so intent she didn't hear Kit come out of the bathroom. But when she looked up to see Padmé Amidala from the Star Wars prequel trilogy, the prettiest girl in all of Naboo, in her Geonosis battle gear, she dropped to her knees, stunned and speechless.

"How'd I do?" Kit asked, doing a slow turn, revealing every beautiful inch of her luscious body. A pure white catsuit covered her, with a low-slung holster, which held her royal blaster pistol, showing off her sexy hips. A silver armband rested just below her biceps, finishing off the costume with perfection.

"How did you know?" Bailey gasped, struggling to her feet. "Most everyone hates Padmé, but I've had a massive crush on her…forever."

"Your screensaver on your laptop. Your desktop is all Doctor Who, but your laptop has about twenty pictures of Natalie Portman dressed like this. I told the guy at the comic book store that I wanted to look like Natalie Portman when she was in some kind of sci-fi movie, and he told me what to buy."

Bailey could feel her chin start to quiver. "If I told people what you've done, hardly anyone would understand. But this means so much to me..." Tears started to leak out, but she willfully stopped them. "You are the best girlfriend in the whole universe. The people of Naboo would be very, very proud of you."

—⁓—

An hour later, they were plastered against each other, trying to dance in a club packed with costume-clad gay people. Kit had been a little freaked out, going over in her mind how she'd deflect any public attention. But after being there for a few minutes, she'd realized that everyone thought Bailey was a guy. She pulled off the Doctor Who costume so well that you'd have to get right in her face to see she didn't have stubble. Kit hated the fact that she'd been worried about being seen, but it was still really early in their relationship. As soon as things settled down and she had some time to come up with a plan she'd start telling people. But for now—she was going to stop worrying about coming out —and think about what she was going to do to Bailey when they got back to the hotel. Bailey could have her fantasy world, but Kit's was much more corporeal. Having Bailey pressed firmly against her body was just where she wanted her.

—⁓—

Bailey lay under her, naked and squirming. Kit had never done any role-playing in her sex life, but seeing how turned on Bailey was at the moment, she might have to whip out the Padmé outfit again if things ever got too predictable. It had surprised her a little when Bailey'd suggested she keep the suit on, but once they got into it, it was pretty cool to do something that worked so well.

Looking up into Kit's eyes, her gaze almost vacant, Bailey murmured, "When I was young, and just figuring out I was gay, I always fantasized about some gorgeous woman from a movie or comic book. But I never, ever imagined anyone as beautiful and sexy as you. You've made every fantasy I've ever had come true—times ten."

"I wish I knew something about who I am, or who I might be having sex with so I could play it up..."

"No need. I'm very, very visual, and your visuals are about to make me pop." She laced her hands through Kit's hair and pulled her down for a heated kiss. "I love you so much, Kit. You're the woman of my dreams."

Giggling, Kit said, "You're the person of mine. And you're way past anything I ever imagined. Nice to know our reality is beating our fantasies, isn't it?"

Bailey sighed heavily. "It's dreamy. Now let's see if that blaster fits any place fun."

Kit laughed at her antics. She knew every inch of her lover, and the blaster was not going to fit where her eager fingers wanted to be. Thankfully. Some things were too much fun to give up.

—⚏—

It was late—very late, but Kit had a hard time relaxing enough to sleep. Bailey was lying in her arms while Kit continued to trail her fingers down her back. They were both naked, the sheet and blanket bunched up at the foot of the bed. "Don't fall asleep until I get the covers over you," Kit whispered. "You're hot now, but that won't last long."

"Mmm…" Bailey snuggled closer. "I love being warm. Especially when you make me that way." She placed a kiss on Kit's sternum. "You sound awake. You okay?"

"Uh-huh." She continued to rub and pat her gently. "Just thinking."

"'Bout what?"

Bailey was clearly struggling to remain alert.

"Nothing big. Go to sleep now, sweetie. You're exhausted."

As her head lifted, Bailey's eyes gained some alertness. "What is it? Tell me."

Kit laughed. Her lover was constitutionally unable to let things be. "I was just thinking about your suggestion that I put my blaster someplace fun." As a silly grin lit up Bailey's face, Kit added, "Like I'd put some cheap plastic toy that was probably made with lead into you."

"I was kidding. You knew that, right?"

"Yeah," she said, nodding. "But I started to wonder if you weren't entirely kidding. If maybe there are things we're not doing that you want."

Now clearly alert, Bailey rolled onto her side, then braced her body against her forearm. "Just one thing," she admitted, looking surprisingly serious. "I wish you had the ability to transport yourself to when I was about…oh…seventeen. I

243

would have flunked out of high school, but it would have been sooooo worth it."
She grinned like a kid, with her whole face lighting up.

"I'm being serious," Kit said. "You asked if I ever wanted you to use a sex toy
on me, but I never asked you."

"I thought I made it clear in Pennsylvania that I wasn't into toys." She leaned
over and placed a long, lush kiss on Kit's lips. "There is nothing…not one thing I
want that you don't give me." She lay back down, now supporting just her head
with a hand. "That's one of the most amazing things about being with you. We
like the same things, and our kink levels seem to match."

"We have a kink level?"

"Uh-huh," Bailey said, looking serious once again. "Ours is really low. At
least it is if you've told me everything you need."

Kit pulled her close and whispered into her ear. "I'm so glad your kink level is
as low as mine. I've had some lovers who wanted…" She stopped herself from
continuing. Revealing details of past relationships was sort of tacky. "Let's just
say that their kink level was much higher than mine. I tried to be a good sport…
but it's tough to act like something's hot when it isn't the least bit sexy in your
mind."

"I'm perfectly happy…make that I'm perfectly satisfied with our sex life.
Frequency, content, level of enthusiasm. Everything. But if I ever think of
something I'd like, I won't be afraid to tell you." She poked Kit in the chest. "But
you have to do the same."

"It's a deal. But I can't see the need to add a thing." She pulled Bailey close
and kissed her eyelids. "Now if my terrific lover will just close her pretty eyes, we
can get some sleep so we're ready for our first session in the morning."

"Steampunk," Bailey murmured, a delighted smile settling on her sleepy face.
"I love steampunk."

Kit scooted down to grasp the sheet, then cuddled Bailey up next to her body
and kissed across her shoulders. She had no idea what steampunk was, but she
knew she'd be learning in the very near future. As long as Bailey was there, it
would be fun—she hoped.

—∞—

They were both tired on the train ride home, but Kit had been working
something out in her head and thought she'd better take the uninterrupted time

to discuss it. "I've been thinking about making some changes," she said quietly, after making sure the people in front of her didn't look like Washington insiders.

"Changes?" Bailey'd been watching something gory on her tablet, but she paused it mid-dismemberment and removed her earphones. "What kind of changes?"

"When we first got together, I said having two compulsive workaholics could be a good thing. But I'm thinking I might have been wrong."

"I can cut back!" Bailey said, much too loud for the venue.

"No, no," Kit whispered. "I meant me. For the first time since I started the newsletter, I'm unable to keep up. But I'm not willing to do more. I actually want to do less." She leaned closer and spoke right into Bailey's ear. "I want to be with you every evening and every weekend—without worrying about the newsletter."

"How can you do that?"

"Well, I ran into a woman I respect the other day. A real pro. She's being pressured to take a buy-out, but she doesn't want to. And, knowing her, she's not the type to teach at a journalism school or write a book. She's a reporter. The kind of person who's happiest when she's interviewing people and figuring stuff out. Kind of a loner."

"Okay... How does that relate to you?"

"I was thinking about offering her a job. I'd restructure so that she'd be responsible for the overnight and weekend desks. Solely responsible."

"But...you said you have people doing that."

"No, I have people who do a good job of presenting me with their ideas. They do all of the legwork. But I still make the decisions. If Margaret will take the job, I'm going to bow out. She's a bit older than I am and has been doing this since I was in grade school. I trust her instincts. The kids on the desks now are good—but they're green. They'd both benefit from working with Margaret."

Bailey looked very pleased. "And you'd do this just to have more time with me?"

"Yeah. When I was single, I was happy to work as hard as I did. Now—not so much. I want to have dinner together, and I want to take off for the weekend without feeling guilty."

"That's super, Kit! Really! I'll try to cut back too."

Kit patted her leg. "You don't need to. I've seen how your projects go. You only have to really gear up for limited periods. You have to do that—and I'll never give you a hard time about it. Of course, if you want to take fewer projects —I wouldn't complain."

"I could afford to," she said thoughtfully. "I just wanted to be busy when I was feeling at such loose ends."

"I didn't say I could afford this," Kit said quietly. "I'm going to have to pay Margaret a pretty good buck, and that comes right off the top. It's gonna be touch and go for me financially."

Bailey removed her glasses and blinked her big, blue eyes slowly. "And you'll do it anyway? Just to have more time for me?"

"Of course. I'd do anything to make this relationship work." She leaned closer and placed a quick, but sincere kiss on Bailey's lips—after taking a look around to make sure the people behind them couldn't see. "Anything."

"Then I'd better keep taking new jobs. I'm going to have another mouth to feed." She tickled the corner of Kit's mouth with a finger.

"I don't need you to support me. But I'm not going to be able to go out as often."

"No, no, no… It's good for us to go out. So I'll pay for our entertainment. You just let me know if you need me to cover anything else. I can," she insisted. "And I'd be happy to."

"Just to have me around more?" Kit asked, batting her eyes.

"I'd support you totally if you wanted to quit. Having you around means everything to me."

Kit looked into her eyes, so clear and bright. "I love you more every day."

"Me too. Now get back to whatever you were writing so I can watch this zombie finish this guy off." She chuckled, put her earphones back in and let the carnage recommence.

—⁂—

A burst of creativity and focus combined to allow Bailey to finish the project she'd been working on almost a month early. It was for a right-leaning think tank, and there were all sorts of bonuses involved for early performance. She wasn't sure why that was, but the Republicans always wanted things done early and were willing to pay for it.

After walking out into the cool, breezy afternoon, she pulled her phone out and read some reviews of highly rated restaurants. A four-star place she'd never heard of had a reservation available for six thirty. That was really early for Kit to pull herself away, but Bailey wanted to celebrate. Kit had been so remarkably understanding during the last ten days—not complaining a word about being largely ignored—that Bailey was ready to fulfill her promise to shoulder their entertainment budget with a splurge.

She thought Kit had said something about being on Capitol Hill most of the day, and was probably unreachable, but she texted her anyway. "Can you get away for an early dinner?"

After waiting a minute, Bailey went to the closest Metro station to head home. Kit replied while she was in transit. "I'm busy until six at the earliest. That work?"

"How about Les Merles at 6:30?"

"I wouldn't have time to go home first. Mind if I'm bedraggled?"

"I like you bedraggled. Meet there?"

"Sure. I'm hungry! XO"

It was just four thirty, plenty of time to run an errand. It had been a heck of a long time since she'd gone to a store in person, but she was confident she could handle it.

—⁂—

The restaurant website stated they required jackets and ties for men. That kind of sucked, but it was too late to turn back now. DC was so much stuffier than Silicon Valley had been. Nothing but conservative suits, white shirts, sedate ties and three-digit haircuts.

No one loved suits more than Bailey, but when you required them people tended to act stuffier. Not that stuffiness was ever hard to find in Washington. So many people seemed to spend their time trying to impress others with how much power they wielded. It hadn't been that way at all in California. There, your creativity and your connection to the latest trends carried the most weight. Both ways were somewhat tiresome, but Bailey much preferred the California style. Plus, in California her look was just a little more quirky than normal. It wasn't odd at all to find women wearing menswear—at least a few pieces. But a woman in a suit always caught people by surprise in DC.

She paced in front of her closet, trying to decide what to wear. A shirt and sweater would let her blend in a little better—something she thought Kit would appreciate. She hadn't ever complained about Bailey's style, but it didn't take a genius to see how hypersensitive Kit was to critical exposure. But the sweater idea didn't seem good. This was a fancy French restaurant, and a sweater would look too plain without a scarf or jewelry—and she'd rather go naked than wear a necklace and earrings.

That pretty much made suits the only option. The blue velvet would be a good choice, since spring was coming and she'd have to put it away until fall. The formal silk shirt she'd worn the night she met Kit looked best with it, and after putting it and the slacks on, she assessed herself in the mirror for a moment. Wearing a tie made her feel like she was dressed properly. But Kit was still getting used to the whole thing. Why make a point of it? She took off the shirt, and replaced it with a thin cashmere turtleneck. That was a compromise she could live with. Then she found the blow dryer Kit had brought to the apartment and used it to properly dry her hair. Leaving it to drape across her shoulders made her feel a little ill at ease. But Kit would probably like having strangers know she was dining with a woman. And pleasing Kit was just about the only thing Bailey was able to focus on these days.

—⁂—

She was sitting at the bar when Kit walked in about fifteen minutes late. She looked a little frazzled, and her dark gray suit bore some deep wrinkles, but she could hardly have been prettier in Bailey's opinion.

She walked up next to Bailey, kissed her on the cheek, and whispered, "Stick a funnel in my mouth and pour alcohol in."

Bailey extended her martini. "Take mine. I'll order another."

Kit squeezed onto the tiny barstool, took the drink and helped herself to a big sip. "I need this intravenously." As if she'd just then noticed, she said, "I've never seen you leave the house with your hair down." She reached out and swept it off Bailey's shoulder. "It looks nice."

"I try to be unpredictable." That was a bold lie. She liked predictability a lot more than most people did.

"This is a nice place," Kit purred after looking around. "I've heard about it, but haven't been here. Is this the kind of place we're going to hang out in now that you're our entertainment director?"

"Maybe. I got a sweet bonus for finishing early for the Original Intent people. You've been so patient with me, I thought it was only fair to spend a chunk of it on you."

"You know I love good food, but you don't have to make it up to me when you're busy. I truly understand." She focused again on Bailey. "No tie?"

"No, I thought…" Now that she had to explain her choices, she felt a little silly. "I thought this looked nice."

"It does. I'd like to rub my face on that soft-looking sweater."

"You can definitely do that later." She almost took Kit's hand, but mentally slapped herself. No public displays of affection!

Kit's smile was like the sun breaking through the clouds on a warm spring day. "I miss you every minute we're not together." She put on a playfully chiding look. "And that's been a whole lot of not together recently, buddy."

"I know. Luckily, my next project won't require me to be on site much. I'll be home for dinner every night for the foreseeable future."

The bartender appeared, bearing two martinis. "Ladies? These are compliments of Senator Brearly."

Bailey watched as all of the blood drained from Kit's face. "Fuck," she mumbled. Pasting on a very plastic smile, Kit turned and searched the restaurant, then nodded at a good-looking guy in the corner. "I've got to go thank him," she said, looking ill.

"I think they're about finished with dinner. Maybe he'll stop by our table." She made eye contact with the hostess, who started to walk toward them, menus tucked under her arm.

"No way. He's a senator. I'm a reporter. I've got to bow and scrape."

"He was your boyfriend for years!"

"Doesn't matter. That's the hierarchy."

The hostess stood in front of them. "I can show you to your table now."

Kit took a quick look at Henry's table and whispered, "Do you want to go with me?"

"Do you want me to?"

"It won't be fun. I've never met his wife."

Bailey put a hand on her back and gave her a gentle push. "You go alone. You can use me as an excuse. Say I've got a medical condition and have to eat every half hour. I'll faint and cause a scene if I don't."

That brought a smile to Kit's otherwise grim face. "Be right back." Then she strode over to Henry's table, chin up, shoulders thrown back. Bailey followed the hostess to their table, continuing to sneak looks at Kit. After the hostess left, Bailey took another long look, seeing several people not-so-surreptitiously watching the interchange. Damn! Everybody was a gossip. What did people think? That they were going to have a slap-fight?

Her nerves were acting up so badly she'd drained both of their drinks by the time Kit came back just a few minutes later. "How'd it go?"

"It went." She put her hand on the stem of her glass. "Did I drink this?"

"I did. Sorry. I got nervous." A laugh she had no control of bubbled up. "Now my head's spinning."

"Good grief, Bailey! Two and a half martinis in ten minutes is gonna have you on your ass!"

"I know. Let's order two for you so your ass is right next to mine."

"Not a bad idea. I thought I needed a drink before I got here…"

Henry and his wife got up and passed through the dining room, nodding hellos to a few people. When they passed by he waved, but didn't stop. "They're gone," Bailey said, given that she could see the exit.

"About time."

"He's a really nice looking guy. Of course, his wife's smokin' hot too. Their kids had better be supermodels or they'll be a letdown."

That broke the tension a little and Kit finally showed a natural smile. "Yeah, I think Caroline's better breeding stock than I was. She's ready to pop with their second, and she practically oozes good genes."

"I'd choose you if I wanted kids. You've got a much nicer face. Not to mention your…" She pointedly cast a look at Kit's breasts. "Those kids would be nursing every two minutes."

"How drunk *are* you?" Kit whispered as their server approached. She turned to him and said, "We haven't had time to look at the menu. Why don't you bring us another round while we do?" She winked at Bailey as he left. "I've gotta catch up. We'll put one glass in front of you, but I'm gonna drink it. If you have any more you might start singing." She chuckled softly. "You do that, you know. When you've had too much to drink you can't stop yourself."

Kit seemed pretty much like herself, but there was an edginess just under the surface.

"How are you? I'm not sure how I'd be if I saw Julie again, but I'm pretty sure I'd be frazzled."

"Add a much younger wife who's bursting with new life."

"Did…have you ever told me about your breakup? Did he… Was he…?"

Kit jumped in. "I generally tell people it was mutual, but it really wasn't. I broke up with him, and I think you know I'm glad I did. But sometimes…" She wore a very winsome expression. "You think about what might have been. It's hard not to go over the choices you've made when you're face to face with your past."

"I really appreciate your offer to let me meet him. I know that wasn't easy for you."

Looking down, Kit shyly shook her head. "No, it wasn't." When her gaze shifted up to meet Bailey's there was determination in her eyes. "I promised I'd be more forthright and I really am trying. It's just…hard."

"Do you trust him? You said the reason you didn't introduce me to those reporters was that they're professional gossipers."

"Yeah, I do. He'll gossip too. He *is* in politics. But he seems to only do it when he needs to. He's never malicious." She rolled her eyes. "Unless he needs to be."

"Do you see him around town very often?"

"Yeah, but usually just on the Hill. We rarely do more than nod at each other. I'm glad for that."

Their server appeared with their drinks, and Kit made quick work of the first one. Then they ordered, and soon Bailey forgot Henry had even been there. Looking at how Kit's eyes twinkled in the candlelight occupied her mind to bursting.

—⁓—

They had a great meal, but as they traveled home Bailey could see that Kit was still a little guarded. Once inside her apartment, Kit started to peel her suit off. "I feel like I've had this jacket on for twenty hours."

"When did you leave this morning?"

Almost closing her eyes, Kit nodded briefly, like she was calculating. "Seven."

"And it's ten now. Fifteen hours." She reached out and unzipped the skirt, slowly lowering it as Kit twitched her hips. This was a good time to pull a little info out of her. She was always more forthright when she was at home and relaxed.

"Did you love Henry?" Damn, that wasn't much of a lead-in.

Kit met her eyes, and Bailey could see a little sorrow hidden in them. "Definitely. But I didn't love his ambition. We were a good pair, otherwise. We met in the middle on most everything." She stopped for a minute, her brow furrowed. "Actually, I won most of the big arguments. I didn't want to get married or have kids, and he definitely did. But he didn't pressure me. He was excellent at letting me live my own life."

"That sounds pretty ideal," Bailey said. "And lots smoother than my relationship with Julie."

"It was good…except for that ambition stuff. He wanted to run for Senate and I didn't want him to. But he pointed out, correctly, that he was giving up important things for me, so I needed to let him fulfill his goals."

"You were still in Boston?"

"Oh, no. Midway into his first term in Congress I moved to DC to be with him. I'm still amazed I followed him, but I was able to get the *Globe* to let me string. I wasn't on salary, but they paid okay for freelance, and I could take other little jobs as they came up. Since I wanted to follow national politics, DC was the right place for it."

"But you came mostly because you loved him."

"All true. I was happy in Boston and still prefer it to DC. Luckily, I met Asante, so it wasn't too hard losing all of my friends. But after people found out Henry and I were dating, my editors wouldn't let me work on any story that he was even peripherally involved in. I could barely get an inch of type. Eventually that just became too much of an issue. That's when I started blogging."

"Okay," Bailey said thoughtfully. "I have a little bit of an idea of how things were for you two."

"Things were good between us. But once he was a senator…" She visibly shivered. "I could see where his ambition was leading him, and I couldn't hang in there."

Kit's feet were in Bailey's lap and she started to gently rub them, a surefire way to relax Kit enough to make her continue to talk. "Why didn't you want to marry?"

Yawning and stretching, Kit said, "Dunno. It just didn't appeal to me. I'm not religious, so having a church wedding would have been meaningless, and since we weren't going to have kids…." She shrugged. "He had a medical power of attorney for me, and I had one for him. We were taken care of."

"That's kinda…different. Most people prefer to marry."

Her sweet smile held a devilish cast. "I'm not most people."

"Was the breakup bad?"

"Yeah. He was hurt. Very hurt. It took over a month to untangle, and he spent most of that time trying to talk me out of it. He was certain I'd get used to being in the spotlight. I. Would. Not. Have."

The words all fit together, but they still didn't make sense. There had to be something missing from the explanation. "Just being in the public eye made you break up? Only that one thing?"

"It was like water torture, Bailey. Chronic. Unrelenting. I was at the end of my rope…snapping at him over things that I normally wouldn't have even noticed. I started staying in the apartment much more than I should have. When we went out together, I made him leave first, so anyone who wanted to take his picture would get him alone. After a while, I flatly refused to go to any official events. That's not ideal for a senator, since nearly everything is an official event."

Clearly, this was a big deal. A very big deal. Kit sounded phobic about the whole thing. "Not to be rude, but why didn't he break up with you?"

Her devilish smile emerged. "I'm just too cool."

"Yeah, yeah, you really are. But maybe you should have gone to couples therapy or something."

Kit waved a hand in the air. "Therapy for what? I'm just private. Really, really private. I'm always going to be a private person. That's not a mental illness."

"No, of course it's not. But if it interferes with your life…"

"It doesn't. I simply hate being the focus of attention for strangers. If I could be anonymous again I'd do it in a second."

"Do you think you OD'd on unwanted attention with Henry?"

"Maybe. But I was prickly about standing out in a crowd long before we dated." She let out a soft grunt. "I've never told another soul about this, but I blew a final exam I could have nailed because I didn't want to be valedictorian of my class. I would have had to give a commencement speech, and I just couldn't do it. Being second was so much nicer."

"Damn, Kit, who convinced you it's bad to stand out?"

"No one. That's just how I am." She sighed. "You're hinting that I should go spill my guts to someone. But I'm not a therapy type of person. I'm happy with who I am. I just want to live quietly."

Bailey held her hands up in a sign of surrender. "Got it." She got up and extended a hand down to Kit. "I'll stop trying to examine your head." They stood toe-to-toe and Bailey dipped her head and kissed her gently. "But I've only started to examine your body."

—∞—

Since her big project was finished, Bailey didn't bother to set an alarm. She assumed Kit would wake her when she started scrambling around the apartment in the morning. But that didn't happen. When she finally pried her eyes open, it was after eight and Kit's side of the bed was cold.

She sat up and reached for her glasses, finding a sheet of paper lying atop them. Kit had printed something out, and Bailey held it up and blinked a few times to focus.

The headline read, *No Hard Feelings?*

After scanning the blurb below she went back and read it again, carefully.

There were plenty of knives available, but neither the handsome, hunky, soon-to-be running for the big prize pol, nor his former long-term squeeze tried to stick a shiv into each other at Les Merles last night. The new wife looked on, already adept at making a fake smile look slightly less fake.

Ms. Lonely Hearts hasn't managed to snag another VIP, now forced to dine with a gal pal.

She had to pee, but this was too important to ignore. After grabbing her phone, she pressed a button and said, "Call my girlfriend."

"Hi," Kit said when she picked up. "I hope you didn't need me to wake you for anything."

"No, no. I'm fine. How are you?"

"Just more junior high for mean people bullshit," she grumbled.

"Will people know this is you? It's awfully vague…"

"Not to insiders. Hell, your nephew would know it's me if he reads this crappy site." She let out a sigh that made it sound like the world rested on her shoulders. "Things like this shouldn't bother me. But it gives me the creeps to have strangers watching me and running to tell other people they've seen me."

Bailey didn't remind Kit that a significant portion of her income came from doing that exact thing to other people, who probably didn't like it any better than she did. "Well, the good news is that you don't run into Henry very often, right?"

"Right." She sounded a little puzzled.

"That made the news because of him, right? I mean, this hasn't happened before…"

"Right."

Hmm. Something was bothering her. But what? "Are you sure you're okay?"

"I'm fine. Pissed off, but fine. Hey. How about meeting for lunch? I don't have much scheduled this afternoon, but tonight I've got to go to some dumb gala honoring a knucklehead who managed to resign from the cabinet before he was indicted."

"Gosh, that sounds like fun. How'd you get roped into it?"

"Paybacks. Just like everything in this town. I pay to go to this for a friend who works for him, then she pays to go to something I actually support." She laughed softly. "If we'd all just give money to the things we like, we'd save thousands of hours and leave millions of shrimp floating in the ocean where they belong."

"Got it. Glad I don't have to do it, but I understand. But what's that got to do with lunch?"

Kit didn't reply immediately, and when she did, she sounded a little tentative. "No big deal. It's just that lunch is the only time I'll be able to see you. But it's cool if you don't have time."

"I have time," Bailey said quickly. "I always have time for you."

"Great. I'll call around noon. I missed breakfast because I stayed in bed to cuddle with your comatose body, so I'll be starving."

—⁓—

Kit's prediction of her availability didn't turn out exactly like she'd hoped. But by one fifteen the White House press secretary was wrapping up. She was sitting in the back of the briefing room, whispering jokes and snarky comments to a few of her friends, and as soon as he left the podium she hightailed it out of there, beating the crowd. It took a few minutes to exit the building, but getting out was much easier than getting in. Wrangling her phone from her purse, she dialed Bailey. "Hey. Still hungry?"

"Starving. Where should we meet?"

"How do you feel about a steakhouse? It's walking distance from your apartment."

"I'm so hungry a steak sounds great. Text me the cross streets."

Kit decided to walk, and by the time she got there Bailey was pacing in front. She looked totally cute in her huge parka and fur trapper hat that Natalie had given her for Christmas. If she lived anywhere that actually got cold, she'd turn into an icicle. "Hi," Kit said when they hugged briefly.

"Hi there. This is fun. We've never had lunch on a workday."

"I rarely have time. But since I won't be home tonight, I decided I had to carve out a little time for my valentine."

She opened the door and before they'd gone two feet a very friendly, effusive man called out, "It's so good to see you, Ms. Travis!"

Kit extended her hand. "It's good to see you, Louis. Sorry we're a little late for our reservation. Can you still squeeze us in?"

His hand fluttered in the air. "We always have room for you. Can I take your coats?"

"Sure." Kit helped Bailey off with hers, smirking to herself at her puzzled expression. Louis held onto the coats and guided them to a booth where he presented menus.

"This is my favorite booth," he said, winking. "And you know why."

"Thanks," Kit said. "You're very kind."

"Your server will be here before you can count to ten." He leaned over and nearly whispered, "You should come here for dinner. No one tells tales on our guests." Then he scampered away, and Bailey turned her head to watch him leave.

"Uhm…do you come here a lot?"

"Not a whole lot." Kit smiled at the server who rushed over with water. "Yes, tap water's great," she said before he had a chance to ask.

He poured, then said, "Do you have a set time you have to finish, Miss Travis?"

"We're not in a hurry," she said. Looking to her left, she added, "I bet every one of those lobbyists is, though. Feel free to take care of them before they have a collective stroke." He dashed away, and once again Bailey watched him leave.

"Uhm…you don't come here a lot?"

"Like I said, not a whole lot." She started to scratch her nose, then redirected her index finger to the wall. Bailey followed where she was pointing, then turned to face Kit, clearly dumbfounded.

"That's a drawing of you."

"A caricature, actually. But, yes, that's me."

Bailey looked at it again, then slowly turned her gaze back to Kit. "You're a lot more famous than you say you are."

"I've told you—I'm famous for Washington. I swear it's just like junior high. The cheerleaders think they're at the top of a very big heap, but they're forgotten ten minutes after they graduate. Same here. My star's on the way up, but it'll crash the minute I don't have my newsletter."

Bailey took another long look at the caricature. "Yours looks new. Some of these other ones…"

Chuckling, Kit said, "Everyone around me's dead." She squinted at the drawing a foot over Bailey's head. "Except for him. He's in the federal pen."

Now looking very sober, Bailey said, "So last night wasn't because of Henry."

"Probably not. At this point, I'm as famous as he is. But the minute he starts being more overt about running for president, he'll catapult past me."

"Do you like this at all? The fame part?"

"Hate it. Truly. I like being treated well at restaurants, but I'd rather have to grovel for a table and be anonymous again. Actually, if you can slip that drawing off the wall and put it in your messenger bag, I'll be eternally grateful."

"I'm not going to do that, but I'd love it if you'd scoot a little closer so I can take a picture of you and your drawing." She winked as she took her phone out and aimed the camera. "I promise I won't post this anywhere. But it's going to be my new screensaver."

Chapter Fifteen

BEING IN LOVE WAS so damned fun. Bailey had forgotten how cool it was to have a good portion of your brain dedicated to thinking of your lover; to have your heart race when she texted you; to look forward to just getting a pizza with her. She wished every day would fly by, and that they could use those extra hours at night, letting her and Kit luxuriate in the sensation of merely being alone together.

Now that they were officially a couple, they'd stopped texting every day, negotiating where and when to meet. The new habit was that whomever got free first went over to the other's apartment. That made things simpler, more predictable. And there was nothing Bailey liked better than predictability.

Once they were together, they figured out what to do that evening. A few nights found one or the other sitting alone until eleven, but that was okay. They both did it—and both knew it was simply a hazard of their jobs.

One evening, after finishing a piece of a puzzle she was working on, Bailey closed her computer down, took a shower, got dressed and took off for Kit's. It was a little early, only six, but she didn't want to tempt fate by even considering looking at the next item on her agenda. That's how hours flew by—with no dinner and no Kit.

Now that they each had a key, Bailey was able to wave at the night doorman and sail right by him. After opening the door, she followed a soft voice, winding up in Kit's bedroom. Her lover was wearing nothing but a bathrobe, with a suit lying on the bed, obviously having just been removed. Bailey waved, and felt her heart swell with happiness when Kit's face lit up in a grin at seeing her. Nothing beat making a woman smile just because you showed up at her apartment. Kit was obviously on a business call, and Bailey put a finger to her lips and started to back out of the room.

But Kit beckoned her in and patted the spot next to her. Bailey moved to the bed and lay down, with Kit then scooting around to use her body as a backrest.

"Yes, that makes perfect sense. I might not have done it that way, but I can understand why you did." She looked at Bailey and rolled her eyes.

"I don't foresee any problems. I think you can schedule it." With a free hand, she brought her fingers together and tapped them against her thumb, indicating the person was taking too long to get to the point.

"Of course. I think it'll be business as usual. I wouldn't worry about it." She nodded dramatically. "Okay. Great. Yeah, me too. Okay. Yes, sure. See you then." She hit the End button, then let the phone drop to her lap. "I might only do that once a month, but it sure as hell feels like more than that."

"Huh?"

Kit turned, smiled and leaned over until they were nose-to-nose. "Missed you." Gently, she placed a kiss on Bailey's lips.

"Hope I didn't interrupt you. I know it's hard to concentrate when someone's in the room."

Kit stood and walked over to her dresser. "Oh, I didn't have to concentrate much. Just making my monthly call home."

She'd started to pull out a pair of slacks when Bailey said, "What? That was your mom?"

"Dad. I usually talk to my mom, but she's getting her hair done." She looked up at Bailey. "Are we going out or ordering in?"

"Come here," Bailey said, fighting an uneasy feeling in her gut. When Kit arrived, she took her hand and pulled her down. Now they were sitting side by side, letting Bailey see Kit's eyes. "What's up with your family?"

"Huh? Nothing's up. Same old, same old," She blinked slowly, looking so ingenuous.

"You've told me almost nothing about any of them! We're in love, which to me means we're going to spend a heck of a long time together. But you talk about them so rarely I forget your siblings' names!"

"Emily and Jason," she said, looking completely confused. "I'll tell you anything you want to know."

"What do they mean to you?"

Kit took a quick look at her watch. "Kinda hungry. Any chance of getting a bite to eat?"

Bailey got up and took her by the hand. "You've got enough in your cupboard for me to make a simple pasta. Let's go. I'll cook, you'll talk."

They started to walk down the hall with Kit saying quietly, "I'd rather cook and have you talk."

Bailey started to pull a chair into the kitchen, but Kit jumped up onto the counter. "I like sitting up here."

Smiling, Bailey said, "I'm a counter-sitter, too."

"Maybe that's why we fell in love." She stuck her arms out and Bailey snuggled up next to her for a few kisses.

"Don't think you can kiss your way out of this, buddy. I want some details. You sounded like you were talking to a Congressional staffer, not your father. What's up with that?"

Shrugging, Kit said, "That's how we talk. We're not warm and fuzzy people. We relay information to each other on a periodic basis. That seems to satisfy all concerned."

Bailey filled a pot with water and put it on the stove. After turning on the heat, she paused and looked at Kit for a moment. "Are you bullshitting me?"

"No. Not at all."

Kit certainly looked serious, but what kind of screwed up way was that to refer to keeping in touch with your family? Bailey plucked an onion out of a bowl. As she began to chop it, she said, "So you talk once a month?"

"Uh-huh. I call them. If I go much longer than that, my mom acts a little offended, so I try to stay on schedule."

"They never call you?"

"Nope. I'm expected to call, so I do."

"Okaaaay. How often do you see them?"

"Four times a year."

Bailey snuck a look over her shoulder. "Quarterly? So…every time you pay your taxes you zip up to Boston?"

"No, not quarterly. I have to do Thanksgiving and Christmas, then I usually go twice in the summer. I skip spring and fall."

"Why go twice in the summer? If you don't like going…"

"Oh. We have a summerhouse on the Cape. I actually enjoy those visits since I love being on the water. Depending on the weather, I'll go Memorial Day and Labor Day or I'll wait until Fourth of July if the ocean's not warm in May."

"That's it? No birthdays, Easter…"

"No. We don't make a big deal about birthdays. And they celebrate Easter but I stopped going and no one said anything about it, so I scratched that off the list."

Bailey put some olive oil in a pan, then, when it was hot, added the onion and started to sauté it. After adjusting the flame, she chopped a few garlic cloves and added them as well. While tending the pan, Bailey tried to think of a way to ask a question without it sounding too harsh. "I knew you didn't have a great relationship, but I don't think I understood it was just…an obligation."

"Yeah." Kit nodded, clearly not offended. "That's right. It's an obligation. If I could, I'd just meet up with the whole group on the Cape in the summer and call it a year. That'd be plenty for me."

Bailey took her eyes off the pan to meet Kit's gaze for a moment. "Why do you even do that? Why see them at all?"

She seemed to think about that for a bit. "I think I'd feel guilty if I cut them off. I don't want to be rude, Bailey. I just don't enjoy being with them, so I do the minimum."

After turning the heat down, Bailey moved over to stand between Kit's legs. Thankfully, she didn't look upset in the least. But Bailey was. Her stomach had started to ache thinking about the whole situation. "There has to be more than you've told me. There has to be."

"Not really." Kit looked the way she often did when cornered. Just uncomfortable enough to leave or change the subject. Bailey'd learned she would choose just about anything over talking about something that made her uncomfortable. But Bailey wasn't going to let up. She needed to know what had caused this…rift? Kit continued to look at her for a few moments. "I don't know what you want me to say."

"I want you to tell me what's caused you to have such a distant relationship with your closest relatives." She dashed back over to the stove to tend to her pan.

"I'm not sure I have a good answer. Uhm…" She let her gaze travel around the room, clearly trying to satisfy Bailey, but looking absolutely clueless.

"Have you always felt this distant?"

Her brow furrowed for a moment. "I guess not. I got an apartment in Boston after I finished college. For a while, a couple of years, I spent a lot of time in Needham."

"That's where your parents live?"

"Uh-huh. Where I grew up. Emily had her first baby by then, and she was over all of the time. Jason was still in college, but he came home a lot, too. Hanging out there got to be a habit. My mom likes to cook, and I found myself going over most Sundays for dinner."

"That sounds nice."

"Yeah. It was okay. And after I met Henry, we did most holidays with my family."

"His parents didn't mind?"

"No. His mom's dead and his dad married a much younger woman. Henry was shut out."

"Aww, that was nice that your family took him in."

"I'm telling you. They preferred him."

"I'm not buying it," Bailey said. She found a box of chopped tomatoes and added them to the pan. "No one who really knew you could fail to love you."

Smiling, Kit said, "I never said they didn't love me. But as I developed my own personality and became more mature I found that I had less and less in common with them. We started to argue more, and I can't stand that." She took in a breath and corrected herself. "We don't really argue. Neither my parents nor my grandparents will tolerate disrespect. I suppose I'd say that their lectures and hectoring got to be too much for me to stand. So I stopped sharing things and kept our conversations light and neutral." Her shoulders rose and fell. "When you don't share your real feelings being together is meaningless. It's almost like being with strangers."

Bailey took a quick look at her. "So you backed away."

"Pretty much. I'm not going out of my way for a lecture. When we moved to Washington, I obviously saw them less and found I liked it more. After Henry and I broke up I cut it down even further. Eventually I found the tipping point. If I call every month, and see them for the mandatory holidays—everybody's happy."

After adding a generous grinding of pepper and a few pinches of salt, Bailey lowered the heat on the sauce and moved back over to Kit. She put her hands on her thighs and looked into her eyes. "And that's how you want it?"

She smiled and placed a kiss on the top of Bailey's head. "Of course not. I'd like to have them at least act interested in me and be willing to listen to what I have to say. I'd like it if either of my parents sounded happy to hear my damn voice." She bent over and pressed her lips to Bailey's head, staying right there for a minute. "But I'm not going to get that."

"Have you ever talked to any of them about how you feel? Is there one person you feel close to?"

Kit's laugh was light and brief. "Not really. I thought I was going to have an ally in my eldest niece, but she lost interest when she was about ten or eleven. She barely acknowledges me now."

Bailey couldn't hold it in anymore. "Damn it! If they're that distant, cut them off! They don't deserve you!"

"Aww." Kit held her in a tender embrace. "Don't get all upset. Trust me. There are an awful lot of families just like mine. Thankfully, I realized I was wasting my time, and stopped trying so hard."

Sharply, Bailey looked up at her. "What do you mean, trying so hard?"

It took a minute for Kit to answer, and when she did, she finally showed some emotion. Not a lot. Actually, damned little for a woman explaining why she had, at best, a business relationship with the people who created her, but at least she looked sad when she spoke again. "When I was younger, I tried, hard, to impress my parents. But Emily had always done it better and faster and with more style. I kept trying, though. Kept trying to have someone fucking notice me. But every time I gave it my all—only to get a nod or a 'Nice try, Kit,' I felt bad. About myself. It wasn't until I saw them less that I realized I was happier— in every way—when we had less interaction. Trying to impress them was never going to work. I had to impress myself."

"I'm so sorry," Bailey soothed.

"It's okay. I worked it through. I'm anxious for a few days before I have to see them, and it takes me a few days to recover, but I think it's as good as it can get. Most of the time, I don't even think about them."

"You still haven't answered my question. Why do you bother seeing them at all?"

Kit put her arms around her shoulders and rubbed her face against Bailey's hair. "It's easier. I'd have to have a whole thing if I stopped going home. And that would be much, much more upsetting than the few days of discomfort I have to suffer through when I see them."

"But if you did it once—it'd be done."

A gentle smile settled onto Kit's face. "I don't hate them, Bailey. You don't stop seeing your relatives because they hurt your feelings. No one would ever see their families if that was the litmus test."

Bailey looked into her eyes, trying to see what emotion hid behind those lovely warm eyes. "Will we... If you're going to still see them..."

"Working on it, boss. One day you'll meet the whole crew." She bent and kissed Bailey, showing a sly smile when she pulled away. "And if you like Emily better..." She made a fist and pressed it against Bailey's chin. "I won't be responsible for my actions."

"I won't like Emily better." She knew she was supposed to see the lighter side of the situation, but she didn't feel light. Her heart hurt thinking about how awful it must have been for Kit. How lonely she must have felt, especially when she was a young woman, trying to be noticed.

"Come on now. Cheer up." Kit tickled under her chin. "We'll share your family. I already like them better than my own."

Bailey looked into her eyes, seeing very little concern. "Uhm, how will they react? To us?"

Kit pressed her lips together. "Mmm. Not sure."

"Are they homophobic?"

"Not to my knowledge..." She looked very thoughtful for a minute. "They're not religious, so there's no higher power telling them to hate gay people. The topic hasn't come up much."

"Really? I'd think they'd have opinions about same-sex marriage and things like that, given that they're so political."

"Oh." She nodded. "You think they're like the religious right or the Tea Party. No, no, not at all. They're Cheney-style Republicans. They love money, want lower taxes and less government—except for government programs that benefit them, of course."

"Well, I guess that's good."

"Yeah. The only time I can ever recall my dad mentioning gay people was when Cheney's daughter came out. He said something about how it wasn't anyone's business what you did in bed." She chuckled. "Then, of course, he added that some reporter probably made her come out before they outed her. He's always sure the liberal media's behind everything bad."

"So he won't be as upset about your being with me as he is with your basic beliefs."

"Bingo," Kit said, touching the tip of Bailey's nose. "Now you're beginning to understand the Travis ethos."

—⁊⁊⁊—

A week later, Bailey sat in her apartment, waiting for Kit. Even though she loved being with her, having a night alone was nice. She'd bought a new game at Fantasy Fest and hadn't had any time to play it. It was a town-building game and allowed for multiple players to build together. After sending Zack a message, she sat there for a second, waiting for a reply. He was never far from a device and he immediately joined her. "I can only play for an hour," he texted. "Lots of homework."

She chuckled at that. Weren't adults supposed to make sure kids did their homework? But playing a game with Zack was, in her mind, a perfect way to stay connected with her nephew. She just wished she had something—anything—in common with April. Having a straight, girly niece who didn't have a wisp of nerdiness made things tough.

At the end of his hour, Zack dutifully signed off. But Bailey kept playing. Once she got into something like this, all bets were off. She and Kit were supposed to meet up with Asante for dinner. But it was past nine and Kit hadn't even been able to offer a prediction. On her last text, an hour earlier, she advised them to eat if they needed to. Stocking the shelves of her imaginary grocery store made her hungry, so Bailey went into the kitchen and gathered all of the leftover food they'd compiled in the last few days. Kit didn't need to know she ate out of the carton, never bothering to heat it up. Even though Kit professed to love Bailey's guy-like traits, she thought that one might be pressing it.

Finally, at nine forty-five, Kit sent out a text to both Bailey and Asante. "Sorry! I assume you've eaten. Drinks?"

They both agreed, and Bailey took the Metro over to Kit's. Normally, she would have walked, but it was too damn cold. Actually, she had to admit she was one of the few who acted like it was still freezing. Maybe she'd just had too much of the cold, but she hated to check her phone and find it was below thirty. Tonight, she bundled up with long underwear, a glen plaid flannel shirt, a knit tie, and lined jeans. She hadn't known you could buy lined jeans, but Kit had told her about them, and now she was a convert. Her work boots were rated for twenty below, but her feet were still cold as she trudged the last blocks from the

Metro to Kit's. Why did people choose to live in such inhospitable conditions? Had they never been to California?

Kit looked a little frazzled, but she was ready to go when Bailey got to the apartment.

"Are you sure you want to go out?" Bailey asked. "You've been running full-out for days."

"I'm wired to the teeth. Talking to normal people about normal things while guzzling liquor is just the ticket."

They walked back to the train, finding the platform jammed with people. Kit lived right in the middle of the George Washington University campus, and sometimes the neighborhood got a little wild. Tonight must have been some sort of fraternity thing, since half of the people on the platform were young guys—and half of them seemed lit.

A train glided into the station, nearly full. That was rare for this time of night. They managed to jam on, but it was very tight. Bailey grabbed onto a pole, but Kit couldn't snag one. Instead, she reached inside Bailey's parka and hooked her fingers into her belt loops. That worked well enough as they took off, but in just a minute or two the conductor slammed on the brakes, making Kit bang into Bailey full-force. Trying to steady herself, Bailey jammed a foot down, felt something give, then heard a "Fuck!" A blow to her back knocked her against the pole. "Asshole!"

She turned, saw a fuming guy who looked like he wanted to deck her, mumbled, "Sorry," then blinked in surprise when Kit squirmed past her to slap the guy on the chest with the flats of her hands.

"You don't push people who run into you on the train!"

It dawned on Bailey that they were surrounded by the guy's friends. Twenty-something guys filled her field of vision. Every one looking like he wouldn't mind getting in on the action. Not good. "We're sorry," she said again, trying to make eye contact.

"What kinda pussy lets his woman fight for him?" The guy was clearly drunk. His breath smelled like a brewery and his eyes were severely bloodshot. He snapped his open hand against Bailey's shoulder, making her stumble again.

Kit reached around her and grabbed the guy's coat, but Bailey peeled her hand away. She couldn't stop her from talking, though.

"You don't push anyone, asshole! And just for the record, she's a woman!"

All of the guys had been snickering or making sounds of one sort or another. At that, silence reigned for long seconds as the car started up again. "This dude?" He slapped at Bailey again, then yanked her stocking cap off, staring, confusedly as her braid fell to her shoulder. "What the fuck?"

One of his friends took a long look, finally saying, "She doesn't think she's a woman."

The car slowed, then stopped. As the doors opened, Bailey grabbed Kit by the collar and burst through the crowd, reaching the platform just as the doors closed. She stumbled over to the wall and slid down it, her knees too weak to hold her. "Holy fuck! What got into you?"

"He was hitting you!" Her cheeks were beet red, eyes wide.

"And what were you going to do about it? Fight the whole bunch?"

"If I had to, yes!"

Bailey rolled her eyes and managed to stand. "We're taking a cab," she decreed. "And if the cabbie insults me, please shut the hell up."

—⁂—

Asante sat, listening carefully as Kit told the tale. Finally, he looked at Bailey and said, "She doesn't get it. You're going to have to keep an eye on her. She could go off at any time."

"God damn it!" Kit moaned. "You can't let people manhandle you!"

"Yes, you can," Bailey said. "You try to get away with nothing but hurt feelings." She met Asante's eyes. "How often have you had to suck it up and take it?"

"More times than I can count. I don't want this pretty face to be a mass of cuts and bruises."

"He gets it from the police," Kit said, obviously still fuming. "It makes me crazy!"

Asante laughed, took a sip of his drink, and said, "One time, we were going to my cousin's big Christmas party in some snooty, lily-white town in Virginia. Why he wants to live there is way beyond my understanding, but to each his own. We had to rent a car, of course. Kit was driving, since, as you might not know, she has no sense of direction and needs a navigator."

"Rental cars have GPS you can add-on," she said, wrinkling up her nose at him. "I'll pay extra from now on."

"Anyway," he continued, "we had the interior light on, since the crappy map we had looked like a kid's finger-painting. As soon as we crossed into my cousin's town, a cruiser came up behind us and the lights went on."

Bailey covered her face with her hand. No way this story had a happy ending.

"Cop comes up and shines the light right in my face..."

"Even though I was driving," Kit added, her voice rising again.

"Yes, Kit, you were," he said patiently. "Says there'd been a report of a car-jacking. Same model car. Says they were stopping every dark-colored sedan. Your girlfriend here," he pointed dramatically at Kit, "says, 'The only dark colored thing you're looking for is black men riding in cars with white women.'" He scowled at Kit. "It's been nine years, and I can recall that sentence with perfect accuracy. I thought I was going to be found at the bottom of a lake."

"Cops don't lynch people anymore," Kit sniffed. "They just humiliate them so they stay out of white towns."

"I'd prefer not to test that hypotheses," Asante said. "My mother taught me to say two things to cops. 'Yes, sir,' and 'No, sir.' I'd much rather swallow my pride than my teeth."

"I can't just sit there and let people harass the people I love," Kit said. "I can't."

"I understand the instinct," Asante said. "And I can't speak for Bailey, but I prefer to handle my own issues. Over time you learn how to diffuse things—not make them worse."

"I'm with you," Bailey said. "I'm not up to fighting a bunch of frat boys."

"Wimps," Kit said, finally showing a hint of a smile. "You let little things like loaded guns and big fists scare you off."

—◆—

The snow had melted, temperatures were consistently over forty, and Bailey had put away her flannel-lined jeans. She still wore her long underwear, of course. Kit wondered if she'd wear it to the beach when she dragged her to the Cape if summer ever came.

To celebrate the promise of spring, Natalie had invited them over for dinner. Nat was serving an early Easter feast, and Kit knew she should be looking forward to it. But as she got dressed that Saturday afternoon she was a nervous wreck. She knew it was stupid to be nervous. But Natalie was very important to Bailey, and Kit was desperate to make a good impression. She was pretty certain

Natalie thought Bailey was foolish for hooking up with a straight woman, and she wanted to relieve her of any lingering worries.

Sitting at her vanity, she peered at her image, tilting her chin to see different angles. Sometimes she wished she looked a little gayer—but she wasn't even sure what she meant by that. There was something about many of the lesbians she'd met that made them look like they were in the same club. A club she was sure she hadn't been admitted to.

If she had to be honest, and God knew she hated to be, she had to admit she'd always felt like she was outside looking in. Since the day she was born she'd felt just a little off—a little different. Outside of her family, classmates, even many of her co-workers. But it wasn't like that with Bailey. With her, she was an insider. But that wasn't enough. Just being close would never satisfy Bailey. Kit had to be more open. It was just so hard. Sometimes it felt as if Bailey was demanding she learn French fluently in a couple of months. It was a request she could strive mightily to honor, but would be awfully hard to fulfill.

—⁂—

Natalie and Jess lived in a sparkling, attached row house in the U Street Corridor. The kind of place that made Kit green with envy. Of course, if she had a three-bedroom, two-bath Victorian-style row house she'd have even more pressure to bring in the bucks. At least she'd bought her apartment when the real estate market was in the tank and could afford it—even if ad revenue on her sites didn't keep going up.

Bailey seemed so at ease, so at home. Kit struggled, but thought she was doing a great job of fitting in. Still, it was hard when two of the people had known each other for over fifteen years, and the others for five. You were always playing catch-up.

Natalie did all of the cooking, while Jess was tasked with entertaining. They seemed to have figured out their strengths, and Nat's was clearly cooking. Everything she served was amazing. Nat incorporated a little Mexican depth of flavor into the Easter-based dishes, not surprising, given the way she seemed to easily straddle the Anglo/Mexican divide. Kit's family had been in America for a couple of hundred years longer than Natalie's but Nat seemed more fully integrated. Weird.

After dinner, Jess did most of the cleanup. Natalie went in to check on how she was doing, and after she left Kit saw a wineglass sitting on a side table. "Be right back," she said, jumping up to get it into the dishwasher in time.

She started to enter the kitchen, but stopped dead in her tracks. Jess had Natalie pinned up against the counter, kissing her with deadly intent. Nat's hands were on Jess's ass, squeezing her hard enough to make her growl. It was the most rabidly sexual situation Kit had ever seen with people she knew. Her stomach clenched as she shakily turned again and tiptoed away to seek sanctuary in the nearby bathroom.

She caught sight of her ashen face when she flicked on the light. Heavily, she plunked down on the closed toilet seat and tried to get it together. It made no sense, no sense at all, but it had been like seeing something…wrong.

She'd never seen women—in the flesh—kissing. Maybe the first time you saw any unique sex thing you were in shock. God knows she'd had a hell of a time when she first started going to bars with Asante. But this was beyond strange. There was no reason to have her guts turning cartwheels, but they were. This all made no sense, but one thing was clear. She could never tell Bailey she'd freaked out at seeing women kiss. This was a "take it to the grave" thing. Without question.

Chapter Sixteen

KIT WORKED HARD TO make her pledge to Bailey a reality. Hiring Margaret had taken a much bigger chunk from her income than she was comfortable with, but the freedom she was just beginning to realize was well worth it. Margaret was fully in charge of both the night and the weekend desks, forcing Kit to learn how to relinquish control. Margaret definitely had her own style, which only made sense given her thirty-five years of hard news reporting. But having her name prominently featured on the masthead drew a new class of readers, which boosted page views. She wasn't drawing the younger, more impressionable readers advertisers loved, but Kit was really pleased with the quality improvement. That was worth at least as much as money in her book.

Having Margaret run the show freed Kit's evenings up in ways she hadn't even dreamed. But when something big came up at night or on a weekend, Kit had to dive back in. Especially when she was going to appear on a news show and had to have her facts lined up. One Saturday night, Bailey called at around eleven. "I have a feeling I'm going to sleep alone tonight."

"Probably true. No one thought the president would make his pick for the Supreme Court on a Saturday. He's ruined the weekend for every politico in the country."

"No chance for a drink? A midnight snack?"

"Not a drink. Definitely not a drink. I've got a million things to read. This nominee was on the circuit court of appeals. He's got dozens of published opinions, and I've got to at least be familiar with all of the major ones if I'm not going to look like an idiot tomorrow."

"What show are you going to be on?"

"On Politics. It's not very popular, since it's on C-SPAN, but I've still gotta be prepared."

"Let me bring you some food. I know you haven't eaten."

"We've had pizza and all sorts of junk. I'd love to clear my head, but I can't stop for long. I've got to finish so I can get some sleep."

"I'll bring you something healthy. Be there in a half hour." Bailey hung up before Kit could argue. Kit always fell into bad habits when she worked too much. Getting a few vegetables into her system always went by the wayside, but Bailey often surprised her by keeping an eye on her diet. She was convinced you couldn't think clearly if you didn't consume some minimum amount of vitamins. Kit didn't have facts to dispel that belief, so she went along with it—glad to have someone care enough to make her eat stuff she didn't like.

—⁂—

Bailey texted when she was in front of the building. "I'm here. Where are you?"

Kit didn't answer, but in seconds she exited through the building lobby while she struggled into her coat. She took in a big breath when she hit the sidewalk. "First unfiltered air today."

"Were you in your apartment?"

"Uh-huh."

"I'm surprised. I thought your whole staff would be here." Handing over a bag, Bailey said, "Veggie wrap. I know that's not your favorite thing, but it's got vitamins."

"Veggie wrap?" Kit made a face and tried to push the bag back into Bailey's hands. "There's peppers on the cold pizza in my conference room. That's my kinda vegetable."

"No way." Bailey took the wrap from the bag and peeled off the paper. "Come on. Take a bite."

Kit clamped her mouth shut, playfully insolent. Bailey could just imagine her as a baby, refusing to eat her strained peas. Wrapping an arm tightly around her, Bailey put the wrap right in front of her mouth. "Open up and take a bite or I'll keep you out here for hours. Then you'll go on TV and look like a complete doofus."

Kit shook her head sharply, playfully.

"Come on, now. I'll take the first bite." She clamped down on the wrap, then nodded and purred with satisfaction. "Mmmrf. Vegetables. Good."

Kit twisted around in her grasp and started to make a run for it. They didn't play rough very often, but every once in a while Kit seemed to like to. Like it was a way to release stress. Bailey caught her from behind, locked an arm around her, and put the wrap in front of her again. "Take a bite or I'm gonna have to get rough."

From behind, Bailey saw a flash of color. Then a woman's fierce voice yelled, "I'm calling 9-1-1!"

"No!" Kit cried, twisting in Bailey's grasp to face the woman. "I'm fine, Nia. Fine!"

Bailey dropped her hands and Kit stood up and settled her coat.

"Are you sure? When a guy's got you in a headlock..." She moved closer, peered at Bailey carefully, then said, "You're not a guy, are you."

"No." What could you add when someone asked you that?

"Sorry about that. It was just..." She trailed off, while avoiding making eye contact.

Kit stared at the ground, like she was magically trying to disappear. Finally, when Bailey was certain they'd all stand there in silence until the end of time, Kit said, "Are you heading home?"

"No, of course not. I'm going out for more caffeine. Want any?" She backed away, like she couldn't disappear fast enough.

"No, I've had enough." Kit's voice was thin and shaky.

Bailey tried to get her feelings under control once they were alone again. But it was a lost cause. If she stayed...she had no idea what she might say or do. So she turned and headed for the Metro. Kit's footsteps slapped behind her, and in a few seconds a sharp tug on her coat pulled her to a stop. "We promised we'd stick together and work things out! No more running away every time you get mad."

"We promised we'd work on being open." Bailey leaned over and got right in Kit's face. "I know we promised to at least acknowledge each other's fucking existence!"

"I was going to introduce you! She left before I could."

"Bullshit! We all stood there like idiots for half a lifetime!"

"Bailey, please! I did everything but beg you not to come."

Stopping abruptly, Bailey tried hard to control her racing heart. This all just seemed so fucking simple! It was a struggle, but she managed to speak clearly and calmly. "Then tell me not to come. Say those words. Don't come. I'm too busy."

"But you were so sweet to want to. I love that about you."

"You can't have it both ways. If you don't want me around, you've got to tell me."

"I screwed up. I admit that. But once you were here, I was stuck." She took in a deep breath, looking like she was about to lose it. "Things are really, really frantic. Do you have any idea how much stress I'm under tonight? I've got to read and understand hundreds of pages of complex legal arguments, then go on TV in the morning and sound like I know what the fuck I'm talking about!"

"I understand you're stressed. And I don't want to add to it. I'm taking off. Call me when you have time to treat me with the smallest bit of human dignity."

She strode away, her legs chewing up sidewalk much, much faster than Kit could have ever matched. Not that Bailey regretted that. If they faced off again, she was sure she'd say something she wouldn't be able to take back.

—⁂—

Kit was waiting in Bailey's apartment when she returned home late the next afternoon. Her mouth dropped open when their eyes met, then she turned and started to leave.

Kit jumped to her feet and grabbed the hood of her parka. It peeled right off her, with Bailey continuing to walk.

"Please talk to me. Please."

Bailey wheeled and gave her a look that burned. "I'd like to shake you until I can loosen whatever it is that's got you so fucking stuck!"

"I'm not stuck. I'm just not going as fast as you want me to."

"Bullshit!" Bailey's eyes held so much anger they were hard, steel-like. "It's lying that I cannot...will not tolerate. I. Will. Not. Tolerate. It!"

"I'm sorry, baby. I'm so sorry. I was just so busy. If I'd had you in the office it would have been a big deal. Straight women don't wrestle with their friends late at night on the street. Anyone can tell we're lovers. Anyone. I'm sure Nia figured it out, but last night wasn't the time for me to introduce you."

"Then tell me that! I can adapt. I can adjust. I might not like it, but I can deal with it. I cannot deal with lying!"

"I...I just needed to get through the night. I didn't have time for a big discussion."

"I'm not a big discussion. I'm your lover."

Kit put an arm around her and got her fully into the apartment. "If you want to meet my staff, come to the office on Monday." She knew she looked like she was facing the firing squad, but couldn't make herself even appear to be relaxed.

"Why is this so fucking hard for you? Why is being in a lesbian relationship like being a pedophile?"

"It's not. I swear it's not. Come to my office on Monday. Really. I'll introduce you to everyone."

"But you don't want to." Again, her eyes were like scalpels. It felt like Bailey could pierce right through her to see what was in her heart.

She hated having to be honest about this, but she was in such a corner she had no choice. "No, I don't want to. I don't want to tell anyone anything about my private life. Friends get inside. No one else."

Bailey held her hands up in a gesture of futility. "What do we do? I can't be ignored. I won't be."

"Come up with a list of people you want me to tell. I'll do it now. Right now."

Bailey moved over to the sofa and sat down heavily. "Fuck it. I don't have a list. I want to normalize our relationship in every area. I want to feel like you're proud of it."

She looked so fragile. Like the slightest blow would shatter her into tiny pieces. "I am, Bailey. I've never been with anyone I'm more proud of. I respect you and admire you and…" She closed her eyes, trying desperately to stanch the tears. "I just don't want to share that with strangers."

"They're your co-workers!"

"I know that. I hired every one of them. But I know next to nothing about their lives, and the same's true for me. If you don't give people ammunition, they can't shoot you with it."

Bailey put an arm around her and pulled her close. "You hurt me badly. You promised before that you'd never embarrass me like that again. I don't think I can take another whack like that."

"I'll figure out a way to make it better. I promise."

"You've got to do more than promise, Kit. You've got to do it."

Kit had no earthly idea how to do that. Bailey was asking her to change her personality, the very way she moved about in the world. But she couldn't lose her. She wouldn't lose her. One way or the other, she'd figure out a way to do whatever Bailey needed. No one on earth was more important than the woman she held in her arms. She'd give her life for her.

Their bodies fell together, entangled. Like a damn had broken, Kit kissed her with a passion-filled drive. They grappled on the sofa, holding each other tightly. Kit started to undress her, working as quickly as her hands would allow.

Then Bailey got to work, removing each article of Kit's clothing with swift precision. The cool air chilled Kit as her clothes fell away, but that was a small price to pay to see the interest grow in Bailey's eyes. Soon, they were both naked and they went into the bedroom, where they drew the down quilt up to their chins.

Kit pulled Bailey in for a full-body hug, relishing how parts of her were freezing cold, while others were as warm as toast. They shifted and moved to connect more fully, then Kit held her face in her hands and kissed her gently. Looking into those trusting eyes, she whispered, "I love you with all my heart. I'm proud of our love. I'm just not ready to share it."

Bailey's chin quivered. "I love you, too. So much it scares me. When I feel you dismissing what we have between us, it makes me insane."

"We can get through this. We can get through anything together. Anything."

"I hope that's true," Bailey whispered as she buried her head against Kit's neck. "Promise me."

"I promise we'll work things through. We'll have ups and downs, but the ups will be really, really good. Promise."

Bailey pulled her close for a long, emotion-filled kiss, then murmured, her eyes half-closed, "Make love to me."

Kit had never so willingly responded to a request. They kissed hungrily, then Kit slid a hand down Bailey's body. She knew she'd be ready. Her fingers slipped inside and a wave of emotion washed over her. It was madness, but she felt whole when she was inside her body. Like nothing could hurt her when they were so intimately connected.

She probed her mouth with her tongue, exploring her pussy with the same rapt attention. "I love you," she murmured. "I love you so much."

It had just been seconds, but the stress of the day had clearly worked her into a fever pitch. Bailey grasped Kit's hand, forcing it harder into herself. Her flesh so slick it was like gliding on ice. An explosion of air left her body as she climaxed roughly. Normally it took Bailey a few minutes to come back for more, but this time she immediately climbed onto Kit's body and began to work herself over her thigh. Their bodies skimmed against one another as Bailey snapped her hips sharply.

Kit gazed at her, amazed at the passion in those smoky eyes. This was Bailey at her rawest, most vulnerable self. Kit felt her love for her grow as the seconds passed. She loved this woman with all her heart, and wanted the whole world to know it. One day… One day she'd tell everyone.

—∞—

The next week was a little better. But now Bailey was at a point in a project that was eating up a lot of their evenings. They'd slept together every night, but they'd missed dinner every evening. But Kit didn't complain a bit. In fact, she was even nicer than usual, leaving sweet notes on Bailey's pillow that she found when she climbed in beside a sleeping Kit.

This gig had Bailey stuck in a cubicle on K Street, trying to get a bunch of programmers to make progress on some mission-critical changes. Sometimes you needed to be on site, reminding people that you were keeping track of them and would notice if they picked up another job instead of yours.

On Friday night, Bailey started to pack up at five. They were all going to have to work on the weekend, so she reasoned she had to give the guys a break or they'd mutiny. Before she left, she texted Kit. "Heading home. Dinner out?"

Her reply came quickly. "Come to my place. I'll cook."

Well, that was a nice surprise. Eating carryouts and grabbing sandwiches from the local delis was getting old. A real home-cooked meal could erase the bad taste this week had left in Bailey's mouth.

By the time she exited the Metro there was another text from Kit. "Stop by the office and drag me out of here." Chuckling, Bailey did as she was told. Assuming Kit was alone, she buzzed the office door. A loud click sounded, and Bailey pushed the door open—where a room full of people turned and looked at her.

"Uhm…hi. Is Kit here?"

A woman got up and hustled over to her. The same woman who'd happened upon them the other night. "Kit's in her office, Bailey. She told me to keep an eye out for you." She started to walk across the space, with Bailey following her, almost too stunned to speak.

The room was set up with a few offices along the back wall, then a bunch of desks, without barriers, in the main part. Kit's office was in the corner; bigish and laid out nicely, with room for a sofa as well as a pair of chairs in front of the desk. Kit looked up, smiled, then held up a finger as she continued to speak to a young woman who stood next to her.

"I'd rewrite the first six paragraphs. You did this as a lede, but a nut graph would work better. String it out, make the reader work for it a little. Remember the piece about the teen moms from a few weeks ago? That started out in news style, but we switched it to a narrative and it worked much better. I kept the draft. Compare it to the final and you'll see what I mean." She gave her a collegial pat on the shoulder. "I'd love it if you could get it done before you go home."

"I will." The young woman nodded, then brushed past Bailey on her way out.

"Hi," Kit said, smiling brightly. "I asked Nia to keep an eye out for you." She got up and walked over to Bailey, stunning her with a hug. "I wanted to make sure I didn't do a repeat of last Saturday—when I didn't even introduce you!" She slapped her forehead. "I can be such a moron."

"Your focus can be a little fierce," Nia said.

"Bailey, this is my life-saver, Nia Robinson. Nia, this is Bailey Jones, the woman who's about to drag me away from all of this fun. I'm actually going to cook food."

"It's nice to meet you," Nia said. "And just so you don't think she's got no manners at all, Kit apologized for not introducing you that night."

"Oh, I know she's got manners," Bailey managed to say.

"Do you want to meet the rest of the gang?" Kit asked.

Nia backed away, saying, "I'm gonna sneak out before I get sucked into anything else. See you Monday, Chief."

"Have a good one," Kit said to her back as she scampered away. "Everyone runs out of here like they've just cracked a safe."

Kit seemed perfectly at ease. Absolutely normal. Why was tonight okay when just a few days ago she'd acted like introducing Bailey was the same as sticking her tongue down her throat? "Yeah, I guess I'd like to meet everyone else. Are you sure you want me to?"

After pulling the door closed, Kit said, "I tried to explain that night that you caught me off-guard. I'm not averse to introducing you to everyone I know when I'm prepared. But that night when you were tossing me around like a doll… I freaked, then I froze." She put her arms around Bailey and hugged her close. "It's my problem, baby. I freeze when I'm unprepared. It's not about you. Not ever."

"Okay. I get it. I'll try to put things in context." She put her hands in her pockets and slowly moved around the space, looking at everything. "Why have we never come down here?"

"I guess because it's just an office. Nothing special."

"These are special." Bailey pointed at the plethora of framed photos grouped on the wall. "I never would have pegged you for the kind of person who'd want photos of herself with famous people."

"Everyone has a 'Me' wall. I don't get a lot of visitors, but the ones I do get would think I was trying to be a smartass or something if I didn't have one."

"Really?"

"Yeah. I think so. Like I was trying to be above the fray if I didn't show how connected I was."

Bailey took off her glasses and leaned in close to look at a photo of Kit and Bill Clinton. "Were you in high school here?"

"No," Kit said, laughing. "Just out of college. I met him at a conference in Boston on global health." She flicked the photo with a fingernail. "When people say he's charismatic, they're not lying. Honestly, it felt like just the two of us were in that room."

"Given how he's looking at you, he wishes that was true." She put her glasses back on and said, "What's the chance of you letting your hair grow that long again? It's…" She tried to think of a word that wouldn't reveal her mental image of Kit, naked and horny, with her golden hair draping over her gorgeous breasts. "Very attractive."

"Thanks. I'd say the chances are slim. About the same odds as you wearing a cocktail dress and heels."

"You sure do know how to spoil a girl's dreams."

"If it means that much to you, I'll buy a wig." Kit took her hand, then dropped it a second later when she opened the door. "Let's go meet the crew. I'm going to try hard to recall the interns' names, but if I don't speak up immediately, introduce yourself. I'll eavesdrop," she added, her relaxed smile making Bailey feel they'd crossed a very big barrier.

—⁓—

The next afternoon, Kit texted Bailey, who was still at work. "Got an offer to be on a show tonight. I'll skip if you're coming home."

Bailey studied the message for a second, touched that Kit would give up a job just to have dinner with her. "No, go ahead. I'm gonna be stuck for a while. Record the show for me."

"Like you'd watch it! No one's wearing a costume or has super-powers."

"You do. And one of these days I'm going to let you use them on me. If we're ever awake at the same time."

"This too shall pass. I'll be home by nine."

—※—

It really was a pain to have to do a live remote, especially when the remote set was just rented by the channel the show was on. The cable channel paid the local ABC affiliate for their technical assistance and all sorts of other things that were over Kit's head, but other than that you were on your own.

She'd only done one show like this before, but she knew the drill. After grabbing a cab, she hightailed it over to the TV studio. She had plenty of time, over a half hour, and after she finished her makeup she went out to talk to the technician who was setting up.

A year ago, if you'd told her she'd be on TV, being interviewed off the cuff, she would have thought you were crazy. But once she'd done a few cable shows, she realized how few people saw them. It wasn't until you got on a network that anyone seemed to notice, and that was even sporadic. She could do Ed Schrader's show in the nude and not get many comments.

The theme music began at seven on the dot, and she sat there smiling when the camera light flashed on. That was just a headshot, and she didn't have to speak. To her surprise, there were two other panelists. There were always two guests, but having a third often made it impossible to get a word in. Luckily, besides the guy who seemed to have the second amendment tattooed on his forehead, the other commentator was also a reporter. Not that reporters always played fair, but they tended to be less vitriolic than people who were merely pushing an agenda.

After the opening commercial, they played a canned piece about gun violence. Then Ed, the host, said a few things he obviously hoped would whip them into a frenzy. The Second Amendment guy bit immediately and they were off.

Being on live TV was a strange experience. When the green light was on, it seemed as if time had stopped, but at the end of the segment it always felt as if just moments had passed. Kit wasn't a born performer, but she had to admit that she got off on the adrenaline that pumped through her veins when the camera was on.

The host started to wrap things up, and Kit spared a quick look at the clock, seeing that it was only seven twenty-two. That was way too early to stop, and it took her a second to realize that Ed had planned to run short. "While we have you here, Kit, I'd like to get your reaction to Senator Brearly's recent conversion."

It was clear he was talking to her, and the green light was blazing. But Kit was struck mute. Fumbling, she managed, "Pardon me?"

"Senator Brearly," he repeated, as though she couldn't understand which senator he was referring to. "He was baptized this past Sunday by Pastor Dick Sprague. He's been born again. I assumed you would've known."

Steamed, both by the implication and the fact that he had purposefully thrown this at her without warning, Kit refused to show how flustered she was. "I wasn't aware of that."

The other reporter piped up, "His office said this is just the first step in a long journey of faith. He's also said to be reassessing his support for a woman's right to choose."

It wasn't fair. The camera wasn't supposed to turn to her. They caught her rolling her eyes. She was sure of it!

Ed's booming voice snapped her out of her musings. "You look skeptical, Kit."

"No, no, I'm sure the Lord works in mysterious ways." She almost…almost stuffed a cork in it. But she wouldn't have held her tongue for any other politician, so it wasn't fair to give Henry a pass. "Apparently, the Lord's told Senator Brearly to tack right if he wants to run for president. I guess a moderate Republican has to make a decision. He can either represent the people who elected him, or play to the people who can pull him up the next rung on the ladder."

"Great quote," Ed said, chuckling evilly. "Well, that's all we have time for tonight. We'll see you on Monday, right here in The Bullpen."

The green light went out, but the main feed was still connected. "Can you hear me, Ed?"

"Yeah." He looked positively giddy. "Loud and clear. Good job!"

"Thanks. Go fuck yourself." She disconnected her mic and battery pack, then stormed off the set, furious. If her agent had even a whiff of knowledge about that mindfuck, he was toast.

—∽—

Too angry to speak, Kit paced around her apartment for a good half hour. She was livid at being set up, slightly less furious with herself. She would never talk about her and Henry's relationship in any real detail, but she couldn't just give him a pass—even on television. He was a national figure now, and it was crystal clear that he was going to run for president. It sucked, but the gloves were going to have to come off and stay off.

So why did she feel like such an asshole? She checked her watch, and realized she'd feel like a bigger jerk if she didn't call Bailey. They generally texted, but she thought this time a human voice was required. Bailey picked up on the first ring.

"Did you have any idea they were going to ask you about Henry?"

"None. I never would've gone if I'd known, and my agent swears he had no idea. He said they were quite insistent that they wanted me because of the piece I wrote about the latest gun control proposal. Neither of us had heard anything about the newly born-again senator, so we couldn't guess I was going to be sacrificed."

"You sound really upset," Bailey said quietly.

"I am. I really am. Would you mind if I stayed home and licked my wounds?"

There was a long pause. "If that's what you need to do, it's okay. I'd rather see you, but only because I think getting a little comfort might make you feel better."

Kit knew that should be true. But that really wasn't who she was. Sitting around talking wouldn't do any good. She had to get on the Internet and see how bad this was. And taking an extra half hour to walk over to Bailey's was a half hour she could have been working. "How about comforting me tomorrow?"

"Whatever you need."

What a nice sentiment. That's exactly what you wanted your lover to say when times were tough.

After monitoring every form of social media, Kit was finally able to focus. So far, there hadn't been very many comments about the incident. She'd never been so glad to have been on a TV show so few people watched. But if the story gained any traction, she would have to have a statement ready. So she spent the next hour writing and rewriting a piece. It came down to a combination of a defense of her journalistic integrity and a sincere apology for making a flippant comment about Henry's faith. She was fairly sure that he'd created this new relationship with God out of whole cloth. But that wasn't for her to judge, and she felt like shit for having done so publicly.

—m—

Kit snuck into Bailey's apartment at five in the morning. She hadn't been able to sleep without her, and after kicking herself for the dumb decision to stay home alone just decided to go on over and at least have a little time to cuddle together. She dropped her clothes, slid into the bed and was immediately enveloped in Bailey's embrace—as if she'd been waiting for her. There was no better way on earth to be greeted.

To make up for the evening, Kit offered to take Bailey to a nice place for brunch. She chose a pricey spot not far from the Capitol, but thought it was worth it since they had lots of healthy options—Bailey's favorites. They were just digging into their meals when a guy Kit had an acquaintance with came over to say hello. She knew he worked in the White House press office, but wasn't exactly sure what his job was. As she always did when she was unaware of someone's name, she acted more effusive in her greeting. "Hey! I haven't seen you around in months. How's it going?"

"Things are good." He shot a look at Bailey, then twitched his head toward the entrance. "Can I have a word alone?"

Kit looked down on her steaming hot fifteen-dollar omelet, sighed, and got up. As she saw the expression on his face her heart started to beat faster. "Hey," he said quietly, standing in the doorway, "I don't mean to break your balls, but we have to start a little brush fire with what you said last night."

She grabbed him by the forearm and squeezed. "No! I dodged a big one."

"I know that. That's why I thought it'd be nice to give you a warning." He slapped her on the back as he started to walk away. "Collateral damage. Sorry for the shrapnel."

She moved back over to their table and flopped down into her chair. "There's going to be a public execution. Mine."

—m—

She really didn't want to do it. She didn't even have words to express how much she didn't want to do it. But Kit had to call Henry. It was the bare minimum she owed him.

Her hand was shaking as she dialed his number, hoping that he wouldn't pick up. But her luck was holding at not very good, and his voice rang out loud and clear, "Why do I have a feeling I'm not going to like what you have to say?"

"All good politicians have a sixth sense. I know this isn't my place, but if your staff hasn't told you something's brewing, they're asleep at the wheel."

He was immediately agitated. His voice always started to rise in pitch when he was tense. "I had my cell phone turned off all day. What's going on?"

"I could ask you the same. You don't owe me anything, of course. But when you do something big it would be nice if you'd let me know. Then I might not get blindsided."

"Somebody asked you about my faith?"

"Yes, and the fact that you're reassessing your pro-choice status. That was a real kick in the teeth."

He sounded a little indignant. "You're not in a position to judge this. Once you have a child, you start to realize how precious every one of their lives is."

"We are not going to have this discussion. I just called to apologize for rolling my eyes when some idiot told me about your conversion. I was on television at the time, by the way. I don't feel like I need to confess private eye rolling, which I get the feeling I'm going to be doing more and more of."

"Thanks. Thanks a lot. It's nice to know you're supportive."

"I was very supportive of you when I felt you were trying to do the best job for your constituents. I'm not sure that's true anymore."

"Good to know. I'll take you off my major donors list. Feel free to not call again." The line went dead and Kit sat there, stunned. He hadn't been that upset when she'd broken up with him. What did that say about the quality of their relationship? That was something she had no interest in considering.

—◊—

Bailey rushed to get out of her K Street cubicle on Friday afternoon. When she hit the street, she heard a quick toot of a car horn. A big smile settled on her lips. It was so nice to have a girlfriend who'd drive in Friday night DC traffic just so they could get a head start on their trip. It wasn't much of a trip, in Bailey's mind. She didn't think most girlfriends would look forward to going to

Pennsylvania to watch a twelve-year-old kid play the cello and a fourteen-year-old play the violin. But Kit was a pretty extraordinary girlfriend, and she claimed she was looking forward to going to April and Zack's spring recital. Bailey jumped into the passenger seat, leaned over and kissed Kit's cheek. "Do you mind driving?"

"No. I'll need directions, but it's good to stay in driving shape."

Bailey gave her a puzzled look.

"I haven't been behind the wheel of a car in months. Hold on!"

—∞—

Kit had such a kind heart. Bailey had mentioned, in passing, that her mom was slightly offended by their staying in a hotel when they visited. Now she insisted they bunk in Bailey's old room. The room held two twins, and Bailey needed every inch of the small bed. So Kit jammed herself into the little available space and spent a long time kissing and fondling Bailey, relaxing her thoroughly. Then she placed one last kiss on her lips and whispered, "Good night, my sweet girl," then got up and went to sleep in the other bed.

Bailey turned onto her side and fell asleep in moments, feeling fully and very well loved.

—∞—

On Saturday evening, they sat through a dozen kids playing a dozen instruments in varying degrees of ineptness. Actually, some of the kids were pretty good—for kids. April had been playing for six years, and had some promise, but she didn't have the drive you needed to excel. Zack had plenty of that, but he played mechanically rather than from his soul. You had to give the kid credit, though. He practiced more than he was asked to and had given up all of his other extracurricular activities to give the cello his all.

Afterward, he grabbed Bailey's hand and dragged her over to April's teacher. "Next year," he said excitedly, "Mr. Barrow's gonna be my teacher. He's really good." As they got closer, the man looked up and smiled at Zack, then his eyes locked on Kit. Bailey could actually see recognition dawn. Zack grabbed Kit's hand too and stood in front of the teacher, beaming. "Mr. Barrow, I want you to meet my aunt and her girlfriend."

"I recognize you," the man said, smiling and reaching for Kit's hand. "I'm a big fan. I didn't know you were related to Zack."

"I'm not," Kit said, her cheeks growing cherry-colored. "I'm a friend of the family. Bailey here is Zack's aunt."

Bailey stuck her hand out and shook the teacher's hand. "It's good to meet you. Zack's really excited about continuing with the cello."

"He's a good kid," the man said, ruffling his hand through Zack's fine, blond hair. "So…you and Ms. Travis are…partnered?"

Bailey had what might have been her first coming-out moment of panic. What was she supposed to say? She could feel Zack's gaze, knew Kit was freaking out, and had Mr. Barrow staring right into her eyes.

Kit jumped in. "Like I said, I'm a friend of the family. I'm not related to Zack, but if you know him at all, you know what a special kid he is. I thought it would be fun to hear him play." She put on a remarkably calm smile. "I'm glad I got to hear you, Zack. I'm going to download some cello concertos to listen to on the way home."

Zack smiled at her, but Bailey could see he was puzzled. So was Mr. Barrow, but Bailey didn't have time to reassure everyone in Pennsylvania. Just Zack.

—⁂—

The whole group decided to go out for pie, and Zack ran to Bailey's car. "Can I go with you guys?"

"Sure," Bailey said, locking eyes with Kit over the roof.

They all got in and Zack didn't say anything for a few minutes. Then, quietly, he asked, "Why didn't you want Mr. Barrow to know you're girlfriends?"

Kit looked to Bailey, but she was staring straight ahead, offering no help.

"Uhm…" She turned around in her seat, looking into his questioning eyes. Yet another Kwiatkowski who could break her heart with just a look.

"My mom said you're living together. Every time I talk to Aunt Bailey she's at your apartment."

"Yes, that's right. We are girlfriends, but I'm not…" She looked for help. Any help. But Bailey was still staring into the distance. "When you're a reporter, it's a good idea to keep your personal life very private."

His eyes narrowed as he clearly tried to understand. "But you told him you were a family friend. That's personal, isn't it?"

"Yeah, but in a different way. Mmm… Maybe your mom can explain this better."

"My mom say you've gotta stand up and tell the truth about everything that's important. Some people give me a hard time when I tell them my aunt's gay, but I'm not supposed to let that stop me from being honest." His head cocked, and his wispy hair tumbled into his eyes. "You're not... You're glad you're gay, aren't you?"

Oh, fuck. Bailey finally came to the rescue. She cleared her throat and said, "It's different for Kit. She has to report on all kinds of things, and she has to be careful people don't doubt her motives. The less they know about her, the better."

"But Mr. Barrow's just a music teacher..."

"True. But you know how gossip travels. He might post something and have a lot of people notice it."

"But he's gay too...I think."

"That's not the issue, Zack."

"But if it's not bad to be gay..."

"Sometimes there's a difference between what you can say in your private life and what you can say in your public life."

Zack's clear blue eyes squinted just like his aunt's did. "But doesn't it hurt everyone when people don't tell the truth?"

Kit couldn't take another moment. "Your mom's right. It's best to be honest about who you are. But sometimes it takes a little time for people to get up the nerve to come out. I'm a little slow."

"Why?" He had such an innocent gaze. Why was it so penetrating?

"I don't know, Zack. It's just taking me a while."

—⁂—

On Sunday, the family gathered for a hearty breakfast after Mass. Kit had only been to a few Catholic funerals and a baptism or two, but it was nice to be with the Kwiatkowskis, even though they were worshiping a God she had very little connection to. After the meal, the whole clan walked them out to their car to say their goodbyes. Before Kit got in, Zack threw his arms around her and gave her a crushing hug. She kissed the top of his blond head, on the verge of choking up. She'd never, ever felt so connected to any of her own nieces and nephews.

He looked up at her and said, "I hope you can come out soon. I've had to do it a bunch of times, and it's really not too bad once you're used to it."

"You've had to do it...?" Kit stared at the kid, flummoxed.

His pretty blue eyes blinked slowly. "Yeah. When I tell people about Aunt Bailey. That's coming out too, isn't it?"

"It is," she nodded. Grasping his shoulder, she met his eyes and they shared a smile. "I'm going to try to be as brave as you are, Zack. I'm slow, but I'll get there."

They got into the car and drove away, with Kit saying, "If I still have any juice in DC when that kid's in college, he's gonna be someone important's intern."

Bailey smiled at her, but she'd been unusually quiet since the fiasco with the music teacher. After driving in silence for an hour, only some seizure-inducing electronic music for accompaniment, she finally said, "I…uhm…had a little taste of what it must feel like to be in the closet last night."

"Yeah?" Kit wasn't sure where she was going with this, so she let her go on her own.

"Yeah. I didn't like it." She turned and gave Kit a sad smile. "It felt like I was trapped. I had all of these conflicting thoughts racing through my head, like I couldn't keep everything straight."

"Yeah, I guess it's like that sometimes."

"I feel bad for you, Kit. I really do. I wish you felt like you could just come out and put this behind you."

"I will. I swear I will, Bailey. I just need to work up a plan."

"You could just…do it."

"No, that's not…I'm not that kind of person. I've gotta figure out a way to do it without exposing myself to too much criticism."

Bailey was quiet for a few seconds as a drum machine beat an annoyingly repetitive track. "Why does it matter if people criticize you? Being gay doesn't change who you are."

Kit looked at her for a few seconds. She just didn't get it, and Kit had run out of ways to explain it. "All I have is my reputation. People already label me as a knee-jerk liberal—even though I'm not. If people label my sexuality…" She shuddered. "I want to be able to write about gay issues without having everyone assume I'm advancing a position for my own benefit. It's delicate, Bailey. I swear it is."

"I believe you." She took her hand and kissed it. "I just wish it wasn't."

Chapter Seventeen

JUST A FEW DAYS LATER, Kit stood in the cold rain waiting for a bus. Buses were her second least favorite form of transportation, edging out cabs, but she'd drown if she took a shared bike, and the Metro didn't go anywhere near where she was headed. The bus shelter had an ad showing a beautiful woman wearing a bikini as she lay on a sandy beach. The curvy woman in the bikini didn't do a thing for her. But she could just picture a much more androgynous woman, probably in board shorts, soaking up the sun.

Without pausing to reconsider, she texted Bailey. "Need to get away. Wanna go with me?"

In a few seconds, the reply came back. "Yes. Always."

That made her smile. She didn't even mind that her best black heels were going to be ruined by the time she got to her meeting. The thought of going away with Bailey made little things like that completely insignificant.

—⚉—

She didn't think she'd ever tried to surprise anyone with a trip, and Kit had to admit the logistics were a little troublesome. But she had everything organized by Thursday, including convincing Margaret to keep an eye on the newsletter all day on Friday. Her staff, particularly Nia, had been giving her funny looks ever since she'd told them she was going away for another long weekend. When your whole crew tiptoed around like they were waiting for the other shoe to drop when you simply took a single day off—you'd skipped too many vacations.

Their flight was at nine PM, and Kit arrived, suitcase in hand, at Bailey's apartment at six. Bailey opened the door and stood there, open-mouthed. "I was sure I'd have to come pry you out of your chair."

"Nope." Kit breezed past her. "You're seeing the new, vacation-centric me." She put her case down and walked to Bailey's room. As expected, her suitcase was lying open on the bed. Kit started to remove almost everything. "Won't need it. Won't want it. Won't need it..." When she was finished, the case held only underwear.

Bailey stood in the doorway, watching carefully. "Nudist colony?"

"Why do they call them colonies?" She thought for a moment, and couldn't come up with a single reason. "I'm going to have to look into that."

Bailey walked over to her, scooped up the meager collection of undies and said, "I'll just stick these in my pockets if this is all I'm allowed to take."

"Not a bad idea." Kit smiled at her, finding she loved having this little secret. "Go do something. I'll pack for you."

"Seriously?"

"Yeah. Trust me, you don't need much, but you need more than this." She flicked her hands in a shooing motion. "Go on. Shut your computer down or something."

Shrugging, Bailey turned and started to leave. "No hints, huh?"

Kit walked over to her, tugged her checked shirt from her slacks and lifted her omnipresent silk undershirt. "I guarantee you won't need this for the entire weekend."

"If that's true, I'll be a very happy woman. I've been cold since September."

—⁂—

It was hard to keep the location a secret when the sign at the gate clearly read Miami.

Bailey was grinning like a child, remarkably jazzed about such a short flight. "I've never been to Florida," she said, nearly bouncing.

"You haven't? But you grew up in Pennsylvania. Everyone on the East Coast goes to Florida at some point."

"Nope. Not us."

"No Disney World?"

Bailey laughed. "Way too expensive. We went to Hershey Park almost every year, though. Seemed like plenty of fun to me."

"Ooo." Kit almost put her arms around her, but caught herself in the nick of time. "You've never seen Mickey and Minnie?"

Bailey's smile was especially sweet. "I saw them at Disneyland. You're not the first woman who thinks I had a deprived childhood. Mimi took me just months after we got together."

"I'm glad." Oh, what the heck? She gave Bailey a brief hug. "My nieces and nephews go every year but they're the ones who've been deprived. Love and attention are a heck of a lot more important than mouse ears."

—m—

Kit decisively walked down a row of rental cars, paused, then took a closer look. "White or silver?" she asked.

"Uhm…white. Don't we have to wait for…"

Kit opened the trunk, tossed their bags in, then got into the driver's seat. "I'm leaving without you…" she called out the open door.

Bailey jumped in. "You just take a car?"

"Uh-huh. Express checkout. You make a reservation, find what you want and take off." She was carefully adjusting the mirrors when she gave Bailey a sidelong look. "Don't you travel for business?"

"Nope. Never have. Never want to. I like this system though."

"They try to make things a little easier for frequent travelers. Travel still sucks, though. When I traveled in the press corps for the presidential campaign I never knew where I was. It was truly like six months of my life just vanished."

"Couldn't pay me enough," Bailey decided. "But, as I say, I think I'd like the perks of being a business traveler—just not the travel part."

Kit seemed to know exactly where she was going, and Bailey was about to ask if Asante had been teasing when he'd said her sense of direction was terrible. But then Bailey heard a muted soft voice and she reached over to pluck the earphone from Kit's ear. "GPS?"

"Give that back!" She grabbed the earpiece and stuck it back in. "We'll wind up in the ocean if I don't have that!"

Bailey settled in her seat and let Kit and her disembodied friend lead them.

After fighting through the heavy airport traffic and traveling a few miles on a very busy highway, they crossed a narrow body of water and were soon cruising down a very cool street. "I'm totally loving this," Bailey enthused. "I've seen this street in a bunch of movies and TV shows, but I always assumed it was kinda enhanced for TV. It's really not."

"No, there's a very cool vibe on Collins Avenue. I love the art deco architecture."

Bailey lowered her window. "Feel that," she groaned. "Warm, humid air." She unfastened her seat belt, ignoring the bleating alarm, then leaned over and kissed Kit on the cheek. "My frozen body thanks you."

"Smells good, too, doesn't it?"

"Incredible. Like we're in another country. A warm country. With lots of music!"

"Lots and lots," Kit agreed. "Every place we pass has something blaring. It's nice—if you're not trying to sleep."

"This doesn't look like a place where people sleep a lot. It's only midnight. Shouldn't we go listen to samba music or something?"

"Really?" Kit gave her a puzzled look.

"Nah. I've been up since six. I'd much rather be horizontal. Hey, can we leave our window open? I love to sleep with the window open when it's warm."

"No problema," Kit said, winking. "Get used to it, 'cause I'm going to use all my Spanish while we're here."

"Fantastico."

—⁂—

Bailey waited patiently as Kit checked them into their hotel. Since they had so little, Kit waved off the bellman and twitched her head toward the elevator. "Who's Hannah Smith?" Bailey asked as she hurried to keep up with her.

"Me. Well, any of the women in the office who need to be anonymous when paying for something. Right after she started, Nia decided we needed the ability to pay for meals and hotel rooms and not have to use our real names. I'm not sure how she did it, but I've got a gold AMEX card that says I'm Hannah Smith. Apparently that was the most common girl's name and the most common surname when she cooked up this little scheme."

"Interesting. Do you use it much?"

"Not now. But I used it all the time when I was anonymous. If you ever hear anyone call me Hannah, just play along."

They were whisked up to the fifteenth floor, and Kit slid her key card into the slot. The door opened and she let out a soft purr. "All of those crappy lunches and dinners I've had to pay for the last couple of years were worth it."

"Run that by me again?" Bailey asked.

"Rewards points. I've got zillions of them, but never use them, given that I go nowhere for fun. I think that's about to change."

"This is nice, Kit. Really nice." Bailey went to the floor to ceiling sliding doors and opened one. "Oh, damn, this is sweet! Come out here!"

Kit joined her and they stood together on the breezy balcony. "Maybe we should sleep out here. Those lounge chairs look plenty comfy."

The ocean, just a hundred yards away, was so calm it could have been a lake. The air was humid, as soft as a caress. Some scent tickled her nose. Jasmine? Plumeria? Whatever it was, she loved it.

"Why don't we live here?"

"It's very nice in early spring. Come back in July and let me know if you're as interested."

"Mmm..." She leaned over and kissed Kit's neck. "If you're here, I'd be interested."

—⁂—

The next morning, after a long, leisurely bout of lovemaking, Kit went into the bath and got the shower to the perfect temperature. "Who wants to be scrubbed clean?"

Bailey joined her seconds later. "I love to shower with you. Reminds me of our first day together. Of course, then I was chipping icicles off your nose. This is much nicer."

"I wish you liked the weather in DC better. I really do know you're making a sacrifice to stay."

"I'd rather be cold with you, than warm without you." She moved so the warm water hit her on the top of her head. "But, ideally, I'd be warm with you."

"Breakfast? I thought we'd go out."

"I'm good with that. I kinda thought we'd just stay in the room and sleep on those lounge chairs. But if you want to venture out, I'm in."

"We've got to go buy some South Beach clothes. I know just what I want to see you in."

—⁂—

After brunch, they set off to Lincoln Road to find what Kit was looking for. It took a while, but eventually they were successful. Bailey was decked out in a straw fedora, a sky blue linen shirt and white linen slacks. Very simple sandals took the place of the heavy boots she'd been wearing all winter. Kit's hat had a narrower brim, making it a little more feminine, and instead of a shirt and slacks, she wore a close-fitting, fuchsia colored linen shift.

They strolled down the crowded street, with their DC clothes in their shopping bags. But the most surprising thing wasn't that Kit had insisted on buying Bailey a whole outfit, it was that they were walking hand in hand. As they walked, Bailey could feel her contentment grow. Almost like she was high. Being with the woman she loved, and having that woman act like being affectionate was perfectly normal was better than any drug she'd ever heard of.

They stopped at an open-air bar for a drink, and Bailey studiously read the drink menu. When the server approached she said, "The bourbon, peach nectar, agave and ginger beer sounds good. What do you think?"

"I think you'll love it," the very attractive woman said. "Two?"

"Yep." She took a quick look at Kit. "Complaints?"

"None at all," she said, smiling contentedly.

The server departed and Kit watched her leave. "She took a shine to you," she said, nodding decisively.

"Huh. Really?" Bailey adjusted her hat, then played with her sleeves, which she'd rolled up, making sure they were even.

"You honestly didn't notice?"

"Not really." Now satisfied, she relaxed into the cushy canvas covered chair. "I don't pay attention to other women when I'm in a relationship."

"Really? Like…at all?"

"Yeah. Not at all. There's nothing to gain, so why bother?"

Kit's interest in the topic seemed to be growing by the moment. "Do women flirt with you a lot?"

Considering the question for a moment, Bailey nodded. "Not as much in DC, but fairly often in California. I'd probably do well with the ladies down here, but since we're not moving it doesn't matter."

Reaching out, Kit slapped at her leg. "So women check you out routinely?"

"Mmm. I wouldn't go that far. Once in a while seems more correct."

"Fascinating. You certainly don't give off any flirty vibes. I wonder why?" She chuckled. "Not that you're not fantastic-looking, of course. You just don't look like you want to play."

"I think it's my look. As you've pointed out, I'm pretty unique looking. Women who like women who look like me don't get lots of opportunities, so when they see me, they figure they'll give it a try."

Kit's grin continued to grow. "You're being modest. I think it's just because you're a doll."

"A doll, huh? I don't think I've ever been called a doll."

The server came up beside Bailey and almost got down into a squat. Each of the women wore skirts so short you'd be able to see their cervixes if they weren't careful, and this particular woman wasn't being overly careful. She placed the drinks on the little table, smiled warmly at Bailey and said, "If you don't think these are amazing, let me know. We'll whip something else up for you."

With a half-grin, Bailey took a sip. "Amazing." She pulled her wallet from her back pocket and handed the woman her charge card.

As she walked away, Kit turned in her direction and said loudly, "In case anyone wants to know, I think it's amazing, too."

Bailey lifted her glass and they touched the rims together. "I'm glad you like it. If you change you mind, I can have something else whipped up." She playfully pointed at the bar. "I've got people here…"

"Show off."

"I got no traction when I was single last summer in DC. I should have come down here. I think my look fits better in a more laid-back place."

"Oh, what the heck," Kit said, acting like she was making a major decision. "We might be able to tolerate the heat and humidity. Wanna give it a try?"

"I could work from almost anywhere…if you'll find me jobs," Bailey said. "I'm not great at networking."

"I could hook you up. Networking's my thing…even once removed. But I'd have to start writing about something else."

"They have politics here, don't they?"

Kit let out a soft laugh. "I've heard Miami is pretty political, but mostly local stuff. My beat wouldn't work here. I need to be in Hell's Gate." She showed Bailey a sly smile. "My current pet name for our home." She let her head fall back and a sigh left her lips. "I guess we'll just have to come down here to warm up. Next year," she said, looking over the tops of her dark glasses, "we're coming at least once a month. I can't have you freezing constantly."

"I'm holding you to that promise, but I'll pay. You can save your points for a rainy day." She sighed. "Thinking about the future makes me so happy."

Kit leaned over and placed a soft but much more than friendly kiss on her lips. "If you're happy, I'm happy."

As Kit slid back into her seat, the server returned with Bailey's card. "Let me know if there's anything else I can get for you."

Bailey looked up, a satisfied smile on her face. "I'm as good as I can get. I don't need a thing."

—⁓—

After dropping their shopping bags off at their room, they went out to the beach and walked along the remarkably calm waters.

"Unless my memory's shot, I think today was the first time you've ever held my hand in public. And I'm sure you've never kissed me right when a waitress was bringing me my credit card." She chuckled. "I know you could see her coming."

"Laying claim."

"No need for that. Any woman who was interested in me after she learned I was involved with someone would lose any attractiveness she had. Huge turnoff for me."

"Really? You're saying you're not only a perfect girlfriend, you also have no temptation to cheat?"

Bailey smiled at the teasing. "None. And if you keep kissing me whenever you think someone's flirting with me—it hardly matters if I'm tempted." She took Kit's hand and brought it to her mouth for a kiss. "Not that I mind. Having you act like you're proud to be with me makes me very happy."

"I'm always proud, Bailey. It's just that I feel more relaxed down here. Getting out of the fishbowl was a great idea."

"DC doesn't feel like a fishbowl to me. It feels like the place I live." She stopped and pulled Kit to a halt. "I love being able to touch you and just act normally. Like we're an average couple."

"We're far from average," Kit teased. "One half of us is stupendous. That makes the average..." She held her hand up over her head. "Shoot up here."

"Are you really listening to me? It's important that we figure out a way to be like this—normal like this—at home."

"I'm working on it, baby. I know I'm not going fast enough, but I'm trying."

Bailey slipped an arm around her shoulders as they started to walk again. "I don't mean to bitch at you." She tilted her head and kissed Kit's cheek. Reflectively, she said, "You know, it'd have to be hellaciously hot and humid to make me not want to live here. Are you sure it's bad?"

"I'm positive. But you might not mind it. You're colder than anyone I've ever met." She reached over and tried to grab a handful of flesh, but Bailey's waist had none to spare. "You don't have much insulation." Stepping in front, Kit tucked her arms around Bailey and looked up at her. "And I wouldn't change a thing." She tilted her chin and puckered up. Bailey almost hesitated. Months of holding back had become part of her. Then she leaned down and kissed Kit tenderly, holding the touch for a long time.

"I love you," Bailey murmured.

"And I love you. I'm so glad we came."

"Ditto times ten. Best idea you've had since you decided to investigate the suspicion that you might like chicas."

Kit started to play with the buttons on her shirt, moving up and tugging on the next. "Not chicas. Chica. The most bonita chica in el mundo."

Laughing, Bailey said, "You didn't take a lot of Spanish, did you?"

"Un poco." She grinned like a child. "I only know that te amo mucho, mucho, mucho."

Bailey pressed another long kiss to Kit's lips. "Quiero hacer el amor contigo."

"I think I understood that. But even if I didn't, let's go upstairs and make love until we're too hungry to function."

"You're definitely bilingual," Bailey teased, taking Kit's hand as they crossed the sand. They were nearing the hotel when something struck her. It wasn't just being away from home that let Kit act like she was part of a normal couple. The hat and dark glasses combined to make her anonymous again. Damn! If Bailey could find the person who'd outed her, she might actually strangle them. That little bit of gossip had made things so much harder for both of them.

—m—

Hours later, they'd sated their need for love and were trying to find a restaurant close by that fit Bailey's criteria. Kit was standing in front of the bathroom mirror, blowing her hair dry, while Bailey was perched on the edge of the vanity, scrolling through restaurant recommendations on her phone. "I definitely want something local. Cuban or … What's nuevo Latino?"

"Something you'd like. Book it."

"Mmm…can't get in for another hour." She looked up, smiling. "I'm embarrassed to say you've drained my tank. I don't have another orgasm in me. What'll we do for an hour?"

Kit took a comb and slid it through Bailey's hair. "I'm going to dry your hair, for one thing. I know you'll braid it or clip it up, but at least it'll be dry for a change."

"Okay. Let me sit down so you can reach the top." She sat patiently as Kit started to dry a portion of it.

"I was lying in bed the other night, trying to stay awake—"

Chuckling, Bailey said, "The night I kept saying I'd be done in a couple of minutes?"

"Yeah." Kit tugged on a hank of hair. "Anyway, I had an unexpected hour to blow, and I started looking for images of women who dress like you do."

Bailey looked up and caught Kit's gaze in the mirror. "Really? Why?"

"Just wanted to see if there were many others. There are, you know. Lots and lots."

Shrugging, Bailey said, "That's cool, I guess."

"You really don't care? You're not interested in reading about other dandy or dapper lesbians?"

"Is that what I'm called?"

"Oh, there were dozens of sites. Women call themselves all kinds of things. But those were the two words I saw most often."

"Interesting. But no, I don't really care if this is a trend. I feel good dressing like this, and I'll keep doing it until I don't." She looked up again and gave Kit a sweet smile. "You can dry my hair whenever you want, you know. I don't mind."

"Do you like it?"

"You're touching me. So, yeah."

"Do you... Uhm... How do you feel about your hair?"

Bailey looked into the mirror again, but this time she wasn't smiling. "You mean because it looks so shitty?"

"It doesn't look shitty. It just doesn't match the rest of you." She tugged at some of the medium-length strands that always fell out of her ponytail or braid. "I like that it looks kind of messy most of the time, but the rest of you is so crisp and precise. No comprendo."

Bailey gazed at herself in the mirror for a minute. "I hate having long hair. But..." She looked contemplative while gazing at herself. "If I cut it the way I'd like to, people wouldn't just do a double-take. It'll be a triple or a quadruple-take. I'm not sure I'd be okay with that." She caught Kit's gaze in the mirror. "When it's long, people can see I'm a woman if they give me a second look. That'd be out the window if I chopped it off. I'd be taking their only clue away."

"It's not much of a clue, honey. You've always got it pulled back. Why do that if you want people to see you're a woman?"

"I don't, really. It's just a safety net I hardly ever use. Like the night I blew it dry and left it down when we went out to dinner."

Nodding, Kit said, "I wondered what was going on. That's the only time you've done that."

"It didn't seem worth the trouble to do it routinely. I would have kept doing it if you'd swooned over it, of course." She showed an impish smile.

Kit leaned over and kissed her neck, letting her lips travel all across the skin. "If you ever want to cut it, I'm with you," she said quietly. "I want you to be exactly who you are. If people stare more, they'll just have another few seconds to see how beautiful you are."

"It's not about other people. It's about what I see when I look in the mirror. When it's pulled back, I forget it's long. That works for me."

Kit thought of Bailey's story about the first time she got to wear a tie. Even though a skirt was part of the package, she was able to forget about it and concentrate on the tie. Her hair must have been the same. Selective focus. "The way you look works for me." She leaned over and placed a hot kiss on Bailey's lips. "Every time."

Bailey snuck her arm around Kit and tumbled her onto her lap. "Even if we were stuck in rainy, cold DC you'd be the best girlfriend in the world for saying that. But after you arranged this trip? I guess I'm going to have to give you the best girlfriend in the universe title. Well deserved, Hannah."

—⁓—

At dinner, they tried to stick with their earlier cocktail, ignoring the wine list to have another variation on the bourbon and peach theme. The bartender fixed them up with bourbon, frozen peach slices, peach nectar, a little peach sorbet and some orange bitters. A damn fine cocktail.

"Despite the fact that no one's flirted with you yet," Kit teased, "I think I like this drink even better."

"It's too close to call, but who's gonna complain about a drink with ice cream in it?"

"Not you. Now that you're warm, that is. I bet you're going to eat ice cream every single day until fall."

"I can eat it all year," Bailey sniffed. "I just need hot fudge or hot butterscotch on it in the winter."

"You're very flexible."

"Only about some things. I think you'll agree that I can get fixated on certain topics and refuse to back off." She smiled sweetly. "I'm trying to change too. It's hard, but I'm really trying, Kit. I'm trying to give you the time you need to come out."

Kit reached across the table and took her hand, then held it tenderly. "I appreciate that." She looked around. "I'd appreciate another drink, too. Can you charm our waiter to get him to at least look at us once in a while?"

"I don't have any luck with men. You're going to have to work your magic on him."

Kit shrugged. "Eh… If he comes, he comes. I've forgotten how to work my charms on men. Just as well. I'm saving all of them for you."

—⁂—

They definitely weren't drunk. Probably not even tipsy. But they were both… relaxed. Kit took off her shoes and pulled Bailey down toward the ocean. Bailey got into the game and took off her sandals, and they walked in the warm, sparkly surf for a long time, just breathing in the moist air and relishing the experience of being together—with no critical tasks, or meetings or phone calls.

"Ever been skinny-dipping?" Bailey asked, one eyebrow raised.

"Not in Florida. How about you?"

"Never in the ocean. Wanna try?"

"You're on." Kit started to whip off her clothes. For someone who loved her privacy, she had a real thing about being naked. If she could have, she'd only swim in the buff. Bailey got naked too, then carefully placed her glasses atop her shirt. But she paused at the edge of the surf for a minute.

"Whose idea was this?" she asked, her arms braced tightly over her chest.

"Yours. Come on," Kit urged, trying to pry a hand away. "It's warm. Really warm."

"Not as warm as I'd like."

"Honey, the fish would all be cooked if it was as warm as you'd like. Come on now. I'll get your temperature up." She ran her warm hands up and down Bailey's back. "You'll love it."

"Oh, what the hell. It won't hurt much." She grabbed Kit's hand and splashed through the gentle waves, squealing like a little girl. When they were chest deep, Bailey wrapped her arms around Kit and pleaded, "W...w...warm me up. I'm b...begging you."

"All I've got are these," she teased, starting to place tiny kisses all over Bailey's face.

"More. Distract me from this mind-numbing cold."

There was a sign near the lifeguard chair stating the water temperature that day was seventy-eight degrees. But to Bailey...that was about twenty degrees colder than she liked. So Kit used her only available tool and tried to heat her from the inside. She wrapped her in her arms and lavished kisses on her shivering lips, keeping up the assault until the lips stopped shivering and started responding.

"More," Bailey begged, her hands starting to roam up and down Kit's back.

"All you want." They kissed again and again, the heat of their kisses raising their temperatures—or at least providing enough distraction for Bailey to forget she was chilly.

"Let's make love," Bailey murmured. Then, as if she'd just noticed they were completely alone, she leaned her head back and shouted up to the sky, "I want to make love to you!"

Kit hated to be the bearer of bad tidings, but she thought she'd better. "The ocean's better for foreplay, baby."

"Why?" Even in the dim moonlight, Bailey's eyes sparkled.

"Well, if I did your favorite thing...I'd drown. And saltwater washes your natural lubrication away pretty quickly. I've tried it...and it wasn't great."

Bailey leaned her head back again and shouted, "I want a raft...with a heat lamp...so I can make love to my beautiful girlfriend!"

"We'll shop for one tomorrow," Kit promised. She draped her arms around Bailey's neck, then encircled her with her legs. "I like having you hold me. We should do this at home."

"I'd better hit the gym. Like seven days a week."

"Are you saying I'm fat?"

"No way. I'm saying I'm weak. But I love holding you with a water assist." She placed a gentle kiss on her lips. "And you're warming up my belly. It's all good."

"Would we enjoy vacation as much if we had it all the time?" Kit mused as Bailey bounced around in the gentle surf.

"I'm willing to try. We'll keep rigorous notes, write some kind of scientific paper and be lauded by the scientific community. Trailblazers! Visionaries! Our names will be in lights."

"I'm not sure what kinda lights they have for scientists in your made-up world, but I think I like it. I think scientists would too."

"Realistically, the magic would wear off fairly quickly. You get used to anything—even the best things. But getting bored with being blissful might be fun for a while."

"I like the punch of a good vacation—luckily. I'm a long way from being able to lie on the beach full time."

Bailey grasped her head and pulled her in for a long kiss. "I've got a very nice nest egg and my hourly rate is embarrassingly high. If you ever need a long vacation…or a permanent vacation, just let me know."

"It's a deal. And if you ever need to…let's see…what can I do for you with very little money…" She thought long and hard, but could only come up with, "I can definitely bring you as my date to the White House Christmas party. That's the toughest ticket in Washington."

"More than fair," Bailey said, grinning as she kissed her.

Kit thought about the timeline. She'd clearly just promised she'd take Bailey to one of the biggest political events of the year. It was March and they usually had it early in December. You could almost have a baby in that amount of time. December it was. By then, she'd have to be out and proud. The thought made her shiver. Bailey responded immediately, holding her closer, protecting her as best she could. If only she could do that in Hell's Gate.

—∞—

They fell into their room well after midnight, their clothes soggy, hair windblown and wet.

"I'm beat," Kit moaned. She opened the door to the patio, flopped down on one of the lounges and lay prone, with her arms and legs dangling off the edges. "But not too beat." She turned her head to give Bailey her most seductive grin.

Bailey got onto her hands and knees, and bent over Kit. "You have total mind control over me. I thought I was tired, but…nope. You give me that sexy grin and all I want to do is feast on you."

Kit looked up at her. Bailey was full of it. She was the one with the sexy grin. Actually, it wasn't that blatant. But there was a way, a simple look she showed that got Kit ready to go in seconds. It had happened dozens of times, so it couldn't have been a fluke. But how such a simple look could have her wet and randy could not be explained.

She looked up into Bailey's clear blue eyes. Wait for it… Yep. When she took her glasses off, the fun was about to begin. Damn, she was a gorgeous woman. Kit could barely list the things about her she found attractive. The truth was it was the culmination of a bunch of little things all joining together to make her rabid for her touch.

Bailey gently lowered herself onto Kit's body. Letting out a pleasured hiss, Kit moved her legs so she could drape them across the backs of Bailey's thighs.

She would never tell Bailey exactly how many men she'd been intimate with, but it had easily been enough to get a wide variety of experiences. Even though she'd had some very good ones, very, very good ones with Henry in particular, she'd never been as hungry for any of them as she was for Bailey. And Bailey knew it. You could just see a little bit of cockiness come over her when Kit practically begged her to make love. The fact was, she would have begged. Willingly. Bailey was the most compelling, the most sensual, the most attractive person she'd ever been intimate with. And if things kept going the way they had been, they were going to have a lifetime to explore every bit of that allure. She couldn't wait.

Chapter Eighteen

As ALWAYS, WITHIN A day, all of the magic of the vacation seemed to vaporize. Kit returned to a raft of minor issues that had cropped up in her absence, and she worked until ten that night, fighting one brushfire after another. She finally answered a text from Bailey that she hadn't been able to get to. "We need to choose what we're wearing to the dinner on Fri. Might need something cleaned." Kit stared at the text for a minute, a sense of dread stealing over her like a heavy fog.

ERCF held several formal events every year. They were a big deal for gay Washington, and Natalie held a fairly prominent role in conducting them. She'd been working on their Spring Gala for a couple of months, and Kit had really come through for her. The event was mostly to thank all of their supporters in government. Every year they had a few big "gets," and this year Kit had hooked them up with a couple of doozies.

Along with all of the government people, they gave awards to many of their volunteers. Bailey was going to receive one for all of the consulting work she'd done in the past year, and she was surprisingly excited about being the focus of attention. That meant Kit was going to bask in some of that reflected light, and she had no idea how to handle it.

—⚹—

They didn't get to plan ahead for the event. Both of them were crazy busy that week. They'd have to hope they'd had the good sense to have whatever they chose to wear cleaned after its last wearing.

The night before the event, Bailey lay on Kit's bed at nearly one in the morning, watching an impromptu fashion show. "Yes, that one's nice too," Bailey said, "but I don't think I'm going to change my mind."

"But that dress was for winter. Dark blue velvet just doesn't look right in the spring."

Bailey got to her feet and walked over to Kit. Encircling her in a hug, she nuzzled her face against her neck, making her giggle. "It looks right to me. I want to wear my blue suit again, and that dress looks great with it. We'll be all matchy-matchy."

Kit gave her a puzzled look. "Is that a lesbian thing?"

"It can be, I guess, but that's not my goal. I just want you to wear that dress again. I want to re-create how I felt the first time I saw you."

"I could put it on now…"

"No dice. I want the whole vibe."

Kit's rumbling belly kept reminding her that she wasn't sure how public a vibe Bailey was going for—and was too afraid to ask.

—⁂—

Kit held the bathroom hostage for so long Bailey was afraid she'd have to go to a coffee shop to pee. Bailey had always dreamed of having a girly girlfriend, but now that she had one she had to admit they were fairly high-maintenance. And she had to admit she wasn't exactly low maintenance herself. Two bathrooms were going to be mandatory when they moved in together.

At last, when Kit stepped out of the bath, Bailey decided the extra primping time had been well worth the wait. Kit looked fantastic. Better than that, actually. Delicious.

"You look way, way too good to go out. Let's just put these fancy clothes right back in the closet and go to bed." She put her hands on Kit's waist and looked into her eyes. She had no idea how she'd made her eyes look so smoky, but it was a very good, very sexy look.

"But if I take my dress off, I won't look as good."

"Ha! You obviously don't look in the mirror often enough."

Kit smiled up at her. "Thanks for stroking my ego. I really do like to look nice for you."

"I can tell. And I appreciate it." She snuck another look in the mirror to check herself out. "Hey…do you wanna blow my hair out again? Like you did in South Beach?"

Kit stepped back and gave Bailey a puzzled look. "Sure, if you want me to. But wouldn't it have made sense to do that before we were both fully dressed?" She held her hands up. "Just sayin'."

"You don't have to do it. But I thought it might look better…"

Kit spent a moment tucking the strands that had fallen from the braid back inside. "Let's do it. Take off your jacket first." Bailey took it off and placed it on the bed, then sat in front of Kit's vanity. "I've got some combs from when I had long hair. They'd look nice. Wanna try?"

"Sure. I have no idea what you're talking about, but if you think they'd look good, I'm up for it."

Kit leaned over and took a nibble on Bailey's ear. "I like that attitude, Jonesy."

—∾—

It was often hard to tell what was going on in Kit's head. They rode over to the hotel in a cab, and Bailey was sure her lover was nervous. But she denied the charge so many times Bailey had finally stopped asking.

There was a crush of people trying to stream into the ballroom, and when they got closer Bailey saw what the trouble was. A phalanx of photographers was located relatively close to the entrance, a bad decision in her mind, but that wasn't something she had responsibility for. "This is going to be a pain."

Kit looked up at her, eyes wide. "I didn't know there was going to be a red carpet."

"Of course. All of those bigwigs you convinced to come want to be idolized. Having the vice president make the keynote is a big deal."

"I've been to dozens of events here. I know a side way in." With what looked like a forced grin, Kit added, "I want to get inside so I can start kissing butt. Gotta thank all of the people I convinced to come."

Bailey let herself be led away from the photographers. She'd have to have her picture taken later, along with the zillion other award winners. But Kit was right. There was no need to wait in line for that.

—∾—

Bailey had the ability to be social, so long as she didn't have to do it every day. Kit called her an extroverted introvert, and that seemed about right. She flitted from table to table, greeting all of the people she'd met through volunteering while Kit guided Asante around the room, introducing him to anyone who might be of use to a Metro reporter. Bailey itched to join them, but this was almost like being at work for Kit, so she let her wander.

Later, catching her in the line for the bar, Bailey sidled up to her. "If you're up for it, I'd love to dance with you later."

"Up for dancing with you? I'd like to see who could stop me." She was next in line and turned to say, "Buy you a drink?"

"Sure. I want to make sure I'm limber. Just don't get me too drunk or I'll start singing and I know you don't wanna attract that kind of attention."

During dinner, Kit babbled away at Asante and the other reporters at their table. She knew all of them, but Bailey could tell she didn't know them well. Oddly, Kit chatted much more with casual acquaintances than she did with friends. She was a slightly introverted extrovert.

The awards went on for too long, but finally the last one was given out. Then the hotel staff moved things around a little to enlarge the dance floor. Bailey got up to finish off her long list of greetings, and came back to the table some time later. Noting Kit's absence, she said to Asante, "Have you seen Kit?"

"Yeah," he said, tearing his attention from the hunky guy he was talking to. "She said the VP's chief of staff wanted to talk to her. I got the impression the Veep might have wanted to have a minute alone with her." He shrugged. "Sorry I don't know more. She never tells me anything when she's got a story brewing."

"That's fine. I can keep busy." She went over to sit at Natalie's table, and she and Jess talked about how much they both hated awards dinners while Nat held court with a long line of well-wishers.

One of the organizers collected both Bailey and Natalie for another series of photos, herding all of the board members and honorees down to a lower floor. The shoot took forever, and her introverted self was ready to be sprung.

Finally exiting the room, she leaned against one of the balconies that encircled each floor. She was about to text Kit and tell her she'd see her at home when a flash of something caught her eye. Looking up she saw Kit—standing alone—three levels up. It was hard to see her clearly, but she was definitely alone. No chief of staff or anyone else nearby.

It took Bailey just a second to put two and two together. Kit's impromptu meeting didn't occur until it was time to dance. A flush pulsed in her cheeks. Anybody who said she hadn't been patient was full of shit. It had been months, and she was pretty certain Kit hadn't told anyone but Asante about them. She was okay with that, she really was. But she wasn't okay with being lied to. They could work almost anything out if Kit was honest. And just the opposite was true. They had no chance if she thought she could get away with telling a boldfaced lie.

Bailey climbed the exposed staircase, taking the steps two at a time. By the time she reached the proper floor, she was panting. Loosening her tie, then unbuttoning her top button let her breathe a little easier and she forced herself to stop and think. She was upset, very upset, but more than that, she was sad. Things were going so well between them in every way, but she couldn't stand to be lied to. If your lover lied about something so minor, how could you believe her when she told you she loved you?

She was just twenty feet from Kit and she stood there and watched her for a couple of minutes. Kit seemed anxious, scanning the ballroom floor avidly. She'd obviously planned on hiding out up here, then dashing back down when the band stopped playing.

Grimly, Bailey walked up beside her. "Did you make up the entire story? Or did the vice president's chief of staff really want to talk to you?"

All of the color drained from Kit's cheeks. Then her chin began to tremble. "I made it all up." Biting her lip, she took in a few deep breaths. "I'm really sorry."

"About what?"

"About not being more open." Kit looked up, meeting Bailey's eyes. "I know you want me to be. I know I should be. But it's taking me longer than I thought it would."

"That's not it," Bailey said, the harshness in her voice surprising her. "I'm the fucking soul of patience. But I can't stand to be lied to. You made up a lie to avoid having to dance with me." Glaring into Kit's whipped-puppy expression, she added, "I'll give you all the time you need. But you have to admit you fucking need it!"

Kit just stood there, looking as if she was being dressed down by the principal. "I don't know how to handle this. I don't think you understand how difficult this is for me."

"I can't understand anything if you don't talk to me about it. If we don't talk about these things, we have nothing. Nothing!"

"Please don't say that." Kit's jaw started to tremble. "Don't give up on me."

"I'm not giving up on you! But you're not giving our relationship a chance. It's got to be built on honesty."

Quietly, Kit said, "You want me to be honest, but being open is just as, if not more, important to you. I knew you'd be angry if I told you I didn't want to dance with you in public." She looked up, her expression so fragile Bailey's breath caught in her throat. "I know your patience is just about gone."

Frustrated, Bailey blew out a long breath. "Yeah, it is. I've never had to be discrete, and it's…" She struggled to think of words to express how being in the closet was chipping away at her self-esteem. "It's a grating voice in the back of my head that says loving you is something to be ashamed of. That being gay is wrong. That the people who hate us are right."

"That's not true. Not at all," she said fiercely.

"That's how it feels to me! You told Zack that you weren't ashamed of being gay, but you are!"

"That's not true," Kit said, her voice thin but steady. "Being private is second nature to a reporter, and you don't seem to be able to understand that." She took a breath and started again. "Every single thing that people know about me colors the way they view my work. If there was any way I could hide the fact that I'm a liberal, I would. I wish people didn't know I was from Boston, for God's sake. And I definitely wish no one knew I'd ever gone out with Henry. There's hardly a week that goes by that someone doesn't bring it up, and I'm not talking about the anonymous idiots on the Internet who call me Brearly's whore on a daily basis."

Bailey shivered. "I didn't think it was that bad."

"It's a low-level annoyance. But it's chronic. It's all of the fucking time."

"I'd hate that. I'd more than hate it. I couldn't tolerate it. But you're wrong about me wanting you to be out to the world. I'd just like to feel that it wasn't a big secret."

"That's my point!" Kit said, her voice rising. "Things are either public or they're not. Once they're public, they're out there forever. I wanted to dance with you, baby. I really did. But if we'd danced together someone would have posted a picture on the Internet, then someone else would have posted it somewhere else. If it was mentioned enough times some news aggregator would pick it up. Once that happened, mainstream media would say it's a valid topic, even if it was just some dope with a Share Me account who posted it the first time."

That had to be bullshit. Or paranoia. It just had to be. "You're telling me that you're famous enough to have dancing with me be on the news crawl of CNN?"

"Of course not. But people hold onto things they hear about you, and pull them out when they need to. If it would prove a point, some crappy cable show would mention it."

"That's pretty damned speculative."

"I realize that. It's possible, even probable, that no one would ever mention it. But how can I have fun dancing if I'm worried about it?"

"I don't know." Bailey buttoned her shirt and tightened her tie. It felt like it was five in the morning, like she'd been up for days without sleep. "We're not going to resolve this tonight. I'm going to find a cab." She started to walk, then cast a glance back at Kit. "Can you afford to be seen getting into a cab with me?"

Kit dropped her head and followed along, with Bailey feeling like an asshole for trying to shame her.

They got home at one. Bailey couldn't wait for sleep. Maybe a new day would give her a new perspective. She started for the bedroom, but Kit moved in front of her and caught her in an embrace.

After a long hug, Kit reached up and removed the combs that held Bailey's hair in place. The look in her eyes was so tender, so filled with love that Bailey's heart started to beat quickly. Kit's fingers slid through her hair, then gently massaged her. Bailey's eyes closed as Kit pressed their lips together. "I love you," she whispered. "We'll work through this. If we love each other enough, we can get through anything."

Bailey held her in her arms, then let her hand glide across Kit's bare skin. That was the sensation she'd longed for. To hold and caress and move with the woman she loved. To publicly proclaim that Kit had claimed her — heart and soul. Maybe it was egotistic. Maybe it'd be better if everyone kept all their private feelings completely private. But she craved normalcy. And dancing with your lover felt like a universal desire.

Her jacket slid down her arms, then Kit's hands moved up and down her back, making her skin prickle with sensation. As Kit's lips claimed hers, her tie was removed and tossed away, then her shirt swiftly followed.

Bailey's hands found the zipper and quickly eased Kit's dress down, where it pooled on the floor.

Half dressed, they started to dance, moving silently about the room. When it was just the two of them, when no one else intruded, her happiness was unfathomable. But there was always something, someone to remind her that it wasn't just the two of them. Like a knife to the heart, she acknowledged that the person who most often reminded her of the tenuous nature of their love was Kit.

Soon her eyes were filled with tears. The woman she loved was the one person who had the power to destroy their lasting happiness. But then Kit looked up into her eyes and Bailey felt herself believing again. She wrapped Kit in a crushing embrace, holding on for dear life. They started to kiss again, emotion pulsing between them. Decisively, Kit led her to bed, rushing to undress her.

Then Bailey lay on her back, avidly watching Kit reveal the beauty of her body. Soon, they were face-to-face, kissing with a fervor that grew by the moment. After just a few minutes, Kit slid down and settled between Bailey's legs.

Bailey'd only had two other lovers, so her experience was limited, but no one had ever shown such rabid interest in her body. She was used to a lover slowly arousing her until she practically forced their head or their fingers between her legs. But Kit was just the opposite. Just moments after they started to make love she made her way down Bailey's body and settled in, as if that was the most compelling spot on earth. No one had ever seemed to get so much pleasure from slowly turning her on, while watching her for every sign of arousal. For long minutes, Kit simply gazed at Bailey, warm breath and rapt anticipation arousing her at an incredibly slow pace.

Bailey slid her fingers along Kit's scalp, tenderly caressing her. She could feel gentle fingers spreading her open, but Kit didn't make another move for a long time. Bailey strained her neck trying to get into position to see the look on her face. Kit looked mesmerized. Her warm brown eyes were trained on Bailey's flesh, and she slowly touched her most sensitive skin with a finger.

Bailey surprised herself when she heard her thoughts come out as words. "Why do you enjoy that so much?"

Kit blinked up at her in surprise. Despite Bailey's early urgings, they rarely spoke when they made love; both of them were naturally quiet and reflective during sex and trying to get Kit to talk hadn't been possible.

"I… I don't know." She placed a very gentle kiss right in the center of Bailey's sex, never taking her eyes from it. "I feel so close to you when I watch you get aroused. It's like we're entwined."

Bailey petted her head, then dropped back down onto her back. It was crazy to think that Kit could explain away her doubts, her questions. The woman who swore she felt not at all like a lesbian was enraptured by cunnilingus. How was that possible?

It was just a term. Lesbian. It only had the meaning we gave it. But wasn't the same true for love?

—∞—

They lay in each other's arms, exhausted from lovemaking. But Bailey's mind hadn't shut off like it usually did. She was dizzy from the relentless questions that pummeled her. It was clear that Kit was moments from sleep, but she couldn't stay quiet. Sitting up, Bailey ran her hand along Kit's bare shoulder, keeping up the caress until Kit opened her eyes and looked up at her questioningly.

"Is this the life you want?" Bailey asked. "To have to second-guess yourself about the smallest things?"

Those lovely eyes popped wide open. Kit spent a moment struggling to sit up, then she tucked the sheet over her chest. Blinking to focus, she said, "Sometimes."

"Not all of the time?"

"No, not all of the time. Lately, I've been thinking I might have taken a wrong turn. I'm not sure how to turn around again, but..."

Bailey grasped her hand and held it tightly. "What would you do if you could do anything?"

A frown flitted across her features. "I can't do anything. Reporting is the only skill I have."

Shaking her head, Bailey repeated her question. "Don't think about the reality. Tell me your fantasy."

Kit's gaze roved around the room for a few moments. Then it lit on Bailey. "If I didn't need to earn money, I'd do something—anything where I wasn't in the public eye."

"You'd give up your newsletter? Your blog? Willingly?"

Shrugging, she said, "The newsletter supports me. I'm not proud of it."

"But..."

"I enjoy writing the blog. It's like having a regular column in the opinion page, without having to get it approved by the editorial board. The newsletter pays for me to do that."

"I...had no idea. I knew the newsletter was a lot of work..."

"It's not journalism. At least it's not journalism the way I learned it. But go ask Margaret Stevens what happens to real journalists these days. She's over at State tonight, trying to come up with blurbs for my gossip rag." Kit turned to her, searching her face. "Why are we talking about my career? What's bothering you?"

"Just…" She felt like she would explode, but she didn't have words that could clearly express her thoughts. "I was thinking about what you said earlier. About how people watch you. How you can never have a truly private moment when you're outside."

"I'm stuck. I just have to take the bitter with the sweet." She stroked her hand along Bailey's cheek. "What I do is much less important than who I'm with. Being with you has shown me that." Taking Bailey's hands, Kit kissed each one tenderly. "I love you so much. And I'm so sorry I hurt you."

Nodding, Bailey said, "I know. I know you don't want to hurt me."

"Never, baby. I will never willingly hurt you."

Bailey dearly wished that was true. But it wasn't. Kit's closet was hurting both of them. And if she couldn't get out of it, Bailey was going to have to leave on her own.

—⁂—

Kit had been awake for a short time, but she wasn't in a hurry to get up. Bailey was sleeping soundly, her hair splayed across her face. Why she kept it clipped to the back of her head all day, only to let it loose at night was a mystery. But Bailey had all sorts of quirks that just made her more endearing. Routinely waking with a hank of her hair in Kit's eyes or mouth was a small price to pay for the pleasure of sleeping with her.

Kit's cell phone was under her pillow, and it buzzed softly. She slipped it out from its hiding place and looked at the screen. Asante was up bright and early for a Sunday.

"Everything okay in lesbianland?"

Rolling her eyes, Kit texted back. "Not really, but I think we're okay."

"Brunch?"

She took another look at Bailey, noting she looked a long way from waking. Sliding out of bed, Kit grabbed her robe and went into the living room, quietly closing the door as she left. She dialed Asante, and when he answered she said, "What's my window of opportunity on brunch?"

"It's wide, but not gaping. I've got two hours to play with."

"Hmm…I can't guarantee Bailey will be up in two. She was really edgy last night. I think she got up and worked, 'cause she seems dead to the world." She didn't mention that their lovemaking hadn't seemed to relax her at all—a rarity.

"Where'd you disappear to? I saw the Secret Service guys take off just a couple of minutes after you left the table."

Kit sighed and slid down on the sofa to lie on her back and stare up at the ceiling.

"I made up a lie so I wouldn't have to dance with Bailey."

He made a strangled squeak. "That's...wow. That's bad."

"Really? I thought it was a good relationship tip."

"There's no need to be snarky. I'm not judging you."

"I'm sorry. You're just in the line of fire." She sighed heavily. "If we lived out in the wilderness somewhere we wouldn't have a problem in the world. We get along so well."

"DC's a long way from the wilderness. And she's not your garden-variety lesbian. The woman leaves an impression."

"I know, I know. But she refuses to understand how private I have to be."

Asante didn't respond immediately. When he did speak, he sounded slightly tentative. "That's not exactly true. You choose to be private."

"What? I thought I could count on you to understand."

"I do understand. Your life was easier when you were anonymous. But you're not anymore. You have to make a choice; you can keep Bailey hidden away, or you can choose to live your life and let people take potshots at you. They will anyway."

"It's different for me," she insisted. "I'm not a lesbian who slowly gained national attention. I'm a straight woman, who was essentially married to a prominent figure who's about to run for the presidency. If I make it public that I'm in love with Bailey it'll be news. Biggish news. News that won't benefit my career in any way. News that will be tough for Henry to deal with."

"That's probably true. But you're asking Bailey to go into the closet to protect you. That's not fair to her."

"I know that. I obsess over that every time one of these situations comes up. But I still don't feel like a lesbian. If this doesn't work out, I assume I'll date men again. I can't afford to be known as a lesbian if this is a one-shot deal."

He made a more pronounced gurgling noise. "If you've got a brain in your head, you won't admit to that. No one wants to know her lover has an escape plan."

"I don't! I'm all in, Asante. I desperately want to be with her for the rest of my life. My only plans are about what I'll do if she dumps my ass."

"Think about what I said. You don't have to make this into a big deal. You can go about your business and let people talk if they want to. The fallout won't be that bad. I'm sure of it."

"Fine. I'll add that to the long list of possibilities and worries I already churn over in my head on a daily basis. Now let me go peek and see if my sleeping beauty is anywhere near consciousness. I'll text you with an update."

"Great. And Kit? I'm on your side. I know this is tough."

"It's tougher than it should be—that's for sure."

Kit clicked off and lay on her back, staring up at the ceiling for a long time. Maybe this was a drive that only real gay people felt. This need to let other people know they were in love with someone. She knew Asante was the same way, so it wasn't just Bailey. They wanted strangers to know something really personal. Really intimate. But why? Validation? Visibility? She sat up, her mind a hive of activity. Trying to guess why something was important to other people was impossible.

After walking into the kitchen, Kit started to make coffee. Clearly, caffeine was necessary for a little extra computing power. After she finished, she stood at the counter, still unable to put herself in either Bailey or Asante's place. Why would you want to give people more reasons to dislike you? It made no sense at all. If she truly had her way, everyone would think she was a human—of an unspecified gender—who'd been dropped to the earth some indeterminate number of years earlier and had never had a significant experience of any kind. She desperately wanted to be an old-fashioned reporter, who was nothing more than a byline to the world.

———

Natalie's law firm owned a season box at Nationals Park, and one surprisingly warm night in late April she and Jess, Kit and Bailey watched the Nats take on the Cubs.

They'd gotten into the habit of socializing with Natalie and Jess, and they saw Asante, but that was the extent of their circle. Kit wasn't sure why that was, since Bailey had made a number of casual friends. But Kit certainly wasn't going to complain. After the ERCF debacle Bailey had seriously backed off from pushing her to come out. Maybe she was beginning to realize you could have a perfectly happy life while still being discrete. They also hadn't had a single disagreement since that night. Everything was as smooth as glass.

Natalie leaned over and caught Bailey's attention. "Can we run by your apartment after the game? I left our picnic basket there and I need it for tomorrow."

Bailey gave Kit a puzzled look. "Where are we sleeping tonight?"

"My apartment. I've got that thing out at the Pentagon early in the morning." She turned to Natalie. "I'll give you my key to Bailey's place. Just leave it on the counter. The door locks by itself."

Giving her a long, assessing look, Natalie said, "Why are you still playing musical apartments?"

Kit felt a chill run down her spine. Neither she nor Bailey had ever seriously broached the topic of living together. She didn't know why that was, and was afraid it was a bad sign. Long ago she'd learned that bad signs were best avoided. "I'm not sure," she said blithely.

"That's a very good question." Bailey leaned forward so everyone could hear her. "I think it's time we considered consolidating. It's inefficient to do things the way we have been."

Natalie playfully elbowed Kit. "I guess that's as romantic as she gets."

Kit looked at her and smirked. It was just as well that Natalie didn't know what a hopeless romantic Bailey could be.

—m—

Minutes after arriving home, Kit went into the bathroom and turned the water on to warm it up. "I'm going to shower now to save time in the morning. Who wants to get in with me?"

Bailey raised her hand immediately. They didn't have time for tandem showers frequently, but Kit appreciated every one since a shower always led to lovemaking. She'd been thinking about sex all day and was itching to get her hands on her lover.

They undressed quickly, got in and Kit started to wash Bailey's hair, as she did each time they showered together. "One of these days I'm going to take you in for a trim. A blunt cut would look cute on you."

Sputtering when the spray hit her mouth, Bailey said, "I'd still just pull it back. To leave it down and make it look nice I'd have to spend a few minutes blowing it dry and putting something on it to make it fluffy."

"Like I do every morning." Kit reached around and pinched her. "You don't want to spend five minutes looking good for me?"

"That's thirty-five minutes a week. That adds up. Plus, I'd have to get it cut every three or four weeks, and that's a pain." She dipped her head so the spray started to rinse the shampoo out. "I'd rather do something else to appeal to you." She stood up and flung her hair forcefully over her shoulder. "I'll spend thirty-five minutes a week reading a book on how to be more thoughtful."

Kit patted her sharply on the butt. "Oh, you know you're already perfect. You could write that book."

Bailey slipped her arms around Kit's waist and looked at her through the gentle spray. "Does that mean you'll consider moving in together? If I'm perfect, I'd obviously be a good roommate."

"Absolutely. I don't know why we haven't talked about this before."

Somewhat warily, Bailey said, "I haven't wanted to push you. I think it would be easier for both of us to live together, but it's a big step."

Kit thought about that for a moment, worrying she might've been a little hasty in agreeing. "There's no harm in talking about it." She pulled Bailey close and they kissed. A little momentum was building between them, and Kit knew it was time to make a move. She let her hand slide down Bailey's back to caress her butt. "I think tomorrow's early enough to talk. Tonight, I've got other things to do with my mouth."

—◊—

As always, Bailey was a woman of her word. She not only didn't push, she didn't even bring up the topic of moving. Kit carefully considered the various alternatives, and when she felt she had a workable plan she brought it up. They were sitting on the sofa at Bailey's, watching a new show about shape-shifters that she seemed to like. While Bailey was zipping past the first commercial, Kit said, "Would you like it if I moved in here?"

Bailey started, like she'd been nudged in the back. "What?" Her finger slid off the remote, letting the commercial play out. She looked around her living room. "Here? Why would you want to live here?"

"I don't know." Kit shrugged. "You're a little closer to the Metro, and we like more of the restaurants around here. I like the energy."

"But I don't even own any furniture."

"We'll return all of your rented stuff and move my things in. Everything I have will fit."

Bailey seemed completely flummoxed. "If we're going to pick one or the other, yours is the one that makes sense. You own and I rent. Why go to the trouble and expense of selling?"

"It's more than that." The commercial was over, and Kit turned the volume back up. "I'll tell you more when the show's over." But Bailey took the remote from her hands and hit the stop button.

"This is more important." Her eyes took on a fiery intensity. "Tell me again why you want to leave your apartment, the apartment that's in the same building as your office."

This wasn't turning out the way Kit had planned. "I was trying to be thoughtful. Really, baby." She put her hand on her leg, feeling the tension in the muscles.

"You're saying your suggestion has nothing to do with someone on your staff finding out I'm your roommate?"

"You're being silly," Kit snapped. "I was trying to be considerate because I thought you liked this neighborhood a lot. But if you don't, we should get a bigger place than I have. You need an office."

Warily, Bailey stared at her. "This really isn't just you being afraid that someone will find out about us?"

"No! The bigger apartments in my building don't have good views. We can find something much better."

Bailey leaned forward and kissed her. Her eyes lost their sharpness and opened so wide Kit felt she could swim right into their blue depths. "I'm sorry I was…suspicious. I'd love to live in your neighborhood. Let's start looking."

"To buy? Are you sure you like DC enough to make an investment?"

Bailey sucked her lower lip in and worked her teeth over it for a moment. "Honestly? I'm ready to move back to California. I think I've given DC a good shot, but I miss the weather and the more laid-back culture. And to really be honest, I miss working for startups. There's an energy there that I haven't felt at any of the places I've done work for around here. But," she said dramatically, pulling Kit in even tighter, "my girlfriend needs to be here. And I need to be with her. Case closed."

Chapter Nineteen

KIT STEPPED OUT OF the bathroom, distractedly rubbing her hair with a towel. "Honey?" she called. "Do you mind if I take the hair dryer with me?"

"I don't mind." Bailey's soft voice sounded like she was mere feet away. But Kit had left her blissed out with her tablet propped up on her legs, locked in while playing some kind of game. Lowering the towel, Kit gasped when she spotted Bailey sitting on the edge of the bed, lit candles dotting the room, the overhead lights dowsed.

"Planning something?" she asked, smirking. "Or just trying to cut the electric bill?"

"Planning something." Bailey crooked a finger and Kit walked over to her while tucking the bath sheet around herself.

"Yessss?" There was nothing cuter than the expression on Bailey's face when she was trying to be seductive. Kit waited for it…but it didn't appear. Instead, Bailey looked almost somber. "What's wrong, baby?"

Bailey took her hand, then urged her to sit on her lap. Nose-to-nose, she cleared her throat. "Nothing's wrong." She paused for a beat. "Other than the fact that you're going away." Her heart-thudingly beautiful eyes blinked slowly. "I know it's just for a few days, but we haven't been apart since we fell in love."

"Ooo. Are you sad?"

Clearly puzzled, Bailey shook her head. "No, I'm not sad. But I'll miss you. I uhm…thought it'd be nice if we…" Looking up, embarrassment showing on her face, she said, "I don't want to let things just fly by. When our routine changes I'd like to pay attention to it."

"Our routine?"

"Spending every night together. Sleeping together. Being together."

Kit nodded, starting to get the point. "Comings and goings are important. We shouldn't just grab a suitcase and blow out of town without saying a proper goodbye."

"Right. I want you to know I'd much rather have you here than gone."

Kit draped her arms around Bailey's neck and gazed into her eyes for a few moments. "I know that. But it's very, very sweet of you to make a point to tell me." They kissed, with the taste and softness of Bailey's lips zipping straight to her heart. "I love you so much."

"I know." She took her glasses off and tossed them onto the bedside table. "I hope you know how much I love you."

"I do." Kit leaned in and kissed her again, quickly lost in her caresses. Bailey's warm lips traveled down her neck, covering her with chills. "Being loved by you is the nicest feeling in the world."

Bailey wasn't the strongest woman, and Kit worried that she was too heavy for her. But when she tried to rise, Bailey held her still. "I like you right here," she murmured, her voice already low and sexy, her eyes glittering with desire.

"I like it here too. Sitting on your lap, wearing just a towel." A short laugh bubbled up. "Doesn't take much to make me happy."

"You make me happy," Bailey said, staring directly into her eyes. Kit felt like she could see right into her soul. Bailey was, in so many ways, guileless. You never had to guess how she felt or what she wanted. That was such a gift.

Kit burrowed against her body, feeling like she couldn't be close enough. Maybe she was the one who was going to have a hard time leaving in the morning.

"You're going to miss me," Bailey said, an impish smile tugging at her lips. "Your bed will feel really empty without me sprawled all over it."

Suddenly, Kit felt herself mist up. "I am," she admitted, sniffling. She wiped her eyes with the back of her hand. "PMS. I'm more emotional than normal."

Gently, Bailey said, "Maybe leaving isn't easy when you're in love."

"It's not," she said as she rubbed her face against Bailey's neck. "I love our routine. Knowing I'm going to be with you at night has let me filter out a lot of crap during the day." She rested her forehead against Bailey's. "I wish I could cancel and stay home."

"You can't, huh?"

"No. I'm locked in."

"Uhm, I could rearrange a few things and go with you." She blinked, looking surprised that the words had come out of her mouth. "If you want me to…"

"Next time. This conference lasts until Saturday afternoon. We wouldn't have any time together."

"Okay." Bailey nodded. "But you know I'd be there if you needed me, right? Even if I was swamped. You're my priority."

"And you're mine." Kit grasped her shoulders and pulled her close for a heated kiss. "Why don't you take this towel off me and show me how much you'll miss me."

With a smirk, Bailey took the tucked-in portion and started to playfully tug it. "I see skin," she whispered. "Lots and lots of clean, nice-smelling skin." She looked up and met Kit's eyes. "You're overdressed."

The towel fell, leaving her completely naked. Then Bailey lay back, taking Kit with her. Sprawled across her body, Kit said, "Now you're overdressed." They play-wrestled, with Kit eventually getting all of Bailey's layers off. "It's May, baby. Isn't it time to drop the sweater or the vest?" Chuckling, she added, "At least the long underwear is gone, but…"

"All things in due time." She climbed on top of Kit and pressed her shoulders to the bed. "Now it's time for pleasure." Lying on top of her body, Bailey slowly stoked the fire that burned in Kit whenever they were close like this. Her desire for Bailey had never wavered, only growing with each passing week. Bailey lifted her head, her voice already thick with need. "I can never get enough of you."

"I can't either. It…amazes me." She slid her hands through Bailey's hair and held it away from her face. Studying her for a moment, she said, "I'd give a lot to stay home with you. A whole lot."

"Then hurry home. I'll be waiting for you." Her expression turned into a warm, welcoming smile. "Right here."

—⁂—

Bailey was super busy on Thursday and Friday, barely recalling that Kit was away. But on Saturday she finished up a project that'd been occupying a lot of her time, and found herself with energy, free time, and no plans.

She tried to scare up a friend or two to go see the latest 3-D fantasy extravaganza, but found no takers. For a moment, she thought she'd just go alone, as she would have before Kit. But big budget space movies were more fun with company. So she ordered in and lay on the sofa, watching some shows that'd been piling up on her DVR.

Nothing was holding her full interest, so she pulled her tablet computer over and propped it up on her lap. Even though she'd helped start the pre-eminent social media site, she wasn't very engaged with it. But she had an account and tried to check it every week or two. After logging in, she noted a few friend requests, and spent a few minutes trying to decide if she knew the people well enough to accept them.

Bailey was about to move onto another diversion when she noticed the column on the far right of her screen—the one that showed your friends' activity. Kit had a pseudonym that she used for friends and family, and Bailey noticed a post about Kit Boston from just a few minutes earlier. She looked at it, then looked again.

Kit had been tagged in a photo added by Jason Travis. That was her brother. Bailey's cursor hovered over the photo for a moment, then she moved the tablet closer to her face.

A group was posing for what was probably a family photo. An older couple sat at a banquet table, with a very elaborate cake placed in front of them, a stylized *50* atop it. Behind them, Kit, a woman who looked a little like her and a man who could have easily been their brother stood, with their respective spouses at their sides. A group of kids flanked the adults, all smiling for the camera. Everyone was dressed very nicely, with the men in tuxedos, the women in cocktail dresses.

Seconds ticked away as Bailey stared, unblinking at the photo. Drilling down, she managed to ferret out a dozen photos and posts about the party. Share Me could give up a lot of secrets if you knew where to look.

The fiftieth wedding anniversary of Russell and Marjorie Travis was a very big deal. Someone commented that there were over two hundred and fifty people there, the biggest anniversary party they'd ever been to.

Bailey was covered in a cold sweat. Almost like she was guided by instinct, she started searching the web. Something hadn't seemed right to her, but she'd tried to quell the niggling doubt. It didn't take long to uncover yet another lie. She stood, her legs shaking violently. It was late, after midnight, but she couldn't stand being cooped up inside. She had to get some air and clear her mind. Worried she might throw up, she fought through the churning in her guts, grabbed her phone and keys and headed outside.

Wandering around, not paying any attention to where she was going, Bailey eventually found herself in front of Kit's apartment. She was compelled to go inside—to tear the place apart; looking for further evidence that Kit was lying to her. For all she knew she was seeing a couple of guys at the same time. Anyone who lied so easily probably did it all of the time. But she resisted the urge, compelling as it was. It was too late for that.

Feeling like she was wearing lead boots, Bailey started to walk home. Her conscience was barking at her, telling her not to call. In two days she might get over the hurt, or at least be able to have a thoughtful discussion about it. But she forcefully ignored that inner voice. She needed her anger to do what had to be done.

She brought the phone to her mouth, pressed down on the home key for a moment and spoke. "Call my girlfriend."

The computer-voice said, "Calling Kit Travis." It rang, and Bailey flinched with each tone. Kit picked up, asking quickly. "What's wrong?"

"Why did you lie?" Her voice sounded like it belonged to a very old woman. "I gave you so many chances."

"Lie? What are you talking about?"

"Don't be coy. I was checking Share Me and saw the photo of your family. Your brother tagged you. Stupid move to tell me your pseudonym, by the way. Amateurish. If you're going to have a secret life, you've got to learn to cover your tracks better."

"Bailey," she murmured. Bailey could just picture her expression. Contrite, embarrassed, agitated; her eyes shifting as she tried to weasel her way out of the situation. "I didn't lie. I was here for business. I spent two whole days at a boring conference. But I had this family thing tonight. I just didn't mention it. It was just a thing I had to go to. An obligation."

"That's the same as lying to me, Kit. Exactly the same."

"No, it's not. Not at all. I didn't tell you about it because I felt like a jerk for not being able to invite you, but—"

"It doesn't matter. You have your reasons for what you do. But I think I've made it pretty clear I can tolerate almost anything but lying."

"I'm not lying!"

"Yes, you are. But if you insist on calling it something else, call it the thing that I hate. The thing that you know I have zero tolerance for. The thing that we've had major fights about. Call it that," she spat.

"I didn't want to hurt you." Kit started to sniffle. "I knew you'd be angry that I didn't invite you, so I just…didn't tell you."

"That shows you still haven't learned what's important to me. I told you from the start that I needed honesty. The second thing I needed was for you to deal with your feelings as they came up. If you've had any fucking feelings, you sure haven't talked to me about them. It's been six months! Six months of saying you're not in the closet, while I can barely breathe in here with you."

"I can't be in the closet if I'm not a lesbian. I don't have a good category to put myself in, and until I do I don't want to make a big deal about it. Why can't you understand that?"

"Because you're lying." She was so tired. Her bones felt like they were too heavy for her muscles to lift. "You're lying to yourself, but it's still lying."

"What am I lying about?"

"A lot of things. For one, you claim you're not embarrassed if people know we're lovers. That's a lie."

"That's not true! I'm proud to be with you, baby. I swear that."

"Not true," she said brusquely. "You claim you want to find a bigger apartment. There's one on a higher floor in your building with two bedrooms and two baths. There was a big, color picture of the view—much better than yours. You lied about that because you don't want your staff to know we're living together."

"No! I want something with more charm. An older building would be much, much nicer for us."

"Bullshit. You're embarrassed or ashamed or something. We could work on that if you'd face facts, but you won't. And I can't make you. I won't try anymore. I've treated you like an adult through this whole process. But giving you control over how fast you go means you haven't moved an inch. Not a fucking inch."

"But we're happy! We go out with Nat and Jess and Asante all of the time. I always act like myself around them. Just because we don't kiss in public doesn't mean we're not making progress."

"You're treating me like I'm slow. Like you can lay bullshit on me and not have me notice. That won't work, Kit. I'm done. You've pushed me and pushed me, and I'm done."

"Bailey! God damn it! You can't break up with me on the phone!"

"If you hadn't lied, I'd be there with you now, and this would be a moot point."

"Damn it! I couldn't have you come to this fucking party! What would you have worn? A suit and tie? Do you have any idea what people would say if I brought a woman wearing a man's suit and tie? Jesus! You'd be the talk of the whole party!"

Quietly, while wiping tears from her eyes with her sleeve, she tried to get control of her voice. "I'm well aware of that. From the first, you said you liked the way I look."

"I love it! But other people wouldn't. They'd be making comments all night. You'd hate that!"

"You're wrong," she said, slowly taking in a breath and forcing it from her lungs. "I make conscious choices and don't give a fuck who likes them—besides my girlfriend. It's more important to please her and myself than to have the rest of the world think I look wonderful. I've prioritized, Kit. You're the person who matters." She choked up, but managed to get out. "That's not true for you. You let strangers' opinions matter more than mine." She took another, longer breath. It felt like a knife had lodged itself under her ribs, but she forced the words out. "It's time to call it a day."

"Please," Kit sobbed. "Please don't do this. I'll fix it. I'll change. I'll do whatever you want. Just tell me what to do and I'll do it."

"I've been telling you. I've told you over and over again. But you've either ignored me or been unable to follow through. I'm sorry. I can't even begin to tell you how sorry I am, but we're done."

"Please, please, please," Kit shamelessly begged. "I'll do anything! Anything! I love you, Bailey. I truly love you."

"I know you do." She fought to get the words out through her tears. "I wish that was enough. But it's not. I love you with all of my heart, but that won't save us. We're through. I'll pack up the things you've left at my apartment and drop them off with your doorman."

"No! Dear God, please don't do this!"

"I have to. I'm so sorry for hurting you, but I have to." She took in a long, shaky breath. "Please don't call me. We gave it our best, but that wasn't good enough. It's time to give this relationship a decent funeral and bury it." She was crying so hard her shoulders shook, and her jaw cramped from violently quivering. "Goodbye, Kit." She hung up and turned the phone off. There was nothing more to say. Not then. Not ever.

—⁂—

Kit returned to DC on the six a.m. train, after having snuck out to a waiting cab before anyone was up. If she'd let anyone in the family see her they'd know something was wrong—and she wasn't about to confide in any of them about something so devastating.

Bailey wouldn't answer her phone and the doorman claimed she wasn't home. Kit knew she was, but the doorman wouldn't let her up, even though she had a key. Bailey had obviously told the guy to block her. She was cold-blooded when she had a plan.

Standing in front of Bailey's building, Kit looked up, trying to find her window. But her eyes were so swollen and gritty she couldn't even count up to find the right floor. After having not slept one wink, she'd cried so hard and for so long the people near her on the train got up and moved to avoid the histrionics. She didn't blame them at all. She'd lost control, and no one liked to see that. Some jerk would probably put a photo of her on some form of social media, but for the first time in years she didn't care. What did it matter if someone gossiped about your life when it had already been ruined?

After hailing a taxi, Kit went home, where the doorman reached under his desk to hand her a box. Inside was her toothbrush, some makeup, a few sleep-shirts, some mementos from events they'd gone to and dinner menus they'd collected. The detritus of a relationship. She wanted to throw it down the garbage chute, but she controlled her anger and kicked it into the corner when she got into her apartment.

Then she dropped to the sofa and fell onto it face-first. It wasn't comfortable. But she didn't deserve comfort. She deserved to lie there and cry.

—⁂—

On Tuesday afternoon, someone banged on the front door. Kit tried to ignore it, but her visitor was relentless. She put on a pair of shorts and a T-shirt and went to open it, finding a wide-eyed Asante. He grasped her by the shoulders and looked carefully at her face. "I was about to call the police."

She turned and walked to the living room, flopping down onto the sofa when she reached it. "Sorry I didn't answer the phone."

"Answer the phone? I understand not answering the phone. But when you have somebody I've never heard of substituting for you, and your assistant claims not to know what's wrong…"

"I told Nia I had the flu. Margaret called in a favor and had one of her old pals take the day shift." She dropped her face into her open hands and tried to get a handle on things. "God knows all I do is lie. Might as well add Nia to the list of people who can't believe a damn word I say."

Asante sat down and put his arm around her shoulders. Unable to hold it together, Kit draped herself across his chest and cried piteously. Always good at comfort, Asante didn't say a word, he simply stroked her back and let her cry. She'd run out of tissues the day before and when it got to the point that she knew she'd start to drip onto his shirt she yanked the hem of her T-shirt up, wiped her eyes and blew her nose into it.

Asante looked like he might throw up, so she stood and excused herself. Living like a wounded animal for a few days was making her behave in unpredictable ways.

Kit spent a few minutes in the bathroom, applying cold compresses to her eyes, then combing her hair and brushing her teeth. A clean T-shirt had her ready to go back and act human. "It was my parents' fiftieth wedding anniversary party on Saturday."

His head cocked slightly. "You didn't mention that."

"I know. I couldn't take Bailey, of course. That was a non-starter. I could have taken you, but everyone would've assumed you were my new boyfriend. So I'd have to figure out who I could be honest with, while trying to avoid all of the people who would freak out because you were black." She put her hand up and squeezed her head, trying to get the painful throbbing to stop just a little bit. "Because of all that, I didn't tell you about it."

He put his arm around her again and gave her a gentle squeeze. "You know I love you, but you're never going to hurt my feelings by not taking me to one of your parents' snooty parties." He kissed the top of her head. "I'm sorry you waste so much time worrying about things that don't matter."

"They matter to me. Don't I have the right to care about certain things?"

"Sure. Of course you do. What happened at the party?"

"Nothing. It was fine." She shook her head. "It was when Bailey saw a photo that the roof fell in."

"A photo…?"

"Of me. And my family. At the party I didn't invite her to."

"Oh." He was quiet for a moment. "I'm surprised that made her angry. She's been so patient. Expecting you to take her to a big family event seems a little unrealistic."

"It's not that I didn't invite her. I didn't tell her about it." She looked into Asante's eyes, which showed some small amount of confusion.

"Did you just sneak out of town?"

"No, I scheduled a conference for Thursday and Friday in Boston. She knew I was there and that I was going to be with my family. She just didn't know why."

"And that…?" He scratched his head. "Bothered her?"

"Enough to break up with me—on the phone."

"Fuck!" He jerked up so quickly Kit was almost knocked over. "You're shitting me!"

"I would give anything I had in this world to have it not be true. But she not only broke up with me, she won't take my calls or answer my e-mails."

"Because she didn't know about the party." He said it slowly, like it would make more sense if he parsed the words out.

"No. Because I lied to her."

"Oh. Oh." He started to nod. "I get it. Well, you've got to admit she's given you fair warning. Everybody has their hot buttons, and being honest about things is hers."

Kit leapt to her feet. "It's a stupid button! We have a fantastic relationship that she's ready to throw away because I go out of my way to avoid hurting her feelings!"

"Oh, that's a tough one," he said, shaking his head. "You're gonna have to try that one on a different audience. I'm not buying it."

"It's the truth! I could no more take her to a formal dinner with my family than… I can't even think of an analogy."

"That's fucked up, Kit. Seriously fucked up."

"I know it. But that's not going to change. She'd be miserable around my family, and I'd be a nervous wreck."

He leaned forward and turned his body so he was facing her. "That's not what's fucked up. It's you. Your attitude."

"You don't get it, Asante. I know her. She'd want to go just to make a statement that we're a couple. It would be a huge nightmare. One that I have no interest in creating."

"No, you don't get it. You chose to go out with a woman with a unique style. Then you say you can't take her places because of how she looks. That's fucked up." Kit started to speak, but he held his hand up to silence her. "But that's not the big issue here. Well, it's part of it. I guess it all ties in together." He grasped her hand and tugged on it until she sat next to him. His handsome face and warm, expressive eyes reflected a touching amount of empathy. But his words cut like a scalpel. "You're ashamed of Bailey, and you'd rather lose her than deal with the truth."

"That's insane! I love the way she looks. There isn't a single part of me that's ashamed of her. But people can be so narrow-minded! I don't want to subject her to that crap."

"She's not your child, Kit. I'm pretty sure she's dealt with her share of comments and disapproving looks. Getting a few from your relatives and their friends wouldn't cause her to break up with you. But lying to her did."

"I know that. I don't need to be reminded of that. What I want is some advice on how to get her back. I'd do anything to get a second chance."

His voice wasn't cold, but his words were. "What did you do during your first chance? What concrete steps were you taking to be more open?"

"I didn't have any firm plans," she said, feeling her temper rise. "I thought...I thought things would just...settle."

"You were trying to wait her out. You wanted her to get used to being in the closet with you. That's not fair, Kit. Not fair at all."

She sank into the corner of the sofa and stared at him for a long time. "Did you come here just to kick me when I'm down?"

"You know I didn't. I love you, and I'll be your friend no matter what. I feel really bad for you, but I feel bad for Bailey, too."

"It sounds like you only feel bad for Bailey."

"That's not true, but you've basically re-created what Natalie did. The one thing she told you she was afraid of."

"Not true! Natalie couldn't have sex with her. That wasn't a problem for us, Asante. Our sex life was spectacular!"

"That's not the point. The point is that neither you nor Natalie could face who you were, and you both hurt Bailey in the process."

"I am facing it! I'm a straight woman who loves a lesbian."

He looked at her carefully for a minute. "You're sounding like my sister Aisha. She's a very strict vegetarian, but I've seen her grab a piece of bacon off someone else's plate. She says that doesn't make her a carnivore. She's just sampling."

"That's not true for me. I would have happily stayed with Bailey for the rest of my life. I wasn't just sampling."

"You were in a lesbian relationship, Kit, and that's what Bailey wanted you to acknowledge. She wanted you to say you were her lover."

"I know that. I know what she wanted. But she couldn't meet me halfway."

"There is no halfway," he said flatly. "She didn't deserve to be treated the way you treated her. You played her after she begged you not to."

All of the anger drained out of her and Kit started to cry again. Asante scooted over and put his arm around her, speaking softly and soothingly. "I don't want to hurt you, but I love you enough to be honest with you. You really screwed this up, and I don't think you can fix it. But you can learn how not to do it again."

Kit leaned into him, weak from crying. "It won't happen again. I'm not going to get over this one, Asante. When a heart's broken this badly, it can't heal."

—⁙—

Asante came over the next day, just to check on her. When he walked in, he handed Kit a FedEx envelope the doorman had given him. "It's from Bailey," he said quietly.

Heart pounding, she clutched the envelope to herself, grateful just to have something tangible that had recently touched her. But she didn't open it. It wasn't good news. She was sure of that. And she couldn't stand to lose it in front of Asante again. Even the best of friends didn't want to watch you blow your nose on your shirt.

Asante left after just a few minutes. As the door closed, Kit ripped the envelope apart. Inside was a handwritten note. It took a few seconds to read the first sentence. In six months she'd rarely seen Bailey write more than her signature, and her handwriting was angular and hard to read. After studying it for a while, it began to flow:

Dear Kit,

I use that term sincerely. You're very dear to me, and always will be. I don't know if I'll ever stop loving you, but I truly hope I don't. I want to keep you in my heart for the rest of my life. Regrettably, I don't think I'll be able to be friends with you. There's just too much pain to get past.

I know you think I'm being very harsh. I wish I could be gentler. You deserve very gentle handling. You seem very resilient, but I know the real you and know how fragile you are. That's why it was so hard to cut the cord so abruptly. But I think it was for the best. The truth is that it wouldn't do either of us any good to keep acting like things will change. Our relationship was ninety percent perfect, but that last ten percent killed it. And I think you've made it clear you're not able to change that last ten percent just to please me.

I'll admit to being angry. Very angry. You promised me the night we shared our first kiss that being in a lesbian relationship was no big deal. You said you didn't care if your family knew and that you were your own boss, so you had no worries about your job. I never, ever would have kissed you that first time if I'd had even a hint about your homophobia. But I think I know you well enough to know you were unaware of it too. So I'm trying to get over being angry with you. It's going to take awhile, but I'm working on it.

What I'd like is to be able to look back on the six months we shared as an example of what each of us can have with the proper partner. I clearly need a woman who identifies as a lesbian and is open about her orientation. You should probably find a nice guy. Even if you are bisexual, you're not comfortable enough with that term to risk entering another relationship with a woman.

I wish things could have worked out, Kit. I wish that more than I have any way of expressing. I loved you with all my heart, but I couldn't be in the closet. It was a death trap for me. Clearly, some people can live happily that way—I'm just not one of them. I knew that over time I'd start to resent you and that would eat away at what we had. I know it hurts now, but, over time, I hope you can come to see that I had to destroy our relationship to save the memory of our love.

Always your,

Bailey

—⁂—

Bailey had blocked her phone calls, didn't reply to any e-mails, and her doorman even refused the package that Kit tried to deliver. The poor guy looked so uncomfortable that Kit felt sorry for him, but he steadfastly refused. Kit started to lose it again, and when he saw her start to cry he said, "Send it to her in the mail. They have to deliver it."

She left the building, thoroughly humiliated. It wasn't important to return the things Bailey'd left at the apartment. Kit just couldn't stand to throw them away, but they haunted her like they were animate.

She still hadn't been back to work and couldn't see going back soon. The staff seemed to accept her lies, or they simply didn't want to know the real reason she'd been incommunicado. She'd barely looked at the newsletter, but the few things she'd read had been good. Margaret's friend was really sharp. She'd been on the New York beat for years, and had become a freelancer after the Post closed their regional bureaus. Now she worked her butt off pitching stories to every newspaper and magazine in the English-speaking world. There was nothing good about losing Bailey, but at least another struggling journalist got to have a steady paycheck for a while. Thank God Kit had enough money socked away to be able to direct her salary to others for at least a month.

It was getting dark, and she decided to stop and have a drink before going home. Unable to talk herself out of it, she went to Bailey's favorite bar. It wasn't too pathetic to go to your ex-lover's favorite spot, carrying a box of her effects, was it?

It had been a little over a week, but she was still incredibly shaky. Never had she suffered this kind of heartbreak. It had yanked her from her moorings, and she knew she wasn't behaving normally, but didn't know how to stop.

The bartender recognized her. "Waiting for Bailey?"

"No. I'll have a…" She stood there, unsure of what to order. "Surprise me."

Walking over to an empty table, she sat, staring into space. The server came by and dropped off a glass filled with clear liquid. "Sahara dry martini," he said, then squeezed Kit's shoulder. It was bad when strangers urged you to buck up.

Shivering after taking a sip, she pulled out her phone and made a call she'd been sure she'd never make. "Natalie?" she asked when the phone was quickly answered.

"How are you?"

"Bad." She started to cry, angry with herself for having so little self-control.

"You know I can't get involved," Natalie said. "I wish I could, Kit, but I can't."

"Can you at least talk to me? I need to know she's all right. Please," she whispered, throwing all of her pride away.

"Are you at home? I can stop by on my way home from work."

"No. I'm at Hamilton's."

There was a brief moment of silence. "Really? Is that a good idea?"

"No. It's a terrible idea. I…I'm a mess. I don't know what to do."

"I'll be there in twenty. Hang tight."

Kit put her head down on the table. She knew she looked like she'd lost it. Might as well wallow in it.

When Natalie arrived, Kit was still nursing her first drink. She could have gulped them down like water, but adding a hangover to her headache was just stupid. Nat leaned over and kissed her cheek, making Kit burst into tears once again. "I'm sorry," she sobbed. "I just can't stop crying."

"It's okay," Natalie soothed. The server came over with a pair of martinis. Natalie looked up, made a face, then let him put them down on the table. "What the fuck," she muttered as he walked away.

"I tried to return her stuff, but the doorman wouldn't take the box." Kit looked at Natalie, seeing sympathy in her dark eyes. "Does she have to be so mean?"

Natalie put a hand on her arm and stroked it soothingly. "I think she does." When Kit's head snapped up, she added, "She doesn't want to be mean. I'm sure of that. But she's trying to protect herself. She's very, very raw right now."

"But she's all right? I worry about her so much. She works so hard when I'm not there to make sure she eats and gets her sleep." She started to cry again, letting her head drop into her hands. "Somebody has to take care of her."

"Shhh…" Natalie murmured while gently stroking Kit's back. "She's okay. She went to California a couple of days ago. She's going to hang out with some friends for a while."

"Is she going to move back there?" The thought of having her all the way across the country was too much to even contemplate.

"I don't know. I just know she needed a break."

"I guess that's good. She'd flip if she saw us here together."

Natalie's head shook decisively. "I wouldn't have come if there was even a possibility of that. She would not appreciate having the two women who've broken her heart taking over her favorite bar."

"Is there any way I can get her back? I'll do anything."

"I honestly don't know. I guess…" she looked down, then met Kit's eyes. "Whether or not you can ever be together again, doesn't it make sense to figure out why it was so important to hide your relationship? I know a good therapist…"

Kit tried to keep the ire from her voice, but she was fairly sure she'd failed. "I don't need therapy. I just need another chance."

"Then I hope you get one." Natalie got up and took the box Kit held out. "Uhm...do you still have a key to the apartment? I hate to ask but..."

Sniffling like a child being punished, Kit took out her key ring and worked the key from it. Without a word she held it out and Natalie closed her hand around it. Just like that, every tangible connection to her beloved Bailey was gone.

—⁂—

Kit's love of reporting and writing hadn't waned during her break, but she didn't have her usual energy back. Losing Bailey had taken a lot out of her, and she wasn't at all sure she'd ever be the same.

It was Sunday afternoon, and her two-week vacation was at an end. She'd had better breaks. Lying in bed for twelve hours a day, crying like a professional mourner wasn't something she wanted to re-experience.

She poked around her office, reading her mail and listening to messages. It was going to take quite a few days to get caught up, but since no one would notice if she worked all night it almost didn't matter. One e-mail in particular caught her eye. She read it carefully, made a few notes, then got on the phone to do a little more digging. She thought she'd seen everything, but this was a little different. This shit was getting serious.

—⁂—

Her first day back felt strange, and heading over to Capitol Hill was even stranger. She wasn't used to using subterfuge to get to talk to someone, but she couldn't afford to just make an appointment to talk with Henry. So she made an appointment to talk with the senator whose office was right across the hall. She actually didn't have a whole hell of a lot to say to him, but she'd found that politicians always had a pet project, and if you let them talk about it they fascinated themselves. They wrapped up their interview right before lunch and Kit spent the next fifteen minutes pacing up and down the long, busy hallway. Being a good reporter required good feet as much as good instincts.

Finally, she saw Henry barrel out of his office, aides at his side. She hadn't thought of how to finesse this, so she stood in his path. When he noticed her, he gave her an annoyed glance. She couldn't really blame him, but it still hurt. "Have you decided how you're voting on the assault weapons ban, senator?"

He tried to move past her, saying, "The vote's tomorrow. Stay tuned."

She wasn't sure what look she gave him. But it was one that made him stop and move closer to the wall, away from his aides. She stood next to him, facing the wall and speaking quietly. "Meet me at the Jefferson Memorial at six o'clock. It's worth it." Before he had a chance to reply she scampered away, fairly certain that no one had paid any attention to a senator having a few words with a reporter. Even one that he used to sleep with.

—m—

It was a lovely warm late afternoon, with the low sun hitting the marble and rendering it a warm, rosy pink. Kit sat on the steps way off to the side. She was almost certain he would come. He knew her well enough to know she wouldn't waste his time. A few minutes later, she saw him, dressed in running shorts, T-shirt and a Red Sox cap pulled down low. He jogged up the stairs, then sat down next to her, breathing heavily. "Are you Woodward or Bernstein?"

"In this case, more like Deep Throat." She smirked at the puzzled expression he gave her. "I'm giving information, not asking for it."

"I have a telephone."

"I know you do. But someone is trying to set you up and I don't want to take any risks."

His eyes opened wide. "Then why are we out in public?"

"We're hiding in plain sight. Right around dinnertime at a national monument is the perfect place to talk. The reporters are already hunkered down in bars."

"Okay." He looked resigned. "If anyone's following me, they've already made me."

"It's not that bad!" She slapped him on the shoulder. "People are trying to take you down the old-fashioned way — political dirty tricks."

"Is it the Eddie Don Jackson thing?"

"It is. It took me months to get to the bottom of it, but I think I'm there." She took out her phone, and looked at the timeline she'd made. "This is the thing I hate about losing old-fashioned reporting techniques. If I'd rushed to post this story based on what you'd given me, you'd be toast. Or at least you'd look like a jerk."

"Do the old-fashioned reporting techniques require taking this long to get to the point? My staff will never believe I've been out running this long."

"Sorry. I get carried away with my own bullshit."

He gave her a touchingly tender smile. Just like the ones he used to give her when she'd done something he found particularly cute. She'd better make this quick. "Here's the deal. Jackson's people had that sign made. They put it up, took photos, then took it down. I even have the receipt from the sign maker who was told to make it look homemade."

There was something really exciting about watching a guy's face when you told him news that knocked his socks off. Kit guessed she really was a natural reporter, 'cause few things felt better.

"It looks like they wanted you to leak the story, then they had all sorts of local witnesses lined up to say the sign had never been there, making you look like you'd made the whole thing up to make Jackson seem like a racist. By the way, the properties on both sides of Jackson's are owned by family members. They have different last names, and the properties are held by various real estate trusts, so you wouldn't know that without checking. A lot," she stressed.

"He did all of that to try to trick me into making it look like I'm trying to race bait him?"

"Looks like. A lot of Southerners have very little patience at being characterized as people who think lynch mobs are funny."

"Can't blame them."

"Yeah, it must get very old having Northerners throw that in their faces all of the time. Jackson was counting on that. All he had to do was make you look stupid nice and early in this thing. Then he could beat on you for a while, then kick your ass in those early Southern primaries. You would've been out of it before it even began."

He looked at her for a long time, his eyes ranging all over her face. "How much time did you spend on this?"

"A lot. I didn't go down there, but I hired people who could look around without sticking out. You can consider the money I spent as an early campaign donation." She took a folder from her big purse and handed it to him. "You can use all of this if you want. I obviously could, too, but then it would look like I was still on your team, and I can't afford that."

His voice softened, sounding as it did when they were together. "Are you all right?"

"Sure," she said lightly. "The sun's really bright. It highlights all the wrinkles I've earned from chasing guys like you around town."

"No, that's not it. You just don't look like you're doing very well."

He sounded so sincere, so much like the old Henry, the one she had truly loved. And yet, she was amazed when she felt her emotional dam crack and the floodwaters start to pour through yet again. "Heartbreak," she managed to get out. She'd learned her lesson, and now carried a handkerchief which she was still using every day.

"I'm so sorry to hear that. I didn't know you were seeing anybody."

"Six months," she got out between choked sobs. Trying to get hold of herself, she looked up, spotting a few tourists taking photos. "How will we ever explain this?"

"What?" he asked blankly.

She jerked her head, indicating a couple of people holding up their phones.

Clearly puzzled, he looked around. "Are you worried about those... strangers?"

"Yes! If somebody post photos of you and me sitting out here, with me crying like you just broke my heart..."

He barely frowned. "I only have to explain things to Caroline. She doesn't pay attention to Washington gossip."

"Someone will tell her about it, Henry."

"I don't worry about things like that, Kit. I don't play that game."

"How can you not?" She stared at him for a second. He looked so unconcerned.

"I don't get recognized very often, so it doesn't come up much. You're a lot more famous than I am, and you're not that famous." He chuckled softly. "Now tell me about this guy. He must be a moron if he broke up with you."

A wave of sadness washed over her again. "He's not a moron. He's not a he, either. She was an adorable computer nerd who broke up with me because I didn't want to tell people that I was a lesbian."

Henry jerked so hard he was probably going to have to visit a chiropractor. "You're a lesbian?"

"No," she moaned, miserably. "That was the problem. Bailey was the only woman I've ever been attracted to." She shook her head. "That's not doing it justice. I loved her. We were perfect together. But she needed to be out, and I needed to be in."

"You've got to give me a minute to get used to this. If you were a lesbian when we were together, you had a very strange way of showing it. I've never known a woman who seemed as fond of my…" He trailed off, his cheeks coloring. "Well, you know what I mean. We had our problems, but you were into having sex. There's no way anybody could convince me you were just doing it to make me happy."

"That's my point! I'm attracted to men in general, and Bailey in particular."

"I'll admit I don't know a lot about being gay, but I've never heard of that."

"Well, now you have. I tried to make her see that I didn't treat her any differently than I did you or any other guy I'd been with. You know I never made a point of the fact that we were romantically connected. But that wasn't good enough for her."

Henry put his arm around her shoulders and gave her a tender hug. "I'm really sorry. Heartbreak is the worst."

"Someone will see us." Kit scooted away. Why was he being so normal?

"We're not doing anything! Damn, Kit, you've got to get over being so skittish."

"I'm not skittish. I'm just careful."

"When an old friend gives you a hug, and you're worried about strangers being poised to take your photograph… And then worrying those strangers will go to the trouble of posting it somewhere…and then worrying something bad will happen if it gets noticed…you're skittish at best."

"You're not the one who has to put up with being called "Brearly's Whore" every day of her life."

"No, I don't. But if I read everything posted about me I'd never leave the house. So I don't read it. Ever. I think you might want to try that."

"My whole career is based on my reputation. I can't afford to do things that would make people question my impartiality."

"You can't stop them! There's a level of snarkiness that's pervaded every aspect of our lives. It's everywhere, Kit. Like a rising river that soaks through everything. What makes you think you can stop it?"

"I can't, obviously, but I also don't have to ask for it."

"That seems crazy to me. Just crazy. What did this woman want you to do? Come out in your column?"

"No, no." Kit shook her head, irritated. "She didn't push me that way. But she wanted me to introduce her to co-workers and other reporters. And socialize as a couple. Even to dance together at gay events."

He sat back, staring at her like he'd never seen her before. "How can you say you treated her like you treated me?"

"I never introduced you as my boyfriend or my lover. I never told people we lived together."

"But we did live together. And you might not have introduced me as your lover, but it was clear we were together." He paused. "Did she want more than that? Did she want you to make it clear you were sleeping together?"

"No!" She regretted ever having brought this up. "Well, yes, I guess she did. She definitely wanted me to acknowledge we were together. That's the same thing."

"I don't get it. What did your parents think?"

"Nothing. They didn't meet her."

"You didn't take her to their big party?" His head tilted, as though he was trying to see deeper inside her. "You were dating somebody for six months and you didn't take her? Damn, Kit, you took me to your brother's wedding, and we'd only been out twice." Gently, he added, "You can say you treated her like you did me, but that's just not true. This sounds like the textbook definition of homophobia."

Tiredly, she moaned, "You're being ridiculous. You can't be homophobic when you're actively participating in a lesbian relationship."

He held his hands up. "I'm no authority, but I thought homophobia meant you had an irrational fear of homosexuals. And that sounds exactly like what you're describing."

"Homophobia's about hatred. I not only don't hate gay people, I prefer them."

"Again, I'm no expert, but I'm telling you that you don't have your facts straight if you think you treated me like you say you treated her. I always felt like you were proud to be with me, even though your career suffered because we were together."

"I was proud to be with her. I was lucky to be with her."

Once again he tucked an arm around her, this time adding a kiss to her cheek. "Then I'm really sorry it didn't work out."

Just to get off this depressing topic, she said, "Are you really going to turn pro-life?"

He looked pained. "I have to, okay? I just have to. You know I don't believe the government has the right to interfere in our private decisions. But I'd come in dead last in the early primaries if I stayed pro-choice. If I win, I can just ignore it. Paying lip service to it seems to be enough in most cases."

"How do you rationalize that? You couldn't have won your seat if you'd been pro-life."

"I know that. But you have to make compromises as a politician. Big ones." He showed a gentle smile. "I'm going to go off the reservation and make it clear I still support marriage equality. It's not much, but I have to hold onto something I believe in."

Eyes wide, Kit said, "They'll trounce you!"

"I'm not sure that's true anymore. And I'm not saying I think there should be a federal marriage law—I don't believe that. I think marriage should be regulated by the states, and I'm going to urge every state to pass a nondiscriminatory law, allowing every adult to choose who they want to love."

"That will definitely make you stand out in the field." She chuckled. "Maybe out in left field."

"Maybe. But I think there are a lot of people who want to disentangle economic principles from religious ones. Those are the people I'm going after."

"By getting baptized and joining a mega church?" She couldn't help it. She was a reporter, even while sitting on the steps of the Jefferson Memorial.

"No, that was actually at Caroline's urging. She wants our kids to be brought up with some level of faith, and she doesn't think it makes sense to send them to church if we don't go." He shrugged. "We shopped for over a year to find a church that was liberal but not too liberal. I'm not crazy about going, but you need to make some sacrifices to have a good marriage."

"I'm really sorry I called you out on it. It just looked awfully…convenient."

He sighed, then his mouth curled into that boyish smile that she'd always loved. "It was. This country's a long way from having an atheist president. But that wasn't my primary intention in joining. A close second, I'll admit, but not primary."

She put her hand on his shoulder and gave him a good squeeze. "You'd better get going. I don't want you to be in the doghouse."

He stood up and grasped her hand, pulling her to her feet. "And I don't want to see you looking so sad. Maybe Bailey wasn't the right woman for you, but if she was, think about what I said. From a purely outsider's perspective, what she was asking for doesn't sound like much."

She wanted to put her arms around him and kiss his cheek for his thoughtfulness. But a photo like that would stay on the Internet forever. So she clapped him on the shoulder and simply said, "Thanks."

―⁓―

After almost a month spent in California, Bailey stood in a long line waiting for a cab at the airport. A horn honked and she turned her head to scowl at the driver. It was too damn early to be honking. Her scowl grew deeper when she saw Natalie was driving the car. After dragging her stuff over, she poked her head in the open window. "I told you I'd take a cab."

Natalie acted like she hadn't heard the thinly veiled rebuke. "Throw your bags in the back and jump in. I don't want to get a ticket."

Grumbling, Bailey complied, then got in and buckled up. Realizing she hadn't offered even a kiss on the cheek, she released the belt and leaned over for a quick one. "Sorry I'm so bitchy. Red-eye flights destroy me."

"Better snap at me than a cabbie. I won't drive you around in circles to punish you." She spared a quick look. "No sleep?"

"None. Not that that's worth a mention. Sleeping on a sofa in people's living rooms wasn't the smartest way to rest up."

Natalie gave her another long look as they waited for a stoplight. "Would you have slept at home?"

"No. I don't think I'm ever going to sleep again. I took a few sleeping pills, but they just gave me bad dreams." She met Nat's eyes and shrugged. "Again, about the same as normal."

Putting a hand on her leg, Natalie said, "What are we going to do with you, Bails?"

"Don't know. Wish I did."

Natalie must have been feeling very secure now that she'd made partner. Back in the day, when she was trying to impress the "big suits" as she called the higher-ups at her firm, she never would have taken the time to have a sit-down breakfast at eight thirty in the morning.

They sat in a booth at an upscale diner not far from Nat's apartment. Bailey hadn't eaten a thing on her flight, but she wasn't hungry. Eating seemed to take so much energy. Energy she didn't have to spare. She'd been staring at the menu, unable to find anything that appealed to her. When their server approached, Nat whipped the menu from her hands and said, "Coffee for both of us. Then I'll have an egg white omelet, with spinach. No bread. She'll have a strawberry banana smoothie. Add some blueberries, too. Thanks."

Bailey raised an eyebrow. "I didn't know I liked smoothies."

"You're going to start. You've got to eat. And if you won't eat, you've got to drink some calories." Natalie reached across the table and put her hand on Bailey's shoulder. "It'll cost you thousands to have all your clothes altered. Think of how cheap you are before you let your tiny waist get tinier."

That was sort of funny. Bailey could feel her smile muscles try to move. But they seemed to need some lubricant. Not using them for five weeks must've frozen them.

Their coffee was delivered, and Natalie spent a minute getting hers prepared just the way she liked it. "Hey, uhm…I didn't tell you this on the phone, but I met up with Kit a few weeks ago."

Bailey resisted the instinct to leap across the table and throttle her. Natalie was as close as a sister, but she would not allow her to get involved. "Good," she managed to say. "Don't tell me about it."

"We're not hanging out, Bailey," she said, clearly irritated. "Although I felt like a jerk for having to turn my back on her."

Bailey looked up at her sharply.

Quietly, Natalie added, "That wasn't a dig. But she's in bad shape. She tried to leave a box of your stuff, but your doormen followed instructions. They wouldn't take it."

"So you're the only one who won't follow instructions?"

"Yeah, I guess so." She took in a breath. "Look. I know you want to act like she doesn't exist, but have a little heart. She didn't cheat on you and steal your car."

"She might have," Bailey sniffed. "Cheated on me, that is. When a woman lies to you, who knows?"

"That's just stupid. I know she hurt you. It would hurt anyone to have her girlfriend whip up a bag of tricks rather than introduce her. But you tend to go nuclear on people…and I'm not sure that's in your long-term best interests."

"I don't go nuclear on people. I'm damn patient, and you know it."

Their food was delivered, and Natalie looked it over, then said to the server, "Hot sauce?"

"Salsa?"

"No. Like Tabasco. Pepper sauce?"

"Sriracha?"

"Good enough." The server walked away, with Natalie grumbling. "I've gotta start carrying my own." She looked up, must've seen the scowl on Bailey's face and continued, "You're too patient. Until you're not."

The Sriracha was delivered and Natalie sprinkled it all over her omelet. She nodded appreciatively when she took her first bite. "Not bad. It'd be better with jalapeño sauce, but this is serviceable."

"I believe you were assessing my personality," Bailey said while taking a sip of her smoothie. It wasn't bad. And definitely easier to gag down than anything she had to chew.

"I'm not trying to do that. Really."

Natalie could convince you of almost anything when she flashed those big, brown eyes at you, but this time she looked genuinely sincere. "So…what are you trying to do?"

"Just point something out. You've been in three relationships, and you ended each one after your partner did something you couldn't forgive."

Smirking, Bailey said, "That's not accurate. I broke up with Kit, I'll grant you that. But Mimi and Julie were, at the very least, mutual."

"That's not what Mimi told me."

"And she's more believable than I am?" Bailey could feel her eyebrows hike up.

"About things like this? Yeah, probably, given that she wanted you back."

"I wanted to have a damn sex life!" Bailey snapped, way, way too loudly. She whipped her head around, seeing only two people who'd turned to stare at her. Not bad. Much better than the crowd she'd drawn at the coffee shop in Cupertino when she'd put her head down on the table and cried like she'd just lost her whole family. One of the employees actually walked her out to her car and poured her into it. Not too humiliating.

"So did Mimi. She was working on it."

"She wasn't attracted to me!" Bailey hissed. "That's not something you can work on."

"You're being an idiot. She told you she fantasized about other people during sex. And that was a fatal flaw?"

"That meant she wasn't attracted to me!"

"No, that meant she liked to fantasize. And for telling you that, you broke up with her."

"She told me that in therapy—where we had to go because our sex life was nonexistent."

"You got her to admit something she was deeply embarrassed about, then broke up with her because of it. You're a hothead, Bailey. That's the truth. You get hurt in a certain way and you cut the cord."

"Was I supposed to let Kit hurt me the same certain way time and time again?"

"How can I know that? I just know that you put up with a lot—then you lower the boom. No warning. You might want to take a look at that, given that you're repeating a pattern."

"Julie broke up with me. Taking off without even a warning was a big clue she was done."

Natalie reached over and took Bailey's hand, squeezing it tenderly. "But she wasn't done. Yes, it was shitty to leave without you. But that's how she was. She'd rather apologize than wait. But you knew that about her. It wasn't until she told you she didn't trust you to co-parent that you went over the edge." She shook Bailey's hand. "You pulled the plug, Bails. You called me two seconds after you did it, so don't try to dissemble."

"She did," Bailey insisted. "Leaving on our trip by herself was the same as handing me my walking papers."

"Bullshit. You might be able to convince yourself of that. But not me. You'd better spend some time looking at this pattern if you don't want it to happen again."

Bailey took a long drink of her smoothie. "It's not going to happen again. I'm gonna hire sex workers from now on." She rolled her eyes. "If I ever want to have sex again…which I doubt."

—⁓—

Kit no longer felt comfortable going to her old gym. Since Bailey belonged to the same place, there was always a chance she would run into her, and she couldn't handle that. She tried a couple of other ideas to get some exercise, finally convincing Asante to go running with her before their weekly taco night. It wasn't ideal, and they usually wound up stopping some place and getting carry-out, but at least she was getting her blood flowing.

It had been a couple of weeks since she'd spoken to Henry, and Kit was finally far enough removed from the incident that she could look at it with some perspective.

She and Asante were running around a decent sized park near his apartment. It was hot, muggy, and sticky, but both of them were driven enough to stick with what they'd planned on accomplishing that night — even if they were miserable.

After completing eight loops, Kit shuffled to a bench and collapsed onto it. "This is the worst idea we've ever had." She panted like a dog, tongue hanging out.

"And we've had some bad ones. Let's just stay here and have a pizza delivered."

Kit nudged his side with an elbow. "No way. It won't take us more than fifteen minutes to get dinner ready. But we can stay until we catch our breath."

He turned his body and scooted down so he could lie on the bench. "I might sleep here. It's nice."

"Hey, I have a little something that will keep you from falling asleep. I had a chat with Henry the other day and I found myself telling him about Bailey."

Asante's eyes popped wide open. "That must've been weird...for both of you."

"You know, it really wasn't. Sometimes I forget what a good guy he really is." Random thoughts of interactions they'd had over the years flowed through her head. "I think I've been letting his political posturings color my memories of the real Henry."

"I'm glad to hear that." He reached up and ruffled her hair. "That must mean he was supportive."

"Yeah, he was. But he said the funniest thing. He thinks I'm homophobic."

Asante didn't speak; he just cocked his head and looked at her questioningly.

"He said it sounds like I have an irrational fear of gay people, or of being gay or some kind of nonsense." She waited for Asante to laugh, to join her in poking fun at such a crazy comment. But he didn't.

He sat up and looked her in the eye. "I never thought about that term applying to you, but Henry might be onto something."

Stunned, Kit's shock quickly turned to anger. "Are you crazy? I support every major gay rights organization in the country! I've never been uncomfortable hanging out with you or any of your friends or any of the other gay people I've worked with over the years. Damn it, I was banging the drum for gay marriage twenty years ago!"

Very soberly, he said, "You can be supportive of gay people, and hate that part of yourself. I know you've heard of internalized homophobia. Maybe it's time to consider if you have a little bit of it."

"I don't!"

He held his hands up in surrender. "Okay, okay. Forget I said anything."

Glumly, she sat there for a few moments, her arms crossed over her chest. "You know I can't do that, you big jerk. Three people whose opinions I respect say the same thing. Do you honestly think I can ignore you all?"

"I'm sorry, sweetheart. I don't want to hurt your feelings, but there's something going on there." He waited a few seconds, then added, "It's not just the gay thing. You're preternaturally concerned with other people's opinions, and that's not good for you."

She hated to hear the whining tone her voice took on. "That's just who I am. It's a middle child thing."

"It might be that, but I think it's getting worse."

There was something about the tone of his voice and the set of his shoulders that made her sit up and pay rapt attention. "Worse how?"

He fidgeted a little bit, the way he often did when he was trying to work his way through a thought. "I wouldn't normally mention this, but I think it might be connected." He took in a breath and spoke quickly. "In the last couple of years, you've mentioned more than once that you didn't invite me to something because you were worried about how I'd be treated. That's not good, Kit. It's not your job to decide what I can tolerate."

Her heart was racing as he spoke. She grasped him by the arm, staring into his eyes. "I can only remember doing that for my parents' anniversary party. Did you want to come?"

"No," he said, laughing softly. "I didn't want to. I didn't want to go to your grandfather's funeral either, but I offered to."

"Oh, right. Yeah. You did that." She smiled at him. "That was really nice of you."

"That's what you do to help your friends out. To be supportive." He touched her chin, turning her head so their eyes met. "I want to make it clear that I'm a better judge of whether something will bother me than you are."

"I'd do anything in the world to avoid hurting your feelings." She shook him gently. "You know that, right?"

He smiled and nodded. "Of course I do. You're my closest friend, and that's part of the reason why. But you said you couldn't take Bailey to the party because she was gay and you couldn't take me because I was black. I'm pretty sure that neither of us wants you to make that call."

"But some of the people at the party were real jerks," she said earnestly. "You couldn't have found ten people you would've enjoyed talking to."

"Ten's a lot!"

"No. Two hundred and forty's a lot. And that's how many would have been staring at you like you'd snuck in."

He waved his hand dismissively. "I bet your numbers are off. But even if they aren't, that doesn't change my point. If you invite me to something where you know some of the people would be uncomfortable with having me there, it's fine to tell me that. Then let me make my own decision about whether or not I want to put up with it."

"It just breaks my heart when people are rude to my friends. If there's a way I can stop it…"

"There isn't. That's the part that you don't seem to connect with." He leaned close and spoke slowly. "I deal with racism almost daily. Sometimes I know I'm going to have an issue, and sometimes I'm caught completely by surprise. But that doesn't stop me from going where I want and hanging out with whomever I want. What kind of a life would I have if I let my fear of being treated badly dictate my choices?"

"I see your point. I do. But if I'd taken you to the friggin' country club, someone would have said something inappropriate. And you would have been hurt. I'm sure of that, Asante."

"Kit, listen to me." He waited a second, then continued. "No one likes to have someone be rude to him. But that doesn't influence me. At all. If you'd wanted company, I would have been glad to go. That's all you should have considered— whether you wanted me."

"Ah, damn it," she said, leaning against him. "I always want you. I'd marry you, for God's sake, even though you'd never have sex with me. You're worth giving up one of my favorite hobbies."

"Then you love me more than I love you." He reached over and tickled under her chin. "But think about it for a minute. I think the truth is that you're on the lookout for the disapproving looks and rude comments. You worry about them. I don't. And from what you've said about Bailey, she doesn't either. So…you're projecting your worries onto us, and you just don't need to." He paused for a second, and looked a little unsure of himself when he concluded, "You need to consider whether you're worried about us—or about what people think of you for being with a lesbian or a black man."

She bent over and pressed her hands into the sides of her head. "This is giving me a headache. Can we go eat?"

He got up and put an arm around her shoulders as they started to walk back to his apartment. "I don't want to give you a headache, but I really do think you need to do some soul-searching here."

Looking up at him, she said, "You know I'll do little else."

—⁓—

Kit started on her project the moment she got home from Asante's. It was disconcerting to see how many scholarly articles as well as popular books were devoted to homophobia. But there were few things she enjoyed more than delving into something and learning everything she could about it. It would take all of her free time, but she had to spend it somewhere. Might as well learn something.

—⁓—

Memorial Day had always been one of Kit's favorite holidays. Since summer was, by far, her favorite season, its kickoff always filled her with happiness. Until this year.

She sat on the beach and watched the dawn break on what was going to be another chilly, gloomy day. The whole family had been together for three days, and the sun hadn't shown itself once. They hadn't gotten an ounce of rain, though, so she'd bundled up in a sweatshirt and windbreaker and gone for walks on the beach so frequently that even the little kids noticed how often she took off. But she couldn't stand to be inside watching everyone but her mother and grandparents staring at all varieties of computer screens and game consoles. It felt like being at a very nicely appointed public library, with very little noise and even less human interaction.

She'd been sitting long enough that her hips started to ache, so she got up and brushed her jeans off, then started to walk. Surprisingly, she saw her mom leaving the house, heading in her direction.

"You're up early," Kit said.

"Not really. I'm usually awake by six. I just normally stay in bed until your father wants his breakfast."

"Mmm."

Her mom put a hand on her shoulder as they walked along the sand, with the brisk wind blowing their hair about. "What's bothering you, Kit? You haven't seemed like yourself."

"Just…" She almost spilled it. It was so shocking to have her mother ask what seemed like a genuine question that she almost trusted her to listen. But as soon as she felt the words forming on her tongue she shut them off. It was simply too risky. "I don't know. I've got a lot of things on my mind."

"Work? God knows I don't know much about what you do, but…if you want to talk about it, I'll try to understand."

"No, not really." She smiled, feeling a little buoyed by her mother's interest. "I was thinking of calling Asante and seeing if he wanted to come up. He loves to shop, and since the weather doesn't look like it's going to improve…" She shrugged. "I thought we could go from town to town, just checking things out."

"Oh, I don't think he'd enjoy that," her mother said, shaking her head.

"You don't?"

"No, honey. He'd feel out of place up here."

"I know he hasn't spent much time with the family, but he's a great guest—"

"I didn't mean that. I meant on the Cape."

"He'd feel out of place on the Cape?"

"Of course he would." Her mother gave her a funny look, like she was puzzled by Kit's clear lack of understanding. "He'd stick out like a sore thumb."

"Because he's black?"

"Yes. Of course. And Nana would surely say something to offend him." She laughed a little, but the sound didn't have any real joy in it. "Sometimes she offends me with the things she says."

Kit had never heard her grandmother say anything particularly hateful about black people, but she might have had the good sense not to do it while Kit was around.

"If you're not having fun, why not have Asante meet you in Needham? You could have the whole house to yourselves and go into Boston to do your shopping."

"Mmm. I'll think about it." She turned her head to look longingly at their house in the distance. "I'm going to go get something to eat. Wanna head back?"

"No, I like being out here in the morning. Before all of the…" She put on a wan smile. "Hubbub starts."

"Yeah. I understand." Kit turned and strode for the house, glad she'd rented a car in Boston. She could be gone before anyone else woke.

After throwing her things in her suitcase, she left a note for the family, thanking them for a wonderful time. Usually she would have added an excuse for her sudden departure. But she didn't bother this time. As she stood in the drive, she looked at the house with a critical eye. They'd owned it since she was a little girl, and she had many, many good memories of their days there. But something in her gut told her she'd enjoyed the last of them.

Determinedly, she got into her rental and started to drive, thinking of what her mother had said. It sounded so awful…so closed-minded…so racist to hear her mother say the exact things about Asante that she'd said about the party. She was clearly her mother's child. And she had a lot of soul-searching to do.

—⁓—

After a couple of weeks of research and reading, Kit rushed to get all of her supplies ready for taco night with Asante. It had been raining on and off all afternoon and she hoped it continued. Asante was tougher than she was, but even he wouldn't want to run in the rain. He showed up right on time, and she smiled with satisfaction as she saw he was wearing shorts, a cotton dress shirt and his Topsiders. No running! Hooray!

They cooked together, with Asante handling the salad and the margaritas and Kit doing the rest. They'd been talking about her research, and Asante, as usual, peppered her with questions. "I guess it doesn't surprise me that the questions on the 'are you a self-hating homophobe' checklists don't fit. You're not gay enough to have most of them occur to you at all. But you don't have to score high on those tests to still have problems." He gave her a pointed look. "Obviously."

"I guess that's true. But so far the only question that resonates with me is the one about not wanting people to know I'm a lesbian." She slapped herself on the side of the head. "Do you see how hard this is? I was in a lesbian relationship, but I'm not a lesbian. I have no sexual interest in anyone right now, but if my sex drive ever comes back I don't think it's going to be pointed at women."

He leaned against the counter, sipping at his margarita. Nodding sagely, he said, "You've got some internalized homophobia in that head. I'm sure of it. But what you probably have more of is an aversion to sticking out."

"You are correct, sir. I've spent my whole life trying to play around on the margins. Wanting to be in the game, but close enough to the sidelines to jump off the court if the ball came my way."

"Not to speak badly of your parents, but they really did a number on you."

"I don't think that's fair. I've got to own my own views, Asante. I can't blame my family for the stupid, narrow-minded things I think."

"Stupid? Narrow-minded?"

"Yeah. Stupid. Insensitive. Unaware."

He gazed at her thoughtfully. "I think we're talking about more than homophobia."

"We are." She swallowed and forced herself to spit it out. "I had a chat with my mom when we were on the Cape. I heard her say some of the same things I said to you right after Bailey dumped me." She put her fists up to her eyes and rubbed them. "The bullshit I tried to feed you—saying I was only concerned for your feelings when I didn't invite you to things—sounded like backwoods racist crap when my mom said them. I've got to own that."

He put his arms around her, hugging her tightly. "Owning it is the first step in getting rid of it."

"I'm going to try. I'm going to try hard. If it's possible to change—I'll do it."

Chapter Twenty

BAILEY LAY IN BED watching a grim, chilly October dawn break. It had been almost six months, but she still wasn't sleeping. Lethargy was constant. Unrelenting. Every day was an effort to leave the house, so most days she skipped it. Luckily, most of her jobs could be done at home. Still, no matter how hard she worked, no matter how tired she was, she lay in bed at night, just staring at the ceiling. If this continued, she'd have to go on medication.

Everyone had been on her about her depression; even her dad had called to talk to her about it. Her mom had probably dialed the phone for him, but it was still shocking to hear him fumbling his way around the topic. Why couldn't anyone understand that she had a damned good reason for being sad? You couldn't heal broken hearts with drugs. Only time would work. Maybe that was the problem. It had probably been long enough to have gotten a little better. But nothing had improved. Nothing at all.

It was Saturday, and the thought of spending the whole weekend alone was suddenly unpalatable. Since the breakup, she'd been going to Pennsylvania every other weekend. She'd just been last weekend, but she got to her feet and started to throw on yesterday's clothes. She couldn't get out of the apartment fast enough. The only thing that made life bearable was being with her family. Lying in her old bed, surrounded by her childhood effects provided some level of comfort. But it was physical affection she craved. Everyone had stepped up their game. Even April, now a very cool high school freshman, snuggled close when they shared the sofa. If it hadn't been for family, Bailey had no idea how she would have coped.

Damn! Why'd she have to think of that? Kit didn't have that kind of support. No one was doting on her, making a week's worth of meals to tote back to Washington. With effort, she tried to get off that track. It was going to be another long day. Now that it was fall, the days were supposed to be getting shorter. They sure didn't feel like it.

It was just after ten when Bailey pulled into the family drive. Her mother came out, a puzzled look on her face. "Are you okay? We weren't expecting you."

Bailey got out of the car, and instead of her usual greeting she wrapped her mom in a hug and started to cry. The storm door creaked when it opened, and after a few seconds it creaked again. Her dad must have come out, seen her, and gone inside to hide until the tears were finished.

"My poor girl," her mother soothed, rubbing her back. "So sad."

"Y…y…yeah. That's all I am. Sad."

"No, you're much more than that. You're just having a bad spell. Come inside, baby. I'll make you some breakfast. I know you didn't eat before you left."

"No, I didn't. I had coffee, though."

"That's not enough. Come on now. You'll feel better after you eat."

They went inside and her mom started to pull things out of the refrigerator. "Kelly left not ten minutes before you pulled in."

"Yeah?" Bailey sat down at the kitchen table and tried to concentrate. The headache her crying always caused was throbbing.

"Uh-huh. Zack wanted an audience for his big report."

Every conversation felt like white noise. But she had to get back in the game. Feigning interest was the least she could do. "What report?"

Felicia stopped and looked at her for a moment. "The one he's been worried about since school started." She turned back to the counter and started to put some bread in the toaster. "He's such a planner. Just like you were at his age. Since his report's about National Coming Out Day, he made sure he could present it on Monday, since the actual day's tomorrow."

Bailey let her head drop to her crossed arms. "My least favorite holiday. The one that reminds me of why I'm going to die alone."

She felt an arm surround her shoulders and once again she started to cry, unable to get the slightest control over her emotions.

After breakfast, she and her father watched the lead-in to college football. She wasn't a big fan, but her father was, and sitting with him was a good way to bond. The announcers had two hours to kill, and after talking about all of the ranked teams, they worked their way down to the also-rans.

A beefy-looking commentator said, "And don't expect much from Massachusetts today. The Minutemen have struggled to stay respectable, but they were trounced last week by Bowling Green."

"Bowling Green?" Bailey grumbled. Her dad gave her a puzzled glance, and she added, "Kit went to UMass."

"I didn't know that." He changed the subject quickly. "I never see anything about Cal Poly when they're talking about sports. Do they even have a football team?"

"No. You know, she was almost valedictorian of her high school class. Her grandfather, father and older sister all went to Harvard, but she didn't even apply. And it's not that she didn't want to go." She stood up and started pacing. "Oh, no! She wanted to go. But she was sure she wouldn't get in. Wouldn't get in!" She stopped and stared at her father. "Of course she would have gotten in! She just didn't have the confidence to try, and her fucking family couldn't give her the support or encouragement to stick her neck out a tiny bit!" She was sweating, and felt a little dizzy as she glared at him.

"Felicia!" He called out.

Bailey's mom dashed in. "What is it?"

"Bailey's…" He got up and patted her on the shoulder, then dashed away, saying, "She needs to talk."

"What's going on? Why do you look so agitated?"

"Fucking UMass." She found the remote and switched off the TV, then collapsed onto a chair. "I've got to do something, Mom. Find a therapist or take some pills or something. I'm losing it."

Felicia sat on the arm of the chair and pulled her close. "You're not losing it. But you do need to figure out a way through this, honey. It's been six months and you're not a bit better."

"I know. Believe me, I know."

"I might be talking out of my hat…" She paused and Bailey waited for her to continue. When she started off that way she usually had an insight. She just wasn't always comfortable offering them. "Just a couple of months after you and Julie broke up you were well on the road to recovery—and you were going to have a baby with her. That says to me that you're not ready to let Kit go."

"She's gone!"

Bailey started to get up, but her mom grabbed her by the belt and pulled her back down. "You're not letting her go. You're holding on."

"Then I need help in letting go. It's over, Mom."

Their eye color was exactly the same. Every once in a while it was like looking in the mirror when her mother stared at her. And today she was really staring. Unusual for her. She must've been at the end of her rope. "Tell me one more time why you can't give Kit another chance."

Well, that was as blunt as she'd ever been. Slightly stunned, Bailey held up two fingers. "I can tell you in two sentences. One: I can't be in the closet. Two: Kit can't be out of it."

Tenderly, her mother asked, "Do you believe she loved you?"

"Yes. Without question. I know she loved me."

"Do you think she wanted to be open?"

"No. Definitely not. If she had her way, she'd live under an assumed name. Preferably in a country where no one had a TV." She nodded as she thought of Kit's wish list. "And she'd love to be so far away no one in her family would expect a visit. I know she'd like to avoid them as much as possible."

"All to avoid having people know she was gay?"

"No! It's her whole life she wants to keep secret. Our relationship was just a small part she wanted to hide." Her head was throbbing again, but she fought to think clearly. "As outstanding as she is, she hates standing out. For any reason."

Her mom fidgeted a little, then hesitantly suggested, "Do you think therapy would help?"

"No. Not for Kit. She'd never tell a stranger anything personal."

"Well..." She squinted, clearly thinking hard. "It seems odd that she'd take a job where she gets so much attention..."

"Yeah, yeah." She waved a hand in the air. "She doesn't love that part. She loves the part where she gets to write her thoughts. The gossipy thing is just what pays the bills."

"Oh," Felicia said, looking a little puzzled. "So she just does that to support herself?"

"Yeah. She can't live on the income she'd get from her blog. She needs the revenue from the damned *Daily Lineup*."

"And that's why she's on TV all of the time? Because of the *Daily Lineup*?"

Bailey thought about that for a minute. "Yeah, I guess so. No one's ever interested in talking about the longer pieces she writes. They just want her to gossip and guess what's going to happen in Washington. She's a pundit."

"But she doesn't like being a pundit."

Head aching, Bailey thought long and hard for a minute. "She does...a little bit. She liked it a lot when she was anonymous. But she hates being known so much that it's taken the fun out of the job."

"Maybe she should have given up the *Daily Lineup* and tried to get by on less money."

"I offered to do anything she needed. Hell, I told her I'd support her. But I don't think she took me seriously."

"Maybe she didn't." Felicia sat there quietly for a few moments, then shifted her eyes so she wasn't looking directly at Bailey. "Maybe she wasn't sure you meant it. Did you?"

"Of course!" Blood rushed to Bailey's head, feeling like her blood pressure had spiked. "I would have done anything for her, Mom!"

"How much does she make from the newsletter?"

Bailey blinked while trying to get her mind to focus. "I have no idea."

"Then how do you know you could have supported her? What are her monthly bills?"

"No idea. We never discussed it with specifics. I just made the offer."

Now Felicia's pale blue eyes locked on her, making Bailey feel like she was under a microscope. "That's not much of an offer, sweetheart. That's like my saying your dad and I would support you if you lost your job. We would, of course, but...all we could offer was your old room not pay your rent in DC for you." She gripped Bailey's hand and shook it until their eyes met again. "Why didn't you come up with specifics? Ways where she could get at least some of her privacy back and you could be more open?"

"I don't know," Bailey mumbled. "We just didn't. Seemed like every time we started to talk about it I wound up yelling at her about not being out. I've used more curse words in the last year than I have in the rest of my life put together."

"I was going to talk to you about that, but I thought I'd better wait until you were more yourself. Using bad language isn't like you, sweetheart."

"I felt so much, Mom. It was so important. I tried so hard to tell her how much it meant to me. I ran out of nice words and started to berate her."

"Why would you do that to someone you loved?"

Bailey looked at her mother for a few moments. As the seconds passed, the answer appeared to her, as if it had fallen from the sky. "I was afraid. Terrified. I yelled at her because I was so fucking afraid of losing her."

Felicia was absolutely silent for the longest time. If Bailey hadn't known better, she would have sworn she was working out some kind of puzzle in her head. "Here's what I think," she finally said, as she took Bailey's hands in her own. "I think you were afraid of too many things. And instead of working them through, one by one, you got more demanding. You were daring her to fail. To not be able to measure up."

"I don't think…" Her head throbbed with pain. There were too many thoughts, too many feelings, all fighting for supremacy.

"Sweetheart, you expected a woman, a public figure, who'd never considered herself gay to jump in and in just a few months be comfortable telling people she'd fallen in love with a…" She took a breath. "A very distinctive-looking woman."

Bailey could feel her anger about to explode. "Exactly! And she'd never be able to do that because she was embarrassed to be seen with me! She told me she'd never be able to introduce me to her family. Never!"

"It sounds like she doesn't even like them. Maybe it's them she's embarrassed of."

That got in. The thought rolled around in Bailey's head, dimming her anger so fast she was dizzy. "I didn't consider that."

"You wanted her to jump off a cliff with no help. I can't imagine you not coming up with a plan. Little chunks she could bite off to get to where you wanted her to go."

"How do you give someone a roadmap of how to be? She's an adult, Mom. Adults have to figure things out for themselves. No one can drag you into accepting something."

"I understand that. No one understands that better than me." She stood and started to walk back and forth across the room. Like she had to work off some anxiety. That wasn't like her. Finally, she spoke again. "We haven't talked about this much, but it took me years to come to terms with the way you dress. Years, Bailey. And for most of those years, you lived two thousand miles away and I hardly ever saw you."

Fuck. Why were they talking about this now? Weren't things bad enough? But the cat was out of the bag now, and Bailey had to know. "Have you ever been ashamed of me?"

Felicia stopped, turned her back and took in a visible breath. Bailey's heart raced. She knew the answer without a word being spoken. "Yes. I'm sorry to say I have been. I thought…I thought I'd accepted it, but when you started wearing ties and suits…" Tears sprang to her eyes and her voice broke. "I know it's wrong. God help me, I confess every time it happens. It's a sin against you and against God, who made you just the way you are. But every once in a while some busybody at church will see you in town and tell someone else about what you were wearing. I hate that it bothers me, but sometimes it does."

Bailey jumped to her feet, went to her mom and held her in a soothing embrace. "It's okay. I'm not mad. I swear. I know it's hard."

"Not very often, baby. I swear, it's not very often."

"What does Dad think about how I look?"

"We've never discussed it," she said quietly. "I'm sure he has his feelings, but you know he's not one to share."

"Like Kit," Bailey said, a knot forming in her gut again.

"He is a little like Kit. He'd rather jump off a cliff than talk about something that bothers him. But he's the most loyal, kindhearted man I've ever met. Have you ever doubted his love for you?"

"No," Bailey admitted, crying again. "I know how much he loves me."

When Felicia spoke again, her voice was soft and gentle. "You give him the benefit of the doubt. Something it sounds like you were never able to give Kit. When she disappointed you, you took it like she'd hurt you on purpose. Was that fair?"

"She hurt me so badly," Bailey whimpered. "It broke my heart, Mom. I couldn't let her keep stomping on it."

Felicia held her in her arms for a long time. When Bailey could finally pull herself together enough to sit up, her mom looked her in the eye and said, "Here's the truth no one tells you. Every person you will ever deeply love will hurt you badly. All you can do is hope to find someone who'll hurt you in ways you can stand."

Bailey felt like she'd been slapped in the face. "That's...the best I can hope for?"

"Yes. That's the painful, awful truth. You'll never know hurt like the pain you feel when your spouse gets past all of your defenses and hurts you. But every single person who's in a long relationship experiences this, honey. It's universal."

"Dad's hurt you like...?"

"Yes. And I've done the same to him. But we got past those times and moved on. I think," she said, her voice almost breaking with emotion, "that you know Kit's weaknesses now. I know they're tough ones, but you could get past them if you were both committed." She squeezed her shoulders to the point of pain. "You swear you loved her. But were you committed to her? That's the test. For better or worse isn't just a saying. It means something. Something important. Something vital."

Bailey sat there, her head a maze of thoughts, images, feelings. "I've never been so confused in my whole life."

"Think about what I've said, honey. I don't know that Kit was the woman for you. But if she was…" Felicia got up and patted Bailey on the shoulder. "Think about it."

—◊—

Once again, Bailey lay in her small bed, unable to sleep. It hurt like hell to know her parents were embarrassed of her. Maybe she should just give up and try to fit in. Life would be easier in every way.

She turned over and slammed her hand into her pillow, trying to fluff the old thing up. Looking more womanly would never work. She'd be filled with resentment. Being who you were wasn't something you could just wish away. Even when you embarrassed the people who meant the most to you.

As she lay there, a strange sensation gripped her. Like a hand had reached into her chest and grabbed her heart. For a moment, she thought she was having a heart attack, but then it became clear it was just anxiety. Maybe panic. Her heart knew the truth. But it took a few seconds for her head to get the message.

Kit's only sin had been her inability to talk about the things that troubled her. She'd never been embarrassed to be out together. In fact, she'd never, ever asked Bailey to change a single thing. She'd never suggested she skip the tie or femme it up in any way. All she'd ever asked for was time and understanding while she tried to maintain what little privacy she had left. The few shreds of a private life that meant so much to her.

Bailey sat up, a cold sweat covering her body. Kit had tried, very hard, to handle her discomfort on her own. She hadn't made any progress. That was undeniable. But she'd never tried to change Bailey. Not once. What more could you ask from a woman?

She thought of her parents and knew, in her heart, that they'd give a lot to make her…normal. But not Kit. Kit loved her…uniqueness. The things that made other people twitch with discomfort made Kit…happy. Good God. What had she done?

—◊—

Bailey's eyes fluttered open. It wasn't the middle of the night. Had she really slept? She was groggy, very groggy. Chronic insomnia didn't go away because of a few hours sleep. But she also felt a little better. Maybe even hopeful.

The moment she emerged from the bathroom, Zack was in her face, holding up his tablet computer. "Did you see it?"

Damn, what time was it? Kelly never came over early on a Sunday morning. She checked the clock. Ten. Hard to argue that was the crack of dawn.

"No, I haven't seen anything." She went into her room and put her glasses on. "What've you got?"

Zack was bubbling with excitement. Bailey hadn't seen him so wired since he'd gotten elected to his student government.

"Her article!" He started to extend it, but then pulled it back. "I'll read it for you."

He cleared his throat and started to read. "Opinion. I was nearly forty years old the first time I had sex with a woman. Up until a few months before that momentous event, I'd never—not once—had car…" He frowned. "Carnal? Did I say that right?"

"What in the hell are you reading?"

Bailey looked up when she detected movement at the door. Kelly and her mom were all trying to take a peek into the room.

"What's going on?"

"Did you read it?" Kelly asked.

"Give me a fucking second," Bailey snapped. She slapped her hand over her mouth. "I'm so sorry." Meeting Kelly's eyes, she grimaced. "I didn't mean that."

"Read it," Zack urged, extending the tablet toward her.

Bailey's eyes scanned the piece. What was the…oh, fuck. Kit's name was at the bottom of the article. Her heart started to race, feeling like it was banging into her ribs. "Where's this from?"

"The Post," Kelly said. She tugged on Zack's sleeve, pulling him from the room. "We'll give you a minute."

Bailey waited until they were all gone, then closed the door. What in the hell had Kit done?

Susan X Meagher

Opinion

I was nearly forty years old the first time I had sex with a woman. Up until a few months before that momentous event, I'd never—not once—had carnal thoughts about a member of my own sex. So how did a woman who'd always been happily heterosexual wind up in bed with another woman?

I have no idea.

That's a fact. All I know is that I was incredibly attracted to this particular woman, at this particular time in my life. If you're captivated by a person, the technical aspects of sex lose their import. There are plenty of ways to have a very satisfying physical relationship, even with plumbing you're not used to. Hearts, not parts, as the saying goes. As we grew to know each other we fell, easily and swiftly, in love.

What I couldn't admit, because I was ashamed to acknowledge it to myself, was that I was deeply homophobic. I use that term, even though it might seem odd, because I can't think of another that fits. I would hope that no one who knows me would consider me homophobic. I wasn't antagonistic to gay people in any way. In fact, I'd been a supporter of every major gay advocacy group in the country for over a decade. My best friend is gay. Trite, I know, but he is. And yet, when I was put to the test, I hid. I used every excuse to avoid letting anyone, even my own family, know that I was in love with a woman.

My lover was patient with my reticence, but she needed to see that I was making, or was at least trying to make, progress. When I continued to avoid, evade and outright lie about my struggle, she left me. She was right to do that. Not because every person needs to make public statements about their romantic relationships, but because I couldn't be honest about my feelings. It was easier to avoid them, and she saw that as a bar to true intimacy.

She was right about that, too. Having to hide your affection, your delight at being with someone you love takes over your life. I didn't want people to give me funny looks or wonder what I did in bed. I didn't want to have awkward conversations with old friends or family members. I didn't want to risk being shunned or treated poorly because of my relationship. In short, I didn't want to give up my privilege. The privilege of the majority.

I'd internalized society's censure of homosexuality just as surely as if I'd been indoctrinated by negative comments from family and friends, which I had not. Negativity about gay people is almost in the air. It gets in, even to a straight kid who'd never been teased, belittled or taunted in her life.

I lost the most meaningful relationship of my life because I didn't want to stand out. How much harder must it be for people who are targeted for those condemning messages? I can only imagine.

I've learned the lesson in the most painful way I can imagine. The only way to fight homophobia, in my case, the fear of being labeled gay, is to open the door and let the light in. So, on this National Coming Out Day, I'm doing just that. I'm declaring that I will work to banish my internal fears and face whatever adversity comes because of whom I love. We can't control how others perceive us, but we can control how we perceive ourselves.

Come out, come out, whomever you are!

Kit Travis is the founding editor of the Daily Lineup *and* Capitol Ideas, *a political newsletter and blog.*

Bailey stared at the words so long they started to dance in front of her eyes. Good God!

The entire family was huddled in the living room, April and Zack on the floor, at their parents' feet. Six pairs of eyes stared down the hall. Bailey'd never felt so exposed. But it was Zack who couldn't stand the tension. "Call her!"

Bailey wanted to hang a quick right and walk out the front door to her car. If she'd had on more than long underwear and flannel pajamas, she would have done just that. Kelly got up, walked over to her and kissed her cheek. "You're barely awake." She went back to the sofa and pulled Mick to his feet. "Let's give her time to let this sink in. Come on, guys."

Kelly gathered her flock and quickly started to exit. Then Zack ran back in and pried his tablet out of Bailey's grasp. She still hadn't moved or even spoken. Felicia got up, walked over to her daughter and took her hand. "You look like you need coffee."

They went into the kitchen, and Bailey heard her father leave by the front door. He'd be outside until he was sure things had calmed down.

Felicia poured a cup, then set it in front of Bailey. After sitting down, she took her hand. "What do you think? About Kit's article."

With a half-smile, Bailey said, "I was pretty sure of what you were referring to." She took in a breath, still trying to get her head to stop spinning. "I'm too stunned to think anything. I'm amazed…blown away." A smile grew. "Impressed. Proud." She chuckled. "Did I say amazed?"

"You did. Are you going to call her?"

"Call her?" She shook her head. "Her phone will be off. Or her mailbox will be exploding." A thought occurred to her. "I'll check her website. I bet she's going to be on one of the cable news shows. She always posts her appearances." Without even taking a sip of her coffee, Bailey jumped up and scampered to grab her tablet. She hadn't looked at the website since the day they'd broken up, but it was still in her bookmarks. "I was right," she said as she went back to the kitchen. "She's on a show on MSNBC." Checking her watch again, she added, "In ten minutes."

There was a small TV on the counter and Bailey played around with the balky channel guide until she found the proper location. Then she sat, fidgeting, staring at the bumper that announced, *Next Up, Kit Travis, Editor of the Daily Lineup and Capitol Ideas.* "I was less nervous waiting for my SAT scores."

"You knew you'd do very well on those," Felicia reminded her. "This is new territory."

Bailey reached across the table and took her mother's hand. The moments ticked away incredibly slowly, then, finally, the host came on and did a quick summary of the news. Then the camera went to Kit, looking very businesslike.

"Oh, look how cute she is," Felicia cooed, like Kit was a child in a bassinet.

"She's not well." Bailey scanned her like a treasure map. She was drawn, thinner than normal, and her eyes were missing their spark, their warmth. Kit was nervous—that was very clear. But there was more to it than that. She looked like all of the joy had been drained from her, and that struck Bailey like an arrow through the heart. Her chin started to quiver and she whispered, "But she still loves me."

Felicia stroked her back while she leaned close. "How do you know?"

"She's still wearing the ring I gave her. She promised she'd never take it off." The floor seemed to shift as she got to her feet. But she had to move. "Watch the show," she instructed. "I've got to find her."

—⁂—

Hours later, back in DC, Bailey finally had some energy. After months of a crippling fatigue that seemed to settle in her bones, she paced around her apartment, so anxious she thought she might go mad. As she'd expected, Kit wasn't answering her phone. But she had to do something. Anything. Being outside would help. Then, it hit her. She knew just where to go.

It didn't take long to get to Rock Creek, but it was a damned big place when you were trying to find one average-sized woman. Bailey'd only been there once, but she used her phone to locate the creek. If Kit was there, she'd be by water. No question. The problem was the water ran through the entire place.

After doggedly following the creek for what seemed like miles, Bailey realized there wasn't a lot of water left. She followed a bend and came to a relatively untouched glade, where the water burbled along its well-traveled path. It was the most peaceful spot on her entire trek, and now the most beautiful. Having Kit Travis sit on your bank would spruce up the least bucolic waterway in the world.

Suddenly, Bailey was stuck. Kit was twenty-five yards away, her back to the path. She was sitting on the ground, and her shoulders swayed gently. Ahh. She was listening to music. Bright red headphones covered her ears. Bailey scowled. Anyone could sneak up behind her and conk her over the head. But Kit's being unawares allowed Bailey to organize her thoughts. Actually, her thoughts were organized. It was her heart that wouldn't calm down. It was thrumming in her chest so loudly she wouldn't have been surprised if her shirt pulsed, just like in cartoons.

Tentatively, she approached Kit from the side. It took a second for those beautiful eyes to open and shift to meet her. "Bailey," she said, her voice a throaty whisper.

God. It had been so long. The TV hadn't lied. Bailey had taken the sparkle, the life from those beautiful eyes. She'd never forgive herself.

Bailey sat down, then reached out and grasped Kit's cold hand. "I've never been so impressed by anything I've read. But that's not why I'm here."

"It's not?" Kit's eyes blinked slowly as she pulled the headphones off.

"No. It's to apologize. To tell you how sorry I am for the way I treated you." She dropped her head, shame filling her heart.

"You? What did you do?"

"My mom finally got up the nerve to tell me I treated you like shit."

Kit's eyes grew wide. "Your mom said that?"

Bailey chuckled. "Of course not. Her version of that, though. I loved you more than I thought was possible, but I didn't even give you a chance to do what I needed."

Kit's head dropped. "That's not true. You warned me. You gave me months to tell people. That's long enough for anyone."

"Bullshit." Bailey gripped her hand with increasing strength. "You can't make people do things on a timeline. Especially not when they're doing things that are really, really hard. I'm so sorry."

Kit's eyes filled with tears. Her voice quavered with emotion. "You are?"

"I am. I've never been a more self-involved jerk than I was when I broke it off. Never."

"I hurt you," Kit murmured.

"Yeah, you did. And we should have come up with a plan. Or figured out a way to avoid repeating the same trap. But I didn't give you time to do that. I stormed away like a child having a tantrum."

"No, no. That's not how it was. I hurt you too badly. I didn't give you any choice."

"That's not true—"

"It is. I treated you and Asante like kids I had to protect. Like I could make sure no one hurt you. But that was bullshit." She sucked in a breath and as she let it out she seemed to sit up taller, looking more full of herself. "People are going to make snarky comments for millions of reasons. There's nothing I can do about that but hang in there with the people I love. Running away from it was cowardly. I own that now."

"That's important," Bailey said, her voice breaking a little. The respect she felt for Kit bloomed in her heart. "That's...exactly what I wanted you to feel."

"If you hadn't broken up with me, I can't imagine I would have worked as hard on this as I have. I did it because I had to."

The ache in Bailey's chest hadn't diminished. She'd never known emotional pain could make your body hurt this way. "I was harsh. Unforgiving. That's no way to treat someone you love." She took both of Kit's hands in hers. "I was afraid of losing you. Of having you decide it was too hard. So I broke up with you before you could hurt me worse." She leaned forward, resting her head on Kit's shoulder. After taking in a big, deep breath, she managed to say, "Will you forgive me? Give me another chance?"

Kit's arms slid around her shoulders. There was no better feeling on earth. "Will you give me another chance?"

"No." Bailey sat up. "No more chances. Chances are what you give someone you're not sure of." She tenderly kissed the backs of Kit's lovely hands. "When you find the woman you love, you have to commit to her." The fire of her beliefs burned in her veins. "If you'll take me back, I promise to be right by your side, through thick and thin, until the day I die. No matter what, we will work through our problems. On my life, I promise that." Her eyes were tightly closed as she tried to hold the tears at bay. "And I promise to do everything I can to show you how sorry I am for turning my back on you."

Her glasses were lifted from her face. Then warm breath caressed her forehead, then the softest lips imaginable pressed lightly upon her eyelids. Kit's hand slid up and down her thigh. "It's been an awfully long time," she said softly. "Long enough to make these the best jeans in Washington."

Bailey looked down, seeing the creases that had been worn in over the past months. "I didn't know time could move so slowly."

"It slowed to a crawl, then sped up for me. Once I started making changes..."

"Tell me about these changes," Bailey said, fascinated by the way the sun peeked through the trees to render Kit's hair dozens of shades of blonde. "I want to know about every single thing you've done."

"Well," she paused just a moment, looking contemplative. "I went away for a week in August."

"For your birthday," Bailey said, thinking of how she'd spent the day. Filled with a longing she didn't even have words to encompass.

"No. The week before. I went to a silent meditation retreat way up in Maine, on the coast. No cell phone, no Internet, no talking." Her chin tilted up toward the sky just as the sun broke through a bank of clouds. She looked peaceful, a state Bailey had rarely observed in their months together. "It took a while to get used to, but by the end of the week I'd made some decisions and had a plan. On my birthday, I sat my entire family down and told them about you. About us."

Bailey's mouth dropped open.

"Yeah," Kit chuckled, "that's what most of them said. But here's the kicker." She spoke softly, like she was telling a secret. "I told them that I'd give them time to get used to it. And I'd answer any respectful questions. But that I wouldn't..." Her eyes grew fierce, filled with a fire Bailey had never seen in their warm depths. "Tolerate a harsh word about you or us. And while I was at it," she added, almost giggling, "I said we were finished talking about politics. We were going to have polite discussions from that day on. Or we wouldn't have any discussions at all." She was beaming with pride and Bailey felt her heart swell with love and respect for the risks she'd taken.

"And? How has it been?"

"I got a note from my mom, telling me she hated to cut me off—but that she had to. Other than that, I haven't heard from any of them since that day." She shrugged, as though it were a minor incident. "They might warm up one day. Or they might not. Their choice."

"God damn, Kit." She wrapped her arms around her and held her tightly. "That must have hurt so bad."

Kit pulled away and gave her a level gaze. "I've been lying to myself for years. There was almost nothing holding us together as a family. We were bonded by chance, not choice. I'm open to changing that, but the ball's in their court."

Bailey put her fingers on Kit's cheek and stroked it gently. "My family would love to claim you as one of our own. You're a Kwiatkowski now." She shook her head, overwhelmed by the onslaught of information. "This started off pretty simply. I just wanted you to acknowledge my presence to people we ran into. Not divorce your family and tell the English-speaking world we were dating. How did it mushroom into this?"

"Truth?" She paused for a second, and when Bailey nodded continued. "I had to do it to be able to look at myself in the mirror." She took Bailey's hand and looked at it for a full minute. "You might not believe this, but I didn't do it to get you back." Their eyes met and Bailey could see the raw pain that lingered in their depths. "I simply did it to get my self-respect back."

"And now you've come out to the whole world...as...not a lesbian." Bailey started to chuckle.

"I am a lesbian."

She said that with such certainty. As Bailey's mouth once more dropped open in surprise, Kit leaned forward and closed it with a kiss. "I'm your lesbian."

Epilogue

KIT PUT HER FEET up on the railing of the deck. The flower-boxes she'd filled still bore bright, vibrant blooms. How was that possible at nearly the end of October? She hadn't even had to put a sweater on yet. During the day, that is. Bailey's long underwear appeared every night as the sun went down and the temperature dropped like a stone.

That same sun now warmed her face, while a light breeze ruffled her hair. Why would anyone live anywhere else? The entire population of the world should move to a narrow band of land nestled between the Santa Cruz Mountains and the Diablo Range. Sometimes, when they were trying to cross the valley, it seemed that might have already happened. But Kit was never, ever going to complain about traffic. The natives could do that. Transplants should remain permanently crushed, always besotted by paradise.

Her paradise sprawled out in front of her. They had a fantastic view. The land beyond the deck dropped away, giving them a huge vista that spanned much of the valley. Bailey had cashed in the vast majority of her options to buy the house, a small bungalow brimming with charm. That was a real estate term for a tiny place that needed upgrading in every possible way. But Bailey didn't mind spending her nest egg on nothing but a view. She was so confident she'd latch onto another goldmine and strike it rich again that Kit had caught her sketching out the cantilevered dream house they'd build one day.

Kit was much more realistic. Grabbing onto a start-up that really panned out was a long way from certain. But Bailey's salary was enough to keep them in the house, even if she never had another strike. And Kit made a little money from her blog, which she now heartily enjoyed. Selling the newsletter to Margaret and two of her fellow reporters who'd been squeezed out of their papers had lifted a burden from her shoulders she'd not even realized she'd been carrying. The time that freed up had let her do something she found she really loved—write a book. She wasn't the first person to write about how the changing media landscape had altered the country for the worse, but she'd gotten very positive feedback from the people who'd seen her first draft. If it did well, they could sock a little money away for a rainy day. She chuckled to herself. Everyone assured her that it did, indeed, rain in California. She'd believe it when she saw it.

The phone dug into her shoulder. How long had she been on hold? It couldn't be as long as it felt. "Building department. Jeremy," a voice finally said.

"Hi, Jeremy. I'm trying to check on a permit. Last name is Jones. 451 Skyline Drive."

"Yeah, I've got it here. Looks like…" He paused for a moment. "We're waiting for a check."

"I paid the fee when I dropped off the application."

"Huh." Their town was small, which was nice in many ways. It wasn't too hard to talk to someone when there were problems. But sometimes it seemed like the city manager's office was made up of volunteers rather than professionals. "Check with your husband. Maybe he forgot."

"I've got a wife, but she wasn't involved. I dropped it off myself."

"Bailey Jones?"

"That's my wife."

"And you're…?"

"Kit Jones."

"Huh." He chuckled. "By your names, you'd never know you were both women."

"Well, we are. Should I put a stop on the check?"

"Maybe your contractor paid the fee. They do that sometimes. What's his name?"

"Her name is Pat Mahoney."

He laughed. "Another one that doesn't sound like a woman."

"I didn't notice that until now, but you've got a point."

"Hey, here's something. I've got a check for the right amount from a Travis."

"That's me!"

"But you said your name was Jones."

"I changed it when I got married. We were so harried when we first moved I must have mistakenly picked up an old checkbook."

"Congratulations. Did you get married married or just a…civil union thing. I have a cousin who did that."

"We got married married. Back in DC."

"Nice. Hey, can you hold for a minute? I'm the only one here and there's somebody at the door."

"Sure. No problem." She was slowly getting acclimated to the pace. It wasn't that people were particularly friendly or polite in Northern California, but it seemed to be bad manners to act like you wanted anyone to hurry up.

Kit walked into the living room to be close to the desk where she kept all of her personal papers. She might need more evidence to convince Jeremy she'd paid. A photo of Bailey, taken on their honeymoon on the Cape, caught her eye. If there was a legal limit to how cute a woman could be, Bailey'd broken it. Citrusy plaid board shorts and a white rash guard made her look like a super cool surfer. And those big, aviator-style mirrored sunglasses let her ogle Kit all day long. What a fantastic time they'd had. Being there together had allowed Kit to reclaim the place she'd always loved. And it had been such a nice break before the stress of a cross-country move.

"Hey! I'm back."

"Glad to hear it."

"Got a question about your name change. Do a lot of gay people do that?"

"I'm not really sure. When we moved I left behind all of the things that weren't working for me. So now I have a new life, new job, new name."

Chuckling, he said, "Got a cousin who did that too. After he got out of San Quentin."

Kit laughed. People told you the strangest things. "Nothing so colorful for me. I just wanted to keep my professional name and my personal name separate. And Jones is awfully easy to spell."

"Nice. Well, we've got the check, and I guess that's all we were waiting for. You can come pick up the permit, or we'll mail it."

"I'll come by. How late are you there?" She walked back out to the deck. It drew her outdoors like a powerful magnet.

"Around three."

She rolled her eyes. The town offices were closed far more than they were open. "I'll be there before that. Well before that."

"Okay." He paused for a second. "Hey, what do you call yourself? Are you Mrs. Jones? Nah, that wouldn't be right."

"We're both Ms. Jones." Kit heard the front door close. She turned and watched Bailey cross through the living room. She looked adorable today. A baby blue linen shirt with a blue and yellow print tie and her freeze-cleaned jeans.

Cool and casual and very handsome. As she hit the deck, the gentle breeze ruffled her super-short hair. The woman had perfect hair. It just needed to be an inch long to reveal its perfection. "I am pledged to the divine Ms. Jones until death parts us. And not a minute before."

"Awesome. I can tell you're newlyweds. Congratulations again."

"Thanks, Jeremy. See you later." Kit hung up and turned to Bailey, now seeing that she had her earbuds in and was talking.

"Yeah," Bailey said as she crossed the deck and put her arms around Kit. "Sure. I'll tell her. And give Jess a kiss for us. Okay. Bye." She pulled an earbud out and let it dangle. "This is from Nat." Her arms closed around Kit, pulling her in tightly. Then Bailey's lips captured hers and she breathed in, loving the scent of her partner.

Finally breaking apart, Kit said, "I didn't know Natalie felt that way about me." She placed a playful kiss on Bailey's chin. "Other than sending an inappropriately sexy kiss, how's she doing?"

"Good. She was all excited because she got tagged in the *Daily Lineup*." She paused, then gave Kit a curious look. "Do you even read it anymore?"

"Not often." Chuckling, she said, "It's kinda like getting the class newsletter after you've graduated. You skim it if you have time."

"Amazing." Bailey put an arm around Kit's shoulders and they stood at the railing, looking out at the valley. "I thought you'd have a tough time letting all of that go. It's hard to believe you were up to your ears in that stuff for years and then completely disengaged."

Kit looked up, mesmerized to view Bailey's gorgeous face with the sun burnishing her features. "I'm not completely disengaged. I love thinking about and writing about the big picture for my blog." She held her hands up in an "X". But no gossip." She gave Bailey a playful push. "How can you call me disengaged when you spent a half hour making fun of me on Sunday when I was glued to the TV watching Hank?"

"You were in the zone," Bailey agreed. "But I was hungry!"

"We got you fed." She put her hand on Bailey's flat belly. "I just couldn't tear myself away until his segment was over."

"I thought you were gonna pass out while you were waiting for him to answer the probing question. 'How did it feel to have your former girlfriend come out as a lesbian?'" She made a dismissive sound. "The guy's running for president and that's what's important to the country?"

"I'm just glad he handled it so well." She laughed at the memory. "I loved the deadpan look he gave the guy. He cut him off at the knees when he asked how intimately he was involved with his past girlfriends. Made the interviewer sound like a stalker." Her heart swelled with genuine fondness for Henry. "I really appreciated it when he said he still cared for me and only wanted me to be happy no matter who I was involved with."

"He seems like a pretty good guy. We should have a drink with him the next time he comes out here to beg for money."

"Ha! His life is scheduled down to the minute. No, we'll have to wait until he gets his butt handed to him in the primaries. Then he'll have nothing but free time."

"You seem awfully sure he won't win a single primary."

"Can't," Kit said succinctly. "Too liberal and he came to the anti-abortion platform way too late. The Christian Right won't trust him, and they determine who the nominee is. Sad, but true."

"That's too bad. We might have gotten an invitation to a State Dinner." Bailey winked to show she was teasing. "Hey, who were you talking to when I came in?"

"A guy in the building department."

As Bailey looked down, intense curiosity showed in her eyes. "Why'd you tell someone in the building department that we're in love?"

"I'm not sure. I've gotten so good at coming out I do it automatically."

Concern colored her gaze. "Is it still hard, baby?"

Kit gave her a quick kiss. "Only for a second or two. I get a sense of panic, then I realize I've got nothing to fear. I guess it'll take a while to get over that knee-jerk reaction."

"Other than coming out to strangers, did you have a good day?"

"Very good. How about you? Given that you're home about four hours early I shouldn't be worried that you got fired, should I?"

"Nope." Bailey dipped her head and lavished a long, sweet kiss on Kit's lips. "I was at a good stopping place on my big project. I sent out my changes to the dozen people who have to approve this next step, and I can't do a thing on it until I get comments back. I could have picked up another thing I'm working on, but I thought an afternoon with my wife made a lot more sense."

"How will Lo-K8R survive without you sailing the ship?" She locked her hands behind Bailey's neck and leaned back. For some reason, this was the perfect angle to gaze up at her. Bailey had retained a little of her tan from their honeymoon, and her hair still bore blonde highlights. Scrumptious.

"They know just where to find me." She chuckled. "That's a joke. Get it? It's a tracking app…"

"I do. Your sense of humor has gotten much sharper out here in California."

"My sense of humor and your hair are both growing in the California sun." She threaded her fingers through Kit's hair, fluffing it. "It's driving you nuts, isn't it."

"Truly mad." Laughing, she said, "But a promise is a promise. You didn't back out of the wedding, so I have to grow my hair out."

Tapping her on the tip of her nose, Bailey said, "I would have married you if you'd cut it shorter than mine and you know it."

"I do. I just like to make my sacrifice sound dramatic. I need to make sure you appreciate me."

"It's not possible to appreciate you more than I already do." Bailey kissed her gently, then paused while looking into Kit's eyes. Then she placed another, longer kiss upon her lips, this time putting some extra heat into it. "You know what we haven't done?"

"What's that?"

"We haven't put some cushions out here, lay down and shared a bottle of wine."

Kit beamed up at her. "I do believe you are correct, my lovely wife. I can't remember the last time we sat on the deck and polished off a bottle of wine at two o'clock in the afternoon."

Soft, sweet kisses rained down on Kit's lips. "We don't have to drink the wine first. I thought we could have it after we made love for a few hours."

"Outside?" Kit pointedly took a look around. They had neighbors on each side who could see onto their deck with very little trouble.

Bailey nodded soberly. "That's the fantasy that's been rolling around in my head."

Kit spent a moment assessing how important this was to Bailey. She didn't ask for specific things very often, but semi-public sex was pretty far past Kit's comfort level. There had to be a way… She stopped her internal dialogue. They discussed things. That was the only way. "I can't do public sex, baby."

Not even a flicker of disappointment showed on her face. "No problem. We'll just—"

Kit stood on her tiptoes and gave Bailey a scorcher. "We just have to tweak the timeline to make it private."

She went inside and found a nice bottle they'd been saving for a special occasion, then picked up some blankets. After taking all of the outdoor cushions from the chairs and making a nice nest in the corner, she sat down and patted the space next to herself. "We'll spend the whole afternoon looking at our beautiful view, talking and drinking wine. Then, when it's darkish, we can cover ourselves with the blankets and go at it like rabbits." She popped her brows up and down. "Who's in?"

Bailey enthusiastically raised her hand. "Want me to go put some sweats on? Easier access."

"No, thank you." Kit twitched her finger, indicating that she wanted Bailey to bend over. Reaching up, she straightened the knot on her tie. "I love to undress you in all of your boyish glory. Don't ruin my fun."

"I wouldn't dream of it." She dropped down to sit so close, Kit almost toppled over. Bailey snuck an arm around her and grinned. "This is going to be a whole lot more fun than doing partitioning algorithms."

"If not, we need to get to a marriage counselor—pronto."

"That's the last thing we need. Unless we don't get that second bathroom fixed up. You take forever to get ready!"

"Oh! I was supposed to go get the permit." She put a finger to her lips. "What to do? Make love to my wife or go to city hall?"

"Again," Bailey said, "if you answer incorrectly, we need to rush to that counselor."

Kit narrowed her eyes in thought. "I choose…make love. I will always choose make love."

Bailey wrapped her arms around her shoulders and tumbled her over, so they lay face-to-face. The sharp, alert quality that normally showed in her gaze mellowed a little bit. That happened a lot when they were close like this.

"Being with you was the best choice I've ever made," Bailey said, her eyes filled with a warmth that took Kit's breath away. "And I'm going to make it every day for the rest of my life."

The End

By Susan X Meagher

Novels

Arbor Vitae
All That Matters
Cherry Grove
Girl Meets Girl
The Lies That Bind
The Legacy
Doublecrossed
Smooth Sailing
How To Wrangle a Woman
Almost Heaven
The Crush
The Reunion
Inside Out

Serial Novel

I Found My Heart In San Francisco

Awakenings: Book One
Beginnings: Book Two
Coalescence: Book Three
Disclosures: Book Four
Entwined: Book Five
Fidelity: Book Six
Getaway: Book Seven
Honesty: Book Eight
Intentions: Book Nine
Journeys: Book Ten
Karma: Book Eleven
Lifeline: Book Twelve
Monogamy: Book Thirteen
Nurture: Book Fourteen
Osmosis: Book Fifteen
Paradigm: Book Sixteen

Anthologies

Undercover Tales
Outsiders

Visit Susan's website at
www.susanxmeagher.com

Go to www.briskpress.com to purchase any of her books.

facebook.com/susanxmeagher
twitter.com/susanx